PENGUIN BOOKS

SALT

Jeremy Page lives in London, where he has worked as a script editor for Film Four, the filmmaking division of the UK's Channel Four. *Salt* is his first novel.

Salt

JEREMY PAGE

PENGUIN BOOKS

PENGUIN BOOKS

Published by the Penguin Group
Penguin Group (USA) Inc., 375 Hudson Street, New York, New York 10014, U.S.A.
Penguin Group (Canada), 90 Eglinton Avenue East, Suite 700, Toronto,
Ontario, Canada M4P 2Y3 (a division of Pearson Penguin Canada Inc.)
Penguin Books Ltd, 80 Strand, London WC2R 0RL, England
Penguin Ireland, 25 St Stephen's Green, Dublin 2, Ireland (a division of Penguin Books Ltd)
Penguin Group (Australia), 250 Camberwell Road, Camberwell,
Victoria 3124, Australia (a division of Pearson Australia Group Pty Ltd)
Penguin Books India Pvt Ltd, 11 Community Centre, Panchsheel Park, New Delhi – 110 017, India
Penguin Group (NZ), 67 Apollo Drive, Rosedale, North Shore 0632,
New Zealand (a division of Pearson New Zealand Ltd)
Penguin Books (South Africa) (Pty) Ltd, 24 Sturdee Avenue,
Rosebank, Johannesburg 2196, South Africa

Penguin Books Ltd, Registered Offices:
80 Strand, London WC2R 0RL, England

First published in Great Britain by Viking, an imprint of Penguin Books Ltd 2007
First published in the United States of America by Viking Penguin,
a member of Penguin Group (USA) Inc. 2007
Published in Penguin Books (UK) 2008
Published in Penguin Books (USA) 2008

1   3   5   7   9   10   8   6   4   2

THE LIBRARY OF CONGRESS HAS CATALOGED THE HARDCOVER EDITION AS FOLLOWS:
Page, Jeremy, 1969–
Salt / Jeremy Page.
p.   cm.
ISBN 978-0-670-03868-8 (hc.)
ISBN 978-0-14-311412-3 (pbk.)
1. Germans—England—Fiction.   2. England—Fiction.   I. Title.
PR6116.A35S25   2006
823'.92—dc22   2006037568

Printed in the United States of America
Set in Dante

For Jacob

Contents

Mud

Finding a man buried up to his neck in mud. That's how it's meant to have started. Him in the mud and her pushing a pram towards him over the saltmarsh. He's on one side of a creek and she's on the other. The pram is full of samphire and there's more of it in her hands and by her feet. Bright green samphire on black, oily mud, the start of this story has very few colours. And against the mud – quite unexpectedly – she's seen the shocking blond hair of the man.

She said she nearly tripped over him. That her wellies nearly kicked him like he was a washed-up fishing buoy, till at the last second – the very last second, which was also their first – he'd smiled politely, and said hello.

It's a pretty start to a story. Across the mud slicks and estuary there's a boat, which was wrecked many years before the man was. It's called the *Hansa*, and because it's sinking in mud and a rising tide the man has felt an affinity with it all morning. He's certainly had little else to look at, and the rest of the landscape fails to make sense – the sky is so watery blue and the sea so cloudy grey that just to look at it makes him feel upside down. Of course, what he cannot see – yet – are the clouds. A thin smoke-signalled line beyond the Holkham Meals. But *she* sees them all right, saw them the second they appeared, and for a moment she doesn't know what to do – should she run? She thinks better of it because she knows it's too late. The story of her and the man she found has already started. And another thing, she's seen the tall wooden figure of a longshoreman on the creek's other side, looking like a cracked mast stuck in the mud, tattered rags of sails blowing from his shoulders.

So this young woman, some kind of creek-hopper, in that instant, with mud on her face and a man's coat on her back, boots on her feet, made a decision. She moved quickly, scattering samphire on to the man beneath her, weaving the muddy roots into his conspicuous blond hair and laying out bundles by the dozen along the bits of his arms and chest where they poked through the mud, and as the longshoreman began to wade into the creek she arranged the last of the samphire on the mound of his belly, finally running out when it came to his 'down there'. No, not even a solitary stalk was unaccounted for. She left that bit exposed, and in the seconds before the longshoreman arrived, she sat on her pile. Three an' six, two shillin' two an' six, she muttered. Needless to say the longshoreman had spent too many years staring at the horizon, talking to fish heads hanging from his hook or herring strung from his belt to notice anything odd about the woman counting her crop.

Though he'd meandered an unnecessary hundred yards across the marsh to see my grandmother, he had nothing in particular to say when he arrived. That being the usual path in Norfolk and this being the usual way of the marsh. They got by in silence, listening to the larks. The longshoreman sniffed, shifted his weight, moved off again. The young woman kept a wary glance on him and the herring swinging from his belt as he began to splatter some drops of weak piss on the mud, and as he shook himself dry she looked at how the fish hanging from his belt danced, their wide-mouthed expressions so close to a smile.

'Guess what I seen,' he began.

She continued the samphire count.

'Guess what I seen yes'day.'

'What?'

'You ought a guess.'

'Why?'

'What I seen.'

'Well, what was it?'

'Ain't you guessin'?'

Ill at ease, he ground his foot into the mud like all marsh-men do.

'I ain't told no one.'

'Thass because ain't no one listen to you.'

The longshoreman frowned and sucked his breath in. 'You put me off my count, thass trouble,' she said.

'Last night,' he said, 'I seen a man fell right out the sky. Out the moon maybe. Fell right out down here an' I been lookin' for him.'

She saw tufts of that blond hair poking through between the samphire. 'Five an' six, ha'penny . . .'

'What them clouds say?' the longshoreman asked, chuckling to himself. He gave her a wink and began to head off. He was, after all, infatuated.

Halfway into the lagoon – known as the Pit – with the water up to the hem of his waders, he turned back, looking a little more like a drowning man than usual, and shouted *I ain't lying no how!* between the circling shrieks of gulls and terns.

And to the man struggling under her samphire pile she whispered *you keep it quiet now 'cause that one's got a long tongue*. But the man she'd uprooted from the marsh like the samphire itself had other things on his mind. Maybe it's just a story, but the story goes that once he was down there, the man weighed up his options, found to his surprise that this young woman wasn't made entirely of mud, that she was probably still in her twenties, that her skin was smooth and smelled like warm dry flints. The story has it that even while the longshoreman's waders and flapping oilskins were approaching through the creek, the buried man was thinking she must be worth a go, thinking about all a man can think about when he knows his number's up.

But maybe this is already far from the truth. Stories start simply enough, but they soon can't be trusted. What's certainly true is that the man did something to put her hackles up, because my grandmother half-carried half-dragged her man from the shore, across the saltmarsh, along the Morston Channel to Lane End, her cottage. To the one room where she slept, ate and washed. And there, in the middle of her room, she threw down the mud-man in near disgust. Crumpled and guilty, he shivered and coughed on her rug while she unhooked the tin bath and placed it on six raised bricks.

'You stink like cod. Should've gived you to that long-shore-man. I should've chucked you back in the sea on the end of his hook.'

It's possible he never understood a word she said.

For the next ten minutes she talked to herself as she carried water from the standpipe outside, sloshing it on the rug and across the curled-up legs of the man on her way to the tub. The man hid his head in shame as the water and the nonsense and the obscenities poured down round him till the tub was full.

These were the nights when German bombers growled through the sky, their bellies full with steel and cordite. When the moon was low their dark shapes and still-darker shadows came over the coast. Several hours later they'd return again, wearily, lighter in weight, fewer in number, dropping the occasional bomb on the forgotten land of creeks and channels beneath them. On one of those nights it all began for me – crablines and samphire, tulips and bees, fireworks like delphiniums and agapanthus in the sky, smoking fish on racks by the dozen, elm trees and marsh fever, boats and rag clouds and dunes and woods and marshes and the dead sperm whale – war, after all, starts many things, and even though I wasn't born for another twenty-five years, my story, or at least the stories that made my story, began there.

Back in the cottage, the odd couple who just met on the marshes are sitting on the rug. Before them there's the blackened shape of the tin bath, under which my grandmother has placed candles to keep the water hot. The man, perhaps wondering whether he's to be cooked, nevertheless cuts his losses and steps – still with his boots on – into the tub. The steam rises lazily into the candlelight of the room. My grandmother kneels by the tub and begins to soap the marsh off his back, occasionally splashing him with water to make him keep still. She uncorks the mud from his ears and for the first time he listens to the murmuring of distant terns, the stirring of the chimney, a rusty weathervane on top of the roof. A lone bomber goes overhead, and an air-raid siren wails mournfully across the marsh. Blackout curtains hang against the windows and my grandfather must think that this woman lives in a cave. He is safe here. No one will ever see her candles.

It is a moment to savour in my family history.

When he stands, the steam rises softly from his skin like he's a man new made, from the mould. He's an impressive sight, youthful and relaxed, arms hanging calmly by his sides. He has the palest blue eyes she's ever seen. But she doesn't wrap the naked man in a warm towel. In fact, she doesn't have a towel. She has a large bunch of muddy samphire stems, and slaps the man on the back of his shins to get his legs out of the way. He steps out, dripping, and her forearms go to work in the soiled water of the bath, washing out the roots.

He stands there dripping, uneasy, unsure what to do. He's confused, what with the watery sky, the cloudy sea, the creek-hopping woman, the longshoreman, the boiling cauldron and the strange green plant.

But she's not without heart, for lying on the bed is a clean white shirt and a dark suit, which has the smell of a wardrobe and marks on the shoulders where she's sponged the dust.

Where had that suit come from, and whose back had it come off? My grandmother sticks to her story – she claims she'd always had one ready, just for this type of occasion. Every woman, she adds, should have a suit at the back of the wardrobe, just in case. That the man she found was nearly naked – apart from the boots – and buried up to his neck in Morston Marsh – well, that was only incidental, a minor detail, although it certainly proved she'd been right to have a suit hanging up ready. So what happened to the suit, then? Chucked in the sea, my mother says, after he did what he did. Rat, my grandmother adds. Every story heads towards tragedy, given the time.

When the samphire was washed, my grandmother put several fistfuls of the plant into a saucepan set over the fire. The man nervously straightened his collar and waited, unaware of the spells that were about to be brewed. Like all the men in my family, his appetite was to be his downfall. And from the moment my grandmother had spied his ridiculous head sticking out of the mud, she'd known that her cookery would land him. She boiled cider vinegar. With her back to him so that he was forced to peer, she made a white sauce, uncorked an earthenware jar and added a dash of dark brown stock. The vapours rose stealthily into the air like ghosts – chicken bones, fish heads, eyes of cod. She cracked two eggs and poured from shell to shell, letting the muscle and white drip carelessly on to the tiles. The plump yolks went in, and she began a vigorous thickening whisk, while the man's stare became more intent, more desperate, his shoulders beginning to sink with the acuteness of his hunger. She added the vinegar, a slice of butter, and bit by inexorable bit my grandfather was forced to succumb. The air was filled with smooth waves of scent: the creamy almost rancid bitterness of a dairy, the rotten-sweet dust of the summer orchard, the breath of corn, of malt, a whiff of the sea.

My grandmother laid the fleshy green samphire across a large plate and poured a generous puddle of hollandaise next to it. She sat by the man and raised a juicy stem of samphire in front of his eyes. Taunting him. She dragged it across the plate, twisting it like rope to gather the sauce, then she put it in his mouth, closing his hanging jaw with her other hand. She pulled it through his teeth, freeing the samphire and the sauce and the delicious creamy tang from the thin white stem and the still slightly muddy root. His eyes closed in bewilderment, then opened in delight. He was a gonner.

Between them, they devoured the samphire, turning the lush green stems into a pile of stringy roots. The man smelled the suit on his back, he smelled the years of stale air woven into it, he smelled the nets down by the creek, the cheap grease of candlewax and the fear and loneliness that was huddled on this bleak North Sea coast during these long dark nights. He smelled the animals huffing in the stables across the marsh, the children crouching hushed under kitchen tables, and high in the air, he smelled the sweet perfume of engine oil, of dark guns heavily greased and hot to touch, the acrid and compelling smell of war.

The man who would become my grandfather pulled the last stem of samphire through his teeth, wiped the yolky hollandaise off his chin and stared contentedly into the candle-flame. And, for the first time that evening, he took off his army issue boots and placed them carefully side by side under the narrow bed.

2

Days on the Wreck, Nights on the Quilt

Before it's even light, the man who was buried in mud the day before has climbed on to the roof of the cottage. He hugs the chimney like it's the mast of a boat and strains to see over the marshes. The tiles feel damp and mossy, and with his ear to the chimneypot he can just make out the eerie sound of the woman's snores coming from inside.

He needs to work out where he is, this misty edge of England, and little by little the saltmarsh reveals itself as the light spreads. At the foot of the garden, a rough mudslide slips into the Morston Channel. Clearly able to carry a sizeable boat, but draining to a trickle at low tide. Beyond it, a flat mile of saltmarsh until the branchless masts of other boats – there must be a channel there too. Yes, leading to a small village with high flint walls against the weather and the cold North Sea. He recalls seeing it on a map, it must be Blakeney. He sees the first of the luggers there, assembled on the quay, deciding which mud pool to dig their bait. A dreadful living. Beyond them the saltmarsh stretches as far as he can see, making its own horizon in a raised bank, which must mean another river is behind it. The Glaven, he suddenly remembers – it's the kind of thing a bomber can follow on moonlit nights. The river flows through a village called Cley next the Sea, an odd name in any language, past serene reed beds and a picture-postcard windmill. Not that serenity lasts long out here – the storm of 1953 will be sent that way fairly soon. They'll be climbing the trees and smashing holes through the tiles before that night is through.

The man knows that none of these channels, all of which point due north like a trident, actually reach the sea. They all drain into a four-mile-long lagoon called the Pit, and on the other side of the Pit is the Point: a low sweeping bank of sand, gravel, mud and dunes, which joins the land at Cley and stretches along the coast like a giant protective arm. Beyond that is the open water of the North Sea.

At this moment the sun rises miraculously, seemingly out of the distant mud of the saltmarsh, orange-yolked and unreal, and for a second my grandfather is illuminated like a film star, on set, in another man's suit. Blond hair, thin-skinned, with the neat ordered smile of a calm man. Those eyes seem impossibly clear, their sky-blue colour almost doesn't register in the light.

He scans the marshes, passing the place near by where a boat will be wrecked in 1953, Bryn Pugh's *Thistle Dew*. As he sweeps the marshes he lingers briefly on the spot where he was found buried in the mud, passes the oyster bed where I shall be locked in a cage and nearly drowned one day, over to the wreck that he spent all of yesterday morning looking at. Then, near the rising sun, he sees the silhouette of a pillbox, newly constructed. I'll examine the way shrimp have been eaten after a picnic there. Near the pillbox he sees a small oak copse and an isolated huddle of buildings and outbuildings. Not much to look at. More outbuilding than building at first glance – just a cattle shed used in storms and floods. But it has a good chimney, which is why my uncle will choose to make his smokehouse there in a few years' time. There's the lawn where we will cure the hocks, the room where he will build his fireworks, and there's the thick smokehouse door with its unreliable latch. Ah, yes, the latch. Looking at these buildings, you've really got to hand it to him. My uncle was a man of vision.

My grandfather will never know any of this. He will know

nothing about the mouthwatering smell of smoking fish, the massive door with smoke pulling through the cracks like nails being uncurled from the wood, or the fireworks being built in the Lab. But, for the moment, he's happy, he's alive and the sun is shining.

He puts his ear to the chimneypot and listens to the sounds of the cottage. Noises rise up at him like he's listening to a well. A shuffle of shoes on the tiles and, suddenly loud, a spit landing in the fireplace right below him. She must be up. He begins to slide down the roof on his backside, is unable to stop the acceleration, so falls the last few feet to land roughly in the garden. She's at the window glaring at him. Falling out the clouds again. *Where've you bin!* she mouths. He points to the sky. *Thassit!* she says, had enough of you. He smiles back, then brushes himself down – it's not a bad suit after all – and opens the door as if he owns the place. She's already turned her back on him.

Once inside, and not knowing what to do, he finds an oilcan and greases the door's hinges. He goes to the fireplace and closes a link in a chain which is giving way, he fixes the rattle on a window by hammering leather into the crack. He begins to whistle with his happiness. My grandmother doesn't want to acknowledge him, but is getting increasingly irritable with a man who can be so annoyed by little things after less than twelve hours in a place. Juss let him try fix my skillet – he'll know about it then. Just who did this perhaps on-the-run, possibly deranged, compulsive handyman think he was?

She unwraps a loaf-shaped block of cold oatmeal porridge and cuts four thick slices from it, melts lard on the skillet and fries the slices till they're golden brown. My grandfather's fixing spree grinds to a halt as the smell of frying fat fills the air. She's at it again, he thinks. He obediently sits at the table.

A wonky table – but he even misses that, such is the power of the woman's cookery.

'You carry on that fidget and I'll clout you with the broom and that's as solid as bugger,' she began, 'fannyin' round like an old woman. Get your grub in an' go fix the rowin' boot.'

Perhaps he smiles at this point the generous smile of a man grateful for small mercies. His dreamy blue eyes glinting with the sheer pleasure of being alive, being well, being useful. Relaxed by the handiwork and the warmth of porridge he says one word – pointing to himself, he tells her to call him Hans.

'*Hands?*' she replies.

With his belly full of porridge, the hammer was given back to Hands – as he'd instantly become – and he was told to go fix the garden. Get out the house, more like, and Hands knew she meant it. Immediately outside the back door he almost tripped over a small rowing dinghy – the *Pip* – badly in need of caulking, splicing and varnish. Overjoyed with the project he went back to hug the marshwoman, but was met only with her finger pointing 'out' once more. He would need tools and materials, but other jobs needed doing first. So he vanished with a box of nails and spent the morning fastening wires to the fence and pegging the raspberry bushes, and as his sphere of fixing grew ever wider he returned to the roof, where he hammered down some of the loose tiles and finally, mercifully, ran out of nails. While he was up there he saw the longshore-man winding his tortuous way through the creeks like a man trying either to lose himself or find something he'd lost. A man not comfortable with straight lines.

On the roof, however, tiles had been realigned, coping stones raised and guttering levelled. The marsh was obviously sucking the cottage down, twisting its beams and cracking its walls in the process, but Hands was doing his best to polish the rails of the sinking ship. As he reached up for the slanting chimneypot he spotted the longshoreman had arrived and was leaning against the gate. The gate leaned in turn against the longshoreman.

'Goose! You got some bloke up the roof. Goose!'

Her real name's Kitty, but it's never used.

Hands looked down, waiting for the marshwoman to come out, but nothing happened.

The longshoreman waited too, nodded a quiet mornin' to the man with the hammer, then began again: 'Roof, Goose. Got some bloke on the chimney.'

The longshoreman shut up when she came out. He grinned knowingly; not that he knew much about anything.

'What you grinnin' at?'

'You're a rum 'un.'

'You what?'

'You heard.'

'What?'

'What I said.'

The days pass slowly in Norfolk. Hands sat down on his haunches, the hammer idle across his lap.

'Don't you make my gate stink of fish.'

'Got you a dab, ain't I,' the longshoreman said, unhitching a pale flatfish from his belt and holding it out.

'Chuck it down. I ain't coming no closer 'cause of your breath.'

The longshoreman gave his fish a lingering kiss on the lips then chucked it down.

'Thanks.'

'That's got grass on it now.'

'It'll wash.'

The longshoreman pulled out a bit of driftwood from his pocket: 'And that's a bit of wood.'

He chucked it on to a pile of similar-shaped wood and other bits of flotsam, looked up and nodded at Hands, pushed himself upright from the gate, leaned forward into his stride, and left.

And wrapped round the length of driftwood was a strip of fabric – part of the fine cream of a German silk parachute, woven in Dresden, found in a creek bed, hurriedly buried. Or so the story usually went, spoken either by my mother or my grandmother over the years. Though even this is uncertain: there are irregularities, details that change, inconsistencies in chronology. That fish, for one, seems likely to have been a red herring. Sometimes it's a plaice – a flatfish, admittedly – but other times it's been a whiting, a John Dory and, once, a mackerel. Whiting are never caught at that time of the year, and the longshoreman's bag of tackle never carried mackerel feathers.

Hands knew from the start he'd bitten off more than he could chew. However hard he worked, however many things he put right and made level, he knew the woman would sweep him out of the house with her broom one day. And so, up on the roof, I imagine he gazed long and hard at the gleaming roll of parachute silk against the muddy lawn, before turning his attention to the horizon, way beyond the marshes.

That little glimpse of him up on the roof is my invention, I admit, but here my story goes along with my grandmother's: Hands *liked* looking at the horizon. Long-sighted, dreamy-expressioned, whatever you want to call it, she noticed it and didn't like it one bit.

She had a problem on her plate. She had a man in her suit and he was already looking into the distance. What to do? Well, her solution was to regard it as a fault in his eyesight. She made him work on things close at hand, made him hunt for pins on the floor, pointed out a speck of dust and asked him what it was, made him search for crumbs under the table, made him inspect the moles on her back. He peered closer each time, completely unaware that his lovely long sight was being reeled in from the horizon like a sleeping fish at the end of her line. Unaware that his world was becoming her cottage. Eventually, she made him thread needles, night after night, with candles placed further and further off, until he rubbed his eyes and massaged his temples to get rid of the headaches. And after several months she put on his nose a pair of glasses she'd apparently had ready for him since the start, sat him in his chair in the dark and told him he looked *a real turkey*.

She had him by the eyes and she had him by the belly. Early in the mornings he'd be rushing over to light the fire, to clean the skillet, to put two gleaming plates on the table. He'd get the block of porridge off the shelf and put a knife next to it. Oatmealy vapours overran his dreams. Hands would guide the marshwoman to the hearth while she was still practically asleep. He'd put the wooden splice in her hand and ease it through the softening lard. He'd flick the fat on to the hot skillet, and as the sizzle and smell rose, her drowsiness would evaporate. Perhaps here he'd get a whack with the splice for being so meddlesome. A pretty little routine, until one morning, when my grandmother decided to be sick on his clean white plate.

Staring down at the mess, his hard-working and super-efficient hands had for once not known what to do. They rose slightly in the air and his fingers stretched out to grasp the things he didn't understand.

'Thass your fault filthy cud, stickin' me up you sly old devil. Thass what you deserve no less. And don't get no ideas about no runnin' off now you hair. Thar's no more porridge cake for you and no lordin' it round the house neither. I'll have a quilt to keep me warm and thar's a needle in that there box.'

That was how Hands discovered he was to be a father.

Soon after, he was sent out to fill the samphire pram – a ripped fisherman's gansey found on Blakeney Quay, a washed-up laundry sack with Property of His Majesty's Royal Navy on it, a trawlerman's shirt, a sou'wester tied across a duck coop. He robbed a scarecrow of its Anderson tartan scarf and unwrapped the dishcloth Goose had bound her drainpipe with. And, most importantly, he found the main part of a rust-red jib sail, which he quartered, boiled the starch out of and ironed flat. Like the best of dreamers he found pleasure in challenge and beauty in his task. Soon he was threading a gorgeous blanket stitch round his fabrics, marvelling in the design and, with special care, weaving the magic of the sail into the quilt's finery.

As her pregnancy matures, he adds more patches until the quilt reaches the floor on both sides of the narrow bed. Each night they spoon each other, then she falls asleep on her back and Hands watches her belly pushing the quilt higher so that his first task of the morning is to widen the material, now putting in all the scraps of cotton, flotsam and sacking he can find. The parachute is used as a lining – the lightness of the material brought down to earth by strips of blackout curtain he's cut off below the windowsill. Eventually, nimble-fingered Hands works so fast that the quilt begins to stretch over the floor faster than any belly can raise it. The quilt expands across the tiles, becoming a rug, a doormat, even an added layer to pin up over the windows.

Exceeding his duties yet again, Hands earned the right to have time off. He was allowed to visit the pub. That's him in his element, sauntering over the marsh on a balmy summer's evening, pockets filled with tern eggs, which he's been swapping for beer, pitch and caulking putty, humming a German tune. He's learned the best place to hide is to be in full view, sipping this strange warm soapy beer, allowing himself to be roped into a few hands of poker at the Map and Sail. He's got it all planned out. During the day he's taken to going out on the marsh, walking in strict grid pattern, establishing hypotenuse then figuring quadrants. He had no theodolite, and to my knowledge never made a map. The only thing he owned was a knife. Hands always carried a knife.

Following the Morston Creek from Lane End, Hands would walk to the small shore near the spot where he was first found. Perhaps he would squat down there in the mud, pluck a young stem of samphire and chew it while he stared across the Pit. Military fashion, then, he would take off his boots, tuck in the laces, then put them next to each other in order to make a platform. His trousers, shirt, cotton neckscarf and socks would be folded and neatly arranged on top of the boots so that nothing but his feet would touch the Morston mud. In only his underwear, he would walk into the Pit and, knife clenched between his teeth, he would start to swim. Heading for what? Freedom? Not yet.

Five minutes later he would haul himself from the water on the other side of the Pit, sinking all the while into deep folds of wet sand until he could grasp the rail. This was his goal – the wreck he'd seen, when his eyes were just a few inches above the mud. The *Hansa*. In Norfolk, 'hansa' means 'heron', but to Hands it must have seemed magical that the wreck which might have been his last sight on earth was practically named after him.

He stands there, dripping on the weather-blackened planks of the wreck. It's a thirty-two-foot North Sea trawler with a long foredeck and two staved-in hatches to the hold. A double hull and a heavy beam, built in the Nordic design. The deck is at a crazy angle, sinking to starboard, where a hole wide enough to swim into has shattered the hull. At high tide the sea pours in, sloshing about inside the wreck with a lethal black inkiness, while at low tide, looking though the hatches, it seems the cargo has never been anything but the weed-smeared mud of North Norfolk. In the wheelhouse, the glass has long vanished. Gulls have peppered the wheel with their shit and clawed the paint down to bare wood. At other places, the paint has blistered away from the iron like psoriasis. A mizzenmast rises behind the wheelhouse, though there's no gaff or boom, and the rudder has been snapped off by the mud. It sticks out of the marsh, about twenty feet away, wrecked itself, totally without direction.

That summer, Hands would spend his day sitting on the jagged prow of the *Hansa*. He would sit, like myself nearly forty years later, with his naked legs dangling either side of the rotten bowsprit, prising limpets from the wood with the flat of his knife, gouging them from their glistening sockets before putting them in his mouth to chew. Soon all the limpets that had survived the knife would be welded to the hull like rivets. And so my grandfather would take his knife to the gunwale, deck, hatches and hawsepipe of the *Hansa*, and there he'd begin to carve the wood.

The mizzenmast becomes a rudimentary totem pole. The lowest animal is a large grinning whale, although it has more than a passing resemblance to the lesser weever which will nearly sting my mother as she reaches out to pull it off her crabline at exactly the same place seventeen years later. The first and only fish she ever caught. Above that, a beak and then the cruel cold eye of a gull like the one my father extricated from my mother's hair. Then carved wooden waves, then higher still and the waves begin to look like flames, the strange blue glow of St Elmo's fire that grips the mast head before the onset of a storm. Finally, at the top, the carving of a boat with a solitary figure clinging to the shattered prow as it sinks.

Goose didn't like all this time spent on the *Hansa*. Days on the wreck were not a good sign; so, late in her pregnancy, she'd walked down to the Pit and shouted his name. She saw his hands worrying at the salt-withered wood and she watched him cracking his lunch against the windlass heads. When her voice reached him over the calm water, she saw him look back at her with his distant, dreamy gaze. He didn't wave, and he didn't come back.

On 8 May 1945, an unusually strong nor'westerly wind blew over the Morston Marshes, bending the marram and arrow-grass and forcing the terns to sit on their nests. In her cottage, my grandmother sniffed the air and decided she wouldn't go out on the marsh that day. On the way back to her bed, she abruptly went into labour.

Hands, out in the garden, heard the first ugly shape of her screams. He sat in the garden under the quilt – which was getting an airing – while the cries and curses came in fits and bursts. From inside the cottage, all she could see through the open door was a corner of the quilt hanging on the line, swaying in the breeze. She stared at it while the time passed, then saw it being slowly pulled along the line out of her sight, until it was gone completely. There was no sign of the man. Her contractions returned with new intensity, the pain forcing her head back on the pillow and silencing her tongue for once. And as Hands raised his brightly coloured quilted sail on the mended mast of the *Pip*, her waters broke, and she called out for the man even though she could hear him slipping the boat down the muddy bank into the creek that led him to the Pit, the North Sea and a newly backing wind, which took him away for good.

And as my grandfather sailed his rickety craft into the choppy water of the North Sea, the bells rang from the flint churches in the flat country behind him. I imagine him craning his neck anxiously, pulling the sail closer to the wind so that warm air would billow into the patches of grass, marsh, corn, wood and heath sewn into the quilt, hoisted on his mast, rich and beautiful, filling with power and urging him away, telling him to leave, to escape, to stop turning back to a land rippling with the sound of bells like the wind now filling his sail. The bells rang until his boat was a dot on the horizon he so adored. Ringing and ringing, and then the first cries of his child, catching on the wind and following him out to sea. My mother was born and the war was over.

3
The Sail (or the Map and Sail)

The mud swelled and shrank round the house, dislodging the tiles on the roof and knocking the chimneypot *on the huh*, as they say in Norfolk. Inside, the floor buckled on imaginary tree roots. Damp soaked up the wall, making screws fall from the plaster like rotten teeth in the middle of the night, while my grandmother buried her head in the pillow. Soon there was no trace of Hands. Everything he'd touched, fixed, put right, he'd only halted on its path to eventual ruin.

No sign, of course, apart from the ruddy-faced little madam down there in the cot. This unpromising bundle of wet nappies and watering eyes was my mother. It was an uneasy relationship from the start. The baby had screamed, starting from the moment the patchwork quilt was hoisted on the *Pip*, screamed louder when the little boat slipped down the Morston Channel, and louder still for the rest of the day. Exhausted and bloody-minded, Goose had struggled out late in the afternoon to scan the marshes, the Point and the open sea beyond. Where's the bugger gone? Behind her, Blakeney's church bells kept ringing, the occasional volley of a rifle went off, and an anti-aircraft gun blasted a ten-gun salute from the bank. Now some lunatic was down Blakeney Quay firing a musket into the sky. A small celebratory group had gathered while crows circled the town like vultures.

Highly confused at the time, Goose may have thought the militia were out for Hands, had possibly caught the rascal, were at this minute dragging him back from the sandbanks after sinking his patchwork boat. It seemed the whole world

– already gone crazy in the last few years – had entered a new state of insanity.

Goose looked to the clouds for answers and saw extraordinary shapes in them. That morning there'd been cirrus, fine and ragged at the top of the sky. The wind had teased them into long flowing mare's-tails hanging across the marsh with the spirit of wild horses in full gallop. But below them had arrived the solitary puffs of altocumulus, with ribbed bellies and candyfloss tops. They came slowly over the heath and down on to the saltmarsh, sluggish with the weight of so many images of war: refugee clouds filled with people afoot, long marches on blank landscapes, smouldering cities filled with fire, children playing ambush in the wastes of rubble. And there was Hands where she would always see him, fighting the waves in the sinking *Pip*, giant dogfish gnawing at the gunwale. He bashes one on the snout with the end of an oar, but it's a losing battle. And squeezed between the clouds she sees glimpses of her daughter's life to come. Flowers grown in weird patterns, wooden ducks painted in gaudy colours and peppered with lead shot, a boat painted like the sky itself.

Some time late in the afternoon, Goose remembered the baby and went in to find it pink from yelling. The tiny fists were clenched with rage and an angry red tongue flicked in a mouth rimmed with white fury. She carried her daughter outside, pretending to abandon her in the hope it might encourage a fear so great that natural instinct would make it shut up. The baby was laid on the grass to yell at the sky while Goose went down the lane to continue her cloud-watching. There wasn't much sky left. Some clouds were moving against the direction of the wind, jostling for space in the ever-crowding air. And it made sudden sense to her. The clouds weren't about the man who'd just left her, but about that ridiculous war. It must be over.

The clouds became so full of the nonsense babble of good

wishes and hopes that the insights she was hoping to glean about the vanishing of the man or the arrival of the baby were totally obliterated. Through the hawthorn hedge she occasionally spied on her daughter, still lying on the lawn, screaming and punching at imaginary foes. The sounds of marsh, the creeks, the guns in Blakeney and the terrified birds had not stilled the child.

Goose looked again at the glimpse of the open sea and knew the man was not coming back. Hands had stuck his dumb smile out from the mud and politely welcomed that mud-creature uprooting herself towards him; he'd fixed a few things, rubbed his stomach, won a few tricks in the Map and Sail, stitched a quilt, caulked and pitched a clinker boat, then sailed off into the sunset. Gone for good. But long tongues have the way of whipping up clean farewells into all sorts of complicated fictions. Norfolk claims all and confuses all issues. In the Map and Sail the men argued furiously about the stranger who used to fleece them every Friday night: – A poker whiz, yeah, sharp-shooter, reckon he come from Lou-ee-siana on one o' them paddle yachts an' all them furs an' blokes with thin moustaches an' gold teeth – He ain't never been outta Norfolk, you prat! – So where's he gone then, the Seagull? – Don't you mention that place hair, you hair? – He got you too, Arthur, got you good an' proper, hain't he? – Don't you come near me now, he got my watch on his wrist remember, I ain't singin' his praises, juss hope Annie don't never stop believin' that watch got dropped in the creek . . .

As the years passed Hands became everything in turn from a conchy to a chappie sent down from Whitehall to check out Blakeney's fighting spirit, to an agent from the brewery with a sensitive palate for tasting the water Arthur Quail added out back – Din't you never think o' that, Arthur? – On the run, came the answer from the publican. Learned his cards in the nick, din't he. Kept his head down an' din't get pissed an' din't say nothin' to no one, in case we'd blow the whistle on him. Bloke on the run from the MP. I seen his type in 1917. Hour square-bashin' up at Catterick, two days hitchin' rides to get away. You go on the run, where you gonna end up? – Blakeney being the obvious answer – And they'd not be let off the hook yet – you get a train till it come to the end of the line, bury yourself in a load of spuds and get a lift in a lorry, flag down a haycart an' bum a lift in that a while, nick a bike, end up walking you name it till you get to the coast an' can't get no further without gettin' wet. Thass right here. They listen to him, nursing their pints, thinking of the world's cutthroats planning cosy evenings in the Map and Sail. We gotta be on our guard now, you lissen, 'cause I heard 'em talk, I have. I heard 'em in places you ain't been an' they all say this is a good place to hang low. I seen blokes sew 'emselves up in mailbags with a label got Blakeney Quay writ on it. I heard 'em up Norwich, I tell you. Go to Blakeney, they say, you get you a map an' go to Blakeney. Bloke up there named Sammy Craske got a good watch on his wrist an' he play a lousy hand o' cards. Eye starts twitchin' the moment he got him an ace . . .

And causing a stir there's a voice from the back of the room, a voice rising out of his drink like that of some half-drowned mariner. It's the longshoreman, man of the marsh, folded into a pub chair and unafraid of the man behind the bar.

'He got your map, Arthur Quail, don't you forget he got your map.'

It silences the pub.

On 9 March 1945, two months before Hands vanished, Arthur Quail's great map of the North Sea was taken from the Map and Sail. It had hung there for thirty years, becoming indistinct under a layer of smoke and dust. But it was a fine map, with a glorious compass rose in the German Bight, fathom contours, anchorages, wrecks, parallels and meridians. And though it needed updating with the hazards of several million tons of wreckage sunk in two world wars, it was still a working chart, and Hands wanted it, even though Germany was pockmarked with dart holes.

It had probably been put up there in the first place so these Norfolk men would know where the German Empire was, but now, in the dying months of the Second World War, the map itself was causing trouble. Two months earlier, on a Saturday night, Captain Mayfield (retired) had downed his pint, wiped the smears of froth from the tips of a moustache limp with beer, and told Arthur Quail to *take down the map*. A threat to national security. Information in wrong hands. Helping Hun get to Norwich quick and all that.

Arthur Quail had a problem with authority and a great liking for his map, so told the retired captain that if Herr Goering fell through the ceiling on the strings of a parachute the only direction he'd learn would be the way to Mayfield's cottage. A showdown, which Quail – the pint puller – easily won, due to the weary cheer from the other men in the pub. Mayfield stormed out to 'inspect the sandbags'.

Hands, my grandfather, had watched all this from his poker table. A man of few words, and with a clear reason to keep silent, he was a natural card player. Regulars at the Friday-night lock-in: Sammy Craske, oysterman, good with a low hand but liable to panic with a queen or ace – estranged relationship with his mother was said to be behind it; Albie Smee, a good liar, but too mean to capitalize on his natural skills; Soggy Brean, a 'weeper'; and Will Langore, a wealthy farmer and authoritarian, whose two great-nephews – one of whom is my father – Hands will never know.

*

I have a photo from one of these nights in 1945. The bar looks empty, but in the corner beneath the stuffed pike that brought Hands his luck sit the six men. It's a bad picture, scratched on the journey from pocket to pocket over the years, smudged by each finger that has smoothed it flat, surviving under grease and dust, turning the shadowy men into the ghosts they became. It's been passed around a good deal. My grandfather – if that's him – possibly sensed the scrutiny of coming years, so has turned his back to the lens.

There's Arthur Quail's great map of the North Sea hanging over the bar. It's been hung upside down to spite Captain Mayfield, so the photo must have been taken in the first few months of 1945.

And here's Hands, sitting on a royal flush in the Map and Sail. Over the baize, Arthur Quail's sweating, defeated, too broke to carry on, but too weak to walk away. He calls. What with? the others join in. You ain't got nothin' leff, Arthur. Shut it! Go on, as a mate, show us, he implores Hands. The man's silence has him riled. You got an ace an' king, ain't you? – It's too late – I said shut it, Sammy! Juss let me know, eh? And that's the moment my grandfather points to his prize – the map that has hung above the bar for thirty years.

The longshoreman looks hard at Arthur Quail, glad that his comment about the map has brought back all these painful memories. The others in the bar stare into their pints. They know each time the bloody map is mentioned it'll end in tears. The longshoreman lights his pipe and gazes into the smoke, as if practising the cloud skills Goose has been teaching him.

From beyond the horizon Hands pulls a final volte-face. May 1949, and an article appears in the *Eastern Daily Press* titled 'We Just Love Them German Tunes':

What is better now the evenings are drawing out than to take a hearty stroll across the wild marshes of the North Norfolk coast before retiring to the gentle old-world charm of the local pub for a warm pint of beer and a singsong to anti-English wartime German songs.

Alerted to this phenomenon by Captain Mayfield, resident of Gunner Creek Cottage in Blakeney, we dispatched our reporter to the Map and Sail dressed in deer-stalker and binoculars. True enough, as the evening wore on, and tongues became loosened, regulars collected round the piano at the far end of the bar with Mrs Balls at the keys. An instrument probably not tuned since the turn of the century – and hammered ever since – the music began with local favourites of 'The Bold Young Sailor' and 'Shoo Arlo Birds', before 'The Foggy, Foggy Dew' broke out, during which Mrs Balls strained her right hand in the difficult chorus section. Mrs Balls returned to the keys after receiving the appropriate treatment to perform a tune closely resembling 'Jawohl, meine Herren', a cheeky propaganda song of the German National Socialist party.

Our reporter threw off his disguise to confront Mr Arthur Quail, patron, who seemed to express genuine surprise that he had been singing German propaganda tunes of the last war. In his defence he maintained that 'Jawohl, meine Herren' was in fact the lesser known, if not entirely unknown, 'She Were a Blakeney Marvel'. He denied any accusations that Blakeney offers, or had ever offered, clandestine support for the German National Socialist Party, and with short shrift showed our reporter the door.

Outside, Mr Albie Smee claimed the scandalous tunes had been taught to those who frequented the Map and Sail by a vagrant card shark who had holed out there during the war, before disappearing one night after conducting many thefts in the area. Sightings have continued unverified over the last few years. His residence is not known.

Captain Mayfield saw active service at Modder River and

Bloemfontein in the Boer War, and was a discipline instructor during the Great War, though sadly too old to see active service in any foreign theatre.

German tunes were never heard in the Map and Sail again, and Hands was dropped as a topic of conversation. To cover up the truth, it became general knowledge that Arthur Quail's great map of the North Sea had not, in fact, disappeared in the back pocket of the man with the royal flush, but had been eaten by Sambo, an overweight black Labrador famed for his appetite for anything paper and, in particular, the beer-soaked cardboard mats at the Map and Sail.

'Thassit,' Arthur Quail finally answers the longshoreman, 'this pub ain't called the Map 'n' Sail no more. Now on it's the Albatross Inn. Soggy – you get some paint and do the sign, should've done it years back.'

Later that day Soggy's paint covered up the Map and Sail's history under the wings of an albatross, which became popular with birdwatchers because the picture was so clearly of a black-backed gull. But Arthur Quail had made his point all right, he was rewriting the story, in the same way that my family, right back to their origins in the mud of North Norfolk, went silent, went missing, erased and reinvented themselves in times of trouble.

So Hands used the map to navigate his way back to Germany. Wrong. Let my mother describe how she found it when she was a young girl: Yeah, in an old pot, hidden in an old pot well away from prying eyes. Took me half an hour getting that cork out, she says, if there han't been a cork I shoun't have bothered looking in there. She told me that when she'd unrolled Arthur Quail's missing map she'd seen a large round island drawn in the middle of the North Sea, 'big and beautiful with mountains and fjords like old Norway, marshes and creeks and wide empty beaches like Norfolk'. A proper little Atlantis. She did what any naughty girl would do, she hid the map and held her tongue. She thought constantly about that mysterious island. And little by little, her eyes began to resemble those of her father: distant and dreamy and lingering on the horizon. When she was on the saltmarsh with her mother, following mud gullies and clinging to Goose's back as the woman waded over to the Point, there, among the nesting colonies of the birds that blew up into the sky as they approached, my mother scanned the horizon in vain, thinking she'd see those snow-capped peaks of the island in the mouths of the white horses: I never saw it. Not never. Back in the cottage she'd spend the winter evenings dreaming in front of the fire, looking as the burning logs changed into the wave-battered coast of her strange imaginary island. Next to her, my grandmother, possibly staring into the same fire and wondering what goblin of the marsh had cast a spell over her daughter.

Finding the island becomes an obsession. Satchel in hand, there she is, lonely and ostracized on Blakeney Quay, in a raggy grey cloth dress, rubbing her raw scalp after her hair has been tugged hard by the local kids, quietly muttering about her mysterious island until she has a reputation for being strange in the head, like her mother. The kids already have a name for her. 'Lil' Mardler'. The little girl who told tales. Eventually she grasped the nettle. A long evening, rain beating at the window, a plain meal of herring and potatoes on a cold plate – my mother could take it no more. She ran – startling my grumpy, dozing grandmother – to the earthenware jar, rolled the map on to the table and put four small jars of pickled samphire on it to keep it flat.

'I ain't no Lil' Mardler, am I? See. The *island*.'

In her own twisted way, my grandmother must have been proud of her daughter's nickname, but this map meant trouble. According to her version, it was meant to have gone to sea with Hands. She rolled it up.

'Don't you go peepin' no more, you hair.'

No. It's not so easy to brush off Lil' Mardler. The little girl's standing her ground till her mother explains.

'Thass Dogger Bank, thass is. Now don't you go talkin' no more about it.' And before she put an end to it her mother added, 'Thass where your father's gone.'

Murky untruths. Lil' Mardler imagines her mysterious father in a playful mood, his pockets jangling with coins as he crosses the marsh early one Saturday morning, the rolled-up map sticking out of his back pocket. He stops for a minute on the high flood bank overlooking the Pit and the Point and the North Sea. In the pre-dawn silence he's watching strange vapours rising from the saltmarsh. He's thinking about the horizon and what lies beyond. That night he unrolls the map in front of Goose. He tells her how he'd won the map with the last wager of the night before, the one that finally broke Arthur Quail's nerve and then his heart, forcing him to unpin the possession he so loved from above the bar. Hands's fine fingers point out the jagged cruel Norwegian coast, the golden-ripe beaches of Denmark and the Baltic glittering with amber, then the silent brooding mass of Germany so pockmarked with the darts of the Map and Sail. Moving my grandmother's elbows, he shows her the lonely curve of the Norfolk coast, like a great sad eye cast mournfully over the water. Then his finger moves out to the North Sea, sailing smoothly over fathom marks, sandbanks and gullies until he reaches the mischievous shape of his phantom island. What's that, he asks, do you know, you voman of zhe marsh, you zea zalt, you creek-hopper? Got you stumped, haven't I. Made you feel a lemon. What's that island zhere? And my grandmother, furious the buried man was gaining the upper hand, furious that *her* sea might have an island where she knew it to be water, furious that the first bit of rock out there might not be Scandinavia, in short, furious – sucks and chews her finger and finally, desperately, shouts it out:

'Thass Dogger Bank, thass is!'

Goose had hidden Arthur Quail's great map in the earthenware jar. Hidden it because it spoke of a man she'd found and lost in the space of a few brief months. She never intended that map to be found. She'd already told my mother, and anyone else who asked, that *that man's* last known whereabouts was bailing the *Pip* in the middle of a storm, with Arthur Quail's great map of the North Sea pinned to the splash deck. Goose would tell us about the cracks that yawned open in the rotten hull, how the gannets swept down to peck his head, push him under, tweak him by the nose – the rising water above the shin, above the waist, above the neck – the thin silent mouth sinking after the boat into the storm, into the dark, into the dogfish jaws, the lobster claws.

But my mother had found that map in Lane End. And I think about Hands pulling the quilt off the washing line and hoisting it up on the mast of the *Pip*, and I wonder, why go to sea without a map?

Did he sail home, or did he hear the screams of Goose's labour coming from inside the house and was overwhelmed by such panic his dextrous fingers had tied themselves in knots? Thunderstruck with indecision, maybe he'd tried to block out the noise of the woman screaming his name by concentrating his mind on practical work. He sees the up-turned hull of the *Pip* on the lawn next to the mudslide with the patches of repair-work he's completed a few days before. He wonders whether the pitch has dried. Will it be buoyant? Will its passage through water be smooth? Will displacement levels be affected? The breeze buffets his cheek and he instantly gauges it on the Beaufort scale. Already the sounds of the birth are fading. The quilt stirs on the line. The quilt, the quilt is filling with the wind like a sail. No, surely not, this cumbersome patchwork nonsense, which has spread and spread though those long hard evenings, surely it can't contain the wind? What is the breaking point of that twine I used? Did I double the thread? And he pulls the quilt along the line out of my grandmother's restricted sight, pulling the fabric between his hands and examining the hems. His fingers begin to unknot. Just the briefest moment of regret for what he's about to do: *Jeder macht mal eine kleine Dummheit*, he says to himself, and he knows he's absolving all blame too. Then he's watching the fine silk of the dug-up parachute gathering the air. Fabric like this is spun by the angels. Deutsche angels. When the quilt is hoisted up the mast of the *Pip*, Hands has lost himself in the beauty of his science. The boat bobs into the water like a cheeky duckling, giddy with life. Yes, just a quick spin into the Pit, it'll focus my thoughts, get rid of the fallow. I'll take a rope and practise my knots and then, when I return – just see – I'll grab that umbilical cord and tie the greatest, tightest knot that's ever been seen. A knot my child will carry for the rest of its life, and when that child is in the bath, on the beach, dressing for bed, whatever, he or she is going to look down and see that tidy little scar in the middle of their belly and put their finger in and marvel, yes marvel, at their father's handiwork.

The ridiculous lengths one can go to clear the family name. Was it the wind's fault – suddenly picking up in a squall to capsize the boat and send his honourable intentions to the bottom of the sea? Were the fish to blame – did they bite through the hull before he could tack his return to the birth of his child?

My earliest memory was seeing my mother's belly-button. My first crawl was to get away from it. As a toddler I was really terrified, pulling my mother's jumper down when she reached up for the top shelf. Dangling there, elephantine, the double and triple knots grown over with skin. Hands, I've no doubt, would have tied a beautiful knot; but what I've always seen was nothing more than a really magnificent granny-slip.

Of that magical sail there is no remnant, no scrap of the scraps that it was made of, no thread of the threads that tied it together. There are no photographs. The only sail is the sail of my grandmother's stories, much fabricated with the collected junk of the marsh and the sea until it resembled the landscape of North Norfolk: muddy, wooded, sparse in its emptiness, luxuriant in its detail. What became of Hands's sail remains a mystery. Perhaps it sunk in the sea during the storm that swallowed the *Pip*. Perhaps Hands, weeping and lost already, dragged it from the mast and wrapped it round himself as the boat took on water in the final minutes, in the middle of the night. And perhaps – imagining all possibilities – that waterlogged man held fast to the wind for a day and a night, navigating by the stars and his own inner sense, tapping the strength of a well-fixed hull until he saw the low, unassuming coast on the other side of the sea, until he lugged the boat out on to the sandy shore. Did he pull the boat into the softly shifting beauty of foreign dunes, the dunes themselves seeming to him like the waves of the German Bight, slowly rolling inland over the years? The sound of the North Sea would gradually fall away, and Hands would wipe the sweat off his brow, as he makes out a lonely figure walking towards him. A small dog trotting with its nose to the ground by her side.

He would drop the rope and sit, expectantly, on the battered prow of his little boat till the woman came closer, stopping before him. Hands would have gathered together a clump of flowering sea lavender from the dunes, the same plant that grows in the marshes of North Norfolk. He would give it to the woman. The dog would sniff his boots cautiously. He would smile and ask what country it was.

Later that night, after a simple meal of smoked herring and pickles, Hands would remove his boots and place them neatly at the foot of the bed. He'd drag the salty quilt over the sheets, then turn to the woman and hold her tightly, the dog curled up at his feet.

In the morning, when the woman would go to harvest the flowers in the polder, Hands would set to work in the house. New shingles for the roof, plane the doorjambs. He'd see another crooked chimney. He'd prise the solid teak splash deck off the *Pip* and fashion a new washboard for the kitchen; throw the dog's fraying lead away, and in its place he'd plait a new, stronger tether from the boat's painter; the rudder he'd make into a weathervane, which would gently steer an imaginary course through the sky, endlessly turning, endlessly restless, fixed in position, without a course to steer, without a hand to guide it, the centre of a new home.

There are no answers, only questions. Questions and half-truths. The only thing we have is the quilt, living on, not across a bed or up a mast, but in the murk of my grandmother's mind, extending, as her stories got ever longer, until it reached beyond the cottage door, across the untidy lawn, through the thicket hedges and across the marshes. Where Hands finished my grandmother continued, faithfully taking over the stitching of the quilt, adding pieces and patches, new clauses, new asides over the years until none of us who listened could find our way out. The quilt of her stories assumed monstrous proportions, unrealistic dimensions, until we were all lost at sea along with Hands. The bugger stretched for miles, across the dismal marshes and creeks until eventually it covered the Point and wove itself across the wide sand beach into the chilling froth of the North Sea, and all of us who listened realized that what Goose was talking about was not a quilt or a sail or a man who left her in the agonies of giving birth. She was talking about Norfolk itself.

4
The Rag Cloud

Here they come – two beads of torchlight across the marsh. One held slightly higher than the other, both trained on a ground so thick with mud it seems to swallow the light before it's fallen. A mother and daughter wearing four coats between them, leaving the cottage to cross the creeks. Goose has her large salt-and-pepper hair bundled up at the back of her head, a variety of pins and sticks to keep it in place. She sleeps in it like that. Her daughter has tied rags into her own hair, over night, so now she has deep brown ringlets that spring up and down as she walks. The ground stinks with damp and the air is knife-sharp with winter. Not much wind, but the marshes are full of quiet expectant rushes of sound. Molluscs and crabs bubble in the creeks, small animals dash for cover. They press onwards as the sky lightens, picking through the mud and cross-ing the creeks on planks so slick with damp it's as if the earth is full of steam. And when they reach the place on the marsh my grandmother always calls the *tuft*, they sit down with their collars turned up, and face forward like Easter Island statues.

There's some cirrus up there. Feathery and vague, reaching across the whole sky like a heavenly harp. It catches my grand-mother's eye immediately. Breath of the angels, she says. This time of morning it's poached-salmon pink, but soon it'll glow as bright as a bridal veil. See that, Lil', see that cirrus? That come from space, it do, got nothing to do with us. They gaze at the cloud several miles above them.

Cirrus is not just the milky cataract it seems at first glance. At the right time, at the right angle, vast shapes are in there.

No other cloud has the capacity to create such an entire inverted landscape mirroring our own, filled with the dunes, creeks, fields and seas of its own ghostly creation. Goose is clearly in awe of its mystery, its enormity and its completeness, but it is just too far away, too unconnected with the world. She prefers the lower clouds.

Hair – she says – coo-mulus! And here they are. Her favourite clouds. Ain't them fat as turkeys! Right char-ac-ters. Mind, got to be patient with clouds, Lil', they ain't going to give it away first look, 'specially them fluff balls. Changelings, thass what they is, right clumsy too, they come 'cross the marsh like bumble bees too fat to fly. Never got how they float, they shoun't be up there. But like bumble bees, she added, you can trust 'em. They don't tell no lies. Other clouds were far more sly. The strat-o-coo-mulus, said the Norfolk way, for one. Bruise it do, too easy, like bad fruit, an' worse still, thass a cloud don't know whether it want to fly high or low – often try both an' pull apart an' that serve it right. Al-toe-stratus, plain bad tempered – cover the rest like a carpet. Real bastard that one, ain't got nothing to say an' bent on spoilin'.

She went on. Cap clouds, scared of wind, stratus-fratus as giddy as ducklings, bobbing this way an' that an' fannyin' around, drove crazy by that storm what formed them. Spiss-attus, best seen in first light, alto-coo-mulus baked gold as a piecrust. She was getting excited, beginning to make it up now, had names for clouds others had never seen: trawler clouds, you should see 'em, gal, they pass over a ship out there an' they turn porn-o-graphic on account of them bored trawlermen's dirty thoughts. 'Viking' clouds, them come from the nor'-east with shallow bases an' armoured sails, right bristlin' with trouble. Marl clouds, good for the farmers, bad for the fish. 'Gannets' were rafters, fat-bellied an' fast to fall, an' then you got leaf-mould an' beech-nut in autumn, then

October onwards, you got you the fungi – flat caps, double ceps, agaric an' blewit. Proud of all that, she is. I seen scale clouds fall out a mackerel sky, then lissen, 'cause you got all them tidal clouds too, such as the double anvils of high-ebb thunder, full o' bad luck, and those mysterious low-drain feathers. You got your mash cloud, crumble, sprout, beet, lambchop, liver, steakside, plaiceback and gill.

'OK, Lil' Mardler?'

So here comes a cloud, freeing itself from the tangle of trees, heather and gorse from the hill behind Blakeney. Fat, full with rain, a couple of hundred feet above the saltmarsh. Goose's cloud eye is on it straight, her daughter silent and spellbound by her side. It's an odd cloud, because – strictly speaking – it doesn't exist. It's been created purely for my grandmother's eyes, and, according to the rules of meteorology, it shouldn't actually float at all. It's a small, boisterous fractonimbus known as a rag cloud. Rag clouds play a crucial part in my family's story. There's a rag cloud painted on the hull of a boat, and there's a rag cloud in human form walking across a fen, dressed in heavy waterproofs. They're always tricksters. This cloud is the savage last breath of a storm. It has broken away from the rest of the nimbus, whipping up the rearguard of a huge deluge, and can do any of a variety of things. While calmer rag clouds disappear, blowing themselves out, knowing when they're beaten, others are more mischievous; rapidly growing in height and shape and – in true nebula form – they begin to spawn new storms and clouds of their own. This one's definitely a loner trickster and has never had a storm to follow. It's low and dark and dense and – to stir things up – is going against the direction of the wind.

Now Goose knows someone somewhere is playing silly buggers.

It falls lower till Goose is under its shadow and she can take a good look up its skirts. A single fractonimbus cloud like this can hide little from the canny woman's eyes. She's able to turn it inside out, pull it apart, shred it, mix it and send it packing, all in a few moments. But it has a few tricks up its sleeves. She begins with the shape. This one looks like a fishing cuddy at first glance – no, let's make it a living thing – a goat. I'm tempted to make it the sperm whale, because I'd like to know whether she could have predicted the string of events that happened to me after I saw that shape in a cloud. But no – the legs of the goat are already there. A couple of horns, a stubborn look, a wispy beard. I know she likes goats, and my mother does too, so this is a welcome sight for them. But my grandmother doesn't waste time admiring.

This liar cloud has a dark, purplish heart to it and fine white extremities. It's really cheating now. In the belly of the cloud she quickly sees what it's hiding. This rag cloud's chased down many other clouds in its brief, phantom life, and each cloud has left its trace. There's a wrecked boat in there, a bull, some dough-like sculptures, a Saint painted in icon style. There are some lights also – what looks like a burning bush or a tree on fire, some fireworks against a winter's sky. Now my grandmother is really scratching her head. I wonder what she might make of it all. I don't think she's ever seen a cloud quite like it, not even in the ones when her daughter was born.

You know – I think she's stumped.

While this ugly rag cloud squats on top of her, a line of cumulus fractus rolls down towards her. The sky becomes masked with a fine, milky steam of cirrostratus. Some cumulonimbus, up they waft – giddy and rowdy, jostling to get down there too. Out at sea now, some of that North Sea water whips up into vapour plumes: Folkestone Pillars tower along the horizon like as many demonic chess pieces. Festoon clouds, caught up in the Holkham pines to the west. A thick, depressing winter layer of altostratus – inching eastwards from Cromer. There's not much sky left! The poor woman and her child are starting to look very small indeed down there on the marsh. And it looks like they're going to get wet.

'Mum, Mum,' Lil' Mardler says, pulling her mother's arm. The young girl's getting scared, her eyes are darkening with fear. Tarred by the brush of having a weak mind and worried it might be her inheritance. 'Mum, I don't *like* it!'

But Goose is doing her best, of course. Working fast. Assessing individual speed, height, internal movement, light, shape and texture. She's listening to the clouds, hearing all these stories filling her head.

As a final touch, let's pull out the stops, man the pumps, check the gauges and pull a thick pea-souper sea-fret from over the Point and cover the whole marsh. Ha! Got you there. The two figures sink into darkness as the mist rolls round them. All those juicy clouds giving away secrets – and you can't see a thing! There's several million tons of meteorology up there now – all bristling with thunder as the rag cloud whips up a hell of a storm. Lightning forks viciously on to the marsh and the whole scene smells charged with iron and salt and while you two struggle home to the cottage against a terrible squall, here comes the rag cloud's rain . . .

The date when all this is happening – 31 January 1953, and the worst storm and coastal flood in living memory is about to be unleashed on North Norfolk. All the way from the Essex estuaries to the Wash, the North Sea is gathering to leap on the land. Goose and my mother have chucked off their coats and are running to the cottage while the sky takes on an eerie twilight and the sea begins to boil in the Pit behind them.

When they get to the cottage Goose shouts at Lil' through

the teeth of the wind to go get sandbags and the young girl, not yet eight, runs up the lane and straight into the arms of a man clutching a storm lantern yelling into the wind and rain and only when he's got her tightly in his grip does she see he's tied to a rope and all round their feet is cold, icy North Sea water. Lil' Mardler screams for her mother, she thrashes like a fish in his arms, he carries her to the church where the rest of the village are huddled like rags while the men pile sandbags against the doors.

Goose slams the cottage door against the fury outside and runs straight to the window. Water is blowing vertically across the pane in trembling fingers, while each gust of wind brings with it a stinging shingle of rain. She imagines this is how it looks on a trawler as it pitches through boiling storms off the Dogger Bank, staring through the flat glass of the bridge's windows while the sea breaks across the bows, windscreen wipers as fast as scissors but doing no good. Everything is dark, and when the lightning flashes there's no marsh out there, just the angry foam of the North Sea leaping off the backs of waves. It feels like the cottage is already not part of the land any more, but has drifted far out to sea, listing, taking on water.

Still she tries to read the clouds. Sheet-lightning makes the sky flash like an X-ray, letting her see deep into the storm. She marvels at it. Giant boulders and cliff faces and ice-capped summits tower above her. She thinks of all the storms she's seen, tries to remember the shapes she saw, the sound she heard in her chimney each time, the smell they left in the air. Because like the clouds themselves, she believes each storm is unique and each storm has a name, a year when it last visited, and a full inventory of all the lost and drowned it has claimed. Goose believes these storms never blow themselves out, but instead drift into some eternal vortex of the North Sea, waiting to return one day. So the storm that hit North Norfolk a thousand years ago, drowning Vikings by the boatful, could return a few hundred years later to add herring fishermen and Dutch traders to its grisly cargo. In her time she claimed she'd heard shouts in Old Norse across the marsh, heard chainmail thrashing in the breakers, had listened to the sickening crack of wood as longboats hit the banks off Blakeney Point. Danish sailors crying like babies in the mist, and she'd smelled their last meal of herring and oats as the galley-pot tipped when the boat went down. She is familiar with all the storms, but as the waves stave in her front door, she's never known a storm like this.

Further up the lane the last villagers of Morston were fleeing their property, climbing over their sandbags and wading to the church for refuge. From the church windows they might have looked down on the lost cause of Lane End. Might have seen the waves break the front door and a second later seen the woodsmoke cease from her chimney. *Poor old gal . . . ain't nothin' to do now, boys* and maybe the odd disrespectful *can't drown a witch* might have been uttered. Even in a church. Lil', forgotten on the tiles, her hair in soggy ringlets, clutching a now useless pile of sandbag sacking, on the verge of being orphaned. There was no way out – the cottage was already a quarter of a mile into the sea.

Across the marshes, pit props are pulling out of coastal defences like corks from bottles. They jostle savagely in the waves and come knocking on the doors of Cley with the grace of battering rams. The village is already under water – the tide rushed the doors and windows, filled the rooms, failed to leave and now another tide's coming on top. Fish dart wild-eyed through the water, into houses, under furniture, become stranded where the water laps menacingly up the stairs. A table floats below the ceiling, bearing a half-eaten meal and a cat. Outside the wind howls through the cables with an eerie wail, deafening and unnatural, and in the darkness all that can be seen is white foam hurtling off the backs of dark metallic waves and the brief flashes of seagulls as they're spat from the storm.

Then rolling up the high street comes an unearthly vision. It's an iron buoy, clanking viciously between the walls, shattering windows like a wrecking ball – the water looks restless around it, as sinewy as eels – and all over the village there's the sound of tiles smashing as people finally break out of attics to escape across the roofs.

'*Hain't there! Hain't there no more!*' A man is shouting, waist-deep in water – his mouth filling with rain and sea each time he opens it. Torchlight is bent against the wind and in its beam the storm seems full of six-inch nails, driving horizontally. *Help!* is heard again and another torch is lit. *There ain't nothin' there!* the second man shouts to the first as hard as he can – though both men are holding each other and are lashed together with rope. And when the torchlights cross in the shattered branches of a tree they see the ghost of a boy up there, like a wet shirt blown from a washing line. *Haf to get him – he in't hangin' on long!* one shouts, and together they haul themselves back along the rope tied between telegraph poles to an army boat brought down from Weybourne. Six men row or punt and keep their backs down to bail, and at the front they throw an anchor and heave the boat up on it and when they reach it they throw another anchor forward. It's the only way they can move. The sea boils against the boat, reeds whip their faces and distantly someone claims he sees Lonnie Lemmon's haystack – the entire thing – floating down the coast from Salthouse to Glandford, where it'll be found in two days' time. They hear pigs, squealing in the waves, unable to get through the fences beyond the houses. When they reach the tree the anchor is flung round its trunk and the boat slams hard against the bark. Above them they see the terrified boy, as white as his fear, dissected by branches and twigs as though the storm has torn him apart, and throughout the tree they see the branches are covered with rats like as many wet leaves. Some of the rats jump for the boat, the men scream, then more rats fall into the water as if they're coming from the clouds themselves and each rat drowns quickly and without fuss the way things do when there is no hope.

The boy is moving down through the tree. As they grab his ankle he's pulled right out of his own shirt, as if part of him wants to cling up there still. It's the Langore boy, one of them says, recognizing him. John, ain't it? he says, their faces almost touching in the dark. *Kipper*, the boy whispers, the nickname he's called himself. Then suddenly the boy panics, flailing wildly at the men while the boat tips to its gunwales, and one of the men sees through the dark rain the army bo'sun knocking the boy cold with a fist the size of a pile-driver. And though the storm still rages, both men share a big grin at that.

Back at the cottage, Goose claims the same tin bath in which Hands feared he might be cooked or drowned all of a sudden popped up like a life-raft. Into it she went. She rocked about all night long in that thing, shivering against the icy metal sides – sluiced from one corner of the room to the other a couple of feet beneath the ceiling, with bread, pans, cups, saucers, cupboards and all the driftwood she'd collected over the years spinning in a dismal galaxy around her.

Through the night she plundered this flotsam. She ate a

jarful of pickled eggs, oh boy, drank an entire shelf's worth of elderflower wine. Roaring drunk, some time in the middle of the night she began to hear the noises she'd been dreading. Along with the wind, the crashing waves, the surging tide, she heard the moans of all the people who'd drowned in that storm over the centuries. There were thousands of them, going back through history, and before the night was out, there'd be hundreds more. Danish longshoremen caught on a sandbar three hundred years before, tumbling rudely into the cottage, cursing the night away as they clung to what was left of the bed. In Olde English, men calling out the names of their faithful dogs as the waves overran them. Bales of Norfolk wool – five hundred years old – rolling in the waves outside. Sheep too – so she says. And against the awful din of the storm she even claimed she heard the death throes of a mammoth – one of Norfolk's last, she supposed – which had drowned in the same storm fifty thousand years before.

Early the next morning, a sombre line of men tied themselves to each other along a rope, then waded to her cottage through the freezing water to collect her body. They found her snoring *like a good 'un* in the bath, now wrecked on top of the bed.

She lived through that storm and spent years dreading the day it would return. Not out of fear for the tin bath, but because she wasn't keen on meeting the hundred and forty people who died in Suffolk and Norfolk that night: Millie Eccles, stoker of rumours about Goose, who died on her bike; Ned Boddy, whose bungalow was swept away and who Goose owed money to – found standing in a pit with his boots filled with shingle when the water drained away; Jackie Rudd, who'd once bought a dozen bad eggs from Goose – never forgiven. They were all drowned that night, and they'd all be back to get her, she thought.

The last day of January – that's the date of the storm. A night of mysteries, of vanishings and appearances. And as each year passed, Goose was more wary of that date than any other in the calendar. I always thought it was part of her nonsense, until I experienced my own vanishing on that night, many years later.

The flood retreats leaving a filthy stink and a dirty brown tidemark along the fields and marshes, further inland than it's ever been, and when we look closer we see the tidemark is partly made of thousands of rats, mice, voles and rabbits. A rat won't be seen for years to come. And the same tidemark threads its way through Cley, Blakeney, Salthouse and Morston. On tree trunks and flagpoles, the tidemark is there – it even runs halfway across the sign of the Albatross Inn, and finally, about a foot lower than the ceiling, the same tidemark girdles inside Goose's cottage.

She looks at this mark, and knows ill things arrive on a high tide. Demons are left floundering in such places. She walks along the tideline to a newly washed-up boat – the *Thistle Dew* – which now sits lopsided on the marsh a couple of hundred feet from her cottage. It's going to be a significant place for her, and me, in its time. But she doesn't stop there, she continues along the tideline picking up drowned rabbits for an early supper, always on her guard, waiting for what the storm has left, and when she's nearly back at Lane End, she sees it. It's two days after the flood, and she notices a boy crying down by the creek. But he's not crying about the storm . . .

. . . I see my grandmother once again in her cottage, with a young daughter allowed for the first time to sit at the table. The young girl is staring bug-eyed at a length of boiled calf's tongue curling on to her plate. The young child looks up anxiously at the trembling tip of the meat as it winds its way through the air towards her. Other children her age would be running wet fingers along the glass-topped counters of Mather's Stores in the hunt for sherbet. The tongue is still intact, boiled limp and skewered with a steel knitting needle, but the end has unwound itself in the pan and now seems to point accusingly at the young girl's mouth. As the tongue passes over the knife and fork it seems to wriggle before breaking free from the needle and, with vigorous life, springs on to the bare table. There it lies, stunned, before curling slowly – as if injured from the fall – into a foetal position, till it hugs the cool circular rim of the plate.

Apparently the calf's tongue began its journey to my mother's mouth when Goose approached the crying boy down by the creek. The boy was new in the area. Not washed up on the tide, as it turned out, but staying with his great-uncle, who ran a farm on the heath. My grandmother had seen him eating pickles from a jar and beating off flies in August. He was either too weak or too clumsy to use the farm machinery, so had spent his days wandering the pasture as a kind of scarecrow, plucking the grass and bronzing his face, and the evenings with his knees trembling under the dining table of Will Langore, his great-uncle. Will Langore, who'd battled and lost to Hands over the poker table. After several months of forcing the farm's food down the lad, the old man had leaned over the marbled remains of a joint of beef and pinched the boy's biceps till they bruised. Satisfied, the tyrant stabbed a long curved knife into the table and said: ain't a boy no more, best you kill that sick calf next week. Don't kill it in the shed, walk it to the truck first or we'll have to carry it. And that was that. The boy shot a pleading glance over to his older brother, found only betrayal where he'd hoped for support, flung his chair back and ran to the creek, where his tears could be drowned in all that water.

And my grandmother had found the boy as he cried, sat by him, watched him throwing stones into the mud of Morston Creek. Self-pitying rage shook the boy when he thought of the sick calf with the weeping eyes, who refused to suckle from its mother. Just a drink from the udder and it might live, you know. My grandmother made sounds of sympathy – while her mouth watered with the thought of tasty cuts. She'd have to play her hand well. First slaughter? she asked, and when he nodded his head she shook hers. Oh, thass rough, it is. Rough. I ain't never killed nothin' that big an' I don't reckon I ever will.

Calf liver and bacon? Calf-feet fricassee? Calf-head pie? That old bastard Will Langore would claim every ounce of meat an' he'd want the liver too an' this lad ain't up to carryin' a head. Best be the tongue, oh yes, simple, on the skewer. Bit o' salt an' pepper.

Her trap was easily laid. Course you gotta give that tongue away. Don't you go leavin' that tongue in its head or you'll start hearin' that dead calf lowin' every time you slaughter. That ain't no fun I tell you. I seen grown men haunted, oh God haunted, till they take no more of it . . . And the boy looked at my grandmother and maybe she briefly saw the dreamy expression of faraway eyes she'd last seen in the man who'd vanished on the *Pip*. But it wasn't enough to stop her in her tracks, and as the boy's blue eyes flooded with the horror of what the marshwoman was saying, she pretended to slice her own throat with painful, drawn-out agony. An' there ain't no escape, she added, swallowing her spit, thinking the boy was close to taking off that night. Time to be a man, she muttered, turning to the horizon to conceal her grin. And maybe the boy thought of his older brother, grey-eyed and calm with it, well on the way to being just that.

Next morning, my grandmother woke before dawn. She saw the pale wood of her white picket gate swinging open in the gloom, and listened to the heavy tread of the boy as he walked up her path. Out come the knives, pestle and sewing kit. The tongue landed with a slap on the front step, and the boy walked off, leaving her gate wide open, to eat his silent breakfast with the men. That was the boy who gave my mother the tongue. And Goose, you did everything to make that boy stay, and yet just a few years later it would be everything to make Shrimp Langore leave.

5

Lil' Mardler

Lil' Mardler had a childhood with no friends. *She live on the marsh an' there ain't no father. The mum's a rum 'un too – she scare the babies. Lil's diff'ernt, thass all I got to say.* Alone on a saltmarsh among gulls swallowing cod heads on the tideline. She's no longer a little scared girl. She's sixteen. She inhabits a landscape that is so big and flat it seems the edges slope up into the sky all round, where mud meets cloud banks and seems to continue up there till traces of creeks and water can be seen there too – she often thinks she stands in some vast and dreary dish which has no end. She's lived like this for years. She's learned how to walk in mud with her heels pointed down, the depths of the creeks and the strengths of the tide, knows where mud cracks are so deep you might break a leg – it's as if she has it all etched on the back of her hand. She knows the calendar by the buds on sea blite, the flowers on campion and dry seeds on curled dock. By the number of joints on a stem of samphire. And she never treads on a tern's egg, even though its shell is made of shingle.

Sandpipers pass her, skimming the creeks with wing-tips so fast they seem blurred. The tide slowly rises and falls in its long-fingered weave through the marsh. And in the centre of all this is the wreck of the *Hansa*. She knows its every detail, from the gannets and storm petrels carved along the gunwale, to the whale on the mizzenmast and the spirits of the North Sea rising towards its broken top. The grooves of the rough letters cut into the planks, so faint you could easily miss them as scratches: *Jeder macht mal eine kleine Dummheit*: we all have times of a little stupidity.

She's there, in the wheelhouse, her hair long and brown and as thick as rope, tied in a simple knot behind her head. Salt marks on her cheeks and forehead, lips slightly blue with cold. The sulky, defensive expression she used to pull as a child no longer fits her face. In the last year or two her cheeks have lost some of their softness. Her eyebrows have grown fuller and seem to sit on top of her eyes with a permanently hurt expression she can't shift. Her skin is less soft, the salt is finally getting in there too. She's grown tall and strong and with it she's grown petulant, and here, right now, she's fuming.

Because she's not alone. Sitting over by the prow with his chin resting awkwardly on the handrail is a young lad. We've met him before. He killed that calf just after the storm eight years ago, and now he spends much of his time out here, strung up on the wreck, his dreamy eyes not entirely without pain.

Lil' Mardler stamps about behind him, kicks the wheelhouse, slides about on the bones of the pilot's chair while she looks at the sagging shoulders of the boy sitting on the wreck. Her wreck. The wreck *her father* carved. She thinks nasty thoughts but the boy doesn't move. The pilot's chair grinds painfully as she swings it from side to side, then she paces over to him and stands so close a boy his age should go cold with fear that a girl like her might do something unexpected. Laugh at his face, scratch him on the arms, kiss him on the mouth like an adult. Lil' is sixteen and girls write the rules and she knows she'd get away with it, but something about his posture shows she wouldn't win this battle, so she goes back to the wheelhouse and makes the chair squeak like a gallows.

Then a strange thing happens. There, in front of her, she

sees the boy's shoulders tense like someone's wringing water out of them. She looks beyond him and sees something, approaching them – a perfect wake spreading gorgeously across the water of the Pit. It looks like a float on a fishing line being reeled in. Then an arm is raised, followed immediately by another, and a no-nonsense front crawl breaks out. Another lad is heading for the *Hansa*, and my mother grips what's left of the wheel like a storm's coming.

The second lad's older than the first, taller by the inch or so to make all the difference, and where the first boy's eyes are as pale as a dawn sky, his brother's are grey like smoke. He clings to the side of the wreck, breaks a bit of rotten wood off the hull and chucks it in the water and Lil' thinks about kicking him in the face and how it was preferable before and decides to stay in the pilot's chair because he'll know she's done that deliberately. But the boy hardly notices. He's calling to his brother and making a big fuss about being pulled from the water and suddenly she's watching the dreamy one hauling the other one out and it seems the two boys have taken over the wreck entirely, because to them that's all it is – a wreck.

The taller boy's got a strong hard body and his face is bony and severe. He sits on the planks and takes some deep breaths to show how good his swim was. His hair's as wet as an otter's and the water streams down his back in fast, quick lines. Then he turns to her and grins and she's immediately disconcerted – because the boy grinning at her seems, for a second, to be entirely different from the one who climbed up on deck. Same person, same features – but two faces in one.

'Mornin', cap'n, where we heading?'

Lil' Mardler pulls her ugliest most sarcastic smile and looks away.

'I'm Kipper and he's Shrimp,' he says. 'You got a name?'

'He said his name was George,' my mother replies.

'Well, it isn't.'

'My name's May.'

'No it ain't. You're Lil' Mardler, everyone knows that,' the boy says, laughing out loud. Even the dreamy one smiles at that.

'And you're the boy they had to fish out the tree in the storm, ain't you,' she says. 'Cryin' like a baby, they said.'

She's drawn first blood. Good on you, Lil', you used to give as good as you got.

Talking of first blood, earlier that morning, Lil' had been peeling potatoes over a bucket when she nicked herself badly with the knife. A thin line of blood had threaded into the water, turning it rust red. She'd thrown the knife in and run to the marsh, leaving Goose to finish the job and wonder what was going on with her daughter. Years had passed since Goose used to take Lil' out each day to pick samphire, pushing her out in the pram, filling it up, making the young girl walk back when it was full. Now, they got on like cats in a cage. Goose consulted the clouds, didn't like what they said, began to feel a growing sense of doom. She began to be suspicious of her daughter and this kind of thing with the spuds and the bucket was just the tip of it.

Lil' was preoccupied. She spent her days on the *Hansa*, watching from the wheelhouse as the brothers ate limpets and whelks, then more and more she sat nearer them, hearing them talk about the farm they lived on and how they'd leave it to rack and ruin one day. We ain't going to fill the old bastard's shoes. They were more interested in competing with each other than paying her much attention. In the mornings they'd swim across the Pit with knives between their teeth like a couple of pirates, in the same way Hands had done, seventeen years before. Then they'd throw stones, dive off the bow, race each other along the shore; all that boys' stuff and it all seemed endless wasted energy.

Shrimp was smaller than his brother, but was more easygoing. He had a broader back and a soft smile of puppy-fat above the waistband of his trunks. Light hair, and a face which seemed a little clumsy, all the features with their own edge of hap-hazardness. Said to look like his mother, though she'd died while they were so young neither of them remembered her. Shrimp put less effort into the throwing contests, but his stones went further. His older brother threw stones with a jarring action which changed style with each delivery, and though he chose his stones carefully, it made no difference. Shrimp's stones kept falling further away.

Knots were a different matter. Kipper excelled at them, had his own length of rope which he strung round his neck in the same way I've hung my notebook for most of my life, could tie a Spanish bowline with his eyes closed, or an armpit bight with three twists of his fingers. He once tied eight half-hitches to a masthead bend and crawled it across the deck like a crab, so my mother told me.

After so many solitary years as a marshgirl, she must have enjoyed the company. The Langore brothers went to a school their great-uncle paid for, hadn't been born in Blakeney, and so remained a little on the fringes themselves. Kipper hated the local kids, said they were mean and narrow-minded, that the boys were a bunch of women with tits in their shirts and nothing in their heads. He often got in fights, and had once pushed a boy on a bike off the edge of Blakeney Quay and gave no other reason than it was *Saturday afternoon*. It was about the best thing he could've said, because people kept their distance after that.

'Your mum's mad, ain't she, Lil'?' Kipper says. He often tried to goad her with these frank comments. 'She listens to clouds, don't she?'

Right at that very moment, Goose was in Lane End, staring at a frog, which was crawling across her kitchen tiles. She screamed, and began shooing it out the door with a broom.

On the *Hansa*, Lil' is not impressed. She can deal with Kipper Langore.

'We got a saying for it.'

'Who's we?' he says, hardening his look.

'You ain't from Norfolk,' she says, and makes out she's happy to leave it at that.

Kipper waits, knowing Lil' is dying to tell him off, one way or the other. He's mature enough to let the trouble come to him. Eventually she gives way.

'It's in the way it lean,' she says.

'That's it?'

'Thass it.'

Lil' is getting this feeling that once again he has the upper hand. She looks at Kipper and his brother on her wreck and she hates the way they're sitting there, legs splayed out untidy and big and both of them not at all bothered about her.

'So what's it mean?' Shrimp says, casually.

'Well, it mean nothing,' she says, and thinks how stupid she sounds, 'it just mean the truth of something's not in the way he speak or what he do, it's in the way it lean, and this is Norfolk, everything lean one way or that. You got to think differently now, that's all.'

Kipper makes a *pah* sound and lies back on the deck, sucking a bit of samphire between his lips. The light's bright and she can't tell which face he seems to be wearing.

Shrimp smiles warmly at Lil'. 'Well, that made a hell of a lot of sense,' he splutters and both boys start laughing and even Lil' finds the whole thing funny and right then that's when the notorious event happened, that's when the herring gull dived out of nowhere with the force of a missile, diving at some glint of metal or glass on the wheelhouse roof and missing it badly and instead hitting Lil' on the shoulder and head with its own dead weight and quickly it wasn't a flying soaring gull any more but a creature of some kind, hanging off her hair with its wings caught up and stiff either side of her shoulder. Lil' starts to scream and the gull strikes a free wing at her face and its beak darts open; it screams back at her – a loud *kay-ow* and a *yah-yah-yah* that pierces the air and both lads are there at the wheelhouse, not knowing what to do and standing with their hands out as if they're going to catch something. It's an eerie moment. Lil' opens an eye gradually and the gull just hangs there, its talons in her hair, and the boys see her ear is starting to bleed. Her shoulder is covered in shit. The gull starts to pant and scares itself again, kicking her and stabbing its head fast at her arm, then it bites her shirt and pulls at it and the red bead at the end of its beak looks like blood. Lil' tries to lift it but the gull starts off again shrieking, filling the wheelhouse with the flashes of its wings, they seem like blades in the air, while the full-throated *yah-kah-eee* it makes is ear-splitting and unearthly and it's mixed with Lil's own screaming now. Then another sound, a strange sound, and it's Shrimp who's making it – a quiet *cawing*. The gull becomes still and it turns to listen and as Shrimp steps into the wheelhouse the gull turns its head to look at him askance and it opens its beak and they see the sharp knife of its tongue inside. Shrimp keeps making this noise and the gull seems to relax, then Shrimp's holding it by the legs and trying to free Lil's hair, strand by strand. The gull hangs there, lifeless, letting Shrimp work, and then it starts to preen itself below the neck while Shrimp pulls it free. The herring gull hops clumsily into his hands and he holds it up and it doesn't seem to know it's free. Then unexpectedly it takes one lazy flap, glides out of Shrimp's hands, and flies off across the Pit.

She looks at Shrimp differently after that. What he did with the gull was extraordinary. It makes her wonder about him. At night, when Goose is asleep, Lil' goes out and sits by Morston Creek, thinking about Shrimp and looking up at the brilliant Norfolk stars. Among them all, she tries to see Sputnik 2, still orbiting after four years. She spends a lot of time thinking about Laika up there in the satellite, in a tiny capsule with no food or water or any way of returning. She knows Laika's dead but somehow, right there on the Norfolk saltmarsh, that dog is alive again, looking down on her in her patch of darkness, a cosmonaut's hat on its head and heartbeat monitors on its side.

The summer passes and the three of them spend their time fishing off the *Hansa*. Kipper and Shrimp, competing as always – but clearly they've both become interested in trying to land her, the girl between them. All three of them with bare legs dangling off the bow, staring down their lines, the only sound coming from Kipper's habit of sucking air through stems of samphire. The Langore brothers have identical rods and floats, they know about lines and hooks and bait, but it's Lil', with a look of pure satisfaction, who pulls in the first fish. It's an angry thing, flapping and twisting on the end of her crabline. But when she reaches out to grab it Shrimp is there first, cutting her line and making the fish fall into the water. *What did you do that for!* she shouts, thinking he's just as mean as his shapeshifting brother after all, and Shrimp just says it was a weever, a stingfish, it was going to sting you. He carries on looking at his float while Kipper looks at the two of them and he sees her hand reach up and gently touch Shrimp on his shoulder. Thanks, she whispers, and Kipper knows in this simplest of gestures that he's lost.

Walking back to Lane End with a bag of shopping, Goose approaches a hedgehog coming the other way. Middle of the day, on a path hardly wide enough for the two of them. The hedgehog shuffles towards her with the gait of an old tramp. She thinks of bad omens and stories of illness arriving in the form of wandering peasants dressed in rags, knocking on your door at night. While she's thinking this the hedgehog keeps coming, determined and ill. When it's almost under her feet she sees it's blinded with lice crawling on every last spike of its body and over its face and into its eyes. She steps into the verge and the horror escalates, because she steps on a dead rabbit, releasing a cloud of flies rising as one horrid ball of wings. And she runs for it and then she realizes; she stops running and looks over the saltmarsh and thinks Lil', oh no, it's Lil'.

But Lil' is not at home, nor on the *Hansa*. She's up at the Langores' farm, sitting on top of the haybales in the barn. It's dark and dusty and quiet in there, even though it's the middle of the day and old man Langore's down in the yard shouting orders. She can see the lower half of his legs and his boots through the open door. A vet's there too, being as authoritative as he can; he should be used to farmers by now but old Langore's got him riled. The vet keeps raising his voice and using scientific words. The two Langore brothers are in the yard also, trying to separate a cow from the herd; Lil' can hear the cow's hooves slipping on the concrete. The rest of the cows are stamping, the way horses do when they're bothered. *Ha!* Kipper shouts *Ha! Ha!* And she hears the thwack of a stick against cowhide. Langore tries to bribe the vet and the vet says that's it, that's the last straw. Shoot that and with luck you won't lose the herd. A heavy iron gate is clanked shut and the bolt slid, and then something moves near her and she thinks it's a rat and she turns, scared, but instead of a rat she sees it's Shrimp, wriggling through the gaps in the haybales, a wide grin on his face. Lil' kicks loose hay at him and laughs and tries to shush him up when he spits out the hay from his mouth. He crawls right up to her and slaps her on the thigh likes she's the cow in the yard and she makes a big fuss that that hurt then slaps him back and then they fight, her in her flannel shirt, him in his denim dungarees, she smells the cow on him and smelly stuff he's put in his hair because he knew she'd be waiting up on the haystack; she smells a type of sweat she's never smelled before. He pins her down and she giggles and coughs in the dust. She sees him in fragments, the way his hair's trimmed round his ears, the softness round the corners of his mouth, the frayed top edge of his collar, a button stretching in its hole.

Goose wakes one morning to hear Lil' Mardler being sick in a bucket. Lil' is trying to keep it quiet but has reached that point when to keep quiet seems an added burden not worth bothering about. Goose brings her a glass of water and sits next to her on the bed. She puts a hand on her daughter's knee, but that's something both of them feel uncomfortable with so Goose stands up and holds the curtain and at that moment she says something very odd. She closes her eyes and says *locusts* under her breath. What? Lil' says, feeling wretched. Nothin', Goose says, and pulls the curtains apart and there they are, out there above the saltmarsh, a swarm of hundreds of tiny clouds. In each one the insect shape can be seen.

Goose has finally caught up with what's going on. Water

turning to blood, the frog on the tiles, lice on the hedgehog, flies on the rabbit . . . a series of biblical omens. She's heard about the illness in the cattle on Langore's farm and the boils breaking out on the sick cow's legs, how it managed to hail in a thunderstorm a few weeks ago. Now the locusts, up there in the clouds, and she knows that it's all leading up to an exodus and that she's going to lose someone again, like she lost Hands stealing off in the *Pip*, and this time it's going to be her own daughter and she starts to shout at Lil'. The shouting lasts all day. By the end of it the saltmarsh is in darkness and Goose is in Lane End surrounded by the broken crockery and upturned chairs of an all-day argument and Lil's sitting in the passenger seat of a car, heading off for a new life with Shrimp Langore driving a car he's borrowed. All she's decided to take is her crabbing line. While she tries to unknot it in her lap she looks out of the car window at dark Norfolk. She wonders if she can see Laika up there in the sky, somewhere, lonely and forgotten about, forever in orbit with no food or water.

6

Dead, Vast and Middle

A night without sleep, but a night before the depression took hold, before those nights when I'd watch her dreamily walk the length of the corridor, each step along a tightrope forming at her feet. A pale nightdress swaying between the walls, the thin crease of concentration between her brows like a tiny scar. That first night she'd woken up standing on the back lawn. It sounded strange to her out there. No dripping of water in the saltmarsh, no sound of waves curling along the Point a mile away. These were the sounds she'd always known, and maybe at sixteen she thought all the world might sound like Morston Marshes. But as she stood there in the dark, her crab line still knotted with the speed she'd stuffed it in her pocket, strange sounds and scents drifted up from the gloomy country below. Sounds of cars slipping through the dark, of a distant growl of machinery. And somewhere quite near, she felt the presence of a large body of water moving slowly in the night. She must have assumed a tide was rising. Some time before dawn she'd watched a light moving smoothly across the land in front of her and realized it must be a boat on the sea, because the light was so level and moved through the darkness without any deviation. Another part of the coast, but for one thing. She couldn't smell salt. This was an odd, dark sea in front of her, quite unlike the North Sea off Norfolk. It was a sea that smelled rotten.

I wonder if she thought of her mother, of the rawness of anger that had inexplicably started on the marshes and finished here, on the lawn. Or perhaps she thought about the strange unwelcome farmhouse that was to be her home. How it smelled of a man's smell, how damp and unloved it seemed. Did she look up at the window of the bedroom and think of Shrimp Langore in there, exhausted, nervous, feeling his own private sense of dislocation? Was he asleep or was he spending the first night afraid to put the light on, sitting in a chair perhaps, smoking a cigarette, looking at the wild geometric print on the curtains and waiting for dawn to shine through them?

They'd explored the house by candlelight. It was a dreary place which had been rented to a single man for many years. The air was heavy and depressing and full of the man's idleness. A bucket had been knocked over in the hall, leaving a long dry stain covering the carpet like blood. There were empty miniatures of Bell's Whisky and Grand Marnier in one of the rooms, stored in cardboard boxes. Some empty gun cartridges in the bedroom. And on the kitchen table, a mug of cold tea stood next to a pile of crumbs and mice shit.

Stretched out on the bed, exhausted, they'd listened to the candle guttering in the corner and foxes barking in the distance. The candle flickered a nervous unsettling light across the walls as they lay on the damp mattress, and when the candle had finally burned out in the early hours, my mother had woken up outside on the back lawn.

Low, brooding outbuildings with impenetrably dark doorways faced the cottage from across the yard. Spilling out of one of these was a pile of poaching traps, left there like discarded jawbones. She stared at them for a while, and at the greater darkness beyond them, then felt her way round the sides of the house, and as she touched the walls she tensed, realizing she'd been expecting the soothing contours of flints, not the damp, foreign texture of bricks.

I see her there clearly, on the lawn with a car blanket round her shoulders, quietly singing 'The Foggy, Foggy Dew':

'. . . of the winter time, and of the summer too,
And of the many, many times that I held her in my arms,
Just to keep her from the foggy, foggy dew.'

And as dawn approaches she sees a damp, misty landscape in front of her. At first the mist looks like the pea-souper banks of a North Norfolk sea-fret. Then, lifting through the mist, the solid mast of a ship turns out to be a tall brick chimney, several miles away. It's leaning. Soon, more chimneys appear on low huddled houses, dotted across the land. She sees water, not in the labyrinthine pattern of the creeks on the Morston saltmarshes, but water in straight unnatural lines as far as she can see. And the last thing to lift from the mist is at the bottom of the slope beyond the house, perhaps two miles away; the long curling shape of a huge brown river, the one she'd felt moving in the night. The land is absolutely flat, relentless, mud brown and dull green; not the soft level of the marshes, but a rigid, carved geometry of lines, furrows, paths and roads. It is the Fens.

As the pale globe of the sun rises over her shoulder, she hears the tap of Shrimp's finger on the upstairs window. When he's rubbed the condensation away with a squeak, she sees his grinning face in the cold morning light. Brave, now it's the new day. She sees his long shadow approaching hers over the lawn, and then feels a mischievous poke in her ribs.

'You sleep?' he says

'Not sure.'

'Hear the foxes? Going for it, weren't they? Han't heard foxes like that for ages.'

Lil' looks vaguely where she thought the foxes had been calling from, looks back, looks directly at Shrimp to gauge his mood.

'Are we still in Norfolk?'

Shrimp laughs at her and, because the sun's rising higher now, he points out the Fens to her.

'That's Lincolnshire.'

Below them, four small villages were lifting out of the soil, the sunlight slick on the wet tiles of the roofs.

'The Saints them villages are called, Lil'. Wiggenhall St Germans, Wiggenhall St Mary the Virgin, Wiggenhall St Peter and Wiggenhall St Mary Magdalen. It's called the Saints here, everyone knows it as the Saints. It's all ours – and I don't want to be called Shrimp no more. I was christened George, and so I'm George now.'

'George,' she whispers to buoy his spirits. She'd like to be called May, she wants to leave Lil' behind, but she feels this is his moment to feel right about himself, so she says nothing.

Armies of tractors are beginning to crawl into the fields, ploughing, pushing, dragging and sifting the soil as if obsessed with levelling the land.

And Lil' asks again, 'But are we still in Norfolk?'

George puts his arm round her, feels the dew in the blanket wrapped round her shoulders, and leads her inside.

Yes, it was still Norfolk. Norfolk's broad in the beam, full of soft fields and quite up to thwarting an escape. But they nearly made it.

During that first morning the details of George Langore's plan were outlined. Using some connection dug up in his great-uncle's farming past, and his own reputation for under-standing bloodstock of all kinds, a position of gamekeeper-cum-stockman had been created at the Stow Bardolph Estate, a mile away. With it came this tied farm-cottage, three small outbuildings, a pigsty, animal pen, hen loft and lawn, part of which was laid out as a vegetable patch. For the past seven years it had been tenanted by Harold Flott, gamekeeper, who'd been known as a lazy farmer. Lazy and filthy. Year on year the estate's pheasant stock had dwindled, escaped, fought itself in pre-shooting battles and pecked mercilessly at Flott's ankles so that when the call was raised and the beaters marched, only the occasional wild, startled, feather-ragged pheasant took wing. Flott had left the house with a cup of tea still made and ready to drink and the crumbs of his midday snack on the table.

Lil' listened to all this as she lay on a couch drifting in and out of sleep. George talked nervously about pheasant rearing, training, pen design and bloodstock heredity till her eyelids finally fell with accepted weariness. George, at last silenced by the deep breathing of his patient, tucked the blanket round her, and stepped out into the milky morning sunlight of the yard. He did what any man would do: went straight to the sheds to sort the machinery, stocks, junk and rubble, eyeing what was useful, what should be salvaged, repaired, sharpened, tied, folded, turned and burned.

At midday a grey Ford truck drove into the yard and a tall man in his seventies climbed out. A suit of fine worsted wool, leather boots polished like conkers. His companion, a plump, friendly woman, stayed in the passenger seat, cleaning the inside of the windscreen with a small flowered handkerchief.

George came out when he heard the car, and both men leaned against the warm brick wall of the pigsty. Occasionally one or the other dragged his foot in the dirt, picked at the grass and moss that grew in the mortar, or looked speculatively at the cottage, the other outbuildings and the fields beyond. All this while the woman stayed in the car, until the heat of the day made her wind the window down, and George's new employer took his cue and got back in.

A few hours later, a pickup arrived, and two men jumped down from the back and swung some groceries, milk and eggs, blankets, wood and a few laying hens into the yard. From inside the cab, one of the men pulled out a used Gallyon & Sons Purdey side by side 12-bore and put it in George's outstretched hand, along with several boxes of cartridges. It was a heavy gun with a butt of English walnut and an etched insignia of pheasants and geese taking wing along the stock. George breached it several times, looked appreciatively down the polished files of its barrels, then, with a nod to the other men, went into the house and stood it against the sideboard in the breakfast room, where it would stay for the next eighteen years.

Some time in the ashes of the afternoon Lil' stirred, climbed off the couch and stumbled into the breakfast room, the imprint of a badly frayed cushion on her cheek. Perhaps she stubbed her toe on the gun leaning against the sideboard. Possibly the afternoon's heat made her curious belly-button itch, and so she stood there, scratching it at the window, listening to the sounds of George moving rusty metal about in one of the sheds. The image of Lil' standing by the grimy window rubbing her belly seems to fit with things I learned many years later about her. But all that is to come. She stands there, in her olive-coloured button-through shirt-waister dress, staring at four laying hens that had been left in a net in the yard, all of them with their beaks parted in the hot afternoon sun, and then beyond the hens she sees George, dirty George, with his shirt torn and grease down his arm and dust in his hair and a big grin on his face and two very dead and well-hung pheasants strung up and held in his right hand.

It soothed her to rip the feathers off the birds. She plucked

66

them at the kitchen table, listening to the feathers tearing from the skin like plasters from a wound. The down settled softly on to the tiles, and when she went for a bowl the room seemed to come alive as they stirred round her feet. She watched them settle again, then she crouched and blew delicately across the tiles. The feathers charged up in a rolling wave towards the yard and she kept them in the air, blowing and wafting them and with sudden dizziness she breathed life into that miserable house, sweeping the man's dark smell into the attic, the under-stairs cupboard, the corners, replacing it with the warm roast of pheasant, the tang of apple sauce and a creamy mash of potatoes and swede. Silverfish were washed down the sink, out went the boxes of tinned vegetables and corned beef. Out went the empty bottles of beer, the rusty tin-opener, the broken-tipped bread knife, the countless mugs without handles. Stale tobacco leaves were bagged-up, the range de-greased and rubbed down. Kettle descaled. The tines were straightened on forks, the knives sharpened. Plates polished till their rims shone like smiles.

They ate in the yard using their fingers rather than the former tenant's cutlery, gazing at the traps with their rusty open jaws. We don't want them looking at us. Bad omen, George says. Shall I chuck them? she asks, half putting the plate down to show she wants to help him, and he says best not to, you never know, and leaving the traps he turned to the rest of the junk and built a fire, turning all that misery into hot brilliant flames, powdery ash and thick smoke, which couldn't tarnish the gorgeous cerulean blue of a late-summer sky.

What a beautiful fire. The first of the fires – for there will be several more: boats set alight; an elm tree; a hen coop with all its secrets; the festivals of fire on the Norfolk marshes, which always conjured trouble; the fire Kipper Langore harnessed in his fireworks; and the smoke he used to cure his fish. My family's story is of fire in one hand and smoke in the other. Fire to destroy and smoke to preserve.

Often, inexplicably, Lil' woke to find herself standing on the back lawn in the middle of the night, escaping some dark shadow of that house, or in the morning, when George had breezed off to the estate, she might find herself frozen at the kitchen sink, watching soap suds drip one by one from her hands. Sometimes she might catch her reflection in the newly polished curve of a soup spoon, and in it she'd see a life bent beyond recognition for her. As the autumn nights drew in, Lil' rarely got out, whereas George had fallen into the new life at the estate with real gusto. Like the enthusiastic Hands in 1944, George had found plenty to fix and plenty of inclination to do it. Pheasant stock for the Boxing Day shoot had to be laid down. New pens to be built, new feeding runs and fox traps staked out. Pig and cattle bloodstocks had been assessed, charted and examined. Ill or weak animals had been sent to the knacker's yard at Downham Market. New animals had been bought at Lynn and a prize Red Poll bull purchased at Norwich.

George became a success at the estate, sometimes coming home with his hat full to the brim with fresh eggs, or carrying a whole smoked leg of ham. There were tales: 'bout this pig he gets himself stuck in a fen-bog and we gets this rope on him but the only thing gets him out is seeing this sow eat carrots, boy he move. Or the business of digging a star-shaped trench round the roots of a tree and dragging it, leaves 'n' all, into a new hole so now he gets a good view from his library, see? How they might still have to cut ice from a lake come winter; how so-and-so had turned up in an Austin Healey sports car; practical jokes played on a cook who hated touching fish and she scream and chase this lad he turn pale as a sheet 'cause of a knife she's still got in her fist! Other jokes done on a lazy farmhand; how they'd caught a poacher in the Saints by marking some birds. Red-handed, Lil', no two ways about it. It was a world which existed only in the evenings for her, listening while she passed a steaming plate of food to him – a man often too busy talking to eat – and it was a world from which she was totally excluded. She received no visitors, had no phone calls.

'That's the lot, I reckon,' George says. He's in a hide of wicker and branches and all around him is the smell of gunpowder. He pulls his earplugs out and grins at the old boy who's breaching the gun. The stock is hot to the touch and the old man wears soft kid-leather gloves.

'Mind if I take 'em?' George says, 'get 'em fixed up?' And he vaults the hide screen and walks out into the decoy shoot. He doesn't like walking out there, into the field, with all the dead bodies of the birds scattered across the earth. It's like the air has turned poison and the guns might still be pointing at him. Around him the retriever runs in excited dashes across the furrows of the field, breathing heavily, sneezing with the dirt, rolling head over the bodies of the birds then gathering them softly in his jaws.

'Gull,' George says, encouraging the dog he's just bought from a neighbouring farm not to embarrass him. A young dog. With age comes loyalty. Keep lifting those birds gently. That's it. And while Gull brings the birds in, George picks up the ruined decoys.

He put the decoys on the kitchen table. Painted drab brown and shot so often that parts of their bodies were missing, were burned, or were so peppered with lead bore their flanks had a dull metal shine. Painting those decoy birds occupied Lil' through that first winter. Beaks might have blown away with the force of the blasts, and she'd gently carve a new replacement and glue it in place. Lead shot was picked from the wood with tweezers and she'd fill the holes with gesso, then sand the whole body. She gave the birds a general undercoat, then began to paint on the feathers, layer upon layer of acrylic, until they began to glow with colour. The purple blue of the mallard's chest, the fiery red and gold of the pheasant's neck.

A week or so later, the birds would come back, riddled with shot, beaks shattered, heads blown away. It never upset her. She ran a field hospital, recarving pieces of wood and gluing them back. With a fine brush she'd repaint the feathers, going over paint she'd already applied and then adding more feathers till her new repairs joined up with the old and the bird was complete and ready to send to the shoot once more.

No one saw her that winter. And six months after they'd arrived, Lil' was admitted to the Quaker Cottage Hospital, Emneth Hungate. The hospital had a small capacity to treat paediatric, orthopaedic, maternity and geriatric patients in four wards, plus three rooms set aside for *psychiatric rest*, and it's in one of these where they put her. Away from the unfriendly house and the long, isolating winter, to be laid out between the crisp white sheets of a cottage hospital bed. A bed close to the window, overlooking the barren void of the Lincolnshire Fen.

Where that hospital was is now part of a large broad field growing rape in late spring, in Marshland Fen between Rands Drain and the Middle Level Main Drain. A row of slender poplars borders the field on two sides and a row of electricity pylons strikes across the sky at a diagonal. When the wind eases, it's possible to hear the hum. The hospital vanished, and with it my mother's stay there could so easily have been hushed up, had it not been for a loose comment made by Ethel Holbeach, whom we're about to meet. I was eight at the time and Ethel and Lil' were cutting delphiniums in front of Elsie and myself. Ethel mentioned Lil''s *illness* and her voice tightened on the last syllable, trying to snip the thought along with the flower. But by then it was too late. She'd let the cat out of the bag. And Ethel Holbeach, whose starched white apron had marched down the hospital's corridors that winter Lil' was there, she knew it all.

Sometimes, when I want to be with Lil' again, when I want to return and have a few private moments with her, I conjure up the image of her in that hospital room. Alone, preoccupied, her head facing the window. The sound of the poplars shivering outside. She's still sixteen. At night the bewildering smells of the fen drift in through the window, reminding her how far from home she is. The dark, decaying rot of cabbage leaves, woody scents of turnips and the sickly tones of beet, the sweetness of carrots. The close, watery smell of freshly cut soil. I regard this bleak, sterile hospital room as a special place, a place where I may always find her, those deep brown eyes wet and unreflective, an arm outstretched towards me – the child she was to love.

About three weeks later George turned up in his car, and helped Lil' into her seat. By the shape of her back as she climbs into the car I can tell her heart's been broken. A son knows his mother's back like no other. I imagine they drove home in a silence made by the unfamiliarity of being together again. And though the road was straight – relentlessly straight – George is there wishing there's a quicker way to cross Marshland Fen. He's staring too far ahead; she's staring too close for comfort. As they pass Wiggenhall St Mary the Virgin, Lil' sits low in her seat, hiding her face from the casual glances of people she's never met.

George makes a miserable cup of tea for her when they arrive back, the sense of real panic in his mind as he realizes he may not be able to cope with this woman in this house. Then the way he hangs his head when she approaches him, when she walks past him, dreamlike, with the hot mug of tea burning her hand, though she'd never notice, and going upstairs to the bedroom where she removes a blanket and makes a bed in the spare room for herself.

That was Easter, 1962. The year left little trace, bar a photograph taken in October, of the same year. The date is written on the back. When I imagine that period in their lives, I see them always alone, moving about that strange little house like a couple of dispossessed spirits. And that's why this photograph seems so odd, because, in fenland terms, it's full of people.

The photo is taken on the steep grass bank of the Great Ouse. To the left of the image the calm water stretches into the distance, and on the right, above the high flood bank of the river and looking like it's sunk into the fen, is the dark tower of the church of Wiggenhall St Peter. It's a sunny late afternoon and the group are all dressed up and dressed for warmth. Some lie in the long uncut grass like it's a summer picnic, others stand, leaning against the steep slope. It looks like a curious fenland outing, but on closer inspection things don't add up.

Lil' Mardler, right in the centre, holding a small posy of late-summer dahlias. Her hair's pulled up in the beginnings of a beehive hairstyle. George, by her side, feels it's right to stand though it looks like he may pitch into the river if he's not too careful. He's raising a flute of sparkling wine with the gesture of a man not used to such a delicate glass and he seems to be urging the others to raise theirs too. Behind him, his brother, Kipper, from Blakeney, looking impatient and wry at the same time. Not one for photographs. Next to George's feet is Gull, younger looking than I ever remember, playfully chewing a slipper he's either found in the river or he's brought from home. Behind them and further up the slope are other faces I remember from the Stow Bardolph Estate. Martha the cook, in a straw hat with pheasant's feathers in the band, those skinny farm lads playing the fool. I look quickly for the *other woman*, but don't see her young face and, anyway, she's not on the scene yet. The only person obviously missing is Goose, and maybe it's that that I see in Lil''s eyes.

Of the whole group, only Lil' and Kipper look directly into the camera. All the others are caught up with the clumsy toast George seems to be organizing. It looks like the wine's going to spill from his glass. Lil' looks calmly into the lens, the corners of her mouth have a haunting, beautifully down-turned look, the angle of her head a resigned pose. She's there in body alone. Behind her, Kipper Langore seems to have a similar look of distance. The look of a man already wanting to get on with other business. The clue is in her hands. In her right she has the posy, on the fourth finger of her left hand, a posy ring. This is George and Lil''s wedding day, if you can call it that.

A small occasion, held at the church of Wiggenhall St Peter a few feet behind the riverbank. As is traditional there, the bride arrives by boat. On this occasion it meant Lil' had to clamber into a borrowed rowing boat at the sluice gate half a mile upriver and be rowed down to the church. I imagine she sat in the stern, watching the church looming up on her right behind the bank and the faces of people who if anything were nearly all George's friends. Even in marriage she seems alone.

After the picture was taken George lifts his newlywed wife

through a cloud of confetti and stumbles precariously into the boat. With little ceremony and a lot of fuss he staggers about the little boat – now rocking in the water with the combined weight of the married couple – until he dumps his wife safely back in her seat and, still standing, begins to fumble with the rope. Someone shoves the boat out with a foot and George splashes around with the oars, spinning the boat and splashing Lil' because it causes a laugh and the boat drifts off down the river and those on the shore hear a lot of muttering and giggling from the boat until eventually he gains control of the rowlocks and begins to row back past the church. More confetti's thrown as they pass again and someone throws a half-full bottle of sparkling wine, which misses the boat and begins to drift off down to the Wash.

As the jeers of the group are left behind them, Lil' falls into listening to the rhythm of the oars. She looks shyly at the concentrated face of her husband and they share a brief, conspiratorial grin. He stops rowing.

'We did it,' he says.

'Did we miss it?' she replies, the whole event already behind her down the river.

Back at the house the guests are waiting under eighty feet of red, white and blue bunting George has stretched across the yard. Lil' loves the colours against the clouds above, but still can't think all this is for her. She's never even met most of them before. After tying her rosebud half-apron, already faded, over her wedding dress, she passes round drumsticks and potato salad sprinkled with dill and gherkins. Occasionally she looks for her own mother, but knows she won't come. She approaches the two Langore brothers with a food tray.

'What's there?' George is asking his brother, noticeably drunk now.

'Nothing much, just a bunch of outbuildings. Used as a storm shelter for cows.' Kipper's bought a smokehouse, George tells his wife. It's clear by the way he shifts his weight and the way Kipper keeps still that George is feeling uneasy. His brother does that to him.

'Not a smokehouse, not yet. But will be,' Kipper tells her. 'Between Blakeney and Cley.'

She hasn't been this close to him for a couple of years. She still can't work out his face and how it can change so entirely from one thing to another.

'What will you smoke?' she asks, the occasion making her too polite.

Kipper grins back. 'Bloaters, eel, salmon, cure some hock too.'

George is drinking too frequently from his glass.

'I'll bring some next time,' Kipper says. 'Shrimp loves bloater pâté.'

George moves away, pretending to laugh, and when Lil' doesn't follow him, he turns back. He points to a wooden box by his brother's feet.

'Now?' Kipper says.

'Why not,' George replies.

Kipper opens the box to reveal five long tubes on sticks. Some of the guests have already heard about him – that he's coming from the marshes of North Norfolk with fireworks that he makes in a shed. He holds them in his hand like a bunch of carrots and George sees how tall he walks with them, deciding where to place them, and how the others naturally fall into a neat shape around him, giving him distance. He's taken charge of the moment, as he always did. He pushes the fireworks into the soft soil and tells people to step back, even though they're safe enough already.

They fizz into the sky with a reedy crack of thunder, and

immediately the clouds answer back with the real thing. The first thick drops of rain fall in the yard, doors slam in the house with the gust of wind, and then the deluge begins.

As the guests run for their cars, the wedding couple are left together in the shadows of the house, the plates and streamers scattered around the living room like they've been ransacked. From here they watch rain like stair-rods pounding the earth and clattering the tiles of the outbuildings. A deafening roar all round them, making the house feel unearthly and silent. The sharp smell of the wet earth. Hurrying, George dashes into the yard to secure a gate which is banging on its hinges and in an instant he's drenched, and when he comes back in Lil' dries his hair with the kitchen towel.

'I'm soaked,' he says.

'Like a fish.'

'I'd best get out of these clothes, Mrs Langore.'

And when he's gone she looks at the puddles of water he's left on the tiles.

He goes upstairs, pauses at the doorway to the spare room where Lil' has now made quite a little space for herself, he smiles at the wedding invite she's kept on her bedside table, and then continues down the corridor to the bedroom with its wild geometric designs on the wallpaper and the ragged curtains against the window. He listens to the gusts of wind hitting the glass, the sound of water overflowing the gutter. He feels the darkened room in all its technicolour glory beginning to spin with the effects of the wine.

An hour later it's completely quiet and he wakes to see his wife's deep brown eyes looking carefully into his. She moves her silent preoccupied face closer, and kisses him gently on the lips, then slowly moves back into the darkness and she is gone. A few seconds later, he hears the door to the spare room closing.

That night he stands in the yard under the shattered bunting. He picks one of the used fireworks that has been trodden into the mud, smells the casing, then throws it in the shed. Bloody Kipper. The only light in the yard comes from the one he's left on in the dining room. The bare bulb shines like a sun on the table, making a pocket of light in there so vivid and awake in all this darkness he thinks it must belong to a life not his own.

7

A Rural Scene, in the Fens

1968, the world in riot, and George Langore attends an auction in Wisbech. It's a mean-spirited occasion drawn out on a car park slick with puddles and slanting rain. The men in groups, hands deep in pockets, with faces set to drive the bargain. In the middle the auctioneer whips up the lots against the crowd's better judgement. George liked all this. He liked the way the men behaved in a herd, how they shifted this way and that, picking up miscellaneous farming utensils and trying to break them with their hands. On this day, whether he'd arrived late or whether the rawness of the spring wind had caused the men to huddle tighter than usual, George found himself on the group's edge while the auctioneer tried to sell a boat. The men jeered the auctioneer, shook their heads to put him off, made false bids as the price fell and fell, told him to hurry up . . . ain't gettin' dryer . . . get you on to the egg sorter, the stack of fence posts, the hundred yard of chicken wire. No one bid. But the auctioneer was already soaked and he wanted a sale . . . c'on, Bill, we all got homes to go to. Fen accents, mingling with the singsong of the Norfolk dialect.

Then, for some reason, perhaps a fleeting memory of the boats in his youth, maybe of the *Hansa* itself, George raises his hand and says *shilling*. The auctioneer and most of the group think this is a great laugh, but faced with no alternative the lot's knocked down and the boat is his. And as the group shuffles off to the next lot, that's when he sees his boat.

*

That evening the *Mary Magdalene* stood proudly and just a little sadly in the centre of the yard while Lil' and George tapped it and Gull sniffed it suspiciously.

'Sweet little rowboat, even got a hole, just like the *Hansa*,' he says, framing his face in the hole and laughing at her.

'We going to keep it in the yard?'

'No we ain't! She's up for fixing.'

Oddly, they realize they want to share something. It's the first time in years and the feeling is sudden for her. It makes her giddy. She's scared she might blush, because after all these years she still doesn't want to give anything away. She laughs nervously, with her hand to her mouth, and says you're a one – a real one.

Now what? she says. The hole's been repaired, the boards caulked and a new coat of paint applied, and the *Mary Magdalene*'s there prow down on a mudchute on the bank of the Twenty Foot Drain. Get in, he says, already pushing it, and they both scramble in at the last moment as the boat plunges into the water with a great rush. Instantly its heaviness is gone. The boat comes up, turns and drifts, and they look at each other in wonder.

Occasionally, when their little boat goes under the shadow of a bridge, Lil' looks down at the water to see the sky's reflection briefly vanish. She rests her hand on the picnic basket to show she's taking good care of it. A precious cargo of rollmops, cheese and pickles. Sometimes she'll look up to see someone cycling along the bank or crossing a bridge. She watches the cyclist pedalling into the distance, until it's no longer clear whether his pedals are going round or whether they're now going up, then down, up, then down. Though it's not the sunniest of days, the summer haze eventually makes the man wobble on his bike, then disappear entirely, as if he's fallen off the edge of the world. George's eye is on the Ordnance Survey map and is struggling to decipher the drains and dykes, at right angles and in parallel, the rivers and the sluices. Their symmetry challenges his right to be in charge, and several times he has to scramble up the high riverbank to stand at the top, scratch his head, and privately curse the idiosyncrasies of a fenland where all the rivers actually flow *above* the level of the fields. It says on the map 'below sea level', but it feels like they're travelling in the sky.

He soon devises his Fenland Steering Method – it's brought about the ingenuity in him, this boat business – where he ties up the rudder so it can't move. They sit at the front of the boat, side by side, away from the noise and smell of the outboard, listening to the water as it passes in a soothing rhythm. And by leaning, in unison, gently – ever so gently – one way or the other, the boat begins to steer itself. And as Lil' leans into George, he leans away, their distance always kept constant.

After an hour, her head lolls on to his shoulder. He stares ahead, taking pride in his task, watching the minuscule shifting of the boat's steering as her body relaxes softly against him. That's it, Lil', you close your eyes. He puts his arm round her and she strokes his side tenderly. He reaches further round her, putting his hand on the opposite gunwale so that the weight of his arm rebalances the boat. Men do things while women sleep – he thinks happily – to rebalance the world.

And like somnambulist lovers, their boat takes them into a dream scene. They're steering down the Middle Level Main Drain to a village called Three Holes. A high pale blue sky, the sleepy colour of a late English summer. Distantly, the sound of larks. The woody smell of cabbage, which must remind Lil' of the weeks she spent at the Quaker Cottage Hospital in Emneth Hungate, not so far from this place. In my mind it all slows down in balletic movement. The humming of the engine lowers hypnotically, the water lulls them towards sleep. Ahead, the top of a small house is seen over the bank. Nothing stirs in the air, not even the soft worn collar of George's twill shirt, or the set dome of his wife's now fully grown beehive. She sighs, sways softly with the motion of the boat, looks up briefly when she hears the sound of a child's giggle somewhere along the bank. He hears it too, and is perhaps the first to see the three figures ahead. He startles from his reverie, begins to fuss with the wooden handle of the rudder, feels the hand of his wife being placed on his and, for a moment, they lock eyes.

'George,' she says. And says no more.

The three figures on the bank are close now. A man and a woman, perhaps twenty years older than Lil' and George, dressed in clothes too heavy for the weather. They've been eating boiled eggs and haslet and cherry tartlets and a bottle of cordial is propped up in the grass between them. They're looking calmly at the boat coming towards them down the drain, but the man abruptly stands and calls out a name: *Elsie! Elsie, come here, darling!*

I imagine the colours bleaching out at this point. I imagine the sun's glare sweeps into the channel like an arc light and I see Lil' and George both looking ahead, their hands raised to shield their eyes. Dazzled and tight-lipped, she glimpses a halo of red light, which turns out to be the hair of a little girl, perhaps five or six years old, playing by the side of the water with an eel-trap. Faintly Lil' hears the man's voice again call for *Elsie! Elsie!* But it sounds so distant, and the girl looks so fragile and beautiful in the light that it surely can't be her he's calling. Lil' reaches out her hand and the girl smiles back at her and the boat gently comes to a halt in utter silence against the soft mud.

Yes this really is a dream. A dream where little Elsie stands boyishly by the rowing boat, with her hands on her hips and the trail of her eel-trap disappearing into the weeds. Elsie is giggling and Lil' is smiling back at her, and George has gripped his wife so tight the ridges of his knuckles are showing and he's trying to fuss with the engine because the steering is still tied up and they're wedged into the bank.

The man and woman are walking unsteadily down the grassy slope towards their child. The man reaches the boat first and squats down on his haunches, one hand on the boat's gunwale, the other on his daughter's shoulder, steadying both and himself, a man who makes caring gestures.

'Hello, Langore, out on your boat?' he says.

'Mr Holbeach. Where are we?'

'Three Holes. Just having a picnic.'

And now the woman has reached little Elsie, and she stands behind her and, with an almost imperceptible nod, the woman greets Lil'. They've met once before, at the hospital.

'This, Mrs Langore, is little Elsie,' the woman says.

Lil' makes a strange little noise in the back of her throat and reaches out her hand to the girl.

'Go on, say hello,' Mrs Holbeach whispers to the child, 'it's all right,' and it makes Elsie shy. She turns her face into her mother's skirts and twists her eel twine into the palm of her hand.

'Have you been catching eels?' Lil' says to the girl, and little Elsie looks back at her and nods. 'Have you caught any?'

'No.'

'Mrs Langore . . .' the woman begins, but her husband looks up at her and she doesn't continue. 'Mrs Langore,' she says again, repeating the name to herself.

'It's all right, Ethel,' her husband says. And oddly the girl starts to laugh.

'What is it?' Lil' says.

'Your boat's silly,' Elsie says, as if it's something the adults have missed.

A rural scene, in the Fens. Hello, Elsie, nice to meet you, in your blue-and-white gingham dress with smocking round the neck, eating a picnic of eggs, haslet, tartlets and cordial. It's so still here; the only movement across the punishing geometry of the landscape has been the boat inching its way down the drain, two people in its prow leaning to keep a straight course. The excited shrieks of a girl as she's dragged her eel-line through the dark weeds, and then the same girl, giggling as she watches this strange couple floating closer.

It's a perfect moment. And then the girl asks her mother whether she can go in the boat and all four adults look at each other, gauging.

Lil' immediately looks at Mrs Holbeach, and realizes in that instant that Mrs Holbeach is one of the kindest women she's ever met. A kind and generous woman who has an aura of trust, of good-will, of peace which has grown over forty years of living on the fen. Mrs Holbeach would make the decision. With her large, slow-moving hands she ruffles the bright red hair of her daughter and then bends to lift up the half-loaf that had rolled down the slope. She picks at the grass clinging to the crust, looks up calmly and says of course, Elsie.

Elsie winds her eel-line and starts to clamber in. Steady, Elsie, be careful now, and Lil' puts her hand on the girl's shoulder and she feels the smallness of the bones there. Then Elsie sits next to Lil' and they hold each other's hands and she tells her father to push the boat off and don't fall in because we're *not* going to fish you out.

★

Elsie's immediately dragging her hand and eel-line fast through the water, not looking back once at her parents receding down the drain. It's unnerving how quickly people vanish in a landscape so large. Lil' and George sit together, near the engine, in a sudden silence made by the presence of this playful child. Lil' looks back once and sees Mr and Mrs Holbeach standing at the top of the bank, shielding their eyes against the setting sun, though it looks equally possible that Mrs Holbeach is in fact crying. And then she looks at Elsie. She looks at the tension of pleasure on her face, the girlish pout of adult front teeth her mouth is yet to frame, the pepper of freckles each side of the nose. At the hair, a deep peachy red, so curly, so vigorous it makes her feel all of life has become new.

The little boat and its odd cargo go another two miles into the fen until they come up to the dark weedy iron of a sluice gate. Elsie wants them to go on, but George turns the boat back to Three Holes. Lil' moves forward and plays with the eel-line, making a cat's cradle between her fingers for Elsie, smelling the girl's hot breath when they laugh together. The shadows lengthen over the water, Elsie huddles closer for warmth, and Lil' puts an arm round her for the half-hour it takes for them to return. Just before they reach Elsie's house, they pass the confluence of three water channels that gives Three Holes its curious name. A place of meeting. They tie up and Lil' climbs out with Elsie, now asleep in her arms. And as they climb up the bank, Lil' sees the Holbeachs' strange little cottage for the first time. A simple Lincolnshire two-up-two-down worker's house, surrounded by a plot of darkly turned soil, immaculately upright in a fen where all the other buildings are twisted as they gradually sink.

Mrs Holbeach has been looking out for them, and opens the door when George, Lil' and the sleeping Elsie are halfway down the path. Lil' puts Elsie into a chair, and they're offered tea in delicate china cups and slices of Mrs Holbeach's carrot cake. A Quaker recipe. It seems like Mrs Holbeach has long expected them. While the tea brews, George comments on the framed photographs of tulips on the walls, awards for the prized tulip bulbs Mr Holbeach grows in his smallholding. One of the last of its kind in the Fens.

When Elsie wakes, her sleep has changed her mood. She doesn't know why the boat people are still there, so she becomes over-polite. She walks round the room, eats white bread and jam in the corner and swings her feet together to make the buckles on her sandals jingle.

'Just tulips is it, Mr Holbeach?'

'Page Polkas,' he replies, 'very striking and very tall.' The men are doing their bit at conversation. 'March,' Mr Holbeach says, sipping his tea.

Lil' continues to sip her tea long after it's gone cold. Mrs Holbeach sits on a piano stool, smoothing her dress over plump knees, suddenly looking tired. And when Lil' and George finally get up to go, Elsie again comes to their aid. Yawning, she says, 'You're nice.' It's to Lil'. 'Can I go in your boat again?'

'Yes,' Ethel says, 'I think it might be all right.'

'George, turn the engine off.'

A week later. Lil' and George, an hour into a trip going down the Great Ouse.

George leans back to the outboard, unsure what's wrong. He cuts the engine and feels the boat lurch to one side, and when he looks back at his wife she's off the bench and is lying flat on the planks of the boat. The *Mary Magdalene* drifts into the sonorous flow of the big river, begins to turn slowly, and still he looks down at his wife, forgetting the old rule of never standing in small boats.

Looking down at her, he watches her fingers unbutton her summer dress, sees the soft, heavy shapes of her breasts in the bra as she pulls the material aside, and the pale, smooth skin of her legs as she begins to pull the dress up to her waist.

And at this point I shall retire to the distant riverbank while they get on with the business of my conception. I leave my father and mother on the rough wooden planks of the *Mary Magdalene*, inches away from the soft fenland water trickling past the hull. A tiny rowing boat, adrift in the muddy swirls of the Great Ouse as the river makes its lazy, final pouring out into the Wash.

That's where I started, on 30 September 1968.

8

Weightless and Soundless

I'm there, behind the weird cockscomb of my mother's belly-button, and I must admit I'm a little apprehensive. I know how things will turn out. It was the first few winter months of 1969, and Lil', my mother, was acting strangely: tasting mustard powder on the tip of a spoon, sharp fermented cider vinegar licked from a finger, salt and lemon off the back of her hand. As spring comes she eats radishes by the dozen, a whole raw goose egg sprinkled with paprika, the bitter leaves of wild horseradish. Then she turns to sweet and sour: the heady darkness of molasses syrup, the sweet tang of rollmop herrings, of pickled capers and, once, the beguiling tastes in a spoon of green tomato chutney – fresh onions, cut across the grain, floury tomato pips, soft plump raisins and the sad brown taste of autumn apples. The exotic fire of a single red chilli. She was throwing me off the scent, distracting me from hearing that far-off note which beat like a second distant heart, her own soft boom-boom of secret sadness.

In the spare room she had changed the wallpaper, repaired the bed, replaced the mattress. Unlike my father's room, where the wild curtains still hung like an angry noise, the spare room became immaculate. She could sit by the window and look down the slope to the high fen of Black Ditch Level, Marshland Fen and Stow Bardolph Fen, even further away, with their rigid lines of dead-end roads and drainage channels and isolated sluice-pump cottages. She hung a North American Indian dreamcatcher she'd bought in a bric-a-brac shop in King's Lynn on the window and looked through it like a target.

George, my father, didn't get a look-in during those months. I was *in there* and she was *out of bounds*. He was not wanted. In their separate lives my father had revamped a cupboard off the living room, which had last been used by the previous tenant, Harold Flott. Flott had stacked the shelves with jars of screws and nails, but the screws and nails had been replaced now by books on animal husbandry, balls of string had become journals on veterinary studies, bundles of yellowed magazines had become estate-organizational records on breeding, selecting and bloodstock management. My father had bought a lamp for the evenings, and a desk for his leather-bound science journal, given to him by Kipper on his wedding day. A beautiful book of pristine white paper bound with the softest calfskin. A small brass lock held the album shut. With a tender gesture my father would wipe the front of the journal every time he entered the room.

Each evening, his mind slightly addled with alcohol, my father would sit there and smoke a pipe until he heard the door of the spare room close upstairs. He'd sit among the gently rising curls of his smoke like the proverbial punished man and contemplate the silence of the house. A dying marriage is a calm place to be, and he resigned himself to it, like giving in to illness.

On 20 July my mother went into labour. Unlike Hands, twenty-four years before, my father wasn't stricken with panic. He didn't feel the wind in the air and dream of lost horizons, he didn't work out his escape route on a map with his finger. What he did was make the necessary call to the midwife, and then he set up the black-and-white television in the living room. While he fiddled to get a reception my mother gasped for air by the window of her room.

The midwife came within minutes to what must have

seemed a deserted house. Gull skulked in shadows by the barn, a solemn heat seemed to fill the rooms, flies turned sharp corners in the air above the breakfast table. Going into the living room she found my father crouched in front of the television where the crew of Apollo 11 were passing under the grey southern hemisphere of the moon. He turned to her, the excitement in his face giving him a deranged, wild look. Ain't it marvellous! he said. She gave him a brief, professional scolding for not being with his wife, then went upstairs with a matter-of-fact purposefulness that scared him to the bone. Just, whenever you need, you know, he whispered, too late, from the bottom of the stairs, before being drawn back to the mesmerizing TV.

It is a long night. At four in the morning the whole world falls silent in front of those flickering pictures. A distant voice and cracks of static perforate an emptiness which seems to stretch from Norfolk right up into the deep void of space. *The Eagle has landed*, says a voice abruptly and is answered with a relieved *roger, we copy, it was beautiful from here, Tranquillity . . . we can breathe again*. My father looks up at the ceiling wondering about all the things going on above his head. He's drinking himself crazy. The sheer magic of the footage continues. Unexpectedly, a bulky shape gleaming in harsh sunlight appears on the side of the landing craft. Half man half refrigerator clings dreamily to the rungs of the ladder. And it all begins to happen fast now. The crackle of Armstrong's intercom sounds once, twice, we hear his breath and my father holds his. My mother screams once, then falls silent, staring up at the light-fitting above her bed. The midwife turns to the window and sees the moon framed in one of the panes. Downstairs he looks in awe as that clumsy body seems to float down the steps without touching the rungs does the foot go down has it finally happened and that's when the midwife remembers the job she's there to do. She turns back to my shocked mother and she sees me lying there, between my mother's legs, swapping the weightless dark of her body for an appearance in the midst of a worldwide drama.

From downstairs a hoarse cheer as the astronaut's famous announcement is declared and a rigid American flag is bent into shape, and then an excited silence, as all in the house remember why they're there and try to listen out for a baby's cry. But the only sound comes from the overlapping gabble from the TV and the faint sound of the radio upstairs. Soon, the anxiety spreads to my mother, she lifts her head because she can't hear me, and sees the midwife tying a professional no-nonsense never-to-be-undone knot in the umbilical cord, so unlike that crude granny-slip hanging down across my mother's belly, and then she sees the nurse wrapping the hot, sticky body of the baby in a soft white towel. A baby refusing to cry.

There's a hesitant knock on the door and my father pokes his face into the room.

'She done it, George, better late than never. A little boy.'

And my father breaks into tears.

That first day I was weighed, measured, checked from head to foot and dusted with talcum. The midwife would call back later. I was carried round the house, the garden, pointed out to Gull, who was sniffing the front door nervously. And all that time my mouth remained shut. When the midwife called in that evening my mother told her I'd made no sound all day. Birth shock, she was told. Get to sleep 'cause the young 'un's going to bawl his eyes out all night. But the night arrived and my parents fell asleep in their separate rooms in a house that sounded no different from the one two nights before. Both of them listened out for their baby's cry, but it never came.

90

On the second day I was declared the best baby the midwife had ever delivered, and on the third she arrived with an anxious doctor. The doctor looked in my eyes, ears and mouth with his ophthalmoscope, and – less professionally – tickled me to get a reaction. Under the arms, the soles of the feet. A reputation at risk. The next day he phoned a consultant with the admission he was calling because a baby in his ward, who was in otherwise perfect health, was sleeping through the nights and seemed fit and happy during the day, had totally stumped him with its refusal to cry. He was told to wait. Wait for a baby with a real problem.

Towards the end of that first week my father was eating a boiled egg at the kitchen table with me next to him in a Moses basket.

'She ought to know.'

My mother continued eating her egg, waiting to see if he'd say more.

'It's just, she's got a right.'

'I han't spoken to her for eight years, George.'

'It's different now. Ain't it, Lil'?'

'It's too late.'

'No it ain't. She'd like to see the young 'un.'

'George, I can't. Eat your egg.'

'I'll call tonight. Shall I call tonight?'

He did. From the phone box in Wiggenhall St Germans by the Great Ouse. He called the Albatross Inn and got one of the lads there to cycle across the marsh to fetch Goose and accept no excuses if she refused to come. My father sat on the bank of the dyke while the errand was done. Some time later, crouched in the red phone box, his head in his hands with tiredness, he finally spoke to Goose.

★

As the coach pulled up three days later the doors swung open with a thump and she was already climbing down, already talking nineteen to the dozen, complaining of stiffness, draught, braking, exhaust fumes. The sandwiches. My father stood the assault, sensed the woman was nervous, then silenced her by raising his hand. I got to tell you, he said, things ain't right. I ain't talking about you kicking Lil' out. That's all under the bridge and I ain't going to say my pitch, but things with Lil' and the young 'un. He hasn't made a noise since he was born and that's near breaking her heart. He ain't right. And I don't want you mixing it or making things worse or I'll send you packing.

She leans forward and when he kisses her cheek he feels it's warm from the bus but slack with age. Her hand on the luggage has a lattice of purple veins on it. But he knows the last thing he wants is to feel pity for the old girl.

'You're fatter,' she says. 'Don't worry, boy, I won't cause no trouble.'

Goose and Lil' manage a limp hug on the doorstep, which proved to be such an important moment my father snapped it with his Kodak Retinette. I still have the picture. Is the surprised expression on my mother's face because her hands have overlapped so easily across Goose's back? The woman has shrunk like the marsh she lives on, and her hair's grown bigger, tied up at the back of her head in an awkward knot very similar to the granny-slip in my mother's belly-button. Her eyes had been brown, but they've begun to go grey. As they release each other Goose looks at the house, the yard, the life she's never been part of. She knows not to draw attention to her absence from Lil', but needs to say something none the less. What's with the flowers? she asks, looking at the odd arrangements that have been planted across the garden. And my mother reacts with a knowing-but-not-telling smile – the kind of gesture that has always wound Goose up, and both women know it.

I expect I was shown to my grandmother a few seconds after the picture was taken. There, on the kitchen table, my hand in my mouth. And when the hand was removed no noise came out.

'He's called Pip,' my mother said, a little unsure what else she *could* say.

'After my boat!' Goose snorts, before thinking better of it. *Well, blow me!* She tries to conciliate: don't you worry – he'll start bawlin' soon. Lil', you cried solid the whole week, day 'n' night – turn me ragged, you did . . . My mother listened tensely at the ease with which Goose dragged up the old stories. It was a mistake to have invited her. But she said nothing and as the story continued past the images of clouds and Hands's disappearance, she felt a sudden relief to hear all this again. So that bastard pull the quilt off the line, he did, use it as a sail . . . and my mother thinks Goose is right to use her stories this way. After all, stories have bound them from the start. This baby is just the next step in the myth. It makes her look at me afresh, held in the dry leaves of Goose's hands. Seeing me, there, it was a moment of real love. I was silent, but I was hers. Her baby, and all was fine.

'I ain't got no ideas.'

'How long's it been?'

My father's in a storeroom at the Stow Bardolph Estate. There's a young woman in there, eating an apple and sitting on some stacked trestle tables. With each bite my father looks at the tiny bubble of juice on her lower lip; he leans against the cool white plaster wall, his body so relaxed after a day's work he has the look of a man entirely at ease. Which he isn't.

'Long enough.'

'There's not much I can say, George.'

The girl has the habit of deliberately using his name. He wonders why. She's what – twenty, twenty-one? He doesn't even know why he's sharing all this with her. She looks at him with a level gaze while all that moves is the hair she's swept up from her face, falling slowly across her forehead like silk.

On the last night of her visit, Goose stood on the back lawn and stared at the sky and then at the moon. Behind her, the eerie silence of the house where a baby should have been crying. My mother came out and stood by the old woman. The clouds passed dreamily in front of the moon, and some-where up in that view, the astronauts had left their cardboard flag ahead of their long journey home. The moon was empty again.

'I wonder if they looked at us,' my mother said.

'These clouds ain't clouds,' Goose replied. 'All fortnight the clouds been buggered up by this moonstuff. Bad enough up Blakeney, but hair . . . I don't know. These fenland people got dull dreams, that they have.' And the old girl turns to my mother and says, 'What I don't understand is why you married him.'

My mother feels she shouldn't have to be asked. 'For Pip,' she says.

Goose lets it lie, but something still brothers her: 'You still han't told me about these flowers.'

My mother smiles darkly in the night. She's full of secrets.

My mother had planted a garden where the flowers grew taller, straighter, had more blooms and lasted longer than anywhere else in the area. Closer to the Wash the salt air burned the petals, while down in the Fens the habit was always to plant edibles. But she'd gone against this local wisdom. Cornflowers and sweet peas wrapped the house in an unbroken garland, while delphiniums, deep blue in the August sun, ran in a straight line across the back lawn. Daisies and marigolds fringed the windows, a hedge of lavender meandered north-east. Beyond them, a single sunflower stood like an obelisk.

On the day my father had brought back his first screaming middle-white piglet, my mother planted flowering sage around the pigpen. Pigs were wise, and sage would improve the keenness of their minds. When he had built a hen-coop – ah yes, the coop that would mean so much to me – my mother dragged it over to the tarragon bushes. Wherever he stood, my mother followed with her trowel, changing his designs with the subtlest of touches. He let it be, and he kept moving.

But anyone stopping by the farm was less tolerant. *That lavender can't hardly be seen from the house*, they said, and *what's that line doing heading off to that bit of ole scrub?* Likewise, delphiniums cut straight through the heart of the lawn, generally bothered the eye and *how the hell she gets the mower round them I don't know*. To the side of the house was the stench of a stinkhorn, growing under my father's study window. *How he put up with her I ain't saying. Fen folk don't piss around like this*. A feeble mind. They still remembered the odd food she ate in the pregnancy – stuff that *poisoned that young 'un though God forgive me saying such a thing*.

More than bees, ladybirds and butterflies, my mother was trying to attract another visitor to her garden. And one day, just after my first birthday, as she was carrying potato peelings across the yard in a bucket in one hand, me under her other arm, the visitor arrived. A car drove up and out climbed Mrs Holbeach.

From under her armpit I glimpsed the satisfaction that flickered across my mother's face. The same expression I imagine she had when she caught the weever before the Langore brothers did.

'May.'

'Ethel.'

'About time I came by. Brought some scones.'

'Pip loves scones.'

'So does Elsie.'

And in the car we see her messing around with the steering wheel. Clumsy and excited, her fiery hair like the sunflower's ragged petals. And I pictured my mother, in her bedroom, gazing through her dreamcatcher at the petals of her own sunflower, and beyond it, miles away in the fen and in the centre of the dreamcatcher's web, the Holbeachs' cottage at Three Holes.

Those two women became the most notorious flower arrangers in the Fens. Each Saturday they stood in the cool dusty calm of the church, all their flowers smelling green and wet on the tiles where Elsie and I searched for fossils. My mother in her utility dress with the faded rosebud half-apron tied round it, the shine of sheer tights below it, her only concession to luxury. One of the women would go to the church Bible and call out the Sunday service readings and gospel. Ethel Holbeach, big as a turkey behind the lectern, turning the pages of the Bible and her voice sounding nervous just because she's up there talking even though it's only my mother, Elsie and me listening. *Vanity of vanities, sayeth the preacher, all is vanity,* and my mother says stop, I've got an idea. It's the final passage of Ecclesiastes and it's a difficult one to pull off. How's it go again? my mother says from the back of the church. *God shall bring every work into judgement.* The other bit. *The preacher sought out to find acceptable words?* Yeah

– that's it. And my mother's piling up the flowers on the floor. There are thistles and thorns and if you can get beyond them you can find the fragile early buds of a lone agapanthus. Ribbons round the base, distracting and false like serpents' tongues, swirls of gypsophila like as many misleading clouds, but if you try hard enough you'll find it, you'll find the beauty. It's going to be a good one, my mother says, and Ethel Holbeach grins, showing her poor fenland teeth.

Elsie spent more time at the farm, sometimes with her mother, more often alone. She had her own stool in the kitchen, and as time went by she and my mother developed their own shorthand communication: the silent exchange of ingredients, a hot spoon passed to be tasted, a sauce to be stirred. Horseradish grated from the root, folded into sour cream and wine vinegar, Elsie squeezing the lemon – hand in front, love, don't let it squirt in your eye – driping tabasco in like a scientist. Arranging it on the plate next to warm peppered mackerel and sourdough rolls. Go and get Pip now, my mother says, wiping her hands on the worn rosebuds of her half-apron. Little Elsie dragging her stool round the kitchen, standing on it in her busy little T-bar sandals as she reaches for the jars, the pots, the ladles and packets before my mother even asked her. And when all the business was done Elsie would watch me eat.

'There, see, he likes it, I *know* what he likes.'

I kept my silence. In my first three years a stream of Ear, Nose and Throat consultants and child psychologists tackled my case. Just how many times was I crept up on and tickled in the ribs, or balloons inflated and popped by my ears? I was shown animals and encouraged to moo and baa in imitation. A dog's bark, a cat's meow. My parents were told to talk all the time to each other, and, when they weren't talking, to sing. So at breakfast they filled the room with talk of what they might do later, what jobs they had to complete, how the weather might change, how fat the pig was getting. As my mother cleared the plates away my father would walk outside, singing a tune until he got into his car, turn the ignition, and fall silent at the wheel.

Forcing a conversation that wasn't there was a great effort. For a month they kept it going for the sake of the child psychologist until my father called the office to tell him it wasn't working only to hear that the psychologist had been transferred to another district anyway. This bit of news was relayed to my mother that evening over cod fricassee and that was the last thing they said that night.

Goose had her own ideas on how to break my silence. She sent recipes containing tongue and, increasingly, laxatives (bunged up at one end, bunged up at the other). Coffee powder stirred into soups, chocolate sprinkled on prune puree. Raw fish for breakfast. Some foods were specified with certain types of weather. Eel broth in fog. Suet pudding in rain. But when the postcard arrived saying I should be fed mackerel heads, uncooked, under a high-mackerel or leg-of-mutton sky, my mother knew the game was over. I'd won the day. The two women had repaired their differences, and my mother knew two things: one, there was nothing physically wrong with me; and two, her son was silent, had been silent from birth, and – as she told me once, bending down to see me and touching my lips with her finger – she preferred it that way.

But my father felt my silence was unnerving. It mocked him. It needed to end. That's why – after sending my mother to Lynn on an errand – he took me to the feed-shed across the yard, looped some rope over one of the game hooks drilled in the wall, and then bound it tightly round my ankles till I felt the heat of the rope. I was left there, where he hung his pheasants, wriggling against the cruel rope and straining to see if he was still around. For an hour I hanged, blood pounding in my head, occasionally getting a whiff of his tobacco, knowing he was by the pigsty, smoking his pipe. Waiting for me to cry out, or for my mother returning in the car. Whichever came first.

Late in the morning he came in and tapped his pipe out against the wall, the weariness of yet another defeat clouding his face. That's enough, he said, I guess you ain't going to say nothing. Never.

That evening as my mother bathed my swollen ankles in a bowl she listened to my father's explanation that I was a growing lad and my boots were already too small. After a while he left the room and went to read his books in the study, and she whispered to me.

'We'll get the bugger back. Some day.'

He's in the storeroom again, under the bare light bulb. The girl's in there too, laughing at a joke he's made, and when she moves her head a girdle of light shines on the woven flatness of her hair. He can hear the bubbles rising in the cider in their cups. One of the lads calls her peaches and cream. He's never heard the expression before, but it makes total sense.

While he's in there, my mother is telling me the events of her youth, and before them, of Hands and Goose on the edge of the marsh. She tells me how bleak she felt when she had to leave North Norfolk and about the first night she spent on the lawn behind the house. About the half-drunk cup of tea, the crumbs of stale bread and the mice shit on the corner of the table, all that was left of the previous tenant. She tells me my father had started off being a great dreamer like my own vanished grandfather, but that as the years passed he was becoming lost to something, though my mother didn't know what. She tells me about Norfolk's skies, the saltmarsh, about fish and crablines, meals of tongue and samphire. We're in the garden, where Elsie and I had been given a strip each to make our own. She'd planted tulips, putting the bulbs in like her father, and when they didn't grow as well as his, she'd dug them up and planted onions instead. I'd filled my plot with glass and metal, mantraps to keep the others out.

My mother calls us over and there, in the soil beneath her, she's parted some large fleshy leaves to reveal a perfect white cauliflower. The leaves squeak when she moves them. Now the sun will get to its crown, she says. And as we marvel at the wonderful vegetable, she begins retelling the story of Hands, my grandfather, whose head had been found sticking out through the black mud of the Morston Marshes. It's the first time Elsie's heard it, and she giggles at the description of the longshoreman wading through the channel, the morning's catch jangling at his belt. At how Hands had rolled his eyes in fear when Goose had covered him in samphire, and how he'd kept his boots on in the bath. She ends where she always ended – with the story of her own birth, of the magnificent clouds in the sky, the quilt disappearing on the line, and the grotesque granny-slip her mother had tied into the umbilical cord. At this, she lifts her jumper and shows her belly button while Elsie stares with wide-eyed horror at the rotten knot that wouldn't last in a washing line but which has somehow taken graft in my mother's skin.

I felt angry that this story was being told to Elsie. It wasn't her grandfather, after all. What about her own grandfather – wherever he was – with his long Quaker beard like Father

Christmas? Jealous of Elsie and my mother, and still hearing Elsie's thin laughter, I ran into the house and lay on the floor, banging the tiles. I picked a stump of crayon and ran it round the skirting board. Then I drew another line with it. The line became shapes – zigzags, parallels, circles – then I saw my mother, standing in the doorway, eyes glistening with a cry of joy she was holding in, her hand to her mouth because she didn't want the joy to leave her.

That first crayon soon wore to nothing as I covered the furniture, walls, tiles and bricks. Wherever I went, my mother followed, translating as quickly as I scribbled, like her own cloud-chasing mother. The line I drew around the room was taken as the Fens' horizon, the clumsy round shapes above the line were claimed to be the sun, the moon, even cloud formations. The skirting board was covered with the dark shapes of those things that live in the earth. The carrot, the beet, the potato. Poplars grew up across the plaster in long straight lines as high as the sideboard, as did the funereal shapes of my mother's garden flowers. There were people too, shadowy people leaning against gates, drawing up in decrepit cars, skulking below the brims of wide summer hats, hiding behind trees. Pigs and bulls fought each other in running battles across the kitchen, chickens roosted unperturbed on chair backs. Around the doorjamb of my father's study there were a series of curving zigzag lines. I spent several days completing them, the crayon sweating between my greasy knuckles, my teeth clenched tightly. The solitary stinkhorn was sketched on the plaster where the wall had blown with damp, tulip heads and bull's horns fought it out on my father's car. Dogs and seagulls wheeled round each other, chasing their tails along the bricks of the house.

Each evening my mother interpreted the drawings for my father, who must have felt as though a kind of free insanity had broken out in his house. How I'd written about food behind cupboard doors, drawn the smells of the cooking as she stirred the pot. How I'd written Gull's name and she hung it round his neck. And one evening, I have a dim memory of finding my father crouched with a torch on the living-room carpet, peering at the drawings leading to his study door. Sometimes I reconjure him there, with a J-Cloth and soap erasing what I'd done a few hours earlier, sometimes I see him with a stub of crayon himself, changing what he sees before him into more recognizable, less revealing images before his wife has a chance to see them. Always I imagine him with a guilty expression as I stand fierce in the light of the open doorway, the well-worn stub of crayon indignant in my hand.

Hanging the name round Gull's neck may have been the last straw, because as soon as he ripped it off he produced a letter he'd been concealing about plans for my education.

A month later – with my hieroglyphs as high as the ceiling in some places – he announced a special-needs teacher from the outskirts of Lynn would be coming to visit. Mrs Crowe, he said to me. Mrs Crowe, whose first gesture when she entered the house was to raise her eyebrows and look down her nose at the graffiti. Who held her skirt carefully so as not to get any crayon wax on it. As you see, Mrs Crowe, my father began shyly, he do want to learn. He want to speak, really, so if you can change all this wild scribbling into half-decent copperplate I reckon you're the one for us.

My mother was stunned by the betrayal. Mrs Crowe was allowed into the house, but with suspicion, not least because my mother had no role in appointing her. My mother tested the teacher by leading her around some of the hieroglyphs, pointing out a goat here, a river there, cloud formations, malformed vegetables. She showed the empty space of wall around the spot where my father leaned his Gallyon & Sons shotgun, and the halo of what looked like flames spreading away from this space along the plaster. She made the rotund teacher kneel down and peer at the shadowy people hiding behind the legs of the dresser till the round fenland face of the woman became flushed. All this time I stood behind my mother's legs, clutching at her skirt and hiding my crayon.

Eventually Mrs Crowe stood up and stared calmly at the mother and child before her.

'And you say he doesn't speak?'

'Never.'

'He's had tests?'

'There's nothing wrong with Pip, Mrs Crowe. Medically. He'll speak if he wants to. When the time comes.'

'But you want him to write?'

'*He* wants to write.'

Mrs Crowe looked down at me. 'It will all have to come off,' she said, looking at the walls. 'I can't have this.'

Three days a week Mrs Crowe scrubbed my hands, confiscated my beloved crayon, and in its place gave me a brand-new, sharpened pencil. On Monday, Wednesday and Friday mornings at nine o'clock sharp I would open the kitchen door at the moment Mrs Crowe raised her hand to knock. Caught in that silly position, or even at the moment when she was still fussing with her hair, she'd be ushered in. It was my first victory. My second would be stubbing the pencil so hard the lead broke, and then watching Mrs Crowe sharpen it with growing frustration as she found the lead was broken all the way through. Watching the pencil being ground into Mrs Crowe's fist was satisfying but short lived, because soon she began to bring her own, previously untampered-with instruments for my lessons.

Mrs Crowe's first name was Cassie. Cassie Crowe. My father referred to her as Ali. Attagirl, Ali, he'd say, give the lad the jab. Oh shut up, my mother would say. Grow up, George, and he'd laugh even more, looking at the sparkle of the drink he held in his hand and shaking his head.

Crowe would put an apple on the table and tell me the mysteries of the letter 'a'. To me, the shape of the letter she drew already meant 'apple', except it had no leaves on the stalk. I drew them in and passed the paper back to her. She rubbed them off and passed the letter back.

I knew what she was doing – she was teaching me to write words. And as soon as she knew that's what I wanted most, she gave me a notebook to hang round my neck.

'Whatever you want, you write in there. You have a voice now.' A notebook has hung round my neck ever since.

But on the other days of the week the crayon was back in my hand. Instead of the glaring public space of the walls, I found more secret places to practise my art. Like crawling under my father's bed and drawing on the slats, or squeezing in the kitchen cupboards. Between the tins, under the shelves, below the chairs and on the backs of picture frames. Even the insides of book jackets – these were my places. And one by one my father found them all with rattish tenacity. Scrubbing with sugar soap. But he never found the coop. Oh no. That was my secret. Or he knew about it but didn't like chickens – which was odd, considering where he ended up in life. Each day for a month I sat in that grubby coop with the hens and my crayons. The dry, sharp smell of the birds, the dust suspended in the air, the powdered crust of their shit intrigued me. As did the chickens themselves, sitting calmly in the dark, napping, shifting warily on their nests. I wedged myself in there and sat for hours, seduced by the secret calm of the coop and fascinated by the erratic hen lore. Though I spent my days in there, they never got used to me. Only one bird seemed at ease: a Rhode Island Red, which spent its days wedged into a gap behind the boxes. It never went out and never left its space, though it must have managed to eat somehow. In all the hours I was in there, it never stopped looking at me.

At first I drew the hens in their boxes. I drew their dreams of eggs and the cold porcelain egg placed in their nests to encourage their laying. I drew a fox sniffing near the door to keep them awake at night, a bowl of mash and grit to keep them hungry. And on the roof – that's where I painted the sky. Not a sky I'd ever seen before, but a mass of clouds shredded by wind and filled with light. Clouds on clouds, in banks, fronts, storm surges and downdraughts. For several weeks I spent my days in that dingy coop, working and re-working that mural. Crawling out late in the afternoon, I'd look up at the bathroom window and see my mother smiling at me and waving for me to come in.

I was not a cloud reader. But there, in the confines of the chicken coop, something urged me on. I drew a fishing cuddy, falling apart, sinking in a storm, two men stranded on a sandbank. A beehive built from the prow of a boat, a rust-red sail, fish hung to smoke in a chimney, pigs curing in vats in the ground, an oak tree falling like an avalanche in a dark wood, a brightly painted van, a piece of blue driftwood and a razor blade with a charging bull's insignia on its handle. And in the centre of the sky, a cloud in the shape of a sperm whale.

All that has gone, consumed by the fire that is coming closer by the minute now.

One summer evening, while my mother yet again repaired the decoy birds my father had shot to pieces, the phone rang. It was Goose, calling from the Albatross Inn.

'May, I'm worried. Have you seen the clouds?'

My mother turned towards the window and looked up at the high evening sky and the line of strange clouds moving in the direction of the North Norfolk marshes.

'What about them?'

'Look after yourself, May, you promise me that.'

9

Bedlam Fen

She plucked and cleaned a pigeon while I watched the feathers fall across the floor – each feather seesawing through the air giving up its tiny gift of flight. She told me to close my eyes and when she let me open them again the feet had been cut off and put to one side. Together, like a pair of shoes. She cut the pigeon in four and laid the pieces in a pie-dish on thin slices of mushroom, which she described as a mattress, soft enough for any bird. There was ham in there too, in strips, and an egg that had been peeled and quartered. She let me sniff the dish and then she rolled on a layer of pastry, leaving a small hole in the middle on top of which she put a button of dough.

While it was in the oven we listened to my father dragging stores about in the sheds. She smiled at me, but his activity was unsettling her. He shouted at the weight of bags and the mess of it all, and before he'd finished she'd opened the oven and her knife made a dry noise as it prised the button off the pie. She told me to watch out for the pigeon's birdy soul and as she said this a thin reed of steam came out of the hole, and she poured in the rest of the stock as if she was putting out a fire. The pie-dish went back into the oven on a lower shelf and when she closed the oven door – a strange sight through the window: in the yard, the *Mary Magdalene*. For the last three years stored under a tarp in one of the sheds. My father was busy dusting it with the palm of his hand, tapping the hull and very noticeably avoiding my mother's gaze. It was in the way, it was old and rotten, but he knew he couldn't just throw it out. That would mean the dream was over. That they'd never again lean into each other's bodies in the fenland twilight.

They let me sit in the prow with a plastic rifle across my lap. My parents stood by the front porch – the sight of the boat meaning so much to them, they put their arms round each other for support one last time, gazing at me sitting among the cobwebs, fixing them in the gun's sights. And as the fenland twilight did arrive, we smelled the pie – even there in the yard – and we all went inside to eat.

He ate the pie too fast, looked at his watch too many times, urged us along to clear our plates – Don't hurry him George, he's doing his best – Can't keep 'em waiting. Ain't right. Pip, you going to eat them mushrooms? I crammed the last of the pastry into my mouth and then we were walking out, all three of us, past the rotting boat to his car.

Am I all right like this? my mother asks. She's in a check skirt and a mustard-coloured sweater, which is stopping her bending her neck. Course, he replies. Look lovely. But there's a tone of doubt under his assurance and she picks up on it, decides to say nothing, begins to worry. *George* . . . Don't start, Lil', I know you don't want to go but you got to get out. Time you met 'em proper. They're a nice crowd, Lil'.

Ten minutes later we were at the Stow Bardolph Estate, looking at a gleaming orange fondue pot in the centre of the table. Both my parents were stuffed from the pigeon pie as my father had said there'd be nothing to eat at the party, but they didn't want to let anyone down, so they obediently took their places and marvelled at the odd cauldron and the little blue flame and the huge pile of food for their skewers. It was a room off the kitchens. Candlelit and Spartan, and my mother knew everyone was wondering how she'd bear up to the evening.

My father wore a bright orange shirt. He'd waxed his hair back to show off his new sideburns and his face had a scrubbed raw look like he'd just woken up. My mother's face was still flushed from the cooking, then flushed with the first lot of eating, and she drank two glasses of cider so quickly she had to burp several times behind her hand. Then she kept losing her pieces of bread in the cheese-and-wine mix, and my father kept mocking her for not pushing her bread on to the skewer firmly enough. The others at the table laughed too loudly at my father's criticisms of his wife; he didn't know whether to play up to it or not, and his scrubbed face began to take on a waxy, pained look. She's full, I thought. She's going to be sick, and I watched the little red spot on my father's skewer and hoped the piece of bread or vegetable on the end of it would fall off and drown somewhere in the mix. And if only my mother would stop her nervous giggling, if only she'd lift her skewer and all the pieces of bread would be miraculously impaled on it, like the fisherman on the boat who manages to land the whole catch. Remember how you caught the weever, I thought. But it didn't happen. She kept losing her food, and he became more irritated, feeling that somehow he was being shown up by her.

Hair go, George, you got it. No you han't – thass mine. Yeah, you reckon? Lil' – Lil' – put some carrot on that an' give it a go.

Eight people round a wooden table, lit by candlelight and the thin glow of meths. Martha, the cook – her face redder than my mother's – at the end of the table because her laugh was too loud. Never lose that one in fog, they used to say. Two farmhands – rindy, strong men with little to say, simple minds and wiry hearts – and three girls, all of whom worked for the house.

Curiously, my father's red-tipped skewer began to play with

a pink-tipped skewer, which was held by a female hand that didn't belong to my mother, and at the same time the foot of the woman who was not my mother slid out of her shoe and tickled my father's leg. A stockinged foot wriggling like an eel against the thick trunk of his leg.

The meal seemed to be over, and the red-tipped skewer and the pink-tipped skewer leaned next to each other. More wine was being poured, there was talk of raiding the cellar, and my mother was listening to a convoluted tale about someone who was not at the party and how he'd had to take four armchairs to London in a car and when that broke down he'd taken them by train. Sat in them on a King's Cross platform. One of the farmhands was telling the story in a mealy voice, egged along because someone was listening, but not that interested in telling the story again. My mother had just learned to put her hand over the glass to stop it being refilled, but her face looked slack and thin and I knew she was struggling.

I was confused about who'd touched my father's leg, so I began to knock my fork against the side of my chair until my mother broke away from the story to hush me. My father turned to me with a warning expression. I returned his gaze angrily, then continued to stare at the fondue pot while banging my fork on the chair. Eventually I heard a woman's voice say perhaps he'd like to try the fondue. My father's face lit up with the suggestion, and a woman's hand reached in and very consciously chose the pink-tipped skewer and fished out a piece of soggy bread and cheese. I stared at the skewer, at the hand, the arm and finally at the face of the woman who wasn't my mother. Saw her young, small face and her hair swept back behind her head, saw her bouncing enthusiastically round the table with the skewer in her hand. This girl, this girl leaned down in a cloud of her own scent in front of me, her hair falling forward as she did so. I stared at her red lipstick, which outlined the shape of lips on her mouth which weren't exactly her own, at the small pebble of her chin and the creamy sheen of candlelight on her neck. I refused to open my mouth, and watched her growing discomfort as she tried and failed to perform a mother's job.

As we drove back over the estate's pasture, neither of my parents spoke. My family felt threadbare with silence and the toll of the evening. The car bumped along over the fields, the pale eyes of cattle reflecting brilliantly at us in the headlights, the scent of grass and dung and dry earth blowing in through the open windows and the acid lemon smell of an air freshener he'd recently stuck to the dashboard. My father was drunk, and as we approached the hedge he couldn't find the gate. He shone the headlights on the hedge and got out to have a closer look and to take a leak, and when he got back in he said I'm going to sort the sheds. We'll have to get rid of the boat.

But before he was up next morning she was out there, dragging the *Mary Magdalene* round to the chicken coop. Hair stuck to her face, boots skidding in the mud, and me beside her, more hindrance than help, tugging at the rope as though the weight on the other end was round my father's throat.

That boat, dusty, warped, as dry as a church Bible, it was ours. She stripped away the old paint, filled the wood, caulked the seams, rubbed it down, skills she'd learned repairing the decoys my father shot to pieces. Polished the brass, cut in some wood along the rail. I walked up and down the boat in which I was conceived, rubbing grease into the wood, wiping marks off the hull, grinning at my mother as she became dirtier as the boat grew cleaner. Eventually she painted it a pure light blue, growing darker along the keel. And when the paint was dry she began to sketch on clouds: cirrus like gossamer threads, cumulonimbus, strangely shaped, drifting across the hull in a calm warm breeze. Altocumulus like a shoal of fish. Scud clouds racing across the wood in anxious herds. And around the stern a storm of biblical proportions, exaggerated and impossible. Nimbostratus, fractonimbus, rollers and anvils. And in tiny detail, chasing the storm – low on the transom – the ugly shape of the rag cloud. She sketched these in, rubbed them off with screwed-up newspaper, redrew and remeasured them. Then it was finished: a storm and a little bit of bright blue sky sitting on the back lawn.

On a grey late-summer morning she launched this beautiful patch of sky into the Middle Level Main Drain at the appropriately named Magdalen Bridge. A fisherman left his keep-net to see the launch, helping my mother put the little boat in and slapping the gaudy paintwork with amusement. Along the bank more fishermen stood up and cheered as our odd little spectacle passed. One man even dropped an eel when he saw the boat, and a postman riding along the bank wobbled as he tried to look back and wave. My mother loved it all.

At the damp brick bridge by Three Holes, my mother hailed Mrs Holbeach and Elsie when they were still just two oddly sized dots in the distance. One, as large as a beet sack, the other, slim and tomboyish, with a brilliant smudge of red hair.

That day we went along Popham's Eau Canal, where we moored the *Mary Magdalene* to an abandoned tractor engine rusting on the bank. A thin bleed of oil made a rainbow film across the water. Elsie watched me playing along the bank, fishing handfuls of heavy green weed and chasing the eels that tried to wriggle back to the drain.

From a discarded blue flip-flop I made a flimsy boat with a lollipop mast and a crisp-packet sail. I stuck a feather into the top of the mast and put pebbles on the back of the boat, placing one each for my mother, my father, a slightly larger one for Mrs Holbeach and two smaller ones for Elsie and me. They all guessed which one was Elsie; her pebble was brick red.

When I launched it the waterlogged craft drifted half-submerged a couple of feet or so away from the bank. It didn't want to move. I found a stick and gave it a solid shove and in doing so it tunnelled under water, and a smooth glassy wave swept my father clean off before I could grab him. I turned to my mother and Mrs Holbeach and saw a look of conspiracy pass between them, a recognition that justice had been done.

Two weeks later it was all very different. It was dawn and cold and Elsie and I were sitting calmly in the boat while my mother carried bags from the car. She put them round our feet and we could see inside them and we knew it wasn't going to be a normal picnic. There were blankets, clothes, a book or two. A torch fell on to the planks of the boat. My tartan suitcase wrapped up in a plastic bin liner to keep it dry.

I unclipped the notepad and pencil from round my neck and began to write a question, and the letters I wrote seemed to be in Mrs Crowe's handwriting and not my own. As I was looking at them I felt my mother's hand closing my notebook as she said not now, love, let's just get going.

Elsie began to cry ever so quietly and I think my mother did too, though she quickly made light of it and told us she was only crying outside because she was laughing on the inside.

Ahead of us, the sky's reflection was almost perfect in the still water of the drain and I lay down on my back, hanging my head over the side to look up at the sky and clouds and watch the reed beds passing upside down.

*

We continued all day along the Great Ouse, Popham's Eau, through Three Holes – passing near Elsie's house in silence – and into the Twenty Foot Drain. We arrived at the heavy iron wall of a sluice gate, damp and weedy in the afternoon light, and had to haul the *Mary Magdalene* up the bank to launch it the other side, where the water was higher. At the top of the bank, just as the boat was tipping with the urge to slide down the other side, I looked far into the distance and saw a huge bank of storm clouds, roughly in the direction we'd come from. My mother saw me looking and perhaps guessed that I knew what it meant. Look, it's raining at home, she said. Better off here. And with that, the boat lunged down the slope and splashed into the new channel.

The light was going and we were all sitting in the back of the boat. We were huddled together for warmth. My mother had spread a car blanket over us and we'd eaten sandwiches of tongue and cheese, then boiled eggs dipped in a little pillbox of cracked salt. The engine was overworked and smelled of hot wires and oil. Then it started to splutter and my mother shook it and the petrol gauge was right at the bottom. She shook it again and the engine died. The boat glided in the water without direction. I looked at my mother but couldn't tell whether she felt defeated or calm or indifferent to the whole situation. Where we were and what was going on, it didn't really matter to her. She wasn't really moving or trying to start the engine and Elsie was staring down at her lap as if she'd been told off.

We drifted into one of the banks of reed beds and I sat there for a while snapping the dry stalks. No one did anything. We were there a long time. No one passed. Then my mother unclipped the hand-paddle and pushed us out into the channel. She paddled us a hundred feet or so, then turned into a tiny drainage channel, not much wider than the boat. She punted us up this channel till the boat got stuck between the banks and then we just sat there as the night grew round us.

'Can we go back?' Elsie said quietly.

'Soon. We'll go back.'

Elsie took that calmly, an adult sensibility beginning to emerge in her. A share of responsibility between them now, for me.

'And tomorrow,' my mother said, deliberately brightly, 'we'll go in the yard and scrub those dirty pigs clean with baking soda and then paint them whatever colours we want. We can put lipstick on them and dress them up as clowns and Pip can paint a Union Jack on the fat one.'

'Right,' Elsie said. And then she began to cry again, and she said through her sobs, 'We're not going home, are we?'

'No.'

My mother kissed us both and I realized that there, in that tiny, ludicrously painted rowing boat in the middle of the night in Bedlam Fen, at the end of a pointless drainage channel which had run out into nothing, with no space to even turn round, I was at home, utterly at home, with my mother and Elsie. Nothing else mattered. The farm, my father, everything up to that point, seemed so far away. Here, in Bedlam Fen, with the icy wink of the stars above us in the blue-black night and my mother in nervous collapse, this was where we all belonged.

'I wish you were *my* mum,' Elsie said bravely in the dark.

I don't think any of us slept that night. But even though it was uncomfortable none of us complained. I remember how my mother wrapped all the blankets round us and then bound us in a length of rope that Elsie and I could hold at either end to keep our three bodies together. How she tied plastic bags over our shoes to keep our feet warm.

At around three in the morning Elsie said she was hungry and my mother gave us some Scotch eggs and crisps, and a plastic mug of chocolate from a flask. Some time later, I found the torch near my feet and wrote in my book: *Mum, the stars are turning round.* She read the message in the glare of torchlight, then she said turn that off, best we save the battery. We all stared up at the sky and the stars had indeed changed. Over the course of the night Orion had turned on his side ready to sink into the Fens again. Pip, she said, I've got you a present. And she gave me a small seashell like the ones hermit crabs live in. It's from Blakeney Point, she said. Listen to it and you'll always be near the sea, the North Sea, wherever you are.

Just before dawn in Bedlam Fen the first draught of air from the storm clouds reached us in our ditch, followed by plump, uncertain drops of rain. Then it began to pour down in heavy sheets. We could do nothing but get drenched while the earth spat mud around us and the fen steamed and boiled. Elsie climbed out and I ran after her, both of us slipping in the mud and she started laughing and running along the bank, our clothes skin tight and heavy with the water. I remember her hair and how flat it was and the slope of her thin shoulders and how big and wide her mouth looked.

'Auntie May!' she shouted, 'Auntie May, you're soaked!'

'Like a fish!' my mother said.

She sat in the boat, still and grey in the rain. She'd heard the engine of the launch that had just decelerated past the mouth of our drainage ditch. Elsie looked up and fell silent as she saw the men in dark green oilskins picking their way over the fen to where she was standing.

My father arrived first, swiftly ushering the others to grab the painter and drag the boat from the ditch. He took his own hat off and put it on my head and it felt warm and secure and ridiculous. One of the other men gave Elsie his coat and she obediently put it round her shoulders, her hair plastered against her head and the man's trench coat splayed on the mud around her as if someone had partially deflated her. My mother seemed on the edge of all this, but one of the men had given her some sort of large fishing umbrella and so she sat under that, motionless, emotionless, while the *Mary Magdalene* was hauled out backwards.

The boat my father led us to was a proper motorboat with bright windows and the glass all steamed up, like someone was having a bath inside. We walked over the slippery black mud of the fen towards these windows, the only light we could see in the entire misty landscape. Inside, a kettle boiled away in a small galley, and a radio played quietly in the corner. An alien world. Elsie and I were given towels and mugs of hot black tea as the men started the engine and the banks of the drainage channel once more began to slip by. Through the windows the fen looked suddenly dark and forbidding. On the roof of the cabin and down the front windows and as far as we could see the river water was pitted with the lead shot of rain.

The *Mary Magdalene* was dragged behind the boat on a thirty-foot length of towrope, pulling so fast the water curved against its prow in a beautiful glassy wave. And there was my mother, still silent, still gripping the man's umbrella in her tiny patch of brightly coloured summer sky in a world gone completely bleak, the simple wedding band on her finger like the last ray of sunlight.

My father handed over the wheel and came into the cabin. He sat down on one of the bunks and looked at his hands for a long time.

'OK, so what happened?' he asked me.

He looked old, the stuffing knocked out of him.

Then he turned to Elsie. 'OK, what happened, Elsie?'

And the Trees Too

Euximoor Drove, Cotton's Corner, Popham's Eau, Three Holes. Rain and mist driving across the landscape in blowing fogs, tearing through stands of poplar and gusting round farmhouses, pumping stations, labourers' cottages. Plau Field, Low Fen. Buildings without inhabitants in a land without people, somewhere lower than the sea itself, and us, somewhere on that negligible line between earth and sky.

Elsie had stuck to a description of pulling the boat out at the old sluice, how the stars had come out, how the storm had drenched us and of the heavy feel of the man's oilskin jacket she'd worn. My father listened with a patience born out of weariness, biting a hangnail, fiddling with his ear, waiting for her energy to wane. Wondering what he'd do then. Soon, Elsie did stop talking, and my father stared out the front window while he picked with his fingernails at a cork ball tied to a keyring. He never quite knew what to say to her.

Uncomfortable with the unfolding of a serious family drama, the other men had chosen to sit it out by the wheel. I recognized them from the fondue party. The one who'd told my mother about taking the armchairs to London had lost his energy for talk, as if that had been his yearly quota and he'd used it up. Both men zipped their parkas so tight only a small aperture of fake fur remained of their faces, as they passed a hip flask back and forth.

By the time my father had built a small pile of cork shavings on the counter we reached Three Holes. The rope pulling the *Mary Magdalene* went slack and the little rowing boat nudged into our stern with a gentle bump. No one reacted to it and it didn't wake Elsie, who had crashed into sleep in the space of minutes. She didn't wake when my father carried her out of the cabin, passing my mother, who didn't look up once from beneath her umbrella, Elsie's red hair hanging over the green shoulder of his oilskin, her mouth like a collapsed O as he picked his way up the bank. The two men stayed in the wheel-house, deep in their coats. Surely Elsie couldn't just sleep her way out of all this? But she was limp in his arms. And a strange moment there on top of the bank: my father kissed Elsie, once, tenderly, on the cheek, and almost as soon as he did it he wiped it away with his finger. The glass cabin door swung gently to and fro. I decided to follow my father and Elsie but one of the men moved instinctively to the hatchway. Looking up at his big coat and a shadowed eye peering out from his fur-lined hood, I pulled the door closed and went back to my seat. I looked at the cork shavings and swept them off the table.

Half an hour earlier we'd passed the abandoned tractor engine where I had chased eels. I thought of the waterlogged flip-flop with its huddled crew of pebbles clinging on for dear life, and the sight of the one representing my father falling off the back of the boat. Falling off and never being caught. And I imagined him sitting in the front room of the Holbeachs' cottage. Ethel Holbeach, plump and waxy in her morning dressing gown, fussing with Elsie's wet clothes. Elsie, sullen and miserable, being made to stand on cold tiles. Mr Holbeach, as grey as the fens, considering some verse from Proverbs in his head because he had no words of his own.

A similar scene two hours later. From behind tightly shut doors I heard the vented fury of my father, his voice tight with the effort of restraining himself. His sense of betrayal. His whole damned situation stuck in this dreary farmhouse on the edge of the Fens with a madwoman for a wife. Occasionally, my mother sneezed, but otherwise she said nothing, and at lunchtime she went to bed and stayed there all day, knowing the weight of silence would be handed over to my father, and in it he'd hopefully find some guilt for the things he'd said and the things he'd done.

That night I dreamed of the oilskin creatures picking their way across Bedlam Fen. Oily creatures with no faces, the rain dripping off them. Their feet sinking into the marsh. And as they advanced – with each footfall – I heard the house creak. Eerily the dreamland fen sank into my room's shadows, and I realized I was more awake than asleep. The creaking continued. Slow, uncertain footsteps pacing the corridor. Opening the door, I saw my mother standing right outside, her head angled to one side as if she'd been brushing her hair. I touched the hem of her nightie and she pushed me away and then held her hand in front of her. Silencing some imaginary noise. The storm had left a terrible silence in its wake. Her eyes were open but she didn't see me. I just stood there, looking up at the marbled pattern of the moonlight shining through the wet window on to her face.

She moved away, her nightie bone-white in the corridor. Her door shut with a click, and I glimpsed something move at the end of the corridor, and realized my father was standing there, dark and brooding in the shadows. He gestured briskly at me, pointing me back to bed, and then with impatient steps I heard him coming down the corridor to make sure my door was closed as I climbed back beneath the blankets.

From then on I spent most days at the Stow Bardolph Estate, where I'd watch how my father priced a cow by the feel of its spine, or how the angle of a sheep's neck became a mark in a ledger. The marks built up into impressive accounts. How disease, vermin, seasons and gate prices bowed the beauty of his tables. How livestock, fowl and game – the whole array of animal nature – tabulated in columns on the one hand, fox, mole, badger and rodent on the other. Figures in red and black over several books, corralled into one irreducible number. Profit.

Only in the bull-pen did I see the dreamer he'd once been. The man who'd known animals before he'd known himself. I was allowed to sit on a high ledge where I could look down at him as he stroked and examined the bull. It was the Red Poll, about a ton in weight, and a deep tan in colour. My father had no veterinary training, but it was clear he was trusted more than anyone to treat the animal. He and the bull had an understanding, and I sat on my ledge in awe. Often he'd un-chain it from the hook and lead it round, the bull taking a stumbling solid walk, only a few steps till its flank pressed against the bricks. It was an old brick shed rising up to black-ened roof timbers, with two high windows – and in the mornings shafts of sunlight would fall into the otherwise dark pit. It was a very calm place. The bull breathed heavily while being led, its breath mixing with my father's pipe into a heady evocative cloud. The bull had a wild pink eye hidden in the curls of its head, and it would glance once at me on my ledge and then look at me no more as it passed between the sunbeams. My father spoke to it all the time, close by its ear. A lulling sound full of that's it . . . fine . . . come on now . . . easy, until the animal seemed to be at one with his leader's somnambulant whispers. Sometimes the Red Poll would swing its square head to one side and my father would be flung back on his heels, but he never raised his voice. The animal trusted him, a tamed giant, bending its spirit to walk in staggered circles through the straw as if wisdom were being passed from man to beast. This was the man who as a boy had killed a calf and cut out its tongue – an act that earned him the right to speak with bulls.

Then my father would disappear somewhere, and I'd wait in the kitchen making models out of dough. I made all the farm animals, and watched them grow deformed in the heat of the oven, and at the end of the day I filled my father's silent car with the sweet smell of bread.

My mother would take these loaves humorously, but when I closed her hands round them, I often noticed a tremble in her fingers which had not been there before. Her eyes, always sad, seemed to have grown duller. The food was still on the table for evening meals, but she didn't speak to my father any more, and when she spoke to me it was with a cracked, quiet voice. It was a silence that eventually drove my father to eat in his study, taking the food quickly from the table and washing his plate alone at the sink later. No mention that we ate the same thing on several nights running, or that it had lost its taste.

No one really knew what she did during the days. The garden became overgrown and eggs stayed in the coop. Only a kitten, Pepper – found as a stray on the estate – lifted her at times from the depression, as it ceaselessly chased bits of wool, ambushed my mother from behind chair legs and pounced on her hand to bite or scratch a finger, her hands becoming covered with tiny scars.

The sleepwalking continued even after my father fitted a lock on her door. She would bang on it, waking us and herself, and as she was in such obvious distress he removed the lock and let her wander free. Sometimes I'd hear a noise from outside and see her standing on the back lawn, looking silently out over the fens until my father came to guide her back inside, being careful not to wake her.

The storm at Bedlam Fen had been the start of it, but now the silence descending on the house and my mother's gradually worsening illness seemed to spread across the entire landscape. It was called Dutch elm disease, but to me the sight of these trees dying in an agony of curling leaves and peeling bark – it all seemed part of the same marsh fever that had claimed her.

The great elm trees at the estate were monitored weekly, then daily as the disease spread. When it was spotted, the branches would be lopped, cut up and burned. Leaning against the wet wood of a five-bar gate, with me sitting on top, my father told me these were some of the tallest in the land, the trees that had made England strong because the wood never split, and that this was a disease sent from the Continent in revenge. That was when he could still joke about it. Goose's take was that the elm suffered from a great arrogance. Like the oak, they had little sense of humour. It was a simple matter of them changing their ways. Whatever the reason, the country was gripped with hysteria as the landscape changed so brutally, and my mother's marsh fever went unnoticed. In the silence over the dinner table at one of our increasingly rare family meals, my father eulogized the dying elm as the saddest, most tragic thing he'd ever witnessed. He couldn't imagine a land without elms. And at a moment of real frustration he spat out God! Why not the ground elder! Even my mother smiled at this, then served the food in silence, the muted stab of the wooden spoon against the sides of the casserole dish the only sound. It was clear – from my side of the table – that the real tragic loss in my father's life was happening right there in that room. Under his nose. But unlike his efforts to conquer the elm bark beetle, he did nothing to save his wife from fading away. Unable to contemplate a land without elms, a land without her was swiftly approaching. Entire country, my father continued, only tree I care about's that elm in the forty-acre. Two hundred year, maybe older. Ain't going to get that one.

But it did.

It happened, even though he thought he could outwit the beetle. Even though he tried to become a scientist.

Parcels and books had been arriving wrapped in brown paper and smelling of glue and ink. Sometimes he made a phone call to London, and I'd sit in the corridor pretending to practise my writing while I listened to him pronouncing Latin names in his Norfolk accent. Ceratostomella ulmi had too many long vowels for him to say convincingly. He often had to repeat what he said, altering the pronunciation and sounding nervous.

Other times the phone would ring, I'd hear my father laughing, but when I went in the living room he'd say hang on a minute into the phone then cup the mouth-piece and snap at me to go out and shut the door behind me.

I took letters to my father from Antwerp and The Hague, and he let me stand in his study while he read them. A new feeling of importance for him. It felt quiet in there; the books silenced the air. I smelled their spines and their dusty paper and saw the corners of the pages where he'd nibbled the paper as he thought. Every one of those books, partly eaten. Tacked to the window frame was a solitary cockchafer, held by a pin. I touched its wings and they felt like paper and my father said careful you don't break him, he's fragile. He flew a long way to get on that pin. It seemed strange an insect might fly anywhere only to be skewered on to a piece of wood. On his desk was his pipe and several twigs of elm with the bark stripped clean. He had a glass demijohn full of elm leaves.

There was a strange metal toy he called a gyroscope, which he used as a paperweight, and he let me spin it while he read the letters, and after he finished he tore off the stamps and gave them to me.

Leaving the study one evening, putting the stamps in my pocket, my mother looked at me from the scullery. Her eyes were glassy. And I knew that while I'd been in there her own disease had spread.

A car has drawn up in the yard. My father rushes out to meet one of the farmhands and hears the news he's been dreading. The lad says something about the forty-acre and my father hitches up his trousers and picks a burr off his shirt. Preparing for the worst. He drives off in the car and doesn't come back till after dark, and when he does it's only to tell us he wasn't hungry and get in the car – we've got to go right away.

By the time we reached the estate a crowd had collected round the great elm tree in the forty-acre pasture. Car headlamps had been trained on the tree while wooden pallets were piled round the trunk. When that was done, my father went forward with a jerrycan of paraffin and poured it round the base. The lights from the cars overlapped each other on the trunk and the wood and on my father's back. Above him, the silent tree rose motionless.

He said something to the tree in the timber man's custom of asking forgiveness for what he was about to do, then he lit a ball of newspaper and threw it at the wood and I watched the sudden whoosh of blue flame erupt like a ghost of the tree. The blue flame rose and vanished into the feathery mass of the leaves and with it I hoped this one act might cleanse the tree. But soon the pallets were alight and crackling with the sound of the wood splitting. The fire rose and the people moved back from its heat. The leaves singed, curled and withered as the whole tree seemed to shiver like a fountain.

My mother watched from the passenger seat with the door open, her face warmed by the death of the tree. I imagined the fire reflecting in her dark eyes, and I wanted it to burn there, purifying her while above us the tree filled with the strange haunting sounds of fire. Of sap boiling and fizzing, of the breath of gases through the canopy, of twigs spitting as though a sudden rage had gripped the tree after two hundred years of peace. One of the cars began to reverse across the pasture and I watched it weaving into the darkness. Beyond it, about a mile away, another elm was on fire; its blaze a golden candle of yellow against the black woods.

My father made his way over to me, his face stern but his emotions under wraps because he was there to tend the fire and not make a scene. He bent down to me and I smelled the fire in his hair and he told me never to forget what we were watching, and then he walked off wearily towards a group of people standing by a Land Rover. I wondered if he felt he'd failed everybody; with his demijohn of leaves and his half-eaten books and his letters from Europe.

I followed him, trying to step in his footprints in the long damp grass while I watched my own shadow flicker round my feet. The people by the Land Rover were staring at the tree and chatting to themselves, smoking cigarettes. My father went to the rear of the car. It moved down as he sat on the back step, then a woman came to him and the car bounced down again, slightly less this time. She was on his lap. And then her voice.

'You smell of smoke.'

He didn't answer.

'George.'

'Yeah, s'pose we all do.'

Whoever was sitting on his lap shifted closer to him.

'It's got to be this way,' she said.

'I know.'

'Saw you say something. What was it?'

'Wish.'

'George, what we going to do?'

I ran off into the dark middle of the pasture and looked back at the scene. At my mother, in her car, by herself. At the raging fire of the still-burning tree. At the Land Rover. My father, with the girl from the fondue evening sitting on his lap. Her head nestled in his shoulder, and I imagined her – like me – smelling the fire and the paraffin there. My father seemed limp with exhaustion, his arm round her waist, leaning into her, the wounded man. His hand on her leg. Never forget, I heard him say.

Fire, which punctuates my life so often. My father kept that blaze alight, burning all the other diseased wood in his life, starting the next morning, when the *Mary Magdalene* was dragged into the yard and set on fire. Straight after breakfast, with little fuss, as if he were bagging up rubbish. My mother showed little interest, knowing intuitively he was testing her. Challenging her to do *something*.

He waited for that moment when a fire can't be extinguished to save the wood, and then left for the estate. Gull, excited by the fire, followed his car as it slewed through the mud. I was the only one to stand in the yard while the boat and the dreams of my parents went up in flames. Those clouds, painted on the hull, blistering and peeling like bark, exposing the dark green of the undercoat before that too burned through. I began to think of a small rowing boat amidst the muddy swirls of a large, powerful river. Of a man standing up in it. Of an engine dragging idly through the water. I thought of a young woman slipping off the seat and lying supine on the planks. Of thin summer dresses and the lapping of water.

And slowly the scene replayed through the jaws of the flames. As the wood split. As the keel crashed softly in two.

Either he lost interest in taking me to the estate, or he had his own reasons for not wanting me there. It suited us both – he went off in his car, chased by the dog, and I rode around on a bike. Three Holes was eight miles away. When I first cycled there I leaned the bike against the brick bridge and walked along the top of Popham's Eau till I was behind the house. I sat, tying grasses together and wondering what to do. There was no movement from the house. I pulled out my father's gyroscope and spun it, watching the centre wheel revolving so fast it looked like an insect's wing. It pulsed drunkenly in my hand. It was early spring and the Holbeachs' acre was immaculate. The soil was as dark as treacle, prepared, turned, broken, turned again and raked flat. And in its centre, the house looked like it had landed there overnight, without proper root there, waiting for the moment when hundreds of prize tulips would break the soil.

When Mr Holbeach came out he didn't see me. He only ever had eyes for the tulips. I watched him loosening soil around their stems, counting how many had broken the ground, examining an area where there seemed to be no plants growing and then marking off a patch of earth with a length of white string. When he pushed bamboo canes into the soil I imagined my mother pushing candles into a birthday cake. My ninth birthday. Pushing candles into the cake and asking me whether I was going to tell her any secrets. Just a whisper now, that's all we need. And then Mr Holbeach was straightening up with the sound of his knees cracking and I was back in his dismal fen, feeling more determined than ever to see Elsie.

Elsie. There she was, standing on a stool in the bathroom under a bare light bulb, her hair as bright as copper wire. On and off went the light, several times, then I slid through the grass so old Holbeach wouldn't see me, and as I reached his picket fence Elsie was there at the back door. I sprinted over the soil and was still wondering about my footprints when I noticed the door closing and she unexpectedly pushed me against the corridor wall and kissed me. On the lips, like an adult. I tasted her breath and felt her hair brush quickly against my face and it wasn't copper at all and I jolted back and knocked my head on the wall. She was pulling me forward then, and we were running up the stairs and through the window I saw the crouching figure of Mr Holbeach still scratching away at the soil with his finger. Elsie pushed me into her room and shut the door.

Before I really knew what was happening she's dived at me and together we fell against her bed with a big soft crumpling sound and her head knocked clumsily against mine. There was a sudden pain in my ear and I panicked because I knew she'd bitten me there. Only a year since I'd seen her being carried up the slope in my father's arms in the rain. Now she was big, with arms that were powerful and long and strong.

'I *wrote* to you,' she said, urgent and hushed. 'And to Aunt May.'

I tried to reach for my notebook, but it had twisted behind my neck, so I had to shake my head in answer.

'You never got the letters?'

No! I gestured, completely at sea as to what was happening. A crazy girl.

Elsie read the look in my eyes and started to giggle. She quickly pulled her skirt up so she could sit on my stomach, a leg either side of me, then grabbed my wrists again so I couldn't move. I'd never been this close to a girl before. Tiny bronze hairs were growing above her knees. She seemed heavy and boisterous. I could still taste her breath.

'Shall I kiss you again?' she said, then abruptly she let me go and swung herself off me and sat on a chair. She got some paper and a pencil for me from her desk.

'I'm nearly sixteen,' she said, and gave me the paper to write on.

Get off me! I wrote, then crossed it out and wrote *Mum's ill*.

I showed it to Elsie, then wrote as fast as I could, describing the silence and the time I'd seen my mother crying when she was making jam, and then about how weedy the garden was and when was Elsie going to come to see her.

While I was doing this she rested her chin on her knees and pushed her lips into a pout.

'I can't,' she said. 'Mum and Dad would go mad. They said I could've died that night in the fen. I can cycle as far as the Ouse but not any further, and you can forget about going in any boats.' When she stopped talking she re-formed her pout, sucking in her chin till it made a tiny crease below her mouth. Her lips were red and I knew there must be lipstick on my mouth and its film felt sticky and I thought I might sweat and I knew I couldn't wipe it away, not while she was staring at me.

'Why isn't she talking to anyone?' she said.

The phone rang downstairs and after it rang a second time I heard not Mr Holbeach but – surprisingly – his wife's voice saying yes that's right we have you down for three dozen.

'You've got to go when she calls Dad in,' Elsie said, springing to the door. Again, she looked big and clumsy in a room so small. She reached into a glass jar on a shelf and gave me a mint humbug.

'That's Aunty May's. For her throat.'

She opened the door a crack and peered down the stairs.

Holding her hair back with one hand. In the shadow of her armpit I noticed the elasticized whiteness of a bra. A decorative herring-bone stitch running along the top of the hem.

'Now!' she said, and as I went to the door I sensed movement at the bottom of the stairs. For a second I imagined Mrs Holbeach was down there in stockinged feet, lying in wait with a rolling pin. Murder in her Quaker heart. And then Elsie was gripping me and I saw the exotic beetle's back of a second humbug in her hand.

'For you,' she said, unwrapping it. I opened my mouth only to see her pop it between her own lips and in the same movement push me against the door till it banged shut. A sudden kiss, again, knocking my teeth with her teeth, and I tried to close my mouth and she pushed her teeth hard against my lips and gums. It wasn't her teeth but the glassy surface of the humbug, and as I struggled against her the sweet was suddenly in my mouth and it tasted of mint and it tasted of Elsie. Then it was all over and she was pushing me away from her and down the stairs and telling me to come and see her again.

That afternoon I gave the first sweet to my mother. *From Elsie*, I wrote, a little angrily. She stared long and hard at the mint, at my note, then finally at me. She put the sweet in her mouth even though I knew she didn't like humbugs and in a hoarse voice she whispered you're everything I could have wanted. Do you know that? You're my angel. A real angel.

It made a single tear roll down the curve of her cheek, and I felt guilty for that. It gathered in the crease near her mouth, then slowly dried from her eyelid downwards, as if she willed it to go.

She didn't ask how I'd seen Elsie, or when, and a whole month passed without any more reference to what I'd done. Until one morning, when I was putting on my shoes ready for the estate, she pressed a small note into my hand. *Will you?* she asked. I tried to stay calm, pretending we'd planned nothing else the whole month. I folded it into the front pocket of my dungarees, and patted the pocket in the same way my father did to remind himself he'd remembered his wallet, and immediately I felt ashamed to have used the same gesture.

On a chair in the larder, while my dough shapes were baking in the range, I read it: *My dear Elsie. I love you. I'm thinking of you. Thank you for my sweet.*

The farm was decaying. Dust covered the egg grader, oil cans popped and leaked as they expanded in morning sunlight, rats threaded their way through the outbuildings, eating everything. Cow parsley, hogweed and alexander grew as tall as a man in the yard. Days and days on a bike, circling the yard, the house, the sheds, the fields, forever moving, forever pedalling, stop and the weeds might claim me, stop and there's my mother, in her bed, a kitchen ghost, a sleepwalker. Stop and my father will get me, not let go, send me away. And rapidly I was cycling too close to something colourful on the ground by the copse and I saw it was someone lying down. A woman lying on a fallen beech tree, stretching her arms above her head along its smooth trunk. Her fair hair bunched to one side, framing her face like ears of barley. She was lying in the full heat of the morning sun with her knees drawn up and her shirt tied into a loose knot over her belly-button. A little way off, my father was sitting on the grass, whittling a stick with a knife. She stretched along the trunk and turned her head in my direction. A flash from the blade as he folded his knife away. She swung her legs off the trunk and they began to walk back over the pasture. Him rolling his shoulders and her carrying her sandals.

★

I shut my eyes and imagined myself standing in the parlour at the Holbeachs' cottage. With Elsie just run in from outside. Run in because she always seems on the verge of action. Legs long and clumsy and full of life, hands clenched into fists like she always did as a child. An uneasy gesture, unsure whether she's an adult or a girl. Her shirt has a knot in it over the belly-button like the woman on the fallen beech tree. Elsie's belly is as bronzed as fresh bread. She's full of expectation – her face is stretched with it – the creases which mark the points where her nostrils meet her cheeks have the sunken curve where the stalk enters the top of a peach, ripe with life. There's a smell of baking in there, of suet and flour, and a carbolic cleanliness which connects Mrs Holbeach and this house with the hospital where she used to work. A smell of violet water, from a bottle, though there are several thousand flowers outside. And I lean forward, thinking of herringbone stitches and shadows in armpits and I try to kiss Elsie and she pushes me away so violently I hit my head on something large and soft and I turn to see it's Mrs Holbeach, cheeks red with the anger she's always swallowed and I think her body must be filled with years of it, and I see that deep within her there's a dark curl of temper like a bramble she can't kill. What are you doing here? she says. Elsie has vanished and Mrs Holbeach seems to grow larger, all the lines in her face are soft and curved. She says in a calm, gentle voice, what's the matter with her, Pip, your mother's ill, isn't she? She needs help, my love. And I run at that moment, run to my mother, across the pasture and dry stubble, and at the outbuildings I hear a strange, muffled noise coming from near the pigsty. Careful of the large pile of rusty poaching traps my father stored in there fifteen years before, I climb on to two sacks of feed and peer over the internal wall into the next shed, only to see my father, grimacing with some sort of pain, leaning against the wall. Above him was the hook he'd hung me from, all those years ago. It seems his pain is private, until he breaks into a broad smile and at the same instant I realize he is not alone. I see the blonde hair being shaken to the side and once more I see her face, pressed against the wall this time, her eyes still shut tight like they had been that morning. It is her who is making the noise. A sharp, regular intake of breath. Together they are pushing against the wall, my father's hand either side of her flat against the brick and now holding her by the shoulders and pulling her shirt off her shoulders as he leans his weight against her and she buckles softly against the wall. He pulls the shirt to the side and quickly I see inside her blouse and her breast is as soft as cream, and one of his rough hands reaches for it and I see the dust from the dry brick wall on his fingers as he holds her there. And she seems to wince with pain and she bites her bottom lip and nearly laughing and screwing her eyes tighter till suddenly she gasps as if someone has struck her and she opens her eyes and stares right through me. Right at me.

She Went This Way

A sickly smell of boiled eggs and hot butter. For the sandwiches. Some have been left for me on the corner of the table but I leave them there. I want no part of their lunch. Tonight there'll be bread-and-butter pudding bubbling like lava in the big glass pot, and I'll eat that.

My mother has made the sandwiches, dutifully, and she's taken some cold beer for them because they'll be parched. All the doors are open to let any kind of breeze shift the relentless, scorching heat of a late-summer afternoon. As I watch her go, the wheels of the car stir up a fine cloud of golden dust.

It's the day they harvest the twenny-acre. A big job, and they'll be out there till late, ten, maybe half ten even. Everyone from the estate gets involved. It takes two to drive the combine it's so fierce. The damage you could do with a machine like that. I go to the window and even though I can't hear the combine I see the yard's filling with dust. The whole air is quietly glowing, as if it contains some strange flame, some form of inferno. It's like the end of the world.

As the dust settles behind the car I go quickly to the end of the dresser. I look at the Gallyon & Sons shotgun leaned against the wall. I touch the metal. Heavy steel. In all this heat it seems cool, really cool, as if somehow the gun has remained unconnected with everything else. And yet that metal could be hot. When they'd last done the rabbits I remembered watching the rifle lowering to my height, being told to feel how warm the barrel was in front of the stock. They all laughed when I burned my finger.

I lift the rigid weight of the gun, then turn it slowly round the room, gazing down the sights, calmly placing it on a chair and lodging the butt under the edge of the table. I'd never breached a side by side. I push down harshly and the gun twists like a broom handle. Locked tight. My hands smell of old metal.

Again. This time the stock snaps at the breech leaving the barrels swinging on their hinge. I quietly open the drawer of the dresser, find the dry cardboard box and pick out two cartridges. They slot into the breech and when I touch their flat shining ends the metal is so smooth it feels greasy. I lift the Gallyon, gaze down the sights, then begin to walk, like that, gun raised, one eye shut, into the corridor. I feel for the safety with my thumb, find and disengage the lever, hear the click close by my ear and go into the living room. So quiet in there, looking through the twin sights. The target wanders casually along the walls, over the furniture, comes to rest on the bureau. A photograph of my parents on their wedding day, sitting in their boat after the service. Brylcream hair, smooth skin. My mother's fledgling beehive haircut. I aim at him, at the bastard and his stupid grin. I feel the pressure of the trigger, the harsh edge of the metal cutting into my finger. The shot explodes into the room knocking me back against the settee and the gun thrashes up towards the ceiling and I notice confetti flakes of plaster falling all around. Along with the photo, a pair of glasses has flown into the air, its rims twisting like surprised eyebrows. There's a smell of gunpowder, acrid and sweet, a smell of burning wood and still the sickly smell of eggs and butter. The bureau is beyond even my mother's woodwork repair; in a cone shape around where the picture had been it is splintered and peppered with shot, long grooves scored into the wood, smoke winding upwards, the photo itself, gone, smashed against the wall harder than any anger could throw it . . .

Unexpectedly something moves by my leg and I see it's Gull, woken from his afternoon nap. I see the tiny scars on his forehead where the ticks have bitten him, and I realize I'm not in the living room at all, that I'm still sitting at the dining table instead, by the uneaten sandwich. Across the room the shotgun leans quietly against the wall, untouched.

The car will be back soon in this long blazing day.

I'll be at the table, waiting.

But there is no bread-and-butter pudding that night. My father returns, exhausted, grimy with the thick make-up of sweat and dust. Someone else's face on his own. He sits at the kitchen table drinking a can of lemonade. Through the open window he looks at his wife as she stands out there by the edge of the corn. He sighs.

'Lil',' he says, flatly, 'come on in now.'

In front of her the burnished crop rises far into the distance. A low sun, heavy and smouldering in the sky. Every now and then a breeze forms in some part of the field and she gazes at the tall stems beginning to sway, their movement confused, then she sees them settle, as if a wave has drifted through them. The breeze seems to come from nowhere, but when it rolls towards her it's hot and dusty, and she must be able to smell just how ready the crop is.

In her hand she has a box of cat biscuits, and she shakes it again, once, twice, then for a continuous length of time as her desperation mounts. The kitten's in the corn, and if it doesn't come out before morning, the combine will take her. The rattle that the box makes sounds so insignificant, so ridiculously quiet against the swirling hush of the field. Does it unnerve her to look out across the wheat? I don't think she ever quite got used to it, living there, that crop so full of its own movement, so close.

I see her look at the picture on the box: a cat approaching a bowl of cat biscuits, one paw outstretched. She begins to shake the box again with renewed vigour. Come out, come out of the corn. Tears fall down her cheeks. It's her last chance. The sun's so low now the tops of the corn shine like broken glass.

Her heart is breaking; I think, right now, I'm watching my mother's heart break.

Some time that next day, when the combine turned so close to the farm buildings its hot exhaust of dust and diesel gusted against the windows, Pepper must have run into the gatherer while the jungle of brittle stems snapped around her. Perhaps she found a corner of the field which had felt safe, far away from the shaking ground and the whirring metal. Perhaps her last movement was to chase the dancing patches of sunlight which would come swiftly at her as the combine approached. We never found the body, or the bodies of the mice that Pepper had been chasing. From a glinting sea of corn in the evening light, there was nothing but sharp stubble and brown soil twenty-four hours later, with the combine itself, giant and exhausted in the field's centre.

As night began to fall the only lights in the field came from the vast headlamps of the combine shining across the stubble. My mother walked out to the men with their supper of warm potatoes and a stew of lamb. The men were thoroughly exhausted, quiet. They knew about her hunt for the kitten the night before and read in her face that the kitten hadn't returned. Each one of them thanking her silently, handing their empty plates back to her, then watching her return across the destroyed field in the glow of the headlamps.

Winter brought ice, covering my bedroom window like a cataract. Ice on both sides of the glass. Each morning I'd sit in front of the one-bar electric heater in the middle of the floor, and hear its deep comforting hum of electricity. I'd crouch and lean forward till the thin cold metal of the grill almost touched my chest. The bar itself was oxidized and old, but slowly its ash-grey surface would turn brown, then start to glow through a series of rust reds. The heat spread quickly across the bare skin of my legs and belly. A sharp smell of dust burning. Each morning, there by the heater, bowed over it and collecting all the warmth it could give until the bar glowed fiery orange and all I could breathe was the airless smell of dry heat. And then shuffling back on the carpet, rubbing at my legs and chest to stop them burning. When the bar was hottest, I'd spit on it and watch the drops sizzle in little black spots like the poker's mark on glowing coal.

Snow had been falling for weeks, snow on snow on snow. On the first morning I'd made my snowman from it, and he'd grown lumpy under fresh falls and his carrot nose had turned black as wood with frostbite.

Inside, I remember that chill. The chill of a house deep in the throes of winter. Sometimes a feeble breeze would stir and the ice would tinkle in the trees outside. Stove and fires burned all day long, but the wallpaper stayed damp and chilly to the touch. The snow reflected a harsh white light into all the rooms, making surfaces appear flat and cold. And there, by the kitchen table, her face like marble, sits my mother. A mug of tea cupped between her hands. She's whistling a tune almost too quiet to hear.

With the kitten gone, the rooms seemed more still than I'd ever known them. My father moved about the house like a caged animal, not raising his eyes to look at anyone, grunting the business of the day over a supper which he often heated up to eat by himself. Even my daily dough scupltures failed to have any effect on her. She'd hold them preciously, turn them softly in her hands and then put them back on the table and stare into mid-space. Each day I'd work and work at my sculptures to make ever more elaborate shapes, anxiously watching them rise in the oven to see if it might be the one that woke her from her dream. But none of them worked.

I wasn't there when it happened. I was at the estate, making one of the most complicated dough sculptures I'd ever attempted, with plaits, twists and glazes of egg yolk and sprinklings of poppy seed. I wasn't there when it happened, but I knew when it happened. The exact moment.

Her car was found parked on the middle of the bridge at Wiggenhall St Mary Magdalen. Pointing back towards the farm road. I was in the kitchen, by the warm stove, my hands raw with scooping snow off the railings outside, and now white and greasy with uncooked dough. But I saw her in my mind. I saw her getting out of the car and stepping into the deep snow that had fallen on to the road. I heard the crump of the snow as she walked to the railings of the bridge and looked distantly along the frozen ice of the Great Ouse Drain. This was the point where the *Mary Magdalene* had often lurched into the water, its planks covered with picnics and flasks of coffee and cordial. That same launching slope, once dazzlingly bright with summer flowers, now dark and icy, with the mud cut up and frozen. And she looks at the river which dissects the punishing flatness of the Fens, vanishing to a distant level, going nowhere. Hers is a gaze that has been passed down to her from her own father's love of horizons.

The dough pulls elastically between my fingers. And my mother steps on to the ice that covers the river. Below her, the mud and reeds are frozen in a twilight world of their own. Even the water itself seems sluggish and congealed between the stems. My mother steps cautiously till she stands in the middle of the river, the banks twenty feet away on either side. No one is about. Again, that incredible silence, across the ice, along the banks, in the fields. The entire Fens are one single object to her, with this solid, twenty-mile piece of ice shining like a dagger through it.

She begins to walk, her feet scuffing the snow which has settled on the ice, walking in a straight line down the drain towards a horizon which is never going to get any closer. Occasionally the ice grows black and watery where a tired current's churned it from below. The only sounds come from the pressure of her foot as the whole twenty-mile sheet of ice bends with her footsteps. Strange stretching noises as the ice bears her weight. Muffled squeaks like wood beginning to split.

I reach into the oven and remove my golden dough sculpture and put it on a cold white plate. My fingers touch the chilled, smooth porcelain, and I watch the heat from the baked dough spread a breath of condensation around its base.

There. I wasn't there. A mile away from her parked car, twenty feet from either bank, the jagged shape of split ice. Shards of frozen river rising into the air where a small brown pool marks the end of a straight line of footprints. A mile of footprints. I've often thought about them. How long it takes to make them, how unwavering they were. How they melted into the river some time during the next day and there wasn't anything to be done to stop that happening, because water holds on to nothing.

Sometimes I hear that great crack as the ice gives way. I see the scything movement of broken ice slipping away from a sudden hole, and spreading like blood on to the ice is the dark, glassy water of the river.

Her body was discovered near the bridge where she'd left the car. A mile back downriver, she had floated under the path of her footprints. That was the bridge where she'd climbed out of the small rowing boat in the arms of her newlywed husband, and half a mile downstream, the church where she'd been married. The church where she was also buried. Confetti and ice and footprints – the river's taken it all away. And on the dark polished wood of the coffin I placed the elaborate shape of the dough sculpture I'd made to cure her marsh fever.

Get in! my father says, his face close to mine. I've been led out of the church and there's a raw wind blowing over the Fens. Get in! I don't want to leave her in there. He's pushing me towards a car and the few people walking out of the church have naturally formed a space around us. They're all in black. Their faces look cold and grey with the stress, reddening with the wind. Goose is there, able to deal with the wind but clearly not the occasion. She's in a cheap black coat and has brought a walking stick with her. She looks like an old American Indian, wise and smoky, bowed under a pressure only she can understand. She has a keen eye on my father and a tight grip on the stick, as if it's about to be raised at him.

'Whass your plan, George Langore?' she says, the wind tearing at her words but not her determination. That's beyond question. A hard edge of flint in all this watery landscape.

I'll get him home, my father says to the crowd, ignoring the black crow in its centre. She takes a step forward and my father seems to shrink as his grip on me tightens. I can see the redness of my wrist where he's holding it. But I'm still not wanting to leave the church with that smooth coffin in its aisle. Goose hardens with another comment but is calmed when Kipper steps forward, as tall as an undertaker, impossibly upright and commanding. He gives a nod to my father – those Langore brothers at it again.

Now my father has his arm round my shoulders and he's dropped down to my height. He hasn't shaved. He's smiling oddly because people are watching but I see there's a crazed look in his eye. He feels cornered by the occasion. All right, lad, he goes, let's not make a scene. He's been drinking all morning from a hip flask and the smell of the warm alcohol mixes with the cold air. Too late for a scene, I thought. You're years too late.

And I see Ethel Holbeach bundled up in her fen-coat lean forward when my father pushes me to the open car door. Mr Holbeach, holding her back with the thinnest of smiles.

Then I'm in the car and I start kicking the dashboard and slamming my fist at the door and he's driving me out of there as fast as he can. He swings off the church track on to the road and nearly hits a car and he shouts abuse out the window at the driver. Then he slews on to the verge and back on the road and that's his mood, that's it set for the rest of the day.

Back at the house he slams all the doors and I slam mine and he shouts at me and at my mother and then he starts emptying her room, making a pile of her clothes and burning it in the late afternoon. So bitterly cold out there but my father's just in a T-shirt because his blood's so up.

He gave up work. He didn't sleep. In the night I could hear him pacing the corridor, descending the stairs, the click of his study door shutting tight. Gull, old and deaf, thumping the wall with his tail. Sometimes the phone might ring and its sound would charge the air with a strange unwelcome sense of urgency in a house so empty. Neither of us would pick it up. It might ring thirty or forty times before the relieving, overwhelming silence returned.

I should be put in care, they said to him, *just for a while, you understand*, not too long but *till you all get through*. Various women were put forward as possible foster mothers. On one occasion I was taken to a farmhouse where two older children kicked me in my shins and a ruddy-faced girl said she'd *drown me in grain*. My father was called for.

The carpets became soiled, the windows grimy, the air became thick and gloomy. Filigrees of damp grew up the plaster and spider's webs wove their own grey fabric across curtains which were neither opened nor closed. Doors warped gently into their frames. In the evenings I watched television and practised my writing. Each day there'd be a power cut, the image on the television abruptly contracting with a fizz to a solitary, fading dot. I lit candles and continued with my letters.

One by one the light bulbs blew and were never replaced, making the house ever darker, choosing to fade from view, a wounded spirit. In its place, nature took over, with slugs moving dreamily over the carpets and walls by night, their elaborate trails glistening by day, and snails huddled in brittle clusters on the kitchen cupboard doors. I realized it was the house itself, that damp little building in the field, which was asserting its right to change, to rot regardless of its occupants. That house, which had been foul and damp and unloved when my parents had first seen it – which had become clean and warm only as a passing veneer through my mother's attempt to make it a home – had always only ever been one step away from ruin.

Ten years old, I was living my life like an animal, orbiting my father. Was there a summer that year? I don't remember. Autumn came and with it the leaves my mother had seen as buds were now falling in the yard, blowing into heaps and rotting on the ground. And threading through the air as the leaves fell, thin wisps of grey smoke, growing in volume, collecting around the sheds and dashing in low flurries across the yard.

Soon the house smelled of it. The air became woody and foul. I pushed open my father's bedroom door and found the room empty, clothes heaped on the floor, opened tins of peaches and beans on the table, two or three bottles of pills with their caps off and a collection of spirits. He'd been drinking for weeks, but the pills meant something new. I tried to read the strange names on the labels, but as I cleared the door some shape stirred on the bed and I spun round to see Gull snarling. The old working dog was lying on the bed, on his side, as heavy as a pig, faded and smelly, like an old coat. His eyes were milky with cataracts but the jaw wrinkled up with hate. I threw a tin of something at him and slammed the door behind me before rushing into the bathroom.

He was on the lawn next to the overgrown vegetable patch with a dead hen hanging from his hand. It was the first time I'd seen him that day, and he looked stooped and severe. He was motionless, absorbed in watching the fire he'd set. The chicken coop. Long fingers of blue smoke blew from the gaps in the planks, and larger smoke balls rolled out from the hatch. As the heat grew he took a step back, but that was the only movement he made. I imagined my mural of clouds inside the coop – how they would come alive as the smoke grew, painting and smoke one and the same element, both sealed in wood. And I remembered crawling out of the hatch with dry chicken shit on my clothes and feathers in my hair and looking up and grinning at my mother, standing where I was standing now, waving at me through the bathroom window.

The smoke plumed into a solid tumbling core and in a wild flurry of panic a chicken came through the hatch. It was the Rhode Island Red, the one which always hid behind the boxes.

Its back and wing were on fire and it beat the ground – neck outstretched with pain and terror. My father stood, stunned, then hurriedly ran to the chicken and scuffed dirt at it with his boot and when that didn't work he stamped on its wing and he stamped again and then he put his boot on the chicken's back and pressed down firmly and for a long time with as much pressure as he could.

After that, he squatted by its side, with the other chicken dropped a few feet away. He touched the back of the chicken's neck, very softly, then put his hands up and buried his face in them.

I sat on the edge of the cold bath and looked blankly at the basin. I smelled my father's shaving soap and saw the line of his stubble stuck on the china like a tidemark. I thought about the pills in his room. The blade of the razor by the spikes of the shaving brush. The razor had a bone handle with a charging-bull insignia engraved into it. When the kitchen door opened downstairs I stood up and in one movement I was folding the blade of the razor into its bone handle and then I glimpsed my reflection in the basin mirror and I winked at it because for a moment I hadn't recognized myself.

I think he slept for much of the afternoon. I stayed in my room. Some time around five I went back to the bathroom and looked through the window. The coop was nothing but a charred shape in the dirt, a lightning strike in the lawn, with only the stoutest wooden studs burning like ingots in the centre. The burned hen still lay there, to the side of the ashes, but the other one had gone. Perhaps he was planning on eating it, like he had the others.

I waited till dusk, and when I heard some stirring of movement coming from his room, I moved on to the landing, crouching at my end of it, concealed by its darkness.

When he stepped out of his room and began to pull the door closed I was running fast and low at him. The razor was unhinged in my hand and I imagined it glinting like a sleek fish in some deep dark water and that would be all he'd see at first would be this strange gleaming flash of steel flying down the corridor before he realized that it was me, voicelessly lunging at him, and that we weren't avoiding each other any more and that he'd have to raise his hands like he'd done earlier in the day but this time he'd have to be quick. And I smelled the alcohol on his breath or his clothes as I wriggled through the flailing shapes of his arms with the steel fish in front of my eyes now and pushing it forward and flashing it up and down till it seemed to be slower in the air and I knew that the shining blade was cutting on something and I came close to his head now and I saw his hair swinging oddly in front of me and I felt how intimate this action was and how I'd not been this close to him in months. It was utterly without sound. And now he was finding some deep strength somewhere beyond the hazy world of his drink and I was being picked up and flung against the wall, and I was winded and doubled by it but I was still at him and the beautiful fish was wriggling on the line in front of my eyes and I willed it forward and made it dance wildly and again it started to leap at his shirt and then higher and we began to fall down on to the carpet like a couple of drunk lovers and really we should be laughing and laughing at how ridiculous this all was and how we'd gone too far, but not yet far enough . . .

Suddenly the door opened at the end of the corridor and my father stepped out of his room. He saw me at the top of the stairs. He pulled the door shut, took half a step towards me, stopped, then let out a warm quiet chuckle.

Although it was now dark, the window at the end of

the corridor was slightly lighter. He was little more than a silhouette.

'What are you doing up? Can't sleep?' His words sounded unconvincing, playing a father's role he'd long forgotten. The wind pressed up against the window outside and died away.

'It can't go on like this.'

And with that he began to walk calmly down the corridor, drew level with me, and began to descend the stairs. Two or three steps down he stopped, turned, and ruffled my hair like a father should.

I packed straight away: my mother's American-Indian dream-catcher, her recipe book, the shell she gave me so I'd always be able to hear the North Sea, the crabline she'd brought with her seventeen years before. The photo of Hands, the one of my parents on their wedding day. It all went in my tartan suitcase alongside my notebooks filled with all the words I'd never spoken.

My father was nowhere to be found when I went down-stairs. Quietly, in the virtual dark, I made myself a cup of tea and got together a meagre supper of hard cheese and stale bread. I ate it at the corner of the breakfast table, the sights and smells of my mother's wonderful cooking so far away, in another world. It was difficult to eat the bread. My mouth was dry. I had to wash it down with gulps of tea. All the while I was tense with the effort of listening out for my father, but I never heard him at all. For the first time I noticed the Gallyon & Sons shotgun was missing from its usual place by the corner of the dresser.

Hurriedly, I picked up the tartan suitcase and opened the kitchen door. My last ever sight of that house was seeing crumbs of stale bread on the corner of the kitchen table and by their side the half-full mug of tea, already growing cold.

The same sight that had greeted my parents when they'd entered that damp, neglected place all those years ago. The house had gone full circle. And I was leaving.

12

Fireworks

Don't you worry, nairly home, the lorry driver said in a broad Norfolk accent. It woke me up. The man was large and bearded with a soft cap pulled across his forehead. It had a blue jay's feather tucked into the band. But the big man didn't turn to look at me, or say anything more. We drove along the road and a little while later he reached for a tape and I heard the soft murmuring of country music. He sang in a quiet deep voice for the chorus, and every now and then he spoke out to no one in particular, about nothing in particular, but often saying the name Michele. His hands were large, but he held the steering wheel as if it was the brim of a hat, politely, between the tips of his fingers. The country breeds this kind of calmness and strength.

I settled back in the dark, remembering how the farm had slipped from view as I'd run down the drive. Such a sharp black night. No moon, and so many stars it seemed the lowest of them were hovering just a few feet above the soil, at a child's reach. The sad little house had retreated quickly into the damp fields, a boat which had been sinking for years, and I smelled the ashes of burned elms, then saw their remains, piled and charred in the fields like the bones of large animals. The metallic tap of my shoes on the tarmac. A badger hobbling fast over a field's sharp stubble. Noises in the hedgerows. Signposts stood with the eerie poise of scarecrows, pointing in all directions into the darkness. I'd felt like my father's gyroscope; spinning, drifting, twisting, staying put. Each junction meant a new identity; each step a new resolve. It made no odds to me which direction I went, though, as long as it wasn't back.

I'd reached King's Lynn some time after midnight. The sickly artificial glow of its streetlights replaced the crystal darkness of the country, an unwanted false dawn that made me feel exposed, a ten-year-old with a suitcase and no reason to be there. Questions would be asked. I'd stuck to the verges while trucks roared past, but increasingly the verges themselves felt tattered and poisoned as the road became an industrial area dominated by the brooding shape of the beet refinery and the long angular fences and supply roads that fed it. Once I'd been here with my mother, carrying two orange swedes in a string bag along the Dyke Road back to her car. Even though the road was bad the lorries used to take it at speed, and their crop cargo shook and bounced until various vegetables flew over the tailgate. It was easy pickings for us. Finding a swede in the verge half-caked in Lincolnshire mud and bruised from the fall was like finding some glorious nugget. The beet factory had always been the furthest point of our journeys in the *Mary Magdalene*. It squatted on the soft marsh like a defeated giant. Even at night the huge doors were still open and inside minute-looking forklift trucks moved to and fro in a flood of cold light, like hell was being stoked in there.

Further along the bypass was a haulage depot and, next to it, an all-night truck stop. There was a smell of fat and burning eggs. Several trucks. Names on the lorries seemed like destinations at a train station: Derby Haulage, Worksop Machine Parts, Bromsgrove and International, Norfolk Line . . .

Unexpectedly a car had pulled into the yard and I'd ducked from its headlamps. It stopped, a girl got out, stretched, and went to another door while the driver climbed across to the passenger seat. As it drove off I'd climbed the two metal rungs of a lorry's cab in the same effortless way I'd seen men swing up the ladder of a combine. The door wasn't locked. It was dark and silent in there, with stubbed-out cigarettes on the dashboard and air fresheners hanging from the sun-visors. A CB radio hung from the mirror. I'd hidden behind the driver's seat and listened to the café across the yard. A single rough burst of laughter, a kitchen door slamming shut. I'd felt my heart racing and began to think of what I was doing, how this truck might hopefully take me to North Norfolk or how it might swing round in the car park and drive somewhere else. I'd thought of my father, drinking spirits in his room and shouting at Gull to shift off the bed. And the fields and trees beyond him and the smell of wet damp earth and the gentle crack of a branch splitting somewhere deep in the middle of a wood. Of the delicate sensations of safety and being alone, as a spreading tiredness and a feeling of being beyond reach was falling all around me . . .

I woke again as the engine stopped and watched the man climbing out of the cab with a weary sigh. It was just before dawn. Farmer's breakfast. A quiet street in a small town, with houses made of flint and the name Holt written in neat letters above a grocer's awning. The man was ambling towards a door, pushing the hat back on his head and trying to tuck his shirt in. He knocked on the door and as he did so he cleaned his boots on the back of his trousers. A woman in a dressing gown appeared and immediately began kissing him with both her hands holding his large bearded face. He let out a big smothered laugh and pushed her into the house and shut the door.

As the sun rose I was walking out of the town, crossing empty fields, the suitcase heavy with words from a life I'd left. Such a still landscape. Far away, rooks blew up from some trees, disturbing the air. Horses stood silently in the damp pasture of a field, all of them facing the rising sun, breath steaming from their nostrils. I stopped in some birch woods by a stream collecting in a series of pools. I washed and then drank some of the water, and sat for a while on the bank. A wood pigeon's song echoed distantly – *you . . . dir-ty . . . rott-er, you . . . dir-ty . . . rott-er*, as my mother used to say. Trees, fields, soil dusted with sand, birds flying lazily in the morning air. Eventually a heath where for miles all I could see was a low sea of heather and clumps of dark spiky gorse. I tucked an ash twig behind my ear to ward off adders. Wild lavender grew by the path, and I lay down in it till the sun was higher and I began to feel warm again. It felt like a magical land, deserted and full of a deep fragrant nature. And there, across the heath, were three isolated elms, healthy and forgotten by the disease.

Late in the afternoon I came to the edge of the heath and stretching below me were the wide flat expanses of the North Norfolk saltmarshes. The creeks and pools of seawater glistening in a complicated labyrinth of patterns and beyond was the sea itself. Blue grey and fen-flat. Ships on the horizon, becoming lozenge-shaped as they passed each other. Small, delicate clouds were rolling in off the water, and I imagined my grandmother with her eye on them, sitting on some raised part of the marsh.

There was an aviary on the heath, and as I walked past the cages I could see the birds sitting in them or flitting from perch to perch. Through the wire I saw an ancient moth-eaten Andean condor, which sat rocking in a cage, while sparrows hopped in and out through the wire. Someone was sweeping the floor next to the great bird. He saw me looking through the wire and said his problem is that he lives for ever. Them sparrows are dead in a few years, but this one's got all the time in the world.

The path off the heath led into a village called Salthouse, built on the edge of the marsh, where the front doors had sandbags against them ready for autumn tides. The churchyard had gravestones with skulls and crossbones on them, and a single gravestone outside the church wall with the inscription:

He lived,
And Died,
By Suicide

Along a raised footpath across the marsh, I passed pools of bulrushes and flocks of geese noisily feeding in the mud. Ducks and swans toiled across the pools while terns, gulls and lapwings flew above them purposefully. The whole scene felt electric with life. Cley next the Sea, then the River Glaven, and I thought of my mother telling me stories of Goose and the man Hands who became my grandfather. How this area had briefly united these two very strange people and how Goose had subsequently buried the whole landscape in a complicated fabric of stories, lies and mythologies until no one knew what was true any more.

The sun was getting low in the sky as I reached Blakeney, colouring the bare flint walls of the town that rose from the marshes with a soft pink light. Beyond, the path curved once more on to the marshes, to the hamlet of Morston and the tiny shape of Goose's cottage, Lane End, at its edge.

Dozens of birds flew up in panic as I approached over the marsh, followed by a whooshing sound and a brittle crack, like the sound of a rifle. In the fading light there were two figures out there, letting off fireworks. The man was wearing some sort of heavy iron welding mask, and was releasing rockets at arm's length with large gloves. The woman, a little way off, threw fireworks in the air where they exploded in sharp white puffs of smoke above her head. Each time one went off she leaped crazily before reaching into a bag to throw up more. Fireworks were shooting in all directions, sometimes skidding fast off the mud, or falling with sudden gasps of steam into the creeks. Around them, birds were running and falling through the grass and taking flight. The man was being more scientific than the woman, sometimes holding the rockets until he felt their strength before letting go. In contrast, the woman was losing control, whirling in an explosive cloud of smoke lit up with the brief, neurotic flashes of gunpowder, like some unnatural dervish.

But it was my uncle, taking off his iron mask, who first saw me as I walked up.

'Goose! Goose!' he shouted.

Something exploded above my grandmother's head before she too saw me, dirty and tired, standing a few feet away from them.

'Whass this?' she said. 'Whass going on hair?'

My uncle walked over to me and crouched down. His face was thick with sweat like an actor's under hot stage lights.

'Well, this is something.'

Hurriedly Goose shoved him aside and was down at my level too.

'Where's your father?' she said.

I shook my head.

'He's run off, Goose. Ain't you? Run off like a wild 'un.'

'Shut up. Is that true? You've run off?'

I nodded cautiously, not sure how they'd take it, and both of them laughed.

'Well done,' Goose said, and Kipper ruffled my hair, the same way my father had done less than twenty-four hours ago. His switchblade razor still in my pocket.

'Looks like you've got a night ahead of you,' I heard my uncle say. 'Does Shrimp know you're here?' he asked. I shook my head. 'Right, well, we should let him know. He'll worry. You understand?'

Slowly, in an uncomfortable silence, they led me to Lane End while all around the birds began to settle.

So there I was, standing in Goose's cottage, miles from the Saints and my father, and all that my mother had said about it was true. The tiled floor in brick-red and black squares, the red ones worn down more than the black over the years. The heavily greased cooking range, the curtain she drew across the room to divide it. Her bed, sagging on the side she always slept on, the tin bath in the corner, and girdling the walls, higher than I thought it could possibly have been, the dirty brown tidemark of the 1953 flood.

As with Hands's first evening there, thirty-five years before me, she started to fill the tin bath. I was told to undress, and when I stood before her with my cold skinny body I held my breath so my chest wouldn't look so narrow. She pinched my arm and felt my ribs and cursed my father.

I soaked in the bath, watching my grandmother separate yolks from whites of half a dozen eggs. Birds cried across the marsh outside. I felt waves of tiredness as the heat filled my body, alongside a hazed notion that my grip on what was real had slipped. That I wasn't really there, in the bath. That I was back in the cold barren shadows of the farmhouse, with my father somewhere near but totally distant, or that I'd slipped into a dream where I was half in my life, half in the story of Grandfather Hands, two generations before. Into the stories I'd been told so many times that they had become more safe and familiar and real than the last few months of my life. I was Hands – this is how he must have felt that first night on the saltmarsh. This is how it all began. If I can just start again here I'll be able to tell where it all went wrong. Here in this bath I could float in some unattainable region of warmth where the events of the last twenty-four hours and the story of my grandfather could mix. Time had pulled elastically all around me, layering my new world with overlapping visions, and it was time which now seemed to stretch in wide, silent avenues over the dark countryside of Norfolk, taking me this way and that, linking scenes and stories into which I drifted. Somewhere in its centre I was there, in the bathtub above the candles, the straggly late-season samphire waiting by my side. Soft, fleshy samphire. Even to think the word was a conjuring of beauty. There, my grandmother separating the yolks from the whites. The muscle of the egg dripping down from the shell. And across the floor, the pale marble figure of Hands in the smoke-blackened bath, his dark leather boots lurking under the surface, a perplexed, amused look on his face. My grand-mother, thinking of the suit hung up ready for the man who would some day fall into her life, separating eggs and picking seaweed from the stems of samphire. Hands, like his grandson so many years later, both of them thinking of the previous twenty-four hours and how they'd finally come to be in this strange, warm bath.

Outside, the marsh stretched into the vast blackness of the North Norfolk night, like the endless quilt my grandmother had spun so many years before, so rich in textures. So full with meaning. How Hands had begun that quilt in the dark evenings of his first few months on the marsh. How his horizon-seeking eyes had been turned myopic by the tiny needle-and-thread of my grandmother's design. I thought all was possible, even the sprightly breeze that had woken him during that fateful day in 1945, when he'd raised the quilt on the *Pip*, never to be seen again. And as I left Hands in the middle of the waves, I thought of the lorry man with the soft felt hat, driving somewhere through the darkness, returning to his lover, and the sound of his low singing voice and the sonorous lament of his sighs. His big fingers pulling the wheel. An adventure that only I knew about, already so far away. Of my uncle in his heavy iron welding-mask, the fireworks in his padded gloves beginning to spit a stream of soft red light; and the acrid smell of the smoke as gentle as fog across the marsh, my grandmother lost somewhere in its middle, howling like a banshee. I thought of the cool steel of my father's razor, with its bone handle and insignia of a charging bull, folded in the pocket of my trousers on the floor. Of the long dark nights I'd spent in that house, both of us avoiding each other because that way neither of us had to think about my mother. Too much.

As I drifted in and out of these scenes I listened to my grandmother, talking to herself, sometimes to me. I knew only fragments about this odd woman, with her big grey hair tied up on the back of her head. My mother said Goose had never cut her hair since Hands had left, but that's nearly thirty-five years! It can't be true. But it did look enormous, with all its historic pins keeping it in place. It's just one of the fragments I knew about her. Fragments and unreliable stories. Somewhere across the marsh at his smokehouse my uncle would be phoning my father. The telephone would ring twenty or thirty times in the empty farmhouse. My father roused from a hangover, or standing in the centre of the yard, listening to the ringing phone, a pile of firewood across his arms. Or maybe he'd spent the day searching the country for me in his car, driving till the petrol ran out and slamming the steering wheel with frustration. I saw my uncle hunched over the telephone in his study, the receiver hugging the line of his cheek like a pirate's beard, concentrated and gently mocking, describing a small boy walking over the marsh towards him

. . . carrying that tartan case, you know the one – ridiculous he looked, like someone who'd been shipwrecked . . . But all that is to come. Interrupting the phantom images comes the smell of hollandaise. First the vinegar, sharp and fruity, a smell of apples and onions. Then the warm gold smell of eggs, and I imagined being back in the shadowed calm of the chicken coop. The Rhode Island Red, looking at me from behind the nesting boxes. Never taking its eyes off me. The smell of dust and dried shit on the wood, then the wet taste of a charcoal pencil between my teeth as I cross-hatched the clouds I'd drawn on the ceiling. Then I smelled butter – the rich summery smell of a farmhouse kitchen – and I saw my mother slicing cooking butter with a warm knife. Her mother, pouring in a dark brown fish stock, bringing me back to the marsh where it all began.

Suddenly the samphire was there, laid across two white plates next to the thick yellow hollandaise, then she was dragging the stems through the sauce and then pulling them between my teeth. Hands – how could you ever have left? Goose was telling me something important. There was trouble, she was saying, plenny of it. Maimed a boy with them fireworks. Stupid child, for sure, that one, but who knows. The short is he's got 'em all against him, see. Cley and Blakeney an' all. Burned his hands and he's got this scar up his face like the light-en-in' got him. Only ten, poor bugger. Goose took the plates away and cut me cheese to have with bread. Course they want their fire and they want them fireworks but not any of this. Can't have it all ways. Won't take his fish now, but that don't stop him. He just keep on smokin'.

She leaned back in her chair, out of the pool of light that came from a lamp above the table. Her eyes glinted like knapped flint. I imagined the creases in her face were filled with salt.

'You like that plant, don't you, boy?' she said, satisfied.

★

I was put in a bed in the corner, behind a small curtain screen. I opened my tartan suitcase and pulled out my mother's dreamcatcher and leaned it against the windowpane. Beyond, the dark flat marsh stretched to a dismal horizon. Low grey clouds filled the sky like ships at anchor. I thought of Elsie. Of her red hair and the soft bronze strands of hair above her knees. Then I imagined my father, his eyes raw with lack of sleep, gripping the steering wheel, driving through the Norfolk night. And I felt his switchblade razor in my hand and knew that if he stepped foot in the cottage I would use it.

13

Ol' Norse

I dreamed of Ol' Norse that night, climbing out of the North Sea, drip drip on the shore, a steely look in his eye. The stink from his rotten bones, the scaly skin, the squelch of his footsteps and his salted breath, which can wither a plant. Seaweed hanging from his shoulders. His ancient face, as stormy as winter, as craggy as flint. I sensed him prowling outside then standing with a hunter's silence on the lawn, listening to the waves breaking on the Point, calling his return. I dreamed him first, then I wasn't dreaming, and I was aware it was very dark, very dark indeed, and like a conjured genie there was Ol' Norse himself, in the house, crossing the tiles, coming at me with a staff raised before him and I knew it wasn't Ol' Norse but my father, and the staff had the dull metal gleam of his Gallyon 12-bore.

He stopped halfway across the room, at a half-lean, focusing his gaze in the lethal manner a heron has by the water's edge. His gun behind him as counterbalance. Then he turned and walked back to the door, his weight entirely on his toes. When he opened the door, the air inside the room shifted like it was one solid object. And as he did this, his murderous face changed to that of my grandmother. His shotgun, her walking stick.

'What are you looking at?' she said. 'Get a jumper on.'

She threw me a dark blue gansey and led me outside. We crossed the marsh, my boots getting heavier with the mud, until we stopped at a small raised bank, which was covered with the scuff marks and litter of someone who spent much of their time there. The sky was vast and cold and luminous. This was the *tuft*, where she did her cloud watching.

Distantly, Blakeney's flint walls looked featureless and grey. A few windows shone, and the headlights of a milk float swept calmly across the marsh towards us. A second later we heard its rising electric wail as it climbed the High Street.

Then, as I stared across the great flat shadow of the salt-marshes, there seemed to be ghostly disturbances in its stillness, and I realized two or three figures were walking out along the thick muddied paths. I heard the squelch of their waders and a muted rattle of tools carried in plastic buckets.

'Luggers,' Goose said, breaking the silence she and I had had since leaving the cottage. 'Bait digging.'

As she said this I watched one of the men leave the path and wade straight into the Pit, like Ol' Norse returning from his night-time prowl. The man's walk slowed as the water lapped to his waist. The bucket became buoyant behind him and made a sleek fantail of ripples showing his path. After a couple of minutes the water shallowed, and he dragged himself out on to the other side of the channel and soon vanished in the further darkness of the Point's dunes.

'Voice out there, on the Point,' my grandmother said, 'in the dunes. Ain't heard nothin' like it. Ain't male or female and ain't a bird neither. There's stuff out here would make you scream out loud though you ain't never said nothin'. Every night in the creeks, armies of 'em diggin' new channels. Creatures with shovels an' bare backs, I tell you.' And then she was watching the sky, staring at some wide translucent cirrus, glowing pink in the sunrise. Muttering and nodding like some sideshow fortune-teller as downdraughts pulled the clouds into the giant ribcage of an animal.

'Stop staring at me,' she said abruptly. 'I ain't crazy. You're just like him, ain't you? That one I found buried in the mud.'

She laughed, showing the quirky angled teeth of a madwoman. 'Thass where the bugger was, up to his neck like a broken shrimp-rake,' she said, pointing to a featureless strip of mud-bank and sandy shore by the Pit. Back inland I saw a car drive up to Lane End and a man get out. He knocked briefly at the door, cupped his face to the window and then immediately set across the marsh. A more upright walk than my father's, a poise to it he'd never had, which suggested the likelihood of changing tack at any moment. It made him look untrust-worthy.

'Got an apprentice, Goose?' He stopped a little way off, deliberately looking at the sky, out across the marsh, then at another lugger making his way through the Pit. 'Yep. Rain coming.'

'Juss out disturbin' terns, Kipper Langore?'

'Called him. About the lad.'

'He answer?'

'Said he weren't surprised. Been looking all day but weren't worried.'

'That fits.'

Kipper gave me a sideways smile and bent down to my height. A crack from his knees. His hands smelled of smoke.

'Is he comin'?' she said.

'No. That OK with you, Pip? Stay with your gran a while?'

Kipper had a thin dark jacket on with the collar turned up. Despite living on the marsh he always looked cold. This early in the morning Kipper's skin had a pale hue, like the fish he smoked. His nose was sharp and pinched around the nostrils. A gleam across his cheekbones

'Think I might visit him,' he said. 'Well, you know . . . don't know what's happening really since . . . I don't know. Sounded odd. Think he's giving up and I don't know we'll get answers out of this one.'

'You got enough on your plate,' she told him. 'Luggers givin' you the shoulder.'

'Yeah, Goose,' he said irritably, 'called the hospital last night. They say the kid's going to a specialist place. Burns and that.'

'Missed a good meal of samphire.'

My uncle sniffed and looked across at Blakeney and at the chimney of his smokehouse beyond.

'I'll show 'em,' he said, giving a short brittle laugh and looking down at me with a dark-eyed look of sleeplessness.

She never told me what the clouds revealed that first morning. But for the next few days she virtually lived out there, chewing mints and drinking from a flask. She seemed unconcerned with me, as if I'd been living there for years. Make do and be on with it. Hair's your bed, get you some clothes, and will you stop that lookin' at me! Just like with Hands as he fell into the same life two generations earlier. She was clearly an oddball. Still, she was my mother's mother, and the same place and landscape that had formed Lil' Mardler was now mine, and it felt like home, which was an unusual feeling in itself. But I'm hardly given the time to think, because I hear the sound of Goose's large casserole pot clanking somewhere near and I know she's walking out of Lane End with that heavy pot wrapped in her apron and I have to follow. She's showing me the area and I can't delay it any longer. I must mention the first time I saw the wreck of the *Thistle Dew*. And to think that the first time I saw it, I knew nothing of how I'd end up there. *Don't dawdle!* she shouts. All right, all right. Yes, I see her quite clearly now, my grandmother, in the late-autumn twilight, a little woman on a long muddy path, boots too big, carrying that warm-smelling pot.

The *Thistle Dew* had once been a small boat, a cuddy at

heart, but surprisingly broad in the beam, washed up on a tideline of briars and scrub no sea had reached since the great storm surge of 1953. Over the years it had been a hideaway, a storeroom and a cow shelter, and seemed to be caught mid-capsize. 'Cain't stop sinkin',' Goose said, highly amused. 'That sunk in the Pit, now it keep sinkin' in mud.'

Behind the wreck was a pile of driftwood, in places higher than the boat itself, giving the impression Bryn Pugh was living on the edge of a bonfire about to be lit. Bryn had left his rented flat in Blakeney to live there fulltime, to avoid rates and noise, and to have his own letterbox. He'd spent the summer laying out a shingle path to the wreck, erecting a bizarre bungalow's porch, painted THISTLE DEW – pronounced the Norfolk way as *This'll Do* – in small, neat letters below the gunwale, and supported the side with some heavy timber braces.

Inside, the lean felt stronger. His table, desk and bed were all propped on legs to compensate, but with one row of portholes showing sky and the others showing mud you could still feel seasick in there. I'd never heard of Bryn Pugh before, but Goose's evenings for several years had clearly been spent here; her smoking a pipe and him rolling tobacco, playing draughts and eating soups and stews and bowls of samphire.

He emerges from the piles of offcut wood, sketches, clothes, food, papers and books. His strong suntanned neck and his Clark Gable tache. His banded jersey like a French poet's and the rope tied as a belt round his waist, giving him the look of a castaway. He pats a dog – a long-haired black-and-tan mongrel called Bramble – lying by the stove with a barrel-chest in the air. Mess surrounds them, and on it he puts his cup of tea. The metal sink's at a useless angle with a permanent pool of water lapping at the plughole. Thin ply and Formica cover the surfaces and chintzy curtains hang at the windows, held with delicate, feminine bows. Remnants of the boat's first owners and a woman's touch long forgotten.

Bryn was working his way through the woodpile, turning a job-lot of oak into beer money at the local art galleries. He made most of his money carving seals for the boat trippers visiting the colony beyond the Point. The money's in seals, he said, on account of them being log-shaped to start with. Some trees got seals growin' right out the trunk.

The logs he didn't carve and the ones carved badly went in the stove, making a dense cosy fog of woodsmoke.

'So, Goose, what's in the pot?'

'Herring gull,' she says stiffly, 'caught on the Point with a self-tight-en-in' fish trace.'

Bryn's face sinks. He's partial to tern but the gull, even slow-roasted, is a bastard.

'Poisoned flesh and a poisoned soul,' he says. 'Norfolk vulture.'

I knew she'd been asking around for a gannet, hard to get because it was a rafting bird which never set foot in Norfolk; but the fishermen she'd asked had come back with nothing, were unable to catch such a canny bird, or hadn't bothered, thinking a witch's task inappropriate business to take on a boat.

I hear Bryn asking Goose about the approaching firework display and I return to *Thistle Dew* to see my grandmother pull a large round firework from her string-bag. It's like a cannonball, with a dull wax-black finish, roughly circular, but obviously handmade.

'This I call the bollock,' Goose says matter-of-factly, and the two of them burst out laughing. Bramble thumps the wood with his tail.

'He's a good dog that 'un,' Bryn says, before breaking into song.

'Shoo all 'er birds you be so black,
       When I lay down to have a nap.
       Shoo arlo birds.
       Hi shoo all 'er birds!'

It goes quiet in the *Thistle Dew*, Bryn asks about Kipper, and Goose says there's nothing new.

'He's got trouble up to his ears, all right,' Goose says, 'them fireworks are driving him half crazy and no one's buyin' his fish on account o' that rubbish with the boy.'

'It'll clear up.'

'Who knows what go on in that smokehouse. Ain't right, a grown man calling himself Kipper. Been so long I can't remember he got a real name or not.'

Kipper Langore. He smelled of smoke and fish and he made fireworks and people gossiped about him up and down the coast. *Weren't that smokehouse old Bower's cattle shed? I ain't going there as long as I live.* That, and he had two faces – how could anyone look so cheerful and open one second, so devious and sharp-edged the next? Slippery as eels, Goose says to me. Mind that one. We're on our way to Kipper's house now, following a pool of torchlight trained on the ground, and the lane's beginning to peter out where the track turns into his yard. A one-storey outhouse, that's where he lives. A big lounge and a couple of bedrooms and not much else. Then across the scrub lawn there's the chimney of the smokehouse itself, sticking out of the marsh like a dirty finger, built in old red brick with a thick barn door calloused in black tar and a veil of smoke clinging to its front. And behind the chimney on the other side of the smokehouse, the glass-fronted conservatory where he designs and builds his fireworks, known simply as the Lab.

Kipper Langore's standing on the lawn in the dusk, bags loaded with fireworks by his feet. He's dressed up in a suit and has his hair damped down with oil.

'You ready?' he says.

'Drink first,' she replies, walking past him into the house.

The house is dark and empty, with a long corridor which opens into the large sitting room. Goose goes straight to a decanter and pours herself something from it into a mug. Behind her, Kipper makes an annoyed *hah* sound and snaps on the light, then stands impatiently in the middle of the room, under its shade. He seems taller in there, under the tasselled shade of the light. A man who naturally stoops in inside spaces.

'They ain't happy you doin' the display this yair,' Goose says.

'Like they've got a choice, right?' he says back, grinning. The room seems endless in its shadows and corners, fragrant with the smell of fires and of the logs by the fireplace. There's a hint of fish too, subtle and penetrating, easily brought in and hard to remove.

'Why d'you want to wind people up all the time?' Goose says, getting irritable with Kipper's stiff presence in the middle of the room. He lets out a sigh and looks towards Goose, aware that he's under the scrutiny of the light and she's in the dark by the window.

'You finished?' he says.

Goose puts the mug down.

'Then let's go,' he says.

I'd been there a couple of months, and this was Nor' Sea Night, the most important date in their year. At Blakeney a crowd was collecting on the quayside, which was slightly darker than the marsh itself, a torch threading its way between the coats here and there. Behind them, on the car park, a boat had been filled with driftwood and was being set alight.

Kipper went ahead and we saw him moving fast round the blaze, closer to the flames than anyone else, his face reddened and waxy with excitement like a child's. The shadow played tricks with his features as the firelight flicked across his face. Sometimes hollow-eyed and as long as a knife, sometimes wide and full with happiness – it seemed both of his faces were there, in the same instant, fighting a duel. The smoke began to bend and topple above the fire and then swing in a scything eddy across the ground. As the crowd ducked back, only my uncle braved it out, oblivious to it, before he emerged dragging a log, coughing and grey-faced, the smoke following him out as if it didn't want to let him go. The smoke was trying to claim him, even then.

But for the moment this really was *his* fire. A man who lived in smoke, whose house stank with layers of fish and burning charcoal. This was his life, and this, as he sprang in and out of the flames, his element.

As I watched this shivering crowd I had a growing sense of the logics of the marsh and of those who lived along its soggy edge. In the main they were mistrustful of the saltflats and of anyone who spent their life on them – such as my grandmother and Kipper or Bryn Pugh in his wreck. The villagers had cars and travelled inland, listened to weather reports rather than studying the clouds, watched television with shuttered windows rather than noticing when the wind veered or backed, knew nothing of spirits or storm ghosts or mythical quilts. Realists, all of them. Practical, hardworking and friendly. They buttoned up their jackets and leaned into the winter weather and laughed in doorways when geese tried to lead their brood down the High Street in spring. Bryn had been one of them once, but he'd found the only real life for him was on the marsh. Likewise, my grandmother and Kipper and Lil' Mardler

– perhaps my whole family – belonged out there. Marsh people. They were connected with the landscape in a way the others would never be. Made by it and made a little crazy by it, and the villagers knew it all right. Every once in a while these two worlds would rub too closely against each other, and this had happened recently, in Kipper's firework Lab, when a boy had put green powder where there should have been blue. A flash, a burned arm, and then the added slight that my uncle didn't seem to care. Kipper had been banished, openly disapproved of, marginalized further, and the business he kept was strangled at source. Hain't got a good word for that 'un. The fishermen had refused to sell him their catches, fearing their wives more than their loss of income. *Them pots go to Sheringham, you got that, Jonny Boggis?* But one by one they would return, selling their catch and putting his money deep in their pockets. My uncle's fish would be back in their kitchens, and his smoke would drift through their houses. He'd be in control, once again, and they could do nothing about it.

And with his finger on the trigger he lights the first fuse. A thin whoosh, which turns the crowd to look over the marsh. There he is, with Goose behind him, glowing tapers in their hands. Don't be hasty, old gal, I imagine he says, crouching by a row of rockets. Like we planned it, right? Hot gusty flares of orange and red leap out of drainpipes buried in the mud, while white flashes spark along a length of clothesline curving by a creek. All those evenings Kipper's spent in his study, an Ordnance Survey map of the saltmarshes in front of him, drawing his design in a pool of lamplight. Hair go, you bastards, he mutters, a thin-lipped smile curling up at the edges of his mouth like the line of a child's drawing. Lock up your pets. The crowd seems uneasy with the closeness of the explosions and the surprising glows of vapours rising from nearby pools. Goose has poured a jerrycan of paraffin out there, and the marsh is glowing with the blue-hearted spirits of her stories.

Now the bangs and fizzes grow as both figures work faster and faster in the smoke. Rockets spring wildly from the ground, firing in all directions, changing speed mid-flight and tumbling back to earth suddenly. *Watch it!* a man shrieks, as a shard of burned casing thuds off his coat. He stamps it on the ground as someone shouts *shit! there's children hair!* and the fireworks march closer like an enemy barrage finding their range. Something whizzes dangerously near, parting the crowd like a hornet, before tunnelling angrily into the grasses. More things spit furiously at the ground, unable to lift from the mud and dying where they started. You gotta nerve, Kipper Langore, someone says, pissed-up on beer and excited as a bomb fizzes into the creek off the quayside. *Missed!* he shouts and someone tells him to shut the hell up it ain't no laughing matter. But Kipper's laughing all right, out there, chucking fistfuls of firecrackers at Goose, making her hop and dance, and her laughs come across the marsh like the cry of a gull in a snare. And a row of fireworks shoot up, leaving a dotted line of blue flashes like the bells of a foxglove. A foxglove – no, it's not that, it's a delphinium – one of the tall blue ones in my mother's garden. A row of six, in a line. The ghostly blue flashes of delphinium petals and beyond them the red-hot pokers. Rockets leaping out of a dark fenland lawn. Clouds of gunpowder smoke, drifting across the grass like the rolling bushes of her gypsophila.

My mother's flower garden and the firework display were one and the same, down to the clumps of pansies burning in the marsh and the bowers of sweet peas dripping their flames. These two women had choreographed them together.

'Give it to 'em,' my uncle whispers in my ear, and the great round shot of Goose's *bollock* leaps darkly into fifty or sixty feet of air, before exploding in a bumping sound, which shakes the windows of Blakeney and Cley. The display is over.

Afterwards I stayed till the fire had burned to its core, revealing the rowing boat's bones, just like the *Mary Magdalene* when it had burned in the yard. I smelled the damp ground as it dried. Stars rippled through the thermals as though suspended in a heavy, clear liquid. All around it seemed the blaze had purified the air. The few people who hadn't left for the Albatross Inn stared into the softly crumbling embers, tracing hypnotic glows crawling through the remains of a fire, finding sudden shapes and faces and scenes they recognized in the ever-changing patterns of ash and light.

With sudden energy something caught deep in the embers, and a pall of greasy smoke rose into the air. The soul of the *Mary Magdalene*, I thought. Through it, the emptiness of saltmarsh stretched flat for miles. And then, close by the fire on the other side, I saw a vision of my father, leaning to one side with his arms crossed. Looking straight at me. Again smoke wafted through the milky air above the fire, and I waited for him to disappear. But he remained, the wobbling vision of his body more solid than ever before, standing like he'd done by all the fires: the bonfire of rubbish he'd pulled out of the sheds when they'd first moved to the Saints, the sad buckling shape of the *Mary Magdalene*, the diseased elm tree's brilliant fountain of light, the blaze of the hen-coop.

He lifted his arm in greeting, wearily, and in my pocket my fingers curled round his stolen razor, tracing the engraving of the charging bull carved into the handle.

Goose appears off the marsh and walks straight past my father. He doesn't exist in her eyes, but she knows not to get involved.

She comes up to me and says I ain't never gonna speak to that man again, and she holds my hand to make me listen. Her skin feels gritty and dry and there's a dangerous gleam in her eyes. But it's best you hear him out, she says. Don't do nothin' though. Don't you do nothin'.

She heads off for the Albatross and my father comes round the fire.

We sit in his car looking over the darkness of the saltflats. The air freshener's still stuck to the dashboard, like a dried fungus. He's been drinking. I can smell it on his breath and his clothes and he's sitting slumped in his seat, his pale blue eyes looking out there at something.

'These marshes, ain't nothing like them anywhere. Ain't no light out there but there's this glow, ain't there? Glow over the Point, and once you know this place that's all you need.'

He's full of talk. His hands look heavy and useless on the steering wheel. He has farmer's hands, at last.

'Don't know whether you've been to the *Hansa* yet, but you should. She's an old boat now, about sixty years maybe, left up there on the high tidemark. That's the wreck, you know, the one where your granddad spent his days, to get shot of the old girl. Used to wade over there and sit in the sun and carve the wood. All sorts of things he carved in there with the tide going in and out the boat.

'Me and Kipper and your mum used to go there. Just sit and fish and chuck stones and that. You know, there ain't no reason for me to tell you all this. I ain't going to make sense of nothing.' He gave a brief, half-hearted chuckle.

'I ain't never got on with Goose, but she's got a big heart. Used to right scare me when I was a kid, round here. All them years ago. Suddenly it don't seem – you know – it's like it's all happened to someone else. First time I saw your gran I was up there on a gate by the five-acre, blabbing my eyes out. Field up there. 'Cause I'd got to kill this calf in the morning, you know, the next day, and I couldn't see no easy way of doing it. Never killed squat before, and I guess that's why they was making me do it. So here comes your gran, all covered in mud, and she says – your gran, that is – told me get her the tongue and think nothing more. First time in my life I never slept a wink all night and I still think about it since.' He sat quiet for a while, nibbling the skin by the side of a finger.

'Look, lad, it's all gone wrong and all that, but it ain't too late. Mum was ill, you know. Used to say weak in the head, if you get me. But I don't reckon that's it. She just couldn't cope and that ain't nothing wrong, you hear. Some can't do things like others. It's sad but there weren't nothing we could've done. She went off. That's all. Just, sort of, just had to go. I knew that all right the day I came chasing after you lot across the Fens. Down Bedlam Fen. I knew it then . . .'

Suddenly I'm in the bull-pen at the Stow Bardolph Estate, the sound of my father's low calm words threading between shadows and sunlight. Dust motes stirring as the bull swings his great head. I hear the heavy stumble of those hooves on the dirt floor, and just once, the sight of the bull's pink eye looking directly at me. Me, up on the ledge by the windows. My father's voice, speaking through the shadows, calming, quelling, defusing a natural rage.

In the car now, my father falling silent, listening with a practised ear, trying to second-guess his strange child, stretching his arm again and now pulling the bull's head to one side as he brings his voice once more to the great ear.

'. . . truth is, I ain't cut out for looking after you. Whenever you want you just turn up at the Saints and I'll bake you a cake and all that. But it's best off you stay here. Here with your gran and Kipper. 'Specially him. All right? Don't believe nothing you hear about him, OK? There ain't no truth in any of it. Give you a job someday. And with your gran – just don't take no notice of all that cloud shit.

'I ain't pretending nothing happened but we got to go on, you know, you're so young and sometimes I don't even remember what it was like your age. How I felt and all that. But thing is, you'll grow up and know how I feel now, someday. I ain't saying you got to know now, just that some time, you will . . .'

The bull shakes its weary head, and my father's flung back on his heels against the wall. Dust falls from the bricks, and he looks up and gives me a brief, reassuring grin. He goes to the bull again, digging his fingers deep into the thick curls of hair across its head and I see the bull calm, and I feel once more the touch of my father's hand as he ruffles my own hair in the dark corridor of the farmhouse. Vaguely, I trace the outline of the bull and know it's a drawing I made when I was seven, on to the wallpaper of the farmhouse, and as the drawing fades, I'm standing there once more in the corridor. My father, at the end, silhouetted against the window, the feel of his switchblade razor deep in my pocket. The charging-bull insignia on its handle. I remember the fantasy I had of running at him, watching the gleaming silver fish of the sharp razor in front of me, and I know this is the time to use it and I hope my father will quickly leave, because I can't face much more of this.

'. . . ain't never known. Maybe you'll turn out right. Your gran says it's all in the sky and maybe it is, but it ain't done her no good so don't think that's the answer. Just remember she's a tough 'un, that woman, and she hurt your mother before anyone, before anything.'

He looks at me and gives me the smallest of nods. I open the door and feel the sharp cold of the winter air collect me, strengthening me as I step out and push the door shut. My father, inside, looking trapped behind the glass and leaning awkwardly over the seat where I was sitting, trying to say something to me. I weaken to it, fumbling for the door handle, suddenly anxious to hear what he's saying, and when the door opens again, a thin yellow light goes on and he's smiling apologetically at me.

'You have to slam it,' he repeats.

For a while I watched his car as it sat all by itself on the edge of the marshes. I couldn't see what he was doing inside. Eventually I heard him turning the car's ignition. Four, five times. I listened to the silences between each time he tried, imagining him counting under his breath like he used to at the farm. Counting to thirty before he tried again. Habits are the last things to change.

When I'd reached twenty-five, I heard him try again, the engine fired, and he drove off.

There was a cloud over the saltmarshes. The moment I saw it I knew it was a rag cloud. While I watched, it began to change, spinning like candyfloss around the stick until there it was – the exact shape of a whale. A great sperm whale, turning slowly on to its side and spouting its last, giant breath. Riding on its back, two figures in the moonlight.

14

Saints and Sinners

It's an overcast winter day, the saltmarsh looks the same as
the sky, as grey as old farm tools, heavy and hard-hearted. I'm
ten, and it's my first visit to the *Hansa*. I'm in a thick parka
walking along the Point by the water's edge. As I walk closer
the wreck seems smaller than I'd imagined and strangely
warped at the bow; the tides of the North Sea have over the
years put its nose out of joint. The wood's black as oyster
shells with winter weather, and a dark oily stream flows out
through the hole in its hull. The wheelhouse has sagged on
one side, but most of the deck is still there, and rising from
the centre I see for the first time the broken mizzenmast
covered with Hands's intricate carvings.

The second I've hauled myself on it I lie on the sloping deck
– the only thing in miles of saltmarsh and water that isn't
utterly level – and I think this is *my* boat, the famous *Hansa*,
which has wrecked itself into the stories of three generations
of my family. The mast is amazing. At its base Hands had
carved a pot-bellied, snub-nosed whale, with a great Machi-
avellian grin on its face. Above it, the cruel eye of a sea bird,
and then half-formed marsh spirits climbing like ivy towards
the flames my mother had once described to me on a bright
April day on the grassy bank of the Twenty Foot Drain:
St Elmo's fire, see, clings to a mast before the storm. All those
waves and creatures and things of the North Sea, he carved it
all there on the *Hansa*.

That day in the Fens she'd described all the carvings of the
wreck, but as I remembered it, the flames were the top of my

mother's mast. So why hadn't she mentioned the carving I saw above it now? That of a man in a little boat, reaching up to something that had either never been carved, or had broken off in some winter storm. It was the figure of Hands himself, jostling on the North Sea in the tiny *Pip*.

The soft gurgle of water, the popping of mud, the calm moat of the Pit round the boat on nearly three sides – it is a special place. Hands knew it, spending his days here, avoiding my grandmother, looking to the horizon with a dreamy expression, keeping his knife sharp with a whetstone. And Lil' Mardler too, coming to sit and trace her finger over the carvings and picture the man who'd done them. Even those Langore brothers had a feeling for the place – swimming across the Pit like a couple of pirates – trying to out-swim each other, trying to impress the girl they'd found so abandoned.

A gull lands like a sack of stones on the hollow wood – gripping the rail with metalled claws and staring with a soul full of hate. I think of my father and of the dreamer-boy he'd once been. Out here, on the wreck, alone with the birds. A boy close to slitting his own throat rather than kill the calf he'd reared. A boy who'd grown out of the saltmarsh under the same vast sky, gaining an unnatural ability to connect with animals, understand them, know what they wanted.

At some point he'd changed. Bidding for the *Mary Magdalene* at auction, yes, he must have been a dreamer then. But the dead-hearted marshman dressed in oilskins rising from the mud and storm of Bedlam Fen was a different man entirely. At some point he'd chosen to turn his back on his ill wife and mute child, chosen to lock the study door, chosen to joust improperly with the wrong fondue stick and chosen to burn, burn everything, boats and coops and the dreams he'd once had.

These North Norfolk saltmarshes, they make you dream all right, and they were unlocking something in me. I was beginning to see things from a new perspective, connecting the stories and half-stories my family have long been dragging out of the mud here. I could feel it welling up in me like a tide, persistent and stealthy. I felt the little miracle long before it happened – but the day it happened started there, not on the *Hansa*, but on the marsh, in the glowing whiteness of a sea-fret. It was cold and damp and I was listening to Bryn Pugh's song coming through the mist . . .

'There once were a lass, she were a funny-lookin' lass,
A swimmin' off-a Crom-er . . .
An' there's me up on the sand
Wi' me crabline in me hand.
Thass for being a roamer.

'"I in't ashamed that my face look like a plaice,"
Is what this gal were sing-in',
Wi' a voice what bruk the flints
Which ha' scared me ever since,
Thass for never liss-ning.

'Then along come a boat wi' ol' Frank dressed in his coat,
An' says she in't for sa-vin',
He puts a hook right through her lip,
An he reel her in right quick,
Thass for miss-behavin'.

'Foll-I diddle-I, foll-I diddle-I,
Thass for miss-behavin'.'

. . . and I can't help but be there, in the thick fog of the sea-fret, third behind Goose and Bryn on the raised path. Their coats look bulky and grey and beyond them the marsh is glowing with a milky strangeness, which has made the air too quiet. Goose is as nervous as a horse.

> *'Foll-I diddle-I, foll-I diddle-I,*
> *That's for miss-behavin'.'*

'Pip!' Goose says, urgently, breaking the spell. 'Don't you look too hard out there in that fog. I seen shafts o' light and it's got my hackles up. This ain't nothin' more than a cloud we're in right now – cloud can't float no more so it's down hair on the ground.'

We walk into Blakeney, which looms out of the mist like a lost island. The streets are dripping and the flint walls shine like glass. The village is empty, the streets have an echo I've not heard before. We turn into an alleyway next to the Albatross Inn, where Bryn knocks on a side door of a two-up two-down cottage. Through the bubble-glass of the door a thin man with white hair approaches, his shape rippling as he does so, holding a pair of glasses up to his eyes while he fiddles with the latch and Bryn mutters here comes the saint under his breath. The door opens and Gideon bends his long straight back down to Goose. Good. See you've brought your fine grandson. The kettle is on. Morning, Mr Pugh.

Gideon's house smells of turps and linseed and herbal tea. We sit in the front room, where each wall is covered with paintings of saints, icons and religious scenes. He sells them at country fairs and to occasional visitors, but most of his trade comes in the pilgrimage season where those walking to Walsingham make a detour to Blakeney, pick up an icon of their favourite saint, and finish their walk with it pinned to their chest.

'When it come to money,' Goose says, 'nuns are bitches. You tell him, Saint.' He looks like he's been slapped. A comment like this, so early in the morning. Goose is undeterred – she goes on to tell how she'd watched three nuns arguing in whispers over an icon of Saint Francis of Assisi here at Gideon's cottage, white-knuckled with the stress of it, while Gideon brewed vanilla tea and Goose had smoked her pipe. 'The fat one lost out,' Goose adds, as if it's something to note.

'Yes, it's all true, I'm afraid,' Gideon sighs. 'The others settled for Saint Sebastian and Saint Anthony of Padua.'

Bryn lets out a snort. 'Should paint more Madonnas. Clear as muck that's what they want,' he says, but Gideon won't be drawn by an atheist.

On the walls, Saint Francis and Saint John the Baptist outstrip the Madonnas by a clear margin. Both of them with distinctly pinched Norfolk faces, marching across fields, sitting by rivers lined with rushes and marsh. St John the Baptist stands in the middle of the ford at Glandford, a group of ducks pecking bread by the water's edge and a Morris Minor with a family in it waiting to cross on the far side. Saint Francis stands in beech-woods, magpies and jays perched on his shoulders, badgers by his feet. The disciples are there too, doing the jobs they'd held before Christ chose them: Saint Peter, on a crab-boat at Cromer, pulling in pots and letting lobsters go free; Levi, son of Alphaeus, collecting taxes in the Inland Revenue office in Norwich, looking dreamily at a snowscape paperweight while the forms pile up on his desk. The disciples opt not for a last supper but an afternoon tea at the Pretty Corner Tea Rooms. Christ, in a smock, breaking not the bread but a thick slab of carrot cake – St Peter's greedy eyes on that – while at the end of the table, Judas pours salt in his cup. There are saints running across fields and brandishing sticks at tractors. Seagulls and rooks pecking the sunburned backs of sinners. On Cromer Pier, St Camillus – the reformed gamester – strides past arcade penny-fountains as they spit out coins from their mouth-like slots. Meanwhile, further up in the town of Cromer itself, St Gengulf rescues crabs by lifting them from a vat of boiling water with his bare arm, gratitude clearly seen on their crabby faces. In the background they crawl down Corner Street towards the sea, while a woman backs into a doorway and tries to shoo them off with a walking stick. It's a painting that will have special significance for me – I shall take a second to gaze at it a little longer, just to see if those crabs were revealing their secrets yet.

Bryn has folded the local newspaper with a flourish and is reading aloud an article on Kipper with great glee:

'. . . the boy has made a satisfactory recovery and it is expected he will receive no further treatment. John Langore, known locally as Kipper, released a statement yesterday saying how glad he is this business is now thankfully behind them. He wished the boy a speedy convalescence and urged all to make a fresh start. However, Marge Vickers, aunt to the injured boy, later added a note of caution. "Although Mr Langore appears to be without blame for this sad incident, he is still on the marsh making unregulated fireworks, and I would ask all mothers to think twice about letting their children wander near him."'

Gideon's trying not to be interested. Gossip's an evil practice.

'End of,' Goose says, 'he's wriggled out, all right. Them Langore brothers always did. Mind – he were always the dark one.'

Gideon sagely raises a finger with a simple hijack: 'So we have Cain and we have Abel. Here, on the Norfolk coast.'

It's a platform for him to launch into what was obviously a familiar sermon, as he pulls out a half-finished scene of an old man and two young girls sitting in a Norfolk barn: 'Not far from this humble house we have Lot and his two daughters.

We can see them here, in the barn where the Deed happened. Mr Pugh was kind enough to read me the story from the pages of the *Eastern Daily Press*. Lovely daughters, apparently, but given to drink, and lonely too. And the old man, weakened in the head, I believe. But here is the barn where they got him drunk and I shall not tell you more but this is how it is.'

Bryn takes the painting and frowns at it.

'Is this *before* or *after* they get him in bed?' he says.

Ignoring him, Gideon reaches for another painting.

'Here, on Yarmouth's Pleasure Front we have Leufredus, rather an ill-natured saint it's said, and next to him this tubby woman and her two overfed children . . . well, look, Leufredus has made them go bald after they poked fun at his own lack of hair. See here, the children can't believe their own reflections in their toffee-apples.' The painting has a SOLD sticker on its bottom-right corner.

'Shouldn't the old boy's trousers be down at least?' Bryn continues, still looking at the picture of Lot and his daughters.

We drink herbal tea and Bramble eats digestives on the carpet. Gideon keeps looking at me with great sadness.

'Ahh, silence. Such a . . . such a thing . . . Come with me,' he says, and I follow him into a second room, which had once been a kitchen. Now, like the rest of the house, it's cluttered with frames and canvases. There's a smell of egg. Opened tins of varnish, gesso, acrylic washes, turps and linseed share the cooker with a saucepan in which he's boiled his breakfast.

As with the living room, saints and sinners peer from the frames in a variety of confrontations. Burning bushes and golden calves stand abstractly in fields or in the middle of roundabouts. An old man is being chased by seagulls, his pockets brimming with stolen carrots. In a tall painting leaning against the fridge is Moses himself, making his way between the parted waves of the Wash while seals and cod look on incredulously through the glassy walls of water on both sides. Moses with an easel on his back, a stout pair of waders and Gideon's unmistakable white hair. Saints are being tortured in here; Gideon has graffitied some of the pictures with WHY DIDN'T YOU RUN? or SINS OF FLESH! in bright paints. In here, Lot has Gideon's thin white beard and quizzical expression, being held down by daughters stripped of their clothes and drunk on wine, one pulling his trousers off while her sister pushes him into the straw and kisses him with a fleshy, puckered mouth.

By this time Gideon has vanished between the canvases into a back lobby. I can hear him rummaging from the other side of the wall, muttering to himself and talking to the pictures with affectionate greetings. Ahh! Such a long time . . . Judas, you poor misguided rotter . . . wakey wakey, Lazarus, no point being in that cupboard . . . From the front room I hear Goose laughing with Bryn as he again sings his local tunes – *Always a Dandy, this little Andy, he'll be a naughty boy-oi!*

I feel trapped and hot and confused by a cluttered Norfolk I don't understand.

Gideon reappears with two small pictures painted on boards hinged in the middle. On the left, Mary Magdalene, sitting in a boat; on the right, St Lawrence.

'This man,' Gideon says, 'protects against fire. When they were grilling him to death he said, "I'm done one side, best turn me over." You'll need them both, he says to me, kindly, giving me a glass of water.

And as he leaves the room he whispers in my ear, 'Remember, we all need a map to follow in life. Without a map we've got nowhere to go.'

From the front room I hear Bryn singing 'The Foggy, Foggy Dew':

'She sighed, she cried, she damn'd near died,
She said: "What shall I do?"
So I hauled her into bed and I covered up her head,
Just to keep her from the foggy, foggy dew.'

There by the sink I gulp from the glass and look at the fog outside through a dirty window, partially seeing my mother there, dream-walking into the alley, a crease of concentration on her brow. She comes to the window. Always the worrier, she says, sadly, my little worried boy. She leans her dark head against the glass, wearily. You've brought us back home, Pip, me, your father and you. And something rises through her, bending her body and pulling her softly away from the window. Forever floating under the ice, she drifts away. I'm left with the rising sensation I've had all day. A certainty that something miraculous is about to happen, and then a hot dry feeling in my throat, a feeling of such burning urgent upset, and I lean to the window to stretch for a last glimpse of my mother and I hear the word *muuh*.

For a second, I don't know where it's come from. And then I realize.

I've spoken it.

A Norfolk Miracle, brought about by the ceaseless choreography of tides, creeks, birds and salt. Rising in me and spreading across this landscape like my grandmother's quilt, long past the point when I thought my lost voice and all its words had rotted away like dead leaves. Could they still be there, in me, after all these years, waiting to be spoken? Ohh . . . I wished my mother had heard. I wished she'd heard me speak so I could hear her say well done, my love, I knew it, I just knew it!

*

But it's too late for that. As my first winter there continued, my evenings were in the quietly creaking cottage of Lane End, virtually orphaned, thinking of the wide expanse of marshes outside, holding back the waves with nothing more than mud and grass, of the pure long sweep of the Point as it curved into the North Sea and the calm water of the Pit which it sheltered. How this landscape had turned men into dreamers: Hands with his carvings, Shrimp with his animals, Kipper with his fireworks, Bryn with the seals and Gideon with the paintings. All of those men, and not a father among them.

'Lissen, boy,' Goose said one evening, over a baked ham-and-artichoke pie, 'I din't want a tell you, but I seen your father's car. On Kipper's lawn. You want a make yourself scarce I'd unnerstand.' Goose went over to the *Thistle Dew*, and as soon as she'd gone I cycled along the flood bank to Blakeney, which was shuttered up against the marshes and the night, with small barred windows glowing like fireplaces in the flint walls. I stopped in the High Street and listened to the sound a small coastal town makes, so utterly silent apart from a soft warm noise coming from the Albatross Inn. Somewhere up the street was the sound of water dripping from an overflow into a backyard it'll never fill. A breeze stirring the weeds growing between houses and pavement – curtains behind windows moving in a draught. More draughty inside than out. And other sounds too, of cables snapping against the masts of boats on the quay, of gulls still in flight up there like the ghosts they are, reminding me of where I am and that this town and this place are right there with me, on the edge of things. Then the door of the pub opened and a lone man came out, lighting a cigarette between cupped hands and pulling his hood over like the faceless men of the mud creatures that day on Bedlam Fen, and I cycled on, past the quay, the car park and along the road till the tarmac gave out and the marsh began again. I approached my uncle's house and sheds, and in their centre, a black shape against a blacker sky, the chimney of his smokehouse. My father's car, dull and unreflective, was parked outside.

I left the bike in the rushes and crawled to the spot where the marsh became a rough lawn. I was close to the house and Kipper had no need for curtains. He was standing there, with my father, by a roaring fireplace, scoffing fish and chips from the newspaper in a room largely filled with smoke, and I saw my father blinking with it. Two tumblers of whisky sparkled on the mantelpiece with their own little fires.

From inside the house I heard the sound of a laugh and the fainter sound of a clock chime eleven. At that, Kipper threw his remaining chips into the fire and called to another room. I heard the latch open behind the house, and a young lad with a crew-cut and a pissed-off expression walked across the lawn to the smokehouse. As he opened its door a thick grey pall curled out. He went inside. Then straight behind him, walking across the same line of the lawn, I watched transfixed as the same lad walked again to the smokehouse. Once more, he opened the door, the smoke came out, and he went inside. What was going on? And there, now, outside, my uncle was also standing on the lawn, leaning against one of the windowsills, calmly looking towards me. My father joined him and stood a little way off, staring at the ground. They didn't speak. Then out of the smokehouse came two boys carrying fish strung up on four long pipes. A dozen herrings; identical twins.

'Eel ain't done,' the first twin said, wiping smoke from his eyes with the sleeve of his smock. 'More o' this and the macks'll be dry –'

'OK, Cliff, you've said your piece,' Kipper said, cutting him short.

The first twin, the one called Cliff, shrugged and looked to his brother. They had the same face all right, shadowed under the eyes and thin across the forehead. Cliff had the air of being the elder brother though. He stood with his leg forward and had draped his arm over the pipe like it was a rifle.

'Pint?' the other one asked.

'Yeah,' Cliff said. 'We'll do the hocks in the morning.'

'You crease me up, you do,' Kipper said. 'Off you go then.'

The two lads grinned at each other and walked off towards Cley, leaving my father and uncle on the lawn. My father went to his car, searching for his keys in his dungarees pockets.

'Had too much to drink, haven't you?' Kipper said.

'You can stop that,' my father replied, his cheeks flushed at a half-turn towards his brother. 'You can't speak to me like you do them twins.'

'Yeah?'

'Why don't you just spit it out?'

'Off you go, Shrimp.'

'Don't call me that,' my father said, his back clearly tensing.

My uncle leaned against the wall, apparently satisfied to have riled his brother.

'All I'm saying,' Kipper begins darkly, 'is you lost one woman already. You gotta act responsibly.'

My father went to his car shaking his head.

'Face up to it, Shrimp.'

'I said don't call me that.' And with that he drove off

It was the run-up to Christmas. The pigs were being pickled in vats on Kipper's lawn, the trout was in his smokehouse, and Norfolk was turning effortlessly from harvest to slaughter. Ducks flew off the ponds into an air spitting with leadshot, pheasants were snared in the hedges, geese strangled in farmers' hands. In low factory sheds turkeys were rammed into crates by the thousand, loaded on to lorries and driven to meat processors. A time of year when Gideon cried each day for the shame of it, the sheer crime of all this killing. We've lost our way in life, we have no map.

In the damp winter shadows of the *Thistle Dew*, Bryn carves a figure of Ol' Norse from a beam of sea-defence groyne. His knife works at the hard wood, giving the old devil the wide snarling grin of a dogfish, cheeks covered in scales and bladderwrack for his hair. It's become an obsession, the two of them in that tiny cramped room, spending the winter together, Bryn getting warm by chipping away at the wood, Ol' Norse looking back, grinning at the folly of it like some hideous gargoyle. It's a dance of death. In the larders of Norfolk the pheasants are hung for the meat to darken. The hocks on Kipper's lawn are turned in their graves, drained, salted and finally smoked. And as the face of Ol' Norse begins to emerge from the sea wood – a face of malign intent and utter mischief – the turkeys reach their end, clipped to a moving track, hung by their feet, because a turkey will fight and stamp till the bitter end but when it's upside down it will enter that dream-state so close to death. And close to death they are, because the track moves with a gentle motion to a slaughter that is so simple, so devastating: a pair of pincers, which mechanically removes their heads. Below them a trench as large as a swimming pool fills with blood and is emptied on to the field each night. Someone has to shovel those heads up by the thousand, someone has to open the sluice and gaze at the bird blood as it drains away. The sodium lights of the factory reflect on the pool's surface like a Norfolk sunset, a dark wide stain on the field outside where all this blood has returned, silently, to Norfolk's heart.

Left behind is a county scraped clear of its leaves, soil cracked bare by the frost, woods silent and haunted by their own loss of life. Bark, flint, chalk, all dead, all retreated into a relentless winter numbness. The north wind arrives, bringing with it the menacing scent of the sea, so wild and untamed, sweeping down, marshalling anyone brave enough to bundle themselves up in winter coats through the draughty alleyways of coastal towns. They turn up their collars and lean into it, into all it has to offer, then huddle themselves in places like the Albatross, nursing a pint and sharing their trauma, staring at the warm cosy glow behind the glass panes of the log burner. They complain, remembering other winters, then as the months go on the winter beats even complaint from them.

By February the men have drunk their way through and there's not much left to them. There's salt on their skins. They're fed up. They've forced themselves to survive but there's still an ache out there, all round, the sky's as tight as a drum with a frozenness they can't quite reach, but which all of them know is reaching out for them.

Then something relaxes. They count the coffin dodgers who've made it against the odds. The birds turn up from God-knows-where, oblivious and stupid in their routines.

And whatever the weather, come rain, sleet and driving wind, I'm out on the marsh, running the flats of thrift, purslane, lavender and samphire, jumping the creeks, wading through the Pit to reach the Point. There, among the seas of marram and lyme, surrounded all round by water, I was able to speak. First I coughed up the sound I'd made in Gideon's kitchen, then odd-throated noises like a dog's growl, and slowly, one by one, I shaped the noises till I strung a *gurgh* and an *ell* into *gull*, and, soon after, a *sea-ll*, a *p-it* and, finally, a long-drawn-out *hann-sa*. A coarse noise emerging between dunes and reeds, neither male nor female nor seal nor bird. The very voice my grandmother said had haunted her on the Point all her life.

I'd decided to keep my voice secret. If I started to speak, I'd end up at the local school. Once, and once only, I'd been taken there – Kipper's idea – to see what would happen. He's a tough 'un, Goose, see if he ain't, he says. What happened was I sat at the back of the class, friendless, rubbing the tops of my shoes on the backs of my trousers and thinking the last time I'd been put in glossy polished shoes was for my mother's funeral. The children turned to stare at me when the teacher wrote on the blackboard. I was just the latest generation to come out of a mad family to them. They spoke in unison when the teacher said How do we do? and then flocked to the door when a bell rang. The teacher made me write in the notebook hung round my neck, and then showed the class some of my drawings of birds and seals. Pufter! a girl said, and because she said that I was surrounded at lunchtime by four girls, all younger and bigger than me, who told me my mother was Lil' Mardler, *who always told lies and then she killed herself.*

Yes, that's what happened. Me watching their mean-lipped mouths chanting:

> *'Marshy Mardler lost again*
> *Through the ice and down the drain.'*

Tough luck, Kipper. You're going to learn the hard way about me. It takes more than a half-baked idea to change my ways. And your next idea wasn't so great either, thinking you'd have a go at teaching me yourself, three days a week, like Cassie Crowe, that crayon-stealer who'd managed – against the odds – to teach me to write. Goose wasn't happy, probably because education had never worked for her, and partly because she thought it'd be harder for her to unlearn the rubbish Kipper would fill my head with.

On the first day she not only walked with me to his house, but sat in the living room while Kipper fussed with books and pens and arranged the right chair by a window which had good enough light but not too much of a view. Goose flattened her skirt across her knees and gazed at her hands as if they were an old pair of gardening gloves she was thinking of chucking. She crossed one foot behind the other. An oddly formal pose. Indoor spaces made her nervous. She knocked out her pipe on the fireplace and Kipper turned his smoky gaze on her, smiling and saying get out in those creeks where you belong, mud-woman. Don't lissen to none of it, she said, on her way out. Then we watched her in the yard as she hauled open the smokehouse door and helped herself to a bloater, which she wrapped, still smoking, under her coat.

'Bloody woman,' Kipper said, his voice tight and not quite managing to be humorous. 'I'll tell you straight off,' he added, 'don't you let me down. There's plenty round here ready to string me up for stuff I have or haven't done. Shrimp ain't no use to no one, not you and not himself, so you're up to me now.' Laying down the law made him embarrassed. He picked a flint fossil off the mantelpiece, turned it over in his hands, placed it back, readjusted it to leave no sign of ever touching it. 'Well that's about it,' he said, running out of steam. Then he left.

Two books on the desk:, first, a hardbacked book with gold lettering down its spine: *The Scientific Adventurer*. An introduction that began:

If you have never seen potassium burning pure in a bowl of water, never watched droplets of mercury running into each other, never seen flowers of iron filings on a magnet's poles or grown alum crystals in a jam jar, then I, dear reader, envy you. I wish I could see these things for the first time once again. But our bags are packed and our guidebook is open. So let our adventure begin.

Kipper had underlined the last sentence with a sharp pencil. The second book was a blue-and-white paperback called *Myths and Legends of the Classical World*. I read about Neptune, banished from the land, dwelling in coral caves, stirring up storms, inhabiting a world of water and salt. That's you, Kipper Langore, that's you all right, living on a land you neither like nor trust. Caught in-between the elements in a little fishy puff of smoke.

I sat there, at the desk, in a room that had an evening feel whatever the time of day. Driftwood was piled around here and there, all of it salt-withered, the whole space feeling like it had been preserved, unnaturally, years ago. I felt like the cockchafer impaled on its pin in my father's study. The only disturbances were the flies that circled silently below the main light, moving in strangely straight lines, taking sudden corners as if they were bouncing off an air more solid than they were used to.

I thought of Gideon, whispering his sermon about losing the map in life. That we need a moral map to see our way through. That without it, we are lost. Of his thin fingers pointing to Psalms and Ecclesiastes with a slight tremble, his eyes watery with his message. He's so tormented by Norfolk's biblical landscapes and the saints he sees in them he draws himself into the barn where he imagines Lot's incest still continues. I read about Lot in Kipper's Bible. I read about Sodom's destruction, how Lot's wife had looked back and turned into a pillar of salt, how Abraham had seen the smoke of the country going up as the smoke of a furnace.

Salt in the ground. Smoke in the sky.

I thought of my mother's mysterious flower patterns in her garden, of Goose staring at clouds and determining her life and the lives of others. All of them – even Hands, studying the map of the North Sea so he could escape Norfolk, where had it got him? To the fishes. All of them – with God or without God, searching for the map which will see them through.

In all these stories, with all these predictions from clouds and maps and Bibles, where was my route through it all? *The Scientific Adventurer* had no answer. And the *Myths and Legends of the Classical World*? A secret here – I saw myself as Oedipus, even then, as I read the details of his story. Hadn't I, after all, been hung up by my ankles in my father's shed? We'll get the bugger back. Some day, my mother whispers as she bathes my swollen feet. Hadn't I faced choices at a place called Three Holes, run away from home to avoid my father? Hadn't my hand closed around switchblade razors in my pocket?

I spend the months in that room, reading his books and eating his fish. This strip of saltmarshes between the land and sea has become my home. It's a year since my mother died, and my trousers are beginning to look too short – there's no one to let the hem down any more. I sit there, at my desk, surrounded by Kipper's books, my trouser hem getting shorter and shorter as the months and then the years pass. I'm growing in that cocoon of his.

On a hot day just after my thirteenth birthday, I stumble out into the sunlight of a July afternoon. I remember the day because it's the same day a young woman wolf-whistles me as I pass Blakeney Quay. When she whistles again I see her hair like a sudden burst of flame. Elsie, leaning against a small hatchback car, sucking a lolly.

15

The Hansa

El-see, two syllables of a word I'd never managed to say. *El*, so easy, so effortless to put by *see*, as in *seal*, as in *sea*. But never achieved. Though I tried, out there among the dunes, invoking the thin, reedy voice to conjure the word . . . I'll tell the truth: I never dared to.

And here she is, on the edge of the quay, in the centre of things. In a baggy red velvet coat with soldier's buttons, though it's too hot for that. Bright long blancmange-pink leggings and wrists full of bangles that make a noise when she moves her arms. I couldn't keep her young for ever. I'm thirteen. She's twenty.

I sit in her hatchback car and it's full of sweet wrappers and has the smell of a long warm journey in it. She spins the wheels on the gravel and laughs too loudly at that. Behind us, the stones spit off the quay edge into the creek, but it doesn't matter because Elsie's driving me up the High Street and she's driving like a man, one hand holding the gear stick and the other turning the wheel. Always the tomboy. She smells of cigarettes and boiled sweets and she thinks all this is really funny. Her hair's shorter. It's thicker, less full of the multi-coloured strands I remembered. Life and its colours get tarnished.

'Want a photo?' she says, then she shouts *shit!* as we swerve past a parked car.

'Where to?' she asks when we reach the coast road. Where *is* there to go? The coast road's like a root growing along a wall.

★

All this seems at odds with the girl I'd been writing to over the last few years – the one frozen in aspic – how could I have written so enthusiastically about the marshes, Goose's cooking and evenings spent in the *Thistle Dew*? I'd written about Gideon crying at his own sermon, about the dirty patch of plaster behind Goose's dining chair where she's leaned her head over the years. The 1953 tidemark girdling the walls. The chimneypot that leans like on so many fenland homes. About how Bryn Pugh had begun to smell of the damp, cooped up in *Thistle Dew* carving that block of sea-wood into Ol' Norse. A man losing his spirit. And about Kipper with his salty skin – how when you shook his hand you wanted to down a glass of water – about his two-faced face and the smoke that rose from the burning oak chippings under the fish, which never went out . . . All those letters, but written to a different Elsie. Why *was* she here?

She drives the hatchback too fast down the track to Cley Beach Café, with geese flying into the air and walkers stepping back on to the verge as we pass and Elsie laughing at them through the window.

'I've got a summer job,' she says. 'Cook at the hotel, the Misfits. How's your grandma?'

Same. Mad. I write, though she's not interested in reading.

'Your uncle got me the job. When he was over seeing your dad – few weeks back – I mean, someone had to. Well, we sort of bumped into each other. Mum's in hospital – she's getting treatment, and Dad's just gone AWOL with the tulips. Tulip-land. Probably hasn't noticed I'm gone. You've grown,' she adds, staring closely at me, deliberately. I point at the café and try to open the car door and Elsie has to lean over me and pull the lock herself. 'Wimp,' she says.

Cley Beach Café is an oily wooden shack with small windows and a heavy door, built where Blakeney Point dovetails into

North Norfolk. Next to it, the River Glaven reaches within a hundred feet of the North Sea, before being forced west into six miles of meandering creeks and the open lagoon of the Pit and the sea beyond. Built to fend off sea breaks and winds where the air is as wet as seawater, it's usually empty, apart from red-faced walkers staring into mugs of hot chocolate in a state of stunned trance. In winter it's a steam-filled room with sticky benches, with the ducks sheltering outside from the winds with necks buried in their backs. A generator growls all year long, lighting a few weather-proof fairy bulbs, and keeping an urn of water constantly hot. It's a place famed for its puddings. Always hot, always sweet, always at the end of gruelling walks, the taste didn't really matter. And that's a bonus, because everything served tastes slightly salty. The wood's withered by it, the cutlery stained by it, the notices made rotten by it.

We both have rhubarb crumble. Mine's with custard. She has ice cream.

I've missed you, I write. *I've missed Three Holes and the Saints. But I never want to go back.*

'Nothing's changed,' she says, glancing up at me over her drink, sucking on her straw to emphasize her cheekbones.

Where will you stay?

'Hotel. I mean it's hardly a room.' She chases the last smears of crumble and licks them off her spoon, thoughtfully. 'Still not talking then?'

I shake my head and wonder whether she knows. How can she? It's hard to look her in the eye.

'Meet me tomorrow,' she says, then looks at me with a cool, smouldering gaze – the kind of look you practise – and gathers her hair on one side of her neck. 'Better get back, you know', she says, getting up, and I know she doesn't really have to go.

*

That evening in Lane End, over roast potatoes and two thin sausages, I explained where I'd been, about Elsie appearing at the quayside and about her car and how she'd said the rhubarb was 'tinned' in exactly the same voice Goose had used a few months before. Goose read what I'd written, all the while stroking her chin, and I noticed a few bristles were growing there. Her silence made me tense. Whass she after? she said at last, speaking to the space between us, as if I wasn't in the room. I shrugged, eager to respond, but not knowing what she meant or whether I was even being asked.

I waited for Elsie on the quay. The tide had turned, revealing a dark collar of seaweed along the wharf. My legs ached with standing still, but I missed Elsie throwing the door open – with such force I heard it bang – and I was sure she must have been sacked, already. She ran down the road clumsily, someone grown tall too quickly, then she walked on to the marsh, pretending not to see me. When I caught up with her she was tearing off an apron, which smelled of wet flour and butter.

'One thing they *don't* know about is hygiene!' she shouted, not realizing people always spoke quietly on a marsh. Unless they're on a boat. 'Who's that?' she said, pointing at the *Hansa* over the Pit, and I saw with dismay that Roger was already sitting on it. He was a local lad, quiet and dark-skinned, but no one really cared for him in the village. He'd been going out to the *Hansa* for months, and though initially I went on the wreck only when he wasn't there, we'd begun to sit there together, vying for the wheelhouse chair in the same way Lil' Mardler and the Langore brothers had once done.

'You expect me to strip off, huh?' she said cheekily, knowing we had to swim. I began to take off my shoes and socks. I didn't look at Elsie, at just how far she was stripping down, but went ahead into the Pit, feeling her eyes on my back for several long seconds, then hearing her wince when she stepped into the water. And I thought of Frieston Marsh, beyond the beet factory at King's Lynn, on a mud-walk with Elsie and my mother. How black our bare legs had been, how Elsie had complained about sharp edges of shells buried deep in the mud, how she'd complained about the cold when we'd crossed a creek, and how in short, she'd complained.

'I'm Elsie,' she said to Roger, dripping her way over the deck of the *Hansa* like she was bringing bad weather. He muttered an unconvincing *hiya*, and retreated behind the wheelhouse to set to work on some limpets with his penknife, giving me a cold glance as he did so. This was clearly our boat, and she was clearly a girl. Very clearly.

He didn't hang around. He walked off on to the Point and threw stones in a mud-pool. Elsie only seemed to notice him when he was way off in the distance, calling him stupid, which I agreed with as if I'd been dying to tell someone.

'Like all virgins,' she added.

This was how Elsie took over the boat. We spent most afternoons after her shift on the *Hansa*, sitting on the deck. Sometimes we'd eat a pint of shrimp. I ate shrimp like my uncle, copying how carefully he pulled the body from the head, wiped the spinal column clear, then snapped the tail to ease the skin and legs apart. A final sharp breath to blow the eggs from the belly. Elsie swallowed them whole, leaving only the head between her fingers, and sometimes she even swallowed the head too, actually enjoying the crunchy salt of the skin, and the more fishy taste of the eggs. Sometimes she'd suck the head clean. She claimed it was the best bit. She ate five to every one of mine, and then we'd swim, me chasing her legs underwater as they kicked into the gloom, my eyes stinging with salt.

And with a gentle bump the sandy bottom of the Pit brushes my chest and I begin to swim above its ridges, following patterns of sand that look like a giant fingerprint. Above me, the sunlight falls in ripples through the water. My ears are numb to the world, hearing only the occasional knock and thud of passing outboards. The hulls of moored boats pass like storm clouds above me. I see miniature crabs fleeing my shadow, their shells wet and papery. My hand reaches forward as if I'm stretching through glass, brushing the horned wrack as it clings to pebbles on the estuary bed.

Back on the *Hansa* I would watch Elsie pulling herself on to the wreck, glistening like a fish, her hair flattened across her head and down her face. I remember watching how her skin dried in patches that spread and joined down the length of her legs, as if a new skin was crawling over her. Like my mother as a young girl, sitting on the *Hansa* while she watched the two Langore brothers swimming across the Pit like a couple of pirates. A girl on the wheelhouse, two boys in the water. A girl sunbathing, knowing the boys are looking at her. Boys prising off limpets and chucking stones and scratching words into the wood.

Elsie flexed her ankles, making them click, and then she drew a finger across her forehead, pulling her damp hair to one side. There were dots of moisture on her eyelashes, a dusting of salt like a stain on her cheeks. She kept her eyes shut. Behind me, Roger was again throwing stones into the low-tide mud. Elsie's eyes remained shut, occasionally twitching under the lids, a little shine there, on her eyelids, where the skin was tight. Gradually I let my gaze drift from her face, down the line of her neck, to linger on her front. On the stretched smooth contours of a part of her I'd never dared to look at before, at shapes seemingly held in place purely by the weight of the wet cotton. On her breathing. And as she exhaled, a breeze seemed to stir across the warm wooden deck and with it two small points under her T-shirt began to rise, as if the air itself were lifting them.

The stones still fell into the mud with sickening regularity. I stared at the gunwale, at a carved guillemot, which seemed more monkey than bird, and mocking with it. At the distant marshes and the boats moored in the Pit. All of it drew me back to Elsie. Lying next to me, at the centre of it all.

Suddenly Elsie's dark, liquid eyes were looking at me, then looking through me.

'You wish,' she said, dismissively.

It turned out she hadn't been sacked from the Misfits, and as the weeks went by the menu had more and more of Elsie on it. And more of my mother too. Smoked eel and horseradish leaves, guinea fowl in plum sauce, bluit and fennel soup were all my mother's. There, under the leaves, my mother says, pointing to a clump of bluits in a pine wood. They look like dishrags. The young Elsie bends down, afraid to touch them. My mother giggles and pushes her own fingers under the mushrooms, lifting them gently. Musn't bruise them, she says, lowering them into the bag Elsie holds open for her. They walk off into the dappled sunlight, enjoying the quiet of the wood.

On the wreck, smelling the gulls' fishy sweet shit on the hot planks, we ate the meals my mother had once cooked; letting the tastes take me back across the years to a purer time, a time of my silence, my crayon drawings on the skirting boards, of her sad brown eyes looking at me with love and nothing but love in them.

It must have meant something to Elsie too, eating Auntie May's meals with me, dreaming of a time when we were all together. Sometimes she'd give me a long hard hug after we'd eaten. You stupid clod, she'd say, why am I so addicted to you? Then she'd push me off the deck and break the moment. Roger never got fed. He kept his distance or walked off through the dunes whacking the grasses with a stick. Sometimes, watching him sitting on a bank scowling back at me, I'd imagine he was some spectral reincarnation of my uncle, staring at his brother sitting on the *Hansa* with my mother. Looking at Shrimp with a sullen face, knowing that Lil' Mardler was captivated by his dreaming mind and his affinity with animals. My uncle in the dunes, knowing he'd lost the battle over the girl. Was this how it had been?

'Look, Pip! Who's that?' Elsie's suddenly sitting up on the deck, shielding her eyes from the sun. Across the Pit there's a man swimming in a line towards us. A no-nonsense front crawl I've heard about before. Kipper Langore, acting the kid, coming out to the *Hansa* like he did over twenty years ago. When he gets close he yells at Elsie to drop the anchor and I see Elsie stroking her hair back and I know in that gesture she knew damn well Kipper was going to come out here. She's invited him. Invited him to our wreck. I look down at him and he sticks a cold wet hand up at me – help me up then – and I have to grab him, his bony long-fingered hand, and haul him on to the wreck and there he is, suddenly large and standing right in the middle of the deck. The whole world is his. Elsie leans back on her arms and stares at the sky. You drip on me there'll be hell to pay, she says, cheekily, and he immediately threatens to do so, their game comfortably bypassing me. Small streams of water are draining off his hard thin body, joining up with each other root-like down his legs, giving him a shifting, tricky look. His hair is slick and dark across his head; I notice he's letting it grow a little longer – distancing himself from the crew-cuts of the twins and the grown-out barber's cut of my father. He's a sly one all right, standing there with his feet planted widely on the planks.

'So, what you two been up to?' he says, a gossipy tone I'm not used to in his voice.

'Not been watching us through the binoculars?' Elsie replies, content to carry on in her mischievous vein. She's taking him on, and both of them are enjoying it.

Kipper's undeterred. 'Han't been here for twenty years or more,' he says, looking around him proprietorily, and Elsie's straight back with well, that's a great fat lie. How does she know that, I think?

Kipper sits down and begins to tie an elaborate knot in a length of rope he's brought with him. He grins while he's doing it, knowing he's impressing Elsie, and I wonder whether he's seeing her or whether he's remembering Lil' Mardler, sitting in the same place, all those years ago. He ties five knots together and makes a crab out of them, then throws it to me in a casual, offhanded gesture, as though he's throwing me scraps.

'Leave you to it,' he says, suddenly getting up, quitting while he's ahead.

After that I was less keen to be on the *Hansa*. It was too visible and being there made Elsie behave that way. We started to walk on the Point, losing ourselves in its dry centre of mudflats, grasses and hot silent dunes. There, barefoot on the dream-scape of sand – so warm in the sun and cold in its shadow – I lay down while she poured fine white sand over my legs to see if she could build riges along them. She tutted when I moved and threatened to tickle my feet. There were rumours about us in Blakeney. I knew there were rumours. I saw it in the way the older lads looked at me, because they'd never looked at me before.

I wish I didn't have to mention the piece of paper I have, to this day, which still has a few last grains of white sand in it. The sand is there because I folded it, that day in the dunes, after I had written *I love you* on it. I remember watching a honeybee, filling the air with its soft buzz, brushing the grasses and bending them with its weight. Elsie's body went tense when the bee landed on her hair, then she let it fly off. She spied the paper in my hand and demanded to read it. Reluctantly I gave it to her. She unfolded it and looked at it, knotting her brows to give it extra importance. Then she smiled and said she loved me too, and she always had. But I knew it wasn't the same kind of love, and I wished I hadn't written it.

I have that piece of paper with me now because she gave it back.

And yet if she hadn't would it all have been different? Was this the moment where it all changed for ever – yes – I see the paper coming back to me, my words folded quietly inside it, and I remember the moment I took the paper and the sound of my terrible thin voice as it said her name. *El* and *sie*. Then louder, my *Elsie, Elsie*. And the look on her face – how her skin managed to redden and go white in the same instant, the tiny freckles which seemed to grow more defined like they were being stranded by a receding tide. And I saw clouds in her face too, the clouds which have blown above and through my family's lives over the years as she tried to work out what was going on. I was speaking to her, and she put her hands on her ears as if she was a little girl again who doesn't want to know.

Eventually she took her hands away and I shut up.

'You . . . little . . . shit!' she said, then said *shit!* again. Then, with a touch of wonder, she said *shit!* once more, as if that's all she could or wanted to say. 'Since when?'

It was one thing to be able to speak, but I'd never thought that it would be so strange to be listened to. This was a whole new world and I felt I'd made a great mistake.

'Please, Elsie.'

That night I couldn't sleep, like on so many nights after it all blew up, after the three deaths, after the smoke which had begun in Kipper's smokehouse had spread into all our lives. I lay in my bed listening to Goose's snore on the other side of the room, staring through the window, as Hands had done so many years before me, contemplating the awesome dark shadow of the marsh and the glitter of moonlight on the high water of the Pit. I was haunted by the walk back through the dunes I'd had with Elsie. Kept returning to it in my thoughts. Our feet in the cold sand and a frightening chill between us.

There'd been a full moon that night, and drifting across the sky was a series of flat, evenly shaped white clouds, dimly illuminated. They looked like sheets being hung out, being pulled along clotheslines to drip-dry over the marsh.

Kipper had converted a room next to the smokehouse chimney into a laboratory of sorts, lined with shelves of powders, chemicals, mixing bowls, glassware, piping and boxes of fuses. People knew he made fireworks in his Lab and they thought he was crazy to make them next to the smokehouse. But Kipper knew it kept prying eyes away, which made sense for him, and besides, the chemicals and card would never get damp.

Where my father's study had been a dark place, smelling of

tobacco, books, drying leaves and, increasingly, of his failure against the elm disease, the Lab had the bright sharp smell of acids and powders.

Kipper is placing five such bottles in front of me, all with different-coloured lids.

'Simple rule. Acid's red, alkaline's blue, brighter the colour, worse it gets. Only one colour open at any time. Ever open green make sure nothing else is open, apart from that window there. Same with black. White lids the only things you can touch with bare fingers, apart from that tin, which is full of biscuits. Here's your tea. But don't worry 'cause you're never going to be in here when I ain't.'

He cuts some thick card tubing, about three inches. Moves chemicals off the shelves.

'Always back where they come from.' He spoons two powders into a mortar, places the card tube on the counter, bungs it, lets me pour the granules in.

'Seen a lot of Elsie, haven't you?' he says casually. 'Out on the wreck.' The Lab had a row of windows facing north over the marsh, and across the Pit the *Hansa* floated like a mirage. There was a pair of binoculars on the windowsill.

'Does she eat the limpets?'

No, I wrote, *says they taste of rust*.

'You eat them?'

Roger does.

'Get the runs he ain't careful,' he says, which makes me smile because Roger always stood with his legs crossed and sometimes he disappeared into the dunes for no reason at all.

'Pack all that stuff down now,' he says.

I push the powder into the tube and press it in with a finger.

'Real live wire, ain't she?' he says, forcing the subject. 'Lot of lads got the hots for her down the Albatross.'

I keep packing the powder.

'When you've done with this rocket, you can give it to her if you like. What's her favourite colour?'

Red? I write.

'Course,' he says, reaching for some grey pellets. 'Strontium salts, like autumn leaves. Best mix this with a touch of blue, you'll see. Lot like painting, this.' And he pours in more pellets then lets me stir them with a glass rod.

'Copper sulphate – not too much, mind –'cause it's a hot-head, that one.'

Sunday was hot and airless, and then unexpectedly a sea-fret rolled in. The whole marsh went white and cold and damp and the air halved in temperature. Goose and I walked through it to Blakeney where a group of visitors in shorts were complaining about the weather, then beyond to Kipper's smoke-house. In the fog we smelled the familiar whiff of fish before we saw it, and after that the smell of roasting lamb, thyme, onions and garlic. Goose looked severe. In the kitchen it was obvious she was out to corner Elsie. Her nose went in the oven and her finger went in the gravy. She prodded the potatoes on the tray and pressed the lamb with the flat of her knife to see the juice. And she was silent. Big praise. It took a lot to take the wind from the old girl's sails. Kipper was in an odd mood. Since before the meal he'd been fussing around laying the long table in the dining room, and I thought his shoes had been polished. When he'd finally sat down, I saw him biting his nails, which was a thing I'd never seen him do before.

The twins were the last to arrive, not exactly over the moon coming to their employer's on a day off. They stood awkwardly in the study talking about rabbit traps they'd laid up in the oak copse. They looked too big for the room, standing below the light, bony-faced and heavy-limbed. The kind of lads who wear rough jackets and don't feel the cold, even in crew-cuts. We'll have rabbit next week, Elsie, they joked. And during the meal they kept asking for more because it made Elsie laugh every time they did, and when she cut more meat they grinned at something they'd clearly said to each other earlier. Outside, the fog glowed brightly through the windows, lighting the room with a harsh cold light as if fresh snow had fallen. A distinct light, which had once cast itself over my mother, sitting by the window during the winter before she'd died, sitting by the kitchen table quietly cupping her tea while the snow fell. Knowing her time had come.

My uncle drank a lot of wine and kept filling Elsie's glass too. She drank it enthusiastically and grew boisterous, implying the twins would get fat and then their cuddy would start to take on water. Both twins shifted in their seats to pull their stomachs in – that's how I remember them best, doing things in unison, facing things blindly, reacting on instinct. Both had kept their jackets on. Looking back, I think I knew then that the twins would die together, and that I'd be there to witness it. How *is* that cuddy anyhow? my uncle says, trying to own the conversation. Comin' on, Cliff says, comin' on. Kipper lays his grey hands on the table palm down and begins to tell of an occasion when he was delivering to the hotel in Cley.

'I come across this impromptu meeting in the lounge bar. Mickey Webb's there, two of the coastguards, some bloke from Sheringham. I'm putting these trays of bloater pâté out the back and all I hear is them talking about you two and that boat of yours – *ain't seaworthy*, they says, then one of the coastguards looks down at his pint and says *I'm buggered if I'll go out to pick 'em up when the time come – they ain't got no right building a boat out of the wrecks of other boats – that ain't right*, and this guy from Sheringham says he'll get the council on to it and Mickey says *they ain't got no power.*'

Elsie's cheeks were becoming flushed and she wasn't quite following the story. She said too loudly *you'll get me drunk!* when her glass was filled, and then she cried out *get me drunk!* when it was empty again.

'You tell 'em, Kipper!' she yelled.

'What?'

'Calm down, gal,' Goose said.

'Here, Elsie,' my uncle interrupted, trying to control an unpredictable mood, 'take your apron off.'

'Why?'

'I've got a present for you.'

'What about the story?'

'What about the present?'

'What's it for?'

'For nothing.'

'Keep it.'

And I saw Kipper felt trapped. Caught somewhere between wanting to act young, and knowing he wasn't. It made his hand stay on the packet he'd placed on the table. His hand remained there and I knew he didn't know what to do. Surely you only act like that when you've either got a lot to lose or something to hide? So what was at stake, with his polished shoes and his ironed twill shirt and his bitten fingernails?

Eventually he slid the packet to her. Goose lit her pipe, deliberately puffing dry-lipped to make the embers glow, making a small sucking noise which only made the room seem quieter, and increasingly filling the air with smoke as if she wanted to fog the details of what might be going on.

Elsie made the right noises when she found two silver seashell earrings in the box. For all the hard work, Kipper said, embarrassed they were too expensive for such a casual present. Lucky lass, Goose said, her eyes glinting with a metal darkness. Elsie made Kipper fix the earrings, pulling back her hair and lengthening the side of her neck. Sorry, ain't good at this, he said after a while, his own neck reddening with the effort of it. Both twins looked on, staring at the bare skin of her neck and enjoying Kipper's unease.

'Done it,' Kipper said.

'That you have,' Cliff said. 'You certainly have.'

'Kipper Langore,' Goose said, 'I should a sorted you out years ago.'

Kipper took that well, his position at the party restored somewhat. He slid his chair back and leaned back with it, his chair, his house. That feel good it do, it really do.

Goose walked a few paces behind me, deliberately, on the way back to Morston. She stopped several times on the path, twisting hawthorn twigs off the hedge and pushing them into her hair in a thoughtful manner. When we reached Lane End she said she should go back to that fen, as if that's all there was to say. She sat on her bed and pushed her boots off with the end of her walking stick. Be with her father, poor soul's lost his marbles. I don't trust her and I don't want her round hair.

But I did. I wanted her on the *Hansa*, on the marsh, in her car, anywhere, just to be close. And when she was press-ganged at short notice into doing the yearly open-air theatre show at the Misfits, I gladly signed up too. The troupe's leader was a bony square-shouldered young man called Lloyd, who infected everyone with boundless enthusiasm, loved to laugh and loved to muck in, often treading on toes because he spoke faster than he thought, and often literally treading on toes because he was amazingly clumsy. He drank from a mug with a broken handle, as if to remind himself to be more careful. Guiding this force of nature was his girlfriend, a pale, observant hippy from Norwich called Kat. She made thin roll-ups and seemed to move only as a last resort, and when she did it was with a sleepy long-armed grace, stretching or rotating her joints. She had a piece of driftwood hanging round her neck, like I hung my notebook.

'Awake the pert and nimble spirit of mirth!' Lloyd projected to a hall rather bigger than the Village Hall he was in, his band a reluctant group of waitresses stiff with embarrassment, myself, Roger with crossed arms and a creased brow, Elsie and the hotel's car-park attendant, all of us there because we had to be. 'Anyone read *Midsummer Night's Dream*, then?' he continued with a grin too wide for his face, knowing he'd win us over, and win us over he did.

When it came to the performance, which also marked the end of the summer season, the hotel's walled garden was decked with fairy lights. A small stage had been erected and the pond fenced off. Elsie was dressed in a thin cotton dress she'd made from a sheet with a wreath of laurel, pansies, sweet peas and lavender as a crown. She looked tall and beautiful and mysterious and she was loving being a queen, even backstage. Kat was trying to pull my donkey's head over my own, and kept getting annoyed when I looked towards Elsie. Dumb ass, she whispered, affectionately, and pinched my arm to make me concentrate. Lloyd was drinking brandy from a bottle and doing a tongue-twister, and then, almost as if he'd walked the wrong way, he was unexpectedly on stage, addressing the audience, and the play had started. He on one side, and Kat on the other, taking turns to narrate the action, telling people to imagine the fragrant garden, the foolish players, the mischievous fairies.

And then, dressed in my donkey's head, I was on stage looking through papier-mâché eyeholes at Elsie lying asleep. Lloyd began to sing . . .

> '*The ousel cock, so black of hue,*
> *With orange-tawny bill,*
> *The throstle with his note so true,*
> *The wren with little quill.*'

. . . and Titania was awakening, only it clearly wasn't Titania but Elsie, my Elsie, with her bright red hair and her fawn-like face, gazing into my donkey eyes while a voice off stage, which must have been Kat's, said, 'On the first view, to say, to swear, I love thee.' *I love thee.* And Elsie was guiding me across the grass and I was following her in a dream.

'Lead him to my bower.'

We sat on a seat made of dried flowers and lavender, and Elsie pulled me sleepily to her side. She put her hair across my chest and lay her head on my belly, and as she yawned and fell asleep Kat whispered:

> '*So doth the woodbine the sweet honeysuckle*
> *Gently entwist; the female ivy so*
> *Enrings the barky fingers of the elm.*
> *O! How I love thee; how I dote on thee!*'

After the show the troupe went to the Albatross and some-one bought me a pint. It was the first time I'd sat at the bar. I stared at the space above it where Arthur Quail's map of the North Sea had once hung and thought of the story of Hands winning it in poker and then walking back to Goose's cottage with it rolled up under his arm. Of the Dogger Bank joke he'd pulled on my grandmother, and of Lil' Mardler, my mother, finding it years later.

The beer tasted of soap, and nearly at the bottom I noticed Elsie wasn't around.

When Lloyd and Kat tried to get the whole bar singing a

round, I slipped out, walking up the quiet road back to the hotel, still dressed in my donkey's costume, though I held the head under my arm.

The walled garden was empty and the hotel's sheets had all been hung out to dry. White sheets against the night's sky: the clouds I'd seen blowing across the marsh. So this was it.

I sensed a movement. Then a splash. Someone was in the large pond, lying on their back in the water, staring up at the sky. It was Elsie. I crept closer and quickly realized her clothes were lying next to the edge where she'd taken them off. I didn't know what to do. Elsie was there and she was stark naked, curved like a tusk of ivory against the dark water. She saw me, or I thought she saw me, because she twisted quickly, splashing like a fish as she grabbed for the side. Her head ducked below the brick edge, then all of a sudden she vaulted from the water, running dripping from the pool, not towards her clothes but towards the sheets.

Then everything went quiet – had she seen me? Had she seen it was me? I stood by the pond and looked at her clothes. At the absolute nothingness of her costume, so flat and lifeless without Elsie. At the smudged outline her toes had worn in the leather of her sandals.

She was hiding somewhere between the washing lines. I followed her wet footprints along the brick path, and towards the end of the row I saw a deep indistinct shadow through one of the sheets. A breeze filled the material and Elsie's silhouette moved with it, defining itself, then softly drifting away. I heard her breathing, and saw the shape of her hair as she turned, looking down the rows for me. Gradually I moved the sheet forward till the shadow of her became slender and dark. Swiftly the material went taut along the line of her thigh. The sheet stuck wetly to her skin, wrapping her leg as she turned. Then suddenly the shape of her other leg appeared, like the limb of a tree. She stayed like this for a while, with the cotton sticking to her legs and the points of her fingers pressing into the material in front of me. A game developing. Then her fingers curled into the palm of her hand, and slowly she took a step into the material, so that it stuck to the flat of her belly and the curves of her breasts. She pushed her face and hair even further into the fabric until they made their own relief, and as she did so, I pushed the sheet in between her breasts and felt their weight moving towards my fingers and my hand was trembling but I kept it there and then I lifted my other hand so I could touch her . . .

What I remember next was the clothes pegs flying off the line as she ripped the sheet down, and there she was, staring defiantly, outrage and challenge in her eyes, holding the sheet against her like a matador.

'The fuck are you doing?' she said, angrily emphasizing each word. Her mouth shivered with a cold raw sneer. I stood, deflated, still dressed as a donkey, while she burned her gaze at me. Then, quite unexpectedly, she raised her hand and lifted my chin. The sneer was gone, the anger abating. 'I'm sorry, Pip, you're lovely and you're just a boy,' she said. 'Keep away from me.'

And then she was gone, walking across the grass wrapped up in her sheet, a blur of white against dark bushes, like the ghost of my mother, sleepwalking, never finding peace, finding me and holding me and then vanishing like vapour.

So there I was, a donkey, ridiculed and being ridiculous, because that's all a donkey can be. A stubborn mute ass who would never fit in.

As I walked away from the washing lines I imagined I saw smoke, and I began to blink because my eyes were smarting. Then I smelled it. Not the greasy, fishy smoke of my uncle's smokehouse, but the fragrant warmth of his pipe, and on the ground among the shadows its knocked-out embers, still glowing.

16

Four Gotes, Three Holes

The bus seats had a herringbone pattern in the fabric and it unnerved me. It reminded me of the herringbone brickwork on my uncle's smokehouse and the herringbone stitch I'd once glimpsed running along the hem of Elsie's bra in the shadows of her armpit. That was in her bedroom in the house at Three Holes, and that was where the bus was taking me. It was February, six months after the night at the Misfits. Elsie had gone back to her parents in November and I'd heard nothing from her until her postcard in January.

Through the autumn and early winter I'd continued going to Kipper's smoky living room, sitting at the desk by the window, but he'd lost interest in my studies. Instead of planning lessons he'd spend most of his time in his Lab, preparing the rockets and bombs for Nor' Sea Night. Soon I began to miss the small things he used to do, such as leaving fossil sea urchins or belemnites for me on my desk. We'd eat silent lunches of pork pie and chutney, roe on toast or rollmops and brown bread cut into triangles. And in the afternoon I'd help the twins stack the smokehouse, threading herring on the bars, from mouth to gill, mouth to gill, and because I was the smallest, I had the task of crawling round the back of the smoking racks to drag the oak chips forward, hearing my uncle and the muted clink of glass bottles on the other side of the warm brick wall. Back in his study and smelling of smoke I'd flick through the bookshelves, waiting for the time to go home, noticing unfamiliar changes to his house: a bunch of flowers in a vase on the mantelpiece; a newly washed tablecloth; a tidied boot-rack by the marsh door to stop mud getting in. A woman's touch. And I knew it was Elsie. Spending more and more time here, in the evenings when I wasn't around, cooking meals and drinking red wine, listening to Kipper's stories and the jokes he pulled, winding her hair around a finger near her temple while he talked. A little hiccup. A giggle. An apology. And then some of her capriciousness – an uncalled-for comment – a cruel piss-take, and now it would be my uncle laughing. Fen girl – you're a wild cat all right.

I'd always steeled myself for the time I might see her climbing astride a motorbike and putting her arms round some local lad. Holding him tight as he gunned the throttle around Blakeney. But spending evenings with my uncle was much, much worse. The poor squit, saw me in the pond, thought he'd try it on. Kipper, roaring with laughter and gaining capital from going over the story again. Don't! Don't! Holding his sides. Dirty little sod, feeling me up. Touching me . . . Right here. And she points to the place. She pushes her chest out and points to the place. And do you know he can speak? He's a dark horse that 'un. Been stringing us along all this time.

I saw her only once in that time, and that was through the bonfire's flames on Nor' Sea Night. Her hair impossibly bright. But an inscrutable expression, filled with shadows and secrets. She came to me and led me on to the marsh, pressed her forehead into my neck and I felt the fire's warmth on her skin, the coldness of the marsh on her back.

'Come and visit me,' she said.

'Where?' I said, with difficulty.

'That's so good. So good to hear you. I'm going back to Three Holes. Season's over.'

'El-sie, I miss you.'

'Me too. Look, just don't balls it all up, all right?'

And with that she'd gone, walking first back to the fire and then vanishing beyond, along the roads of dark Norfolk to the greater darkness of the Lincolnshire Fen, in winter, just about the darkest place there is. At the end of January she sent me a postcard: *My mum has died. They found her face down in the tulip beds. Please come as soon as you can. I'm not staying here a second longer than I have to.*

So there I was unexpectedly sitting on the coach to King's Lynn, staring at the herringbone pattern, holding her card in my hand. Through the windows the buildings looked damp with winter, stained like sugar cubes in fields the colour of wet tea leaves. A journey of Norfolk's softness giving way to ever-growing geometry. Power lines and poplars, drainage dykes and roads, all pulled taut over the soil, unimpeded by the earth below till all was flat.

Tydd St Giles, Tydd St Mary, Tydd Gote, Four Gotes. That's where I got off the bus on my first stop, and the first thing I noticed was an overwhelming smell of chickens. By the thousand. A sweet dusty smell of their sweat and shit and bran. An address in my pocket in my uncle's handwriting. The name of a farm, which I could also see hanging from a signpost down the road: FOUR GOTES EGGS. A ragged hedge, and through it I saw the farm opening up into row upon row of chicken coops laid out across a dull earth field. Three sets of power lines stretched in parallel over the soil, and the electricity made a soft wide buzzing sound in the drizzle. There were two or three hundred of the coops, and one man, more scarecrow than I'd ever seen him, but him all the same. My father. The way he chose to lean when he didn't need to, the way he bustled across the mud as if avoiding low branches. He was slamming the lid down on a coop and picking his way between the feeders with the action of someone grown used to pushing his way through chickens. He lifted another lid and let it fall, a second later I heard the sound, then he was jotting something on a clipboard and when he slotted his pencil under the clip he looked up, bang on cue, and gave me a wave, taking the cap off his head like he was on a harbour quay.

Until then I'd thought this would be a surprise visit. Those Langore brothers were still thick as thieves.

The sound of the pylons grew louder above us and we met by a chain-link gate, which clicked with an electric current, and when he let me in he took his cap off again, a polite gesture. He was close to me, holding the cap in front of him, looking at the ground and asking how I was, how Goose was, had the journey been all right.

'You came, then,' he said, abruptly. I looked around at the large bleak field, at the bright clumps of bronze hens making their way back to the coops, at the aluminium feeders the colour of elephant skin and the chain-link fence, dotted with feathers.

'Not bad this. Pays quite well.'

He'd aged. His donkey jacket was torn at the pockets and his boots had a sandblasted look where the chickens had pecked through to the toecaps.

We leaned against a coop and I wrote down that I wanted to see Mum's grave and his new bungalow and the dog. Underneath us the hens stirred and clawed their way round the nesting boxes.

I wrote down *Elsie, her mother's died* and he bent towards the notebook and took a drawn-out breath.

'Yeah, Elsie,' he said, biting his lip thoughtfully. 'You going there?' he added, brightly, and when I nodded he said, 'Well, you know, send her all the best and that.'

He stiffened next to me as he looked towards the horizon.

The sail of a boat was gliding through what seemed to be a ploughed field. River Nene, he said. A tall line of poplars sliced diagonally across the view, and halfway along their row the trees had grown shorter where the soil wasn't so good. I remembered him standing by the burning coop at the farm. How the dead chicken had hung from his hand while the Rhode Island hen had burst burning from its hiding place. And my father's boot as he stamped it dead with a farmer's strength and forthrightness which was all but gone now. His spirit now stamped out of him by monotonous, bleak, hard work. The man who'd quelled the nature of bulls with a whisper. Now nothing more than a pair of boots half-pecked apart.

'Vicious,' he said, catching me looking at his feet. 'Still, pays the bills.'

I wasn't sure what I was doing there; and then he was walking off again, looking round, distracted, used only to hens interrupting his train of thought.

His bungalow was built where no one else would live, under the convergence of two power lines. They fizzed angrily above us as we went deliberately to the back door – as a farmer always does, even when he no longer lives on a farm. Inside, it also smelled of chickens, like fermented beer, hot and enclosed, the smell of a coop. And there was a smell I remember from the Saints – the smell of dampness and wood and the Pears soap that he scrubbed his face with in the morning, and the smell of him in the middle of it all, an ageing man with unwashed clothes and no inclination to open windows. Neglect. Chicken shit was on the patio and on the windowsills outside. The bungalow felt besieged. He didn't take his boots off. Washing-up was piled in the sink, soaking in cold water, the remnants of several meals bleeding into a grease-spotted tideline round the stainless steel. Tins were left open on the side next to crusts of bread and packets of biscuits. With me there he seemed to see the mess of it for the first time. He went to the sink and his shoulders dipped at the sight of it and then his hand rubbed the back of his neck where it was permanently tanned from outside work and his skin had a cracked, sparsely haired look like the skin of a pig. His fingers played with a mole there, a thing I remember him doing when he was studying the elm disease in his study, and he stared at something in the sink for a long time then he turned back to me and we both sat at the table. It was the table from the Saints, the burned ring from the base of a casserole pot my mother had put down on it five years ago still there. Chicken casserole, with tarragon and cider.

No sooner had he sat down than he was up again, saying there was interesting birdlife here – when swans come landing at Welney Marsh you see them flying over several hundred a time. A flight path, that's what it is – they follow the Nene, I reckon. Whooper and Bewick's – sun's on them up there even though it's just gone dark. He opened a packet of Swiss roll and cut several thick slices and put them on a plate. There was a picture of the Alps on the label and it looked odd, so green and snow-capped with a bright blue sky, there, on the table in the middle of the Fens. He didn't like chocolate, as I remember, but he ate the roll.

He made tea and the pot had a top from a different pot on it and he poured mine in a cup and saucer and his in a mug that said Wingate's Agri Seeds on it. I still make a good cup of tea, he said, the faint sound of an old boast in his voice, reviving his spirits. Secret's to scald the pot, most people don't have time for that now. You've got to have time for tea, that's what I say.

Something moved in the room I guessed to be his bedroom and through the doorway I saw Gull, as old as the hills, lying on a blanket. The blanket was so full of the old dog's hair it seemed he was lying on a second skin, the pelt of his own vanished life at the farm. Hates the hens, my father said, looking at the dog. Can't stand them, and Gull gave a single, lazy thump of his tail because he knew he was being talked about. I showed him some sketches I'd drawn of the marsh and one of the *Hansa*, which I gave to him. He told me about the days he'd spent on the wreck with the brother who'd just renamed himself as Kipper, and how they'd been scared at first of the young girl who called the shots. She were a right miss, that's true, used to sit in the wheelhouse with her feet up. He smiled when he told me about all that, and when I wrote down a question about him and his understanding of birds and animals he looked at the notebook eagerly and said yeah, that's something I just can't explain. Always had this way with animals, 'specially birds. Some way I've got of looking them in the eye, make them friendly. There was this time with a gull, 'spect you know the story, that's why I called that old pile of bones through there Gull. This gull lands out of nowhere and it gets all caught up in your mother's hair. She was right scared. He ain't a bad dog, he added, for some reason. We sat in silence for a while. Our tea was finished. Then he said mind you, hens are different, ain't got no way with them, that's for sure.

Outside the pylons spat with sudden loudness as a heavier rain fell, and as I looked up I couldn't even see the wires that had seemed to stretch in such a sinister embrace above the bungalow. He led me into the chicken enclosure and before I went he lifted the lid of a coop and pulled out three warm eggs. He gave them to me, pretending it was a great crime, hiding them with his cap as he dropped them carefully into my pocket, even though it was dusk and no one was watching anyway. Don't tell no one, he said, and then made a noise deep in his throat which sounded like an apology.

I left him there, watching him getting wet while he settled them for the night, halfway through a routine I'd interrupted, a routine which had such a definite start and finish his attention had never entirely been away from it. The coach growled its way into the village and as it approached I watched him a little longer through the hedge. Turning this way and that, ticking boxes on his clipboard. Imprisoned by chicken wire, almost half-bird himself.

Sitting down in the coach after a day of little other than sitting down made me weary. The landscape was entirely flat, but the old bus lumbered and growled its way through the gears, its dark oily engine full of sand. I thought of the life my parents had made for themselves here, of my mother and father driving back from the Quaker hospital – the road too long and too straight for the couple they'd become. The skies all round deepened, stained by the fields beneath them. Gathering, ominous clouds like the storm at Bedlam Fen. A small boat in a vast landscape. Three people in the boat, so unbearably fragile, the whole lot of it.

A couple of large fenland women had hauled themselves into the bus at a village stop and their clothes gave off a damp vegetable odour. I rubbed the window with my elbow, then made the cleared patch into the shape of a neat picture frame, and through the smeared glass I saw the darkening furrows of fields spreading into dusk, the monstrous shapes of root vegetables hidden deep in the earth, buildings collapsing into the fen, then a glimpse of my father, standing by his bungalow in the cruciform shape of a wretched scarecrow, and finally, my mother sinking into the weeded depth of a passing drain, holding her breath and pinching her nose.

I shut my eyes and listened to the women's thick brown accents. Sumbody made rite muck o' that job – called it off till Sat-day – thass right? – says 'e won't cum no more – bess get Tommy down fix it – jokin'! That lazy bugger! – still got that van though. Their talking gave off the iron smell of strong tea, so similar to the rooty smell of the fields and the tobacco odour of the bus seats; their words, their breath, the laboured progress of the bus and its dying engine, all part of the same.

The sign for Three Holes was flashing past the window, and the driver was grinding the bus through the gears while he watched me in his mirror. He left me at the stop and drove off into the envelope of fenland night. No one was about. People were inside their houses, in their living rooms, with heavy-curtained windows, protecting the preciousness of their own individual pockets of light from an overwhelming darkness.

I went to the bridges at the confluence of the three drainage dykes and as I stared down at the water I remembered my mother saying can you see the three holes? The three holes here? Now, some say there's a fourth hole, a secret channel, a secret river going deep into the earth. Where do you think it is? A child's game. And now nothing, nothing but three miserable water channels stretching into the night like the points of a compass. But a compass without direction because it pointed to nowhere. We used to stand on that bridge and love the three holes, at their ability to take you instantly to three different horizons, but there, that lonely night, I felt the drains were not so much leading me away as holding me at their empty junction point.

As I walked off the road, on to the soft mud path, I saw the landscape was glowing with a cold, bone-like greyness. The blank fen had the vertiginous, expansive feel of a desert, with lights dotted in the distance like cattle's eyes caught in headlights. By my side was the dark oily water of the drain and, soon, the black brick shape of Elsie's house, with its rows of tulip beds lit by light spilling from the windows.

A simple gate and a path to the door. And a long time ago, my father and mother, carrying the sleeping Elsie along that same garden path, and the front door opening and there had been Ethel Holbeach, pretending she hadn't been looking out for their return. The same front door opening now, warm interior light flooding out into a vast winter landscape, but it's not kindly Mrs Holbeach with her flushed face this time; it's Elsie. Elsie, who had also been looking out, this time for me. Elsie framed in the glorious soft light of the hall, dark-eyed, her hair wound up tight behind her head.

'Hello Elsie,' I said.

'Hi. I'm so glad you're here. How was the old man?'

'Pecked.'

I hadn't been inside their house for years, but little had changed. And no sign to show Mrs Holbeach had died just a couple of weeks ago. The same photographs, awards and tulip paintings on the walls in rows as neat as the real ones outside. China cups on the dresser like I remembered. A full set of fine bone china, but a feeling that there'd never be guests to use them. The smell of beeswax and ironing. The trappings of a life carrying on regardless. As if Mrs Holbeach had popped out for shopping and never returned, and that that didn't really matter because the chores of the house had somehow continued without her.

Elsie was wearing a pair of faded blue dungarees and her father's tartan slippers. She had made cakes and, unsure about what she was to do with me, sat me straight down at the table. Through the back I could see Mr Holbeach at the scullery sink, running cold water over a shiny galvanized bucket. He lay it on its side, checked the back-door lock, picked up the bucket and began to rinse it again.

'Does he . . . know I'm here?' I said, my voice bringing out a smile in Elsie which crinkled the sides of her nose. She shrugged nicely.

'I doubt he'd be interested. Not my father, anyway.'

'Why?'

'He talks to himself in the tulip beds. Says God'll punish him for not having children.'

'He's . . . ill,' I said.

'It's these fucking fens, more like. Like Auntie May,' Elsie said, then flashed an apologetic smile at me. 'I mean, she didn't really talk any more, did she? Towards the end.' She looked at her father. 'And I don't care about him,' she said, loudly, pushing bits of cake round her plate with the flat of her knife.

'Ill, Elsie. That's all.'

'Pip,' she said, softly, 'we've both lost mothers now.'

I tried to brighten things by telling her where I'd been, and when the words came too slowly I wrote them down. How I'd found my father in a field of chickens and how he'd become so used to chickens that his concentration had been shot to pieces.

'I went to see him,' she said. 'He gave me some eggs. It's really sad, he used to be a funny man.'

Funny? I thought. I'd never seen him that way.

I showed her the eggs he'd given me too.

In the scullery, Mr Holbeach checked the back-door lock again.

I slept on the couch in the living room, listening to the coots on the drain outside and Elsie in her room upstairs. I thought I'd stay up all night, listening to the sounds and silences of a strange house, three people and a thousand prize tulips tucked up in beds. But a stealthy exhaustion overtook me, and I drifted into its warmth and heaviness and felt I was on the edge of knowing something, feeling some shape that was just there, just beyond reach, a shape that had shadows and angles, which had been there all along. Travel had clarified it for me, and as I searched for it I was abruptly awake, some time in the middle of the night, lifting my head from the cushion and seeing Mr Holbeach sitting in the chair opposite me.

'You're the one caused all the trouble, ain't you?' he said in his sad, church-pew voice.

I lay there, looking at him, too tired to reach for my notebook, too uncertain to move, till I fell asleep again. In the morning he was gone.

We ate those eggs for breakfast and then Elsie and I cycled to the Saints and along by the Great Ouse to Wiggenhall St Peter Church. Elsie sat on the floodbank, plaiting grasses, while I went to see my mother's grave. Since the funeral a tombstone had been set. It said 'A Loving Wife and Mother' below her name, chosen by my father from a book of sample inscriptions. May Langore. At least he'd finally used your real name.

I remembered how her coffin had looked in the aisle. How terrified I'd been that at any moment it might start dripping river water.

Elsie walked off down the bank and I put my hand on the earth and in my strange, scratchy voice I said hello. The word felt huge. And after that it was easier. Easier to let the words come out, dropping them on to my mother's grave alongside a couple of tears as surprising and as hot as blood. I told her about the months I'd spent in the farmhouse living a feral life alongside my father's. Of the burning chicken coop and the Rhode Island Red, of the night-time flight to Norfolk and the big man in the lorry with the soft voice. I told her about Goose, her clouds, of Gideon's house where I'd discovered my voice and about practising it among the dunes and that I could speak to Elsie. And then I told her about Kipper, about

228

the things I'd learned, of fireworks and fish, and how I loved the marsh and knew just how she must have loved it too.

I saw Elsie's shadow approaching, weaving between the tombstones. She sat down next to me and kissed my neck. It was a windy day, and her hair kept blowing in front of my eyes, obscuring my mother's name on the stone.

'Is that better?' she said.

We cycled to the Flags Café, about four miles away, built next to a giant sluice which separated the dark muddy water of a drainage channel from the green salt water of the Wash. We propped our bikes up against the sluice and watched flotsam circling in the eddy below. Always polystyrene caught there; like ice from a winter which never thawed. The wind made the iron resound with deep hollow echoes, and closer, putting our ears to the metal, we could hear barnacles below the high tidemark popping in the air. The flags themselves were on a row of poles alongside the A17, so windtorn and ragged from a wind which blew two hundred times a year that some were little more than half their original size.

Inside the café it was full of the urn's steam, frying fat and the smells of sugar and fags. I had a hot chocolate and Elsie had a cappuccino, which I'd never heard of before. The waitress made a big fuss of doing it in the kitchen, and when she came back she brought a black coffee alongside a bowl of whipped cream. Elsie spooned the cream on to the surface then spooned it into her mouth. She told me she was coming back to Blakeney.

'When?'

'June. I can't stand it here. I'll go mad and then I'll have to grow tulips the rest of my life.'

'Your dad,' I said, 'last night.' Then I wrote down: *He said I was the one caused all the trouble.*

'What's he saying that for? He says that all the time anyhow.'

'What's he mean?'

'Meaning he's a mixed-up old man who blames everyone but himself. Don't listen to it. He says all sorts of stuff about me and you.'

'What stuff?'

'You're too young, sweetheart. And I'm not going to tell you,' she said, mischievously, and I wondered whether she wasn't just making everything up as she went along.

We had egg mayonnaise sandwiches and Cornish pasties and three packets of crisps. Elsie put the crisps inside her sandwiches and said they taste so much better that way. I should try it. I watched her eat, aware that I was hunched over my own plate, a gesture of apologizing for something, and I wished that I wasn't doing it. She was wearing the silver seashell earrings Kipper had bought her last summer. Did she think about him when she put them on? It's crafty of him, giving her a present which reminds her of him every time she looks in the mirror.

'We should go away together,' she said, unexpectedly. 'I mean *really* go away. Change our names and rob banks and have lots of kids.'

'OK.'

'You *can* fire a gun, I take it?'

'Course.'

'Would you kill for me?'

'Yep.'

'Wanted, the outlaws Elsie Holbeach and Pip Langore, the silent killer,' and she leaned over the table and kissed me and when I tried to move my head back I felt her hand on the back of my neck, pulling me towards her like a man does. I was kissed again and I felt her tongue lick my lips.

'Cheese and onion,' she said, giving me a wink.

Outside, beneath the rags flapping on their poles, she hugged me for a long time and all I could see was the harvest colour of her hair and the distant shape of the beet factory across the marshes. And while she held me I felt her hand stroke down my back and then she gripped my backside and said *mm, not bad* in the most suggestive way she could. I pushed her away.

'Why are you doing this?' I said.

'Doing what?'

'Touching me.'

'Because I know what's going to happen.' She got on her bike and moved the pedal round ready to push off. 'I've seen it in the clouds,' she said, cycling off with one hand on her handlebars and the other guiding the bike I'd rode. The lorries thundered past her. Very quickly she became a tiny shape, the way things do in a flat landscape. She didn't look back at me once. Some people do, others don't, and Elsie never did.

The coach arrived and I decided to sit in the same seat I'd been in the previous day. In front of me, the herringbone pattern on the fabric – damn it, just damn it all.

The Whale

In June, a whale beached itself on the sandbanks off Scolt Head, and lay in the surf, dying. When he go, they said in the Albatross, his death rattle's gonna shake the windows in Burnham Overy – he's groaning like a bull right now. It's a solemn moment. There's talk about taking a crab boat over there, getting a rope round its tail and dragging it out to sea, but that's all it is so far, talk. We best raise a toast, someone says, and everyone at the bar lifts his pint.

But Roger is full of plans about how he and I can sail there to see it. Forty-five-foot sperm whale, he says, there's this crowd all along Brancaster Beach but they can't get to it 'cause of Scolt Head Channel. We need a boat. And after a pause he adds, and we've got one, pointing to his father's brand-new dinghy, bright white against the mud of Morston Creek. It's called the *Bishy-Barny-Bee*, the Norfolk term for a ladybird. We're sitting by the mudchute at the back of Lane End, and Goose is hanging out washing behind us, trying to listen in. Roger starts to whisper. Plan is, we take her into the Pit, then round the Point, see how she handles. Then tomorrow we'll get some food in and go.

That day we sail across the Pit, the saltmarshes already smelling of the warm rotted-green scent of summer. The *Hansa* drifts in and out of our view, flooded and black, steam rising from the deckbeams and a grin coming from the gash in its side. That's where Elsie sat, the previous summer, as wet as an otter on the dry wood, lying on her back in a bright T-shirt, gazing at the clouds, loving the attention. Goose says she's already back, working at the Misfits, though I haven't seen her yet. The *Bishy*'s dark sail snaps above us and the boat tips forward, stretching the water by our side till it looks like molten glass. So was this how Hands felt that day he raised the quilted sail? The feel of water beneath him, the dry smell of sun-baked wood and of varnish, heating gently. Did he stretch his legs against the slow rise and fall of the sea, his ears deaf to the sound of a baby crying? Did his hand trail in the water behind him – scoring a groove in the sea which was instantly erased as he himself vanished?

The tide curves round the Point with a lethal sinewy motion, more river than sea, arching its back into a stretch known as the Race. The flotsam that has washed out from Blakeney and in from the North Sea clings to us as if boat and rubbish are all orbiting a larger more powerful object. The sail flaps without power – filling and tipping the boat, then relaxing and beating again. Roger's loving it, letting out the sheet so the *Bishy* slides off the Race to meet the North Sea in a long curve of crenulated waves. The boat lowers into them, braking, and we feel the sudden vertigo of deep water below us, dark and green and rising in long broad swells without obstacle. And out to sea, about a mile away, the twins' boat, drifting beyond the banks, ropes trailing for tope. Roger holds the sheet tight like an old salt and looks where the wind pricks the sea. The gap closes quickly now on the twins; their hunched shapes over the side of the cuddy they'd built out of the wrecks of so many other boats. Low and heavy, with a cabin that looks like a garden shed, the twins keep adding bits on, ignoring common sense and building way beyond the necessary. Planks to reinforce earlier bodges, bits of driftwood which have no real use but are too sound to throw away, a green tarpaulin strung beneath the hull to keep it watertight, and which seems to gather the whole boat together and keep it one. Cliff's painted dragon's teeth on the prow, like on a bomber plane, and has written THE BASTARD in bleeding red letters next to it. It looks like a carnival float.

As we approach a strange thing happens. The sea next to their boat buckles, and a second later, after a muffled fizz, a thin plume of steam rises. We're close now, and as we steer in, the debris of dead fish starts to float up around the *Bastard*, more of them rising rigid from the shallows. The twins scoop their haul with keepnets as we go alongside. By Cliff's foot there's a bucket of eels, some herring and a dry box holding long dark candle-shaped sticks. He kicks a sack over it with his foot, but he needn't have bothered. He knows we wouldn't dare mention them. Dead man's fingers they call them, after the grey lungs of the crab. Straw soaked in nitroglycerine and wrapped in wax, made from chemicals stolen from Kipper's Lab.

Roger is afraid of the twins. He knows he has a beating coming from them which sometimes seems distant, and other times more imminent, but the certainty is there, unspoken. One day, he'll walk into some violence from them.

Sandy, the other twin, begins to haul his rope in, hand over fist, until he reaches a thin shaft of metal which has been bent into a rough hook. A chunk of pork belly dangles from the meat like a tongue, and from the skin a baby crab hangs by one pincer.

'Been dragging,' he says to Cliff as he brushes the crab off.

'Sand?'

'Gravel. We should try off the Longs.'

They both look towards the same featureless patch of water beyond the stern.

'New boat?' Cliff says to Roger.

'Yeah. It's my dad's. Moves a bit heavy but she sits well.'

'You're full of shit,' Cliff says.

I'm standing, holding the mast and looking down at them.

Cliff smiles sharp-toothed at me from his stinking boat. There are threads of rolling-tobacco on his lips. They've got a reputation for pulling girls in Blakeney. Even swapping girls halfway through the night, it's said, all done to some signal they pass between each other in their grim flat. Bottle of tequila, a video on too loud, some girl staggering across the living-room floor, pissing herself when she trips up on Cliff's outsized legs stretched across the carpet.

A crab boat is dragging full throttle through the sea a little way off. The two fishermen wave at the twins in unison. The twins nod back and then watch as one of the men hurls a plastic buoy at the other. Sandy chucks a coke can overboard and follows it in with a bright green gob. The sea's a lawless place.

'We got news for you,' Cliff says, looking at me. 'Your girlfriend's back. Came Sunday.'

'And she's well up for it,' Sandy says, creasing up with laughter.

'Well, you don't have to tell that to laughing boy here.'

'Always the quiet ones, yeah?'

Unmistakably, I see a cloud in the half-sunk shape of the twins' cuddy. I feel a rising sense of dread as Cliff starts to speak about Elsie, and in the rag cloud above I can make him out. Cliff, Sandy and two other people sitting in that phantom boat. Ah leave off – he's all right, I hear, shouldn't say that on a boat, anyhow, it's bad luck. They're starting to have a small row. Meanwhile the rag cloud's changing. One of the figures is standing, and while the others watch, the whole cloud splits in two. The men are going to drown. I look at the twins' cuddy in alarm – but all I see is Cliff – staring intently at me and saying . . . I said, did you hear me? *Did you hear me?* Sandy's looking down at his tope-line, not wanting to be any part of this any more. He's muttering for Cliff to shut the hell up. He's shaking his head ever so slightly. I wonder what's going on. What have I missed?

Cliff knows I'm listening to him again. He has my full attention. Then he says the one word that changes my life.

'Sisterfucker!'

Elsie, returned to North Norfolk, in a tiny room at the back of the Misfits, putting her make-up bag on the shelf next to her mirror, hanging her clothes in a wardrobe, lying on the bed with her hands behind her head. Always coming back, staying close to me, but never within reach. Playing games, it seemed, wearing Kipper's seashell earrings and kissing me, playfully, not quite playfully. Just who does she think she is – yes, who *does* she think she is?

I'm at her bedroom window before dawn. It takes a long time to wake her – she's not one for early mornings – but when she opens the curtains she sees I'm upset and knows better than to make a fuss. We sit on her bed for a while. I look at the cassettes she's put next to a stereo, at the travel guides she has on a shelf, and propped against the wall there's a picture of me and my mother sitting in the *Mary Magdalene*, near the bridge at Three Holes. I look at my mother as she in turn looks into the lens, at the camera that Elsie was holding.

She makes small talk about her father, how he's totally lost it now, how he wanders up and down the tulip beds even when it's winter. She's never going back, it seems. She tells me she might stay at Kip's for a while, if the job at the hotel doesn't last. How she's going to save up and go to India, and how, if she runs out of money when she's travelling, she's going to sell her hair.

'Kip's?' I say.

She doesn't answer. She has a way of abruptly falling silent which unsettles me.

'What's up with you?' she says in a level voice.

I don't know. I really don't know, but Elsie's part of it. She always has been. She looks at me for a while. I wonder how similar we look.

'You're growing up,' she says. 'Now, look away, will you.'

I turn to face the back of the door. Behind me, I hear Elsie taking off her T-shirt then pull her pyjama trousers down. The sound of her bare feet padding across the carpet to the chest of drawers. A couple of drawers opening and shutting. In no hurry. She begins to hum. I continue to stare at the door and she sits on the bed again. I hear the strappy sound of her knickers being pulled up her legs, the thin sound of the elastic snapping into place as she again stands up. Something being pulled off a coat hanger.

'I'm decent,' she says, and I turn to see her standing in a thin summer dress with an orchid print on it. 'It's new,' she says. 'So?'

'So what?' I say.

'I'm all yours. Where are we going?'

I suddenly know exactly where we're going.

'We're going to see a whale.'

Elsie steals food from the kitchen and I steal the *Bishy* from the creek. At the last moment I'm full of doubts. I suggest we tell Roger and see if he wants to come along. Yeah, right, Elsie says. It's clearly not an option.

Half an hour later I'm guiding the dinghy out of the Pit into the North Sea. The rust-red sail passes its shadow across me, snapping into the breeze with a smell of old canvas. All that air and wind and a sail will never lose its smell. It's a hot day, and I'm already thirsty. Elsie's on the seat below the mast.

There's a buttery light glowing on her skin, and salt has dried like flour on her cheeks. Her gaze is on Holkham Meals in the distance, with its low sandy islands and banks of fir trees. She's squinting in the light. Her back's a long shallow curve up to her shoulders, and I look at the delicate ridge of her collarbone as it pushes out the straps of her dress from her skin. *A seal!* she yells, pointing, and we watch it alongside us, sad and unblinking, rolling off into the deep again. Occasionally we pass above a sandbank, where the water becomes so shallow we can get out and walk, even though we're a mile out to sea. The sheer oddity of it makes Elsie reel with laughter – she's a fen girl, after all – she jumps overboard to stand on the sandbank while I hold the side of the stolen boat. Then she slides herself cautiously to the sandbank's edge, where it tips down suddenly into deep water again. She reaches out for my hand.

'Remember when Auntie May took us to Bedlam Fen?' she says. 'That was it, I thought, we're never going back. No more Three Holes and tulips or walking along that stinking drain. I didn't know what I wanted, not really, but I knew I loved your mother – really loved her – and I really wanted her to take us away. You know, away from everything. I could've worked in a shop or something. Buy food and cook it for you and save up for a car and teach you to drive . . .'

Was this really my sister? Cliff had said so. But it was still the same Elsie. Here I was back on the *Bishy*, and just from its motion in the water I began to think of another small boat. Of a rural scene, in the Fens. Of my mother and father sitting in the prow of the *Mary Magdalene*, the rudder bolted tight behind them, leaning this way and that to steer the boat between the banks of the sluice drain. The distant horizon – merely a dot between the banks, ten miles ahead, part of the world has been left unmade there. And out of that disappearing point – with no smoke or mirrors – the Holbeach family appearing. Ethel, plump as a turnip, Mr, wordless and preoccupied, even then, eating haslet and drinking cordial while their little girl played by the water's edge. The eel-trap pulling between Elsie's six-year-old fingers. The boat drifting close till it bumps into the bank and all four adults not knowing quite what to do. How to play it.

It was no ordinary meeting. There was something in the air. Something passing silently between the parents. A recognition. A caution. The Fens are darker at night than anywhere else. Stories are made that never see the light of day and who'll believe the things old man Holbeach might say now, to the daughter who never listened to start with?

Look! Elsie whispers. Passing beneath us we see a lion's mane jellyfish, as big as a car tyre, contracting suddenly in a silent cough, then rising, blind and on fire, it seems, with its own sting.

We smell Holkham before we reach it, the breeze has carried over a hot scent of pines and sand, and as the water shallows I jump in and drag the boat on to the beach. Together we tug it up the sand on to the high tideline. It looks conspicuous like that, very much someone else's boat, a long way from its mooring.

Elsie wanders off into the dunes. The fir trees behind them make a distantly unreal sound, like listening to the sea at night. It's a rising sound that rolls along the line of the beach like a slow wave breaking. When she's gone I wonder what's happening; why, in fact, she and I are here together, alone on this enormous beach. She's hijacked the day – it's running to her agenda now, like it always does. I follow her into the trees and find her in a small grass clearing. She's laying out the rest of the stolen food. She eats greedily, rolling radishes and piccalilli in slices of ham and licking her fingers clean. There are Scotch eggs, artichoke hearts in oil, tomatoes, pears, a jar of cooked prawns, chocolate and a bottle of red wine. It smells hot and dusty and there's sand between the roots of the grass. I eat some prawns and artichokes, then place fir cones in a circle round us, and when she gives me the bottle of wine, I have to push the cork in to open it. The wine leaps out in a dark red gout, bruising my shirt and making Elsie laugh. You're wounded, she jokes. I agree. You kill me, I say. We drink from the bottle, taking it in turns, listening to branches cracking somewhere in the wood, and staring out at the golden white of the beach and the glitter of the sea beyond. I've never seen a sight better than the sight of water between trees.

Elsie lies down after the food and stretches out her arms to stroke the ground. Like an angel, she says, stroking my wings. Her summer dress looks thin, and the faint orchid design seems like petals have been scattered on her before they blew away, leaving just their imprint.

I pick at the tines of a fir cone, occasionally stealing glances at Elsie to see how patches of sunlight move across her. Her breathing, rising and falling. The limpness of her ankles. The dusty soles of her feet, the traces of sand under her nails, the slight knitting of her brows and the shine of skin along the ridge of her nose. I think how important it is to remember all this, remember her in so much detail.

We're there until the sun gets low in the sky. I feel slumped with the wine. The boat would be missed by now, surely. I didn't know whether I was capable of sailing it back. Maybe it's best just to leave it here. But then that leaves her, and me, and what do we do?

I crawl over to her till I hear her breathing. I think she's asleep. I smell the comforting fragrance of her breath each time she exhales, and as I'd done before I try to see things in the pattern of freckles you can make out only when you're this close. The tiny pursed shape of her upper lip, still childlike. The two tendons at the base of her neck, between which is a delicate egg-shaped depression as if a thumb has smoothed it there, pulsing gently. Below it, the harder shape of the top of her chest, pushing all away, and the first button of her dress.

It's undone; and so am I.

That button, hard as a fingernail in all that softness. Half-upright where the dress has pulled itself free. The soft frayed edge of the eye that has released it. Elsie looks at me with a watery gaze. She smiles.

'You know what it is?' she whispers. 'It's midsummer's night.'

We walk back to the *Bishy*. The setting sun has made all the colours seem unnaturally saturated. The gunwale looks like lipstick has been run round it, the rust-red sail looks as bright as blood, and Elsie's hair has the colour of ripe corn. We push the boat in and drift round the promontory of the beach. About two miles away we see the outline of Scolt Head Island – little more than a heap of dunes and grasses with wide, empty beaches. All along the coast, Norfolk is sinking into the North Sea with incredible softness, a landscape made entirely of lavender greys, chalk blue and dull green. And against that, one solitary dark shape, its own island in all that evening scene. There's nothing so dark and black as this in the whole of Norfolk. Even when we're a mile away it still seems vast. Out of place. I no longer have any doubts; the light is closing in, we're miles from home, but the whale is magnificent, like a ruin. It's mesmerizing.

Elsie jumps off the boat and wades though the surf to reach the body. It's enormous, lying on its side, flattened by its own dead weight. When I join her she's already running her hand along the old leathery skin. Even though the light is really fading now, there's enough to see how the skin is just a mass of deep scars, calluses, barnacles and folds. Each rock off the coast of Newfoundland, each battle with giant squid, each crossing of the Atlantic has etched a hieroglyph. An entire history written on skin. And are smells too: a strong, musky smell of the sea, a sulphurous smell where the skin has been burned by the sun, and a rotting stench, sickly and overwhelming. A male sperm whale. A row of blunt white teeth line the length of the jaw, which sticks into the sand like a javelin. Above them, the roof of the mouth is pockmarked with sockets, disappearing into the closed muscle of its throat.

Elsie has climbed on to the whale, running her hand along the ridges of skin like it's the bark of an old oak. She looks upset and distant, in her own world. She's stroking the whale and looking at me and she's saying it's so – so sad. So sad. And I climb on to the whale myself, feeling the skin bow ever so slightly with my weight until I'm sitting next to Elsie, not sure if she wants me to be there. The whale feels incredibly huge and completely impenetrable. It has no eye, or not one that we can find. Just wide, flat, thick skin. I think of the line of white vertebrae like a shattered treetrunk, somewhere in there, a giant's ribcage, a vast and silent heart and secret pools of ambergris.

'Midsummer's night,' she says again, and lies her head down on the whale. The longest day, it's a day to be cautious of. I think of the play in the Misfits garden, last summer; of the sheets hanging out to dry across the lawn like the clouds I'd seen over the marsh. And then I'm drawn to that other cloud, the one which I've wondered about for ages – the cloud in the exact shape of a dead sperm whale, drifting over the marshes as my father drove his car away. Here I am, on the whale. A month before my fourteenth birthday. Arrived at the moment.

*

The air is dry and the sky is stunning. I begin to fall asleep, watching the stars swimming in and out of the night. Perhaps I do sleep. The wine's making my head spin very gently, as if the whale is floating out to sea, with memories of the ocean: of calm depths beneath the storms, of surfacing in the mid-Atlantic night, of silent icebergs in the dead calm of Arctic winter. The huge bell-jar of the night's sky above us. I drift with the whale, feeling the sad beat of its heart thump through the flesh, and the long slow rhythm of its tail behind us. And still the stars, glittering above. A shooting star now, etching a brief line across the blackness to mark the moment of its death. And little more than a smudge by my side, a cloud rising into the sky – a cloud which becomes Elsie's dress being lifted over her head. And as I turn to look at her I have the impression that she's asleep too. That her sudden nakedness is nothing more than the soft grey of a faded photograph, unreal and beyond reach. Moving gradually towards me, rolling into me with the motion of the whale until her hair gathers round my face like soft grasses and I feel her weight climbing across me and smothering me and I feel the soft skin of her back with my fingertips and I hear the smallest giggle escaping her mouth. And on her breath I detect the smell that reminds me so much of my mother.

It was cold and grey and Elsie was kneeling by my side, rocking me to and fro. She was in her flimsy dress with the orchid print and she was shivering.

'Pip, I want to go back now,' she said. 'It's time to go back.'

I lifted myself heavily from the whale. Its skin was covered in a fine salt dew. Elsie kissed me on my mouth and sniffed loudly.

'I'm so thirsty,' she said. She looked small and damp and her chin looked sharp with worry. Her eyes were dark and surrounded by a waxy sleeplessness, and she wouldn't look at me.

'Thanks,' she said, steadily, 'for bringing me here. For being with me here.'

My last memory of that place is of sitting on the whale, hugging my legs for warmth, while Elsie walked to the *Bishy*. The beach was misty and ordinary and Elsie looked so thin and lost in the enormity of it, and the whale felt low and slab-like beneath me.

It was a long cold sail back to Morston, both of us shivering and hungry. Gradually the Point loomed ahead, wide and snub-nosed, surrounded by off-lying banks and islands. It was low tide. We sailed against the flow of the race with a hard sail, the current nearly enough to halt us. Then we were in the Pit, and, on the beach where Hands had been found, standing and masking her eyes against the light and then briskly walking towards us, Goose was wading into the water up to the hem of her dress and when she reached the boat she grabbed a rowlock with an iron grip and reached for Elsie with her other hand. She grabbed Elsie like you'd grab a dog, round the collar, and as Elsie's face crumpled with surprise and shock, Goose gave her a mighty shove, sending her backwards and over the side. With Elsie gone and splashing and swearing furiously at Goose, the old woman turned to me, and using the same grip she dragged me from the boat too. I remember watching the *Bishy* spinning behind me as I was hauled over the transom. The bang the rudder gave my knee. The angry snap of the sail as it broke free of the sheet.

I was under water, dragged out again, being pulled on to the shore. Behind me Elsie was falling about and splashing, soaked, trying to catch the drifting boat. And then she was out of sight.

I stumbled along with Goose, looking at the marsh weeds and worm casts in the mud and wondering what was happening. We weren't going back to the cottage. And then suddenly I knew where I was. It was the oyster creek. A long snaking creek on the wrong side of the Morston Channel, filled with low dark oyster cages sitting on the mud. And Goose was kicking open one of the latches with her boot and I was thrown in – little more than a sack of her rubbish. She slammed the top of the cage down and threaded a rope through the latch and tied both ends to a post sticking in the mud. I lay in the cage and pulled at the wood and splashed in the watery mud and at the bottom and all around me I felt the brittle, sharp edges of the oysters. Shells shut against my plight in the midst of their own.

And then it was quiet. Through the net I saw Goose's deep footsteps in the mud leading to the stake. A little pattern of prints where she'd tied the rope, and a single determinedly straight line leading away.

Time passed. Boats swung in their moorings. Rafting gannets drifted inshore. Staithing posts left wakes as the tide gathered momentum. An entire sea lifting imperceptibly against the coast of Norfolk. And a hushed, inanimate tongue of the sea trickled up the creek. All around me the barnacles sniffed the tide and licked their lips, and I was caught in the net, forgotten about, as the water rose around me.

18

Norfolk, Oh Yeah

Trapped in a cage full of oysters – what was going on? What, possibly, could make Goose do this? The water rising, a chill spreading from my fingers to my arms, bringing an ache with it, making my thoughts clouded. I was seeing visions of being naked on the dead whale, the eerie sight of Elsie's dress lifting over her head. The starry sky, the gentlest of giggles in all that vastness. Such intimacy there, such a sense of unknowns. Fleeting sensations of her body, as hard and smooth as beech wood, pushing itself on me, a determination of purpose that was frightening. My sister? I don't know. It's so difficult to be sure – it's so full of fenland secrets and little moments over the years – the thought of my mother, that first day in the Saints, the imprint of a frayed cushion on her cheek and the sounds of George hurling rubbish about in the yard – how she itches her oddly shaped belly-button which could be because of the heat that day or it could be because she was pregnant, with Elsie. A secret gesture, the tiniest of scratches, and I alone, across the years, have seen it now. Or the dreamcatcher she hung on her bedroom window, through which she saw one thing and one thing only in all that grimy fenland distance – the small patch of red tulips in the Holbeach's acre – and it's so difficult to hold on to an image like this and see what it means, and abruptly, with a sneeze, I'm brought back to the oyster net and I see there's not much space above the rising tide left in the cage, and I think I'm going to drown in there for sure and maybe at the moment of drowning I might realize what the truth has been all this time. Elsie . . . my mother . . .

my grandfather – himself buried up to his neck once with a rising tide all round him. How must he have felt? Falling out of the sky, or more likely a German bomber, burying his parachute and flight jacket and keeping his boots – the last thing a man gives up, only to be caught in the mud. All that adventure over Europe and there he was, about to drown in this rotten North Norfolk marsh.

And the tide kept rising, as it has to, and my face was turned sideways to the sky, with the old twine of the net pressing a diamond pattern on my cheek. Below me, the feel of ancient oysters shifting round the cage, opening their slippery mouths. A sand eel shot through the net like a phantom – where you looked it had already vanished. The flow of the creek began to turn my body, floating me as if I'd already lost consciousness, making me feel I was already not strictly part of the world's great living family any more. This was it, this is how it happens, this is how you drown, drop by drop, listening to the pleasant sound of your own breathing, a friend to the last, before an unwanted sound begins to interrupt, a spluttering of water and air. You listen as if it's coming from someone else. A pain, a feeling of heat. A sense of approach – something dark and wide enveloping.

Someone plunged into the creek, pulling the net to wrestle with the latch and briefly I knew it *must* be Grandfather Hands – those nimble fingers working on the knot. But then I was being lifted like a sack and instead of my grandfather's dreamy blue eyes I saw the rough unkempt stubble of Bryn Pugh's chin.

Soon I was inside, standing on the tiles with the marsh and sea dripping off me, shivering, while Goose sat on the foot of her bed, the way you do when you think you're ill, locked into her own world. Bryn, standing behind me, nervous of a situation he doesn't understand. But of the three he knows he must take charge, however hard.

Goose, I've got him here – he's safe. Goose? Less clear him up, heh? Don't do nothin' today but get him cleaned up.

She heard all right but she didn't move. Bryn crossed to her and placed a calming hand on her neck. Her shoulders sank, the effort of the day getting to her. Even her hair, usually tied up at the back of her head, was beginning to unravel – with several of the pins that kept it in place hanging like thorns. Bryn squeezed her shoulder and her eyes flickered with confusion. Kitty, he whispered, we'll get some help OK? Don't rush. You ain't never rushed all your life. He loves her very much, I thought, he must have loved her all this time. And I had no choices any more but to listen to the soothing compelling voice of my own instinct: you must go. You must go now. Take your suitcase, though its handle reminds you of past hurts, of running away, pack your mother's dreamcatcher, her crabline, the photo of Hands and the one of your parents' wedding day. Leave, because everyone in your family always leaves. Pass Goose, small and bewildered on the edge of her bed, don't stop.

Bryn was outside. Where you gonna go? he asked gently. She din't mean it. Din't mean none of it. She ain't right and she need some help, and she din't mean none of it. I strapped the case to my bike and he helped me tie a knot. I could see it made him feel better. He told me he was moving on too. The marsh was a sick place to live, he said. It ain't right, livin' on land that ain't really land at all. He tied more knots on to the knot, tying in his frustration about this marsh life with each pull of the string till the knot was as large as a knuckle. Shouldn't have lived here, not for any time. And with that the knot was complete and sculptured and as gnarly as the one Goose had tied in my mother's belly-button. He looked at me one last time and cracked his face into a smile but there was just too much worry all round so he turned away and sniffed loudly at the marsh. *Thistle Dew*'s all yours, he said weakly.

I cycled towards Blakeney, only once looking back at the tiny figure of Bryn Pugh being swallowed by the saltmarsh. I ate chips on the quay as a blood-red sunset broke through the clouds near the horizon. That was the direction of Lane End, my past on fire again – fire coming for me, always. Below me, the tide which might have drowned me gently flowed out, and the water was itself once more: inanimate, impartial, finding its own level. The twilight came. No wind. Sounds drifted across the marsh on warm, dry air. Terns on the Point. Luggers with their buckets, going to the flats. Everything going about its usual business in the usual fashion. Just an empty coastal town, washed up itself, life at a dead end with nowhere to go.

Everything was quiet when I got to the smokehouse. He'd do the rounds at half-ten, remove the bloaters, restoke, rake and lay a ham for overnight. But as I walked to the house the door opened with an eerie magic, and there he stood, leaning in the frame, neither coming out nor staying in, the orange glow of the hallway light behind him.

'Thought it'd be you,' he said flatly. 'Talk gets 'cross this marsh quick.'

He deliberately blocked the space, leaning the way a man does when he's proving something, his face completely shadowed, making it expressionless and sinister. The light behind him glinted darkly off his flat oiled hair, then a faint reflection of the light picked out the dull shine of his eyes. His pipe glowed as he drew breath.

'Not good, you know. Not good at all.'

He let his words hang. In no hurry.

'Best come in,' he said.

I followed him down the hall and into the lounge, thinking Elsie would be at the table, all held-in and sheepish and ready for a row. But in her place sat one of the fish buyers, a pale thin man who never spoke much and managed to unnerve everyone except my uncle.

'Bang on cue,' Kipper said with a concession of lightness because the other man was there, 'the young adventurer.'

The man nodded casually, then with a bony hand slid me a notepad of A4 paper across the table. He let his hand fall to the side, exhausted by even this. There was a diagram of a fish on the top sheet next to instructions about salt curing.

'I'll tell you straight,' my uncle said, in a louder voice than usual, 'you got a nerve coming here. I ain't saying what you did was wrong or dangerous or nothing, but it ain't right none the less. You understand?'

Where's Elsie? I wrote.

'Now, you want to tell your side of the story, that's fine. That's fine by me, OK? But that's up to you.'

Kipper stood against the fireplace to increase his hold on the room. He rested his arm on the mantelpiece, his hand touching the face of the clock there. Master of time and precision. Behind him was my sketch of him as the exiled Neptune, trident in hand, a smoked fish on each tine.

'You eaten?'

Some chips, I wrote.

'What's he put?' Kipper said, a little impatiently.

'Chips,' the fish buyer said.

'Fix him a sandwich would you?' he said to the man. 'And we'll have a Scotch, right?'

The fish buyer unfolded himself from the table and went to the kitchen. Kipper bent down and spat into the grate. He straightened, looked at me calmly, wiped his sleeve across his mouth.

'She's in bed. An' she ain't well – so it's no good you askin'. She ain't seein' you tonight.'

What had he been told? Just what did they think I'd done? I stared at the pencil and paper. I didn't know where to start.

He waited.

'I've called your dad . . . he says you can stay there a while. Till you – till whatever.'

When?

'Morning. Get the coach. He'll pick you up from Lynn.'

A done deal. A field of chickens, the overwhelming smell of their shit, the depressing bungalow with Gull blind and violent in one of the rooms, and my father making efforts to clear a space in his life for me.

'Sometimes I look at you I don't reckon you've got any Langore blood in you at all. You're from that other side, ain't you – the side of your mother and grandmother. There's madness in you.'

The sandwich came and was put on the table. Slices of white bread on the corner of a farmhouse table, just like the first night my parents entered their new home at the Saints; and the night I left, all those years later. A sign of abandonment, and of flight. I couldn't just give in to it. I didn't know where I was, what I was doing there or what I *should* be doing, numb but for an overwhelming, sudden rush of tiredness. I ran, ran for the door and the marsh outside and the reed bed and its dusty alleyways of stalks and the reeds snapped like fireworks all round me and then I hugged the ground and it all went silent.

Kipper and the fish buyer went after me with torches, but the search seemed half-hearted and they soon gave up. Kipper made the man wheel my bike and suitcase into the house, then I listened to him tending the smokehouse racks. A man gives up when he stops his chores. Till then he'll always be himself. The clock chimed eleven in the lounge behind him. He began whistling a tune, then went inside and drew the curtains.

The light was on in my uncle's bedroom, and though the curtains were drawn, there was enough of a gap to see in. I thought it might have been left deliberately.

I saw Elsie in there, lying in bed with the blanket pulled tight up to her neck. Seeking comfort. Her skin was marble smooth and her hair was like bronze seaweed across the pillow. A mermaid in Neptune's cave. Perfectly still, asleep, but as I watched, the bed beneath her moved, gently – as if a wave was drifting through the room – and I realized Kipper was now sitting at the foot of it. He was taking his shoes off. And in the seconds before the light went off, the tiniest of smiles spread across her lips.

That's how I found out, I suppose. God, what a fool I'd been – all those hours on the *Hansa* while Kipper Langore watched us with his binoculars, his mouth set in a confident grin. Take your time, take your time, don't rush the girl. How he swam out there with his bloody front crawl. What a kid! Climbing on the wreck like he'd done twenty years earlier. Losing the girl then and making up for it now – now, with Lil' Mardler's daughter? Damn your fucking smoke and your two-faced face.

I was in trouble, I realized, real trouble, facing a second night spent out in the open, while Kipper and Elsie were snug in there, behind the curtain. Doing God knows what. There was no place for me there. I walked up the track and into the oak wood behind his house. It was quiet and enclosed in the wood, with the old trees heavy and dark above me. I'd taken a car blanket from Kipper's shed, and I wrapped it tight round me and sat against a trunk. Why does this hurt constantly return in my family? Why are we always having to run away? Hands gets on the *Pip*, my mother gets on the ice, I'm in the wood, looking through the trees at Kipper's house, the smoke from the smokehouse chimney smudging the buildings from view. Goings on, badly erased. I don't want to sleep, but I'm exhausted, so thoroughly exhausted. Even the bark of the oak feels soft. I give in to it, I sleep, and I dream. I dream that I'm walking through the oak wood, looking at a glimmer of light between the trunks, but it's not the lights of my uncle's house. It's coming from the doorway of an old wooden shack. When I get close I can smell beans being cooked on a stove inside, I hear the thin hiss of a primus stove, and I see the white hair of an old man sitting under the acid light of a storm lantern. Briefly it looks like there might be several people in there, because the shadows dance about so quickly as he stirs the pot.

Come in, come in, the man says, then he looks at me and says well, well, my old friend. You need beans, more beans than I think I have. It's Gideon. He peers at me with his distant milky gaze and he adds nice to see you at last. Our paths we've followed – they've come to the same point, have they not?

I dream about eating the beans with some bread and then he heats more beans and pours them over more bread. We have strong sugary tea and he stirs it with a buttery knife and the fat makes little oily pools on the surface. He only has one cup, so we take turns sipping that. It tastes fantastic. The shack's filled with the tins, sacks, newspapers and paints Gideon takes everywhere, along with boxes of chocolate, homemade gingerbread men, fruitcakes and shortbread in biscuit tins. It's like a fairytale. He opens up everything and lets me feast on whatever I like. The Lord's been kind, he says, seeing as I'm partial to malt loaf especially. We have chocolate Rice Krispies in cupcake wrappers, and slabs of carrot cake with cheese sliced on top. Not the place I thought I was heading – but I'm no complainer, he says. And then sadly he adds I'm nearly finished here, you know. My job here in the oak wood. And with this he picks up the large dark shape of a church Bible, little more than its two hard covers of dimpled black leather, with the last few of its loose pages inside. Remember I told you we need a map in life? If we lose that we have nothing? Well, here is mine – the stream outside this shack feeds into the River Glaven, friend, that's my job. I have been floating the pages of this holy book down the stream, one by one. Outside the hut I see the large pages of the Bible have clogged up the stream like old clothes. But! he says emphatically, I shall save Ecclesiastes. That is my Book. That is my map of life. *All the rivers run into the sea; yet the sea is not full; unto the place from whence the rivers come, thither they return again*, he says, stroking his beard into a point. We go to the stream and he tears a page out of the Bible and lets it float in. It's the story of Lot. The paper is so dry after a hundred years of being in a church the water runs over it like mercury. Then he speaks again: Now you may or may not tell me but there was a miracle that day wasn't there? When you came to my house. You see – the lobby's right by the kitchen and I heard you. I heard you say your first ever word and I fell on to my knees, that's right, on my knees and prayed. A miracle – that's what it was.

With this he leads me back into the shed. It feels safe and warm in there. He turns the gas lamp off, and we both sit listening to the owls screeching like banshees in the wood. Something has alarmed them. Suddenly there's a surging of noise and breaking of twigs which rises and grows and rushes at us and with it comes a huge splitting noise of wood. The ground trembles as things fall from the shelves in the dark, then all is still again. The oak tree, Gideon says. I've been waiting for it.

We step out of the hut and see a massive tree, fallen, with

its great branches either side of Gideon's shack in a tender embrace which so easily could have crushed us. Gideon smiles at me, and with a finger wet from the stream he touches my forehead and mutters a prayer.

'Go back,' he said, 'you must return.'

'I can't,' I say to him.

'Then you must find your own way.'

'This isn't real,' I say. 'It's all a dream.'

'It's as real as you want it to be. Now look through there, through the trees.'

'I can't see anything,' I say.

'You will in the morning.'

I wake in the grey light of dawn, against the tree and chilled to the bone, and immediately I remember the dream and look through the trees. There, in a field behind the wood, is a van parked in the grass. A man gets up from a camping stool next to it and does a huge stretch. It's Lloyd, in a large multicoloured jumper, wiping the morning sausage and egg from his mouth on to its sleeve. As I walk up to him he grins widely. Morning, cocker, he says, the day meant for the likes of him. What you up to?

Kat's hanging up clothes, and she's more perceptive. She rushes up to me and I start crying. They sit me down on a camping chair and Lloyd says heh, heh, heh softly over and over again and Kat tells him to get some more eggs cooked.

'Well, I reckon I go and see Kipper,' Lloyd said, certain of his right to speak his mind after reading the barest of facts I'd managed to scribble down.

'Not a good idea,' Kat said, knowing him too well. I'd had breakfast and was now wearing Lloyd's jumper and a pair of his chunky-knit socks.

'At least tell him to call off the dogs,' Lloyd said, conceding. Beyond the field we could all see Kipper's house and the smokehouse chimney. No one had come out yet.

'We'll both go,' Kat said. 'Then what we gonna do?'

I sat in the cab of the truck while Kat and Lloyd went to see Kipper. They knocked on the door and I saw him – slow to emerge – come out in his dressing gown. Lloyd let Kat do the talking. Kipper listened, then looked several times up towards me in the van. He leaned against his doorway and Kat hugged her coat round her for warmth. The discussion went on. Eventually Kipper went inside and a while later emerged with my tartan suitcase. He started to walk with it, towards the van, and Kat stopped him with a hand on his shoulder and he passed the case to her.

That night we parked the truck in a field in the middle of nowhere, with the huge sky of Norfolk stars above us. I looked at the sky and smelled the damp grass and I listened to my mother's seashell. The sea sounded calm and distant, like it had been on the whale just two nights earlier. Just two nights. Had I really seen Elsie lying on my uncle's bed? Had she really curled up the corners of her mouth into a smile?

We'd been to a village pub where Kat, Lloyd and I had had three pints each. Lloyd had explained the deal they'd cut with Kipper – that I could spend the summer holiday with them for as long as I wanted. But after that I'd have to go back. Then Lloyd had become angry about a bloke Kipper's age carrying on like he did. Elsie Holbeach's worth ten of him any day. A rant developing. Lloyd, Kat said, calming him, now's not the time. Her poise reining him in. I still think someone round here's got to stand up to him – he just takes the piss. The pint glass looked big in Kat's hand. You could do it, Pip, when you go back – it'd be the making of you. Later on Lloyd got embroiled in an argument with a drunken farmhand who'd been propped against the bar eavesdropping and rolling his eyes for his own amusement. It turned out the labourer had been hauling bales all day whereas Lloyd *han't never done a day's work in his life*. When Lloyd said the man should throw his pitchfork away and join the cause the man said fukkin pufter and went off for a piss. That cheered Lloyd up no end.

Later, as Lloyd took his own piss against the pub sign, he told me he'd met the same man in the same pub and had had the same row three years before. He chuckled as he shook himself dry, muttering Norfolk, oh yeah, under his breath.

We toured in that van, parking overnight in fields or pub car parks where Lloyd had the habit of leaving the keys behind the bar so he couldn't be done for drink-driving. Which had happened before. I slept in the cabin where Kat had rigged a curtain to go round the windscreen, but often I sat with the curtain open, looking over the grey fields in front of me, listening to the sound of 'Buffalo Soldier' and the rhythm it lent to the bump and grind of Lloyd and Kat's nightly trysts. During the day we'd drive from one fête to another, doing the carnivals, farm-shows and festivals of the Norfolk summer. I walked round with a sandwich board, took the tickets, prepared the props. The play that year was a two-man retelling of *The Wild Man of Orford*, the story of a half-man half-fish who'd been caught in nets off Suffolk. He'd been tortured in Orford Castle where he cried for the sea every night, and over the months his captors relented, seeing sense in letting this strange man covered in scales have a swim. Only, the man escaped the nets and was never seen again. It made the children cry.

*

'You do have to go back in September,' Kat said to me one morning. First thing, an intimate time between us. Sitting in long grass on two camping stools, neither of us having washed, just the sound of the Calor gas stove and the tap of the porridge spoon stirring the pot.

I can't. There's nothing there.

'There are the people you love. Your family.'

My family's been destroyed several times over. My dad's a chicken labourer, my uncle's hated by all of North Norfolk – he's sleeping with the only friend I've ever had. My gran's gone or is going senile and my mother drowned herself. I push the notebook to Kat like we're playing chess. Her move. It makes her laugh.

'OK – fair point, but it's still who you are. Come September me and Lloyd are back in our semi in Norwich. He's working at an insurance firm and I'll be helping at a nursery. We don't save anything but we've got this thing going and we fight for it. I sometimes think you just don't fight.'

Lloyd would emerge from the van with the loudest stretch in East Anglia. Kiss his girl, give me a wink, then think about the porridge pot. He loved the fact I never spoke – it was the envy of a man who knew he talked too much. Same old, he'd say, checking out the breakfast, sitting on a tree stump in a chunky-knit jumper and rolling his first of the day. A big grin with the wide, straightforward teeth of the innocent, not a crease of concern on his face. Sex, porridge, a pint, all I need, mate.

Gideon had been right. When you think you're lost all you need do is look through the trees for the next path. Here, with Kat and Lloyd, I'd found it. Friendship. And I learned from them that summer. Lloyd felt everything and talked it through, life was simple for him – blacks and whites, rights and wrongs; whereas Kat was a dreamer, smoking thin cigarettes, painting flowers on her shoes and, gently, over the weeks, coaxing out a language between us, not in the way that myself and Cassie

Crowe's fenland education had been a battle of wills, but there, in the back of the theatre van, as the smell of woodsmoke and frying food wafted in from outside, her slender fingers wove magic out of the air. A sign language of mime and shapes and a great deal of patience. While Lloyd brewed the tea outside and split the yolks, we'd sit there, looked down on by the outlandish props and costumes of *The Wild Man of Orford* – lords, farmers, fishermen, soldiers, village virgins, buffoons and clowns. I began to tell her what I could of my life. Of the stories and non-stories. The herrings and red herrings. I told her about the Fens, about boats, about bonfires. Burning elm trees, decoys and bulls, tulip heads, curing fish, fondue sticks, clouds, whales and wrecks. Of stale sandwiches and mugs of cold tea on the corners of farmhouse dining tables.

It was coming to the end of the season. The theatre troupe would do a couple more shows before Lloyd and Kat returned to their Norwich semi; Lloyd would spend the winter dreaming about the summer gone and the one to come while he stared at a typewriter. And I would have to go back.

They dropped me on Blakeney Quay. Kat hugged me and told me to be strong and Lloyd made an awkward moment of it, not finding the right words and eventually muttering well – you know, anyway.

I walked the half-mile to the smokehouse, where Kipper and Elsie had laid out a tea of sandwiches, Bakewell tart and pork pie. Kipper fussed with the teapot and brought plates from the kitchen. The smell of fish and tobacco, the ticking of the mantelpiece clock, the silence of the books on the shelves. Nothing had changed.

'How I see it, we get Shrimp over and talk things through. What you want to do and that,' Kipper said, leaning back in his chair.

'Kip,' Elsie said, 'face it, he's staying, here – I'll make him up a bed in the storeroom. I know we've talked about it and you're not keen, but you're always doing stuff and I'm bored and it'll only help, what with how it is.'

Kipper shifted uneasily and looked away, his eyes as grey as an old photo. He hadn't touched the food.

Elsie reached for a slice of Bakewell and spoke through it.

'I'm the boss now,' she said, a cakey smile on her face, and with it she held out her hand, royally, for me to inspect the glinting newness of her engagement ring.

19

Herrings and Red Herrings

'Came running home with your tail between your legs,' Elsie said, coarsely whispering over the tabletop, 'that's your problem – just can't see it through.'

Cley Beach Café was the same as always. Humid and breathy, with the birders' journal on display – its pages heavy with moisture – and salt-bleached postcards on the wall.

'You've got to grow up,' she said, 'get a life.'

I could do without the lecture, especially from her, shacked up with a man like him.

'You gonna talk or what?' she said.

'Congratulations,' I said, looking at her ring. It stung her.

There was a smell of burned treacle and buttered toast. We were sitting in the corner and Elsie had been fiddling with the salt shaker since we'd sat down.

'That day you ran away, Kipper was so pissed off. Said you should be locked up.'

'I don't care.'

'Just don't start any trouble,' she said, wiping the damp putty of salt round the shaker's chrome top.

'Why not? He's just like my dad.'

Elsie stared hard at me. 'No, he's not,' she said, 'you've got him wrong.'

Behind her the café girl went through to the kitchen after a sniper's glance at Elsie and I knew what would be going on in there, over the saucepan of hot treacle. *She's come here, you know, that girl, could be his daughter and her carrying on like that.*

With that one that don't speak . . . he give me the spooks, he does,
the way he look at you sometimes . . . din't he run off?

Had they noticed the engagement ring? Surely not long till
they did. Then the tongues would really start wagging.

'Elsie . . .'

'Don't, Pip. Please don't ask. Don't make this harder than
it already is.'

Kipper made breakfast at six. Smoked herring, two poached
eggs, sometimes marmalade, like my father, both of them
with the habit of cleaning the knife by sliding it into the soft
centre of the toast. After that the radio would go off and I'd
hear him putting his weather gear on before going outside.
With him gone I'd make my own breakfast. Elsie would be in
her bedroom listening to music. I'd knock on the door and
take her tea. Sometimes I dared to sit on the bed, looking at
her ruffled hair and rosy cheeks and the dark shape of my
uncle's slippers lurking under the bed. His side of the bed was
tidy, hers was messy. His clothes hung along an open rail and
seemed to fill the room with his presence. Hers slept dog-like
on the floor.

Elsie cooked a meal for her boys each evening, Kipper and
me at the same table, stabbing our sausages, for the most in
complete silence. Kipper made a fuss of mopping up the sauce,
lessening the embarrassment. Plate won't need washing up,
he'd joke.

'We should do this place up,' Elsie said one night, out to
cause trouble. 'It's too depressing. Men make depressing places
to live in.'

'Yeah?' Kipper said, warily.

'You can paint, can't you?' she said to me. 'Well?'

I nodded.

'Well then, I'll get some charts and some paint and –' before she finished her sentence she was already crying. Tears welling and tipping with incredible urgency, without any change in the bright expression she'd started with.

'Pip,' my uncle said, 'I think it's best you . . .'

Leave the room. Which I did. And in my storeroom bedroom I listened to the muffled argument they began to have.

That was in November, and it was the beginning of the end.

I started to keep my distance from them after that. Things weren't right. She pretended all was fine, and he pretended he didn't know it wasn't. What would be next? A sudden pregnancy? That would be too much. Would she ask me to make her a quilt like Hands did for Goose, a quilt which would rise on her side of the bed as her belly grew, while on his side he would tuck the quilt's edge between his knees? Not willing to let go of what he had. It can't happen. Not between them.

Sometimes they went on to the marsh together and would eat a picnic against the wall of the pillbox near the oak wood. They'd talk all morning. Left behind them, the pile of fruit pips my uncle had neatly arranged, the heads from the shrimps, the grasses that Elsie always knotted when she sat still. Scuffmarks in the earth seemed to have the footprints of their conversation – how they paced round the issues, dragged their plans to and fro and pushed them into the mud.

And sometimes while they were out there on the marsh I'd sneak into the Lab, using a key which was kept under a flint outside. There were new charts on the walls, diagrams of trajectories, primary- and secondary-burst shapes, colours and timings. Beneath them, a book filled with firework designs with headings such as 'Alignment of Tube on Missile Body for Whistle Sound', 'Cross-section of Pellet Layers', 'Chamber Shapes', 'Necks of Pressure' and, throughout, the necessity of improvements. A big display was planned for the coming New

Year, and Kipper wanted to show Cley just what he could do. He was fed up with their friendliness when they wanted his fish, their disapproval when he turned his back. The back-garden whispers, the fourth-pint rants, the shop-counter glances – he'd had enough. They'd never forgotten the young lad who'd been burned by his fireworks in the Lab, or the inquest where Kipper had been absolved from blame. They'd smelled a rat, and ever since he'd been wreathed in the sulphurous cloud of his own making. Each year on Nor' Sea Night, he'd be making it worse on himself. *And now him carryin' on with a girl half his age. Old enough to be her father. Him stinkin' o' fish an' all.* Nothing was more untrustworthy for the wives of Cley than to have a man in their midst showing their husbands how it could be done. Some of them remembered the night when Kipper Langore as a boy had to be dragged out of the tree in the great storm, the fuss he made, the endless tears. So the circle grew vicious. That he lived on the edge of the marsh, away from the village, and that every-thing he touched turned to salt – it all made sense to them. He was rotten news; always a rum 'un and now a bad 'un. Caught between sea and land and marsh, and yes, the marsh was the best place for him.

A tap on the window and I was caught, caught in the Lab where I had no right to be. But not by Kipper this time. It was Eric, who worked a charcoal kiln at the top of the oak wood. I always knew when he'd been around because wherever he went he'd leave grey fingerprints. On the kettle, the knife, the invoice. Eric was a low-slung man with big eyebrows and creases like coal seams across his face. He'd spent too much time in the wood to speak much to anybody, and was the only person who smelled more smoky than Kipper. He held up a bag of charcoal and gave it a dry shake outside the window.

I carried the charcoal to Kipper and Elsie where they were sitting by the pillbox and my uncle said great and clapped his hands and actually put his arm round my shoulder. He led me back to the smokehouse with an air of being glad to get away from whatever was going on, and because I was with him, because I'd brought him the long-awaited charcoal, he said I should help him out in the Lab and before I knew it I was back in there, listening to him with all that pent-up energy which only ever came out with the fireworks.

'It'll give a gold burst. If that's in a sphere packed round the charge we'll have a thirty-foot chrysanth. How about that, huh, thirty foot?'

As he spoke he ground the charcoal in a pestle and mortar.

'Get the grains smaller,' he said, 'she'll burn faster. Don't want it hanging around. There, glitter for sparkle.'

He was making the biggest show in his life and he wanted these to really burn. Rows of hard-shelled cases were arranged on a shelf like an arsenal. I knew those were the noisy ones – filled with flash powder to explode like flak and burn the retina.

'Coronation of Anne Boleyn, these guys wrap 'emselves up in damp leaves so they don't get burned. They call 'emselves the greenmen,' he was saying, while I looked along the shelves at the trays of different-shaped charges, the sounding tubes labelled WHISTLE, CRY, SCREAM, the colour-coded chemicals: copper sulphate, barium nitrate, strontium salts, a row of traditional Chinese bamboo tubes, a box of fuse-and-pellet chambers, sticks, touchpaper, wax, string, glue. In front of them, my uncle himself, looking less like my father than ever, too much energy in too small a room, mixing dry powders but seeing explosions.

He let me look at his book. It reminded me of the ill-fated science journal my father kept while he tried to defeat Dutch elm disease. The same man whose only writing now was filling in the hen-to-egg ratio on a shit-spattered clipboard. And here was his brother – the designer, the alchemist, still caught in his art, in love with science. There had never really been any fair competition between them. Kipper ran rings round my father. He always had. Yet it was my father who'd landed the girl on the *Hansa*. That must've hurt.

Christmas was close now and I had work in the smokehouse, not doing fish, but the curing of ham. Kipper had bought knuckles of pork by the sackful. From the middle of October the twins and I rubbed salt into the skin of all the cuts we'd got, working hard at the flesh till our own hands were as dry as pumice. We stood on the lawn at two trestle tables – both twins working the hocks, trimming skin, sizing and salting, passing them down to me as if we were rendering the corpses of a whole army. The hams were sunk in large barrels in the lawn, and while they were in the brine we prepared the next batch. After three days we drained them, then worked the skin again, rubbing salt and muscovado sugar into the meat. Kipper would join in at this stage – squatting down on the grass, poking and sniffing the hams, then, with a dash of ceremony, add saltpetre to the brine. Well done lads, my mouth's watering. Saltpetre, which also went into his fire-works, from out the Lab and into the bellies of anyone who ate his meat – both of his industries coming together.

All through October and November I worked this way in the freezing marsh wind, turning the pigs with a wooden paddle in their graves, and then after each batch had had a month, we stacked them in the smokehouse, on a high rack so the fat wouldn't melt. If it did that, they'd be too dry. An ugly stain began to spread across my hands: the dark nicotine of a smokehouser's tan. As a final touch, from high in the chimney I dripped honey over the hams while the twins raked the oak chippings beneath me.

Cliff reaches up and pinches my ankle. 'Nother couple 'o days she'll be ready, he says to his brother. Sandy crawls in beside him and grins wide-mouthed at me. Carve him Christmas Day, what d'ya think? I shift, sending down a cloud of soot to make them back out. *Easy!* they shout, together. That unnerved me, how they thought as one and used their shorthand like all twins do. They spent their time ribbing each other and taking the piss, but when it came down to it they were virtually inseparable. Kipper'll send us all up one day we're not careful, Sandy says, easily the more nervous of the two, about the firework Lab so close on the other side of the wall. Cliff's still staring up at me. He looks at his brother, waiting for a nod to go ahead, then he whispers to me you want to make *real* fireworks? What d'ya reckon? Think it's time you came up the shack, Sandy says.

I know what that means. The shack's where they made the dead man's fingers.

The twins left me there high in the chimney, where the bricks narrowed round me like the throat of an animal. Greasy with rendered pig and fish fat, inches thick with soot. As I scraped away at the blackened wall I revealed the heavily lined carving of a face – a wooden face encased in soot, as ugly as the Lincoln Imp.

Outside I could hear the twins laughing and yanking the smokehouse door by its broken catch. This ain't never gonna get fixed proper, Sandy said.

The face looked like an old man with a thick beard, but it was covered with the wax of fish fat and smoke that had congealed over time. I pushed my knife into the carving till the blade touched the wood beneath, and carefully I exposed

267

the original features: a young man's face with a clean-shaven chin. An honest, clear symmetry to his expression, a dreamy faraway look in his eyes. The face of an angel, carved in exactly the same style as the rest of the *Hansa* carvings. The face of Grandfather Hands.

What was Kipper doing with it? Where had he found it? Had he broken it off all those years before when he spent the summer with his brother on the *Hansa*. Or was it Goose – that other imp – who was responsible for hanging it up there? What better fate for the man who'd deserted her than to have him smoked for years till he grew ugly with age and his dreamy look was lost for ever?

On Friday nights we went to the Albatross. There's Kipper, over by the bar, stooping to avoid the tankards hanging off the beams. Elsie is sitting in the corner with me. She's been drinking Cinzano all evening and she's kept her huge coat on, so her face is flushed. Her eyes look dark here in the pub, and strangely sunken. She's wearing enormous hooped earrings and one of them keeps falling out. She seems nervous.

Kipper's leaning over the bar. A spotlight near him is striking across his face, making him look pretend and untrustworthy, like a waxwork image of himself. He's listening to someone in the back bar. It's Willie Slater and a couple of his mates – I can see Willie's corduroy trousers and the wellies rolled down at the top.

'That ain't the only reason,' Kipper's saying, his voice a little higher than normal. He's trying to keep something light over there. He's smiling and in profile one of his teeth gleams unfortunately, a little like a shark's tooth. 'Yeah, that's for certain all right.' Kipper's agreeing too much. He's trying to force a laugh where there is none, and Willie Slater knows it. There's a loud male shout from the back bar.

'What's he doing, Pip?' Elsie's staring down at the table, the make-up she's put on is too thick. Around her eyes it's given her a permanently surprised look.

'Making a fool of himself,' I whisper.

'He shouldn't get involved. He always rises to it every time.' What's she being so protective about? Let him fight his own battles.

'Elsie. What's really going on with you and him?'

'Oh Christ!' she says. 'You pick your times!' And even while she's saying this Kipper's coming back from the bar, the pint, the half and the odd-shaped Cinzano glass looking as mismatched in his hands as we do in the corner.

'Lads,' he says, sitting down, 'sexual repression in a coastal town. Discuss.' The effort of forcing a joke is still with him. he drinks from his pint and Elsie puts a tense hand on his knee.

Willie Slater comes through, fat and unbalanced on the tile floor. His lips are wet with beer and one of his eyes has become lazy. He puts a whisky down in front of Kipper.

'No offence meant,' he says, staring at Elsie.

'You're all right,' Kipper says.

'You should come out on the speedboat sometime. The both o' you – I mean all three of you,' he says, glancing uneasily at me. I'm part of a mad family in his eyes. 'Else – you'd love it.'

Elsie looks up at him, her chin straight and defined like the edge of an axe. 'I doubt that very much, fat man.'

Willie Slater rolls back on his heels and raises his eyebrows comically, caught between staying and going.

'Ohh, you're feisty, ain't you, lass?'

Kipper stands, his knuckles pressing on the bar table, bridling with anger.

'Time, gent'eman, please!' calls the barman, ringing it out like the ringside bell at the end of the round.

*

On New Year's Eve, Kipper set his fireworks like an artillery range in the marsh halfway to Cley, leaving Elsie and myself in the house. Elsie, standing bloodless by the window, half in shadow, half a shadow herself. We were meant to go to the display but Elsie wasn't going anywhere. She stood by the window and I stood by her, with the lights out, our breath touching the glass in a single misty cloud as the first fireworks leaped up. Hold me, she said, and I put my hand in hers and she stood slumped in front of the window not wanting to be there but doing as she was told as streaks of colour and light shot up into the sky. I imagined Kipper crouching low in the reeds by the firework pen, his expression set on Cley and the crowd building along the bank, the glowing taper in his hand, wondering where we were. The thin whistle of his rockets rising up from his fingertips – their scream turning to agony as they burned out over the rooftops, like the cries of gulls, diving and diving as they hunted eggs. From his boots the low snaps of fireworks crackling through the marsh – leaving blue trails as they search rat-like through the banks of reeds, looking this way, looking that. There's the scatter of birds taking wing. The crowd begins to get nervous. All gettin' a bit close, they think, the lights and bangs advancing on all sides, and now it's rising and gathering pace till the cracks and booms are knocking the windows, waking the children, sending the pets under the beds. All that happening and there was Elsie, kissing me, her lips feeling wet and fleshy on my face. In Cley the sounds of the fireworks are clanging off the flint walls, the men get nervous, like when they hear the lifeboat going out. There are pints left half-drunk on tables. Elsie smiles and I see her face in the dark and I think I'm on the whale again, she's so translucent. There's Kipper, grinning like a devil in the marsh, his smoky eyes set on the village. He's got their attention all right. And now the full arsenal of his Lab goes up. Flash powder cauterizes the air, explosions thud into the marsh. *Here it come!* he yells, *you bastards!* Imagining the Glaven lit up like lava, seeing the flames leap from roof to roof, even the windmill – such a picture postcard – with its sails on fire like a giant roman candle. This was the place where the storm had left Kipper high and dry in a tree, crying like a baby, and now he was bringing it back. *You gutless bunch! I'm here!* And with a sudden, quiet whuump of air, our window shifted in its frame, and the show was over.

'I'm sorry for everything,' Elsie said. 'So sorry.'

'You and me,' I said, and she put her finger on my lips and said don't talk, I don't want you to talk.

We stayed by the window till we saw Kipper's silhouette rising through the dark wave of the riverbank. He vanished as he climbed down the slope on this side. Elsie placed her hand on the windowpane and I wondered whether she was trying to stop him coming. And then he was at the door, stamping the marsh from his shoes and entering the house with sudden speed. The noise of him being inside broke the stillness which until that moment was so perfect, so crystal. He came into the room and shouted *well!* and with it I knew how much he needed adulation, not just for his fireworks, but his fish, his education, his whole scientific approach to life – all there to make us love him. Love this flawed man. Love and loathe him in equal measures, and I felt a darkly turning insight, of being on the outside but able to see in. His two faces, his many sides. How it would end for him. And us by the window said it all. Our breath was still there on the cold glass like a guilty conversation that wouldn't fade.

That night, I fell asleep listening to the rumblings of their argument through the walls. And when I woke, Elsie was lying in bed with me. Perhaps it was the hotness of her breath and the familiar smell of her mouth which made me wake. Her hair had the colour of ash. For a while I gazed at her in the darkness, till I saw the obsidian gleam of her eyes and realized she was looking back at me.

'Come with me. Let's go to the *Hansa* before he's up.'

The saltmarsh was always a soft thing, but that New Year's morning the ground felt crisp with frost and unreal for it. When we reached the lagoon, the water was perfectly still and brilliant, as if it wasn't water at all, but some light liquid metal with the sky trapped down in there, deep in its own reflection. Every few seconds a smooth lap curled along the whole length of the shore, and with it came a small breath of air. Elsie went off to free a cuddy from one of the moorings.

I punted us over with an oar while Elsie stood forward of the cabin. The prow of the boat was covered in frost, and it passed just a couple of inches above the water. There was something about that – that clean white powdery frost, and the water gently stretching next to it, which was so fragile. Just a lip of water splashing on to the deck – the smallest drop – and it would all be lost.

The *Hansa* floated eerily in the full tide, alive and constant in three generations of my family, for Hands, George, Lil', Kipper, Elsie and myself. A part of our identity. Old and black, falling apart, and one of the family. I tied the painter to the gunwale and helped Elsie aboard. She stood on the words my grandfather had carved into the planks. *Jeder macht mal eine kleine Dummheit*, barely visible any more. She seemed excited and apprehensive and I suppose she knew then that this would be the last time for her.

On deck she went to the bow and breathed the salt air deeply. Then just as quickly her shoulders slumped and she began crying softly. I scrambled over and hugged her, realizing for the first time that I was now as tall as her. What was going on? What was happening?

'We had a huge row,' she said. 'Kipper and me – he said these things, Pip, just to hurt, you know, he just wanted to hurt me. He said these things about you and me. I can't take it . . .' She trailed off, sobbing. 'He's going to make me ill – it's already happening. Can't you see – no, you never see, do you – not even your own mother . . .' too upset to stop herself. 'You know, the best moment of my life was on that whale.'

It was just her and myself and miles of sky and water but I felt so watched, so vulnerable. All around us were the carvings. Those grey old carvings my grandfather had done with a German army penknife nearly fifty years ago.

'He's draining my life away,' Elsie was saying weakly.

'Elsie,' I said, using her name as if naming her would make her stop, 'we should leave. Run away. I'll look after you. I'm good at running away.'

She let out a brief laugh. But I didn't want her to laugh.

'Get off this marsh,' I said. 'Let's start somewhere else.' I don't know what I said – it was all coming out in one go – and Elsie wasn't even listening. But by that time I wasn't speaking for her anyway. I was speaking for me and I was speaking for my mother – because it was suddenly so clear I hadn't saved her – my own mother – I couldn't save her – but maybe I could save Elsie. Elsie – the girl who might be my own sister. *It's this marsh.* This beautiful marsh. It will destroy us. It's destroyed them all.

January was terrible. Cold, dark, frozen and silent. On the 31st, after more than two months of fading and fading, Elsie vanished entirely. She left us in the middle of the night. No note. No goodbye. Just gone. It was the anniversary of the great storm of 1953, just as Goose had predicted. A storm's gonna come back, ain't stoppin' till it gets them who got away the first time. And this time, all that was left of Elsie, all that remained, was the smudge of her handprint, still there on the windowpane, like the wave of a ghost.

20

Crabs

The day after my mother went the ice went too. And with it
the mile of footsteps she'd left melted into the drain and
washed away for good. It's odd thinking this way; had the
thaw come a day earlier, would she have stared down at the
water from the bridge at Wiggenhall St Mary Magdalen and
simply turned back? Returned to the farm, made a bread-
and-butter pudding for tea, and we'd have eaten it in silence
and no one would have known how close, how terribly close
she was. Spring's coming, my father would say, and he'd show
us how raw his hands had become over the last few weeks
fixing fences in the estate, nothing colder than a cold length
of wire, he would add. But that didn't happen, and over the
years I've thought that frozen winter was part and parcel of
her own illness, that moments like that wait for us whatever,
that spring would never have come as long as she'd lived.

And now it had happened again, family history circling
like the storms round the North Sea. A cold snap. No mile of
footprints, but the end of a journey none the less. Elsie was
gone.

And she ain't coming back, Kipper was saying, sounding
oddly bullish about the whole thing, building a fire in the
grate, snapping kindling and layering it in a lattice across the
paper. She weren't happy here, we all know that. We'd been
talking things through. That was how he told me, that 1st of
February morning, his back to me as he filled the grate. She'll
write when she feel better about things, there ain't nothing
we can do anyhow, once she make her mind up. Just his back

to me. How can you scrutinize that? And me, plunged once more into silence – because Elsie had gone and with it she'd taken my voice. Best to keep busy, he said. I couldn't tell if he was upset or not. There ain't no more hams – we'll get you work down the crab factory in Cromer. Pay's good. And with that he turned. A grey-eyed look, which said that's that, the deal's done.

Spike yelled at me and I snapped out of the memory. Get that side and don't slip and don't reach too far or you'll do your back in an' that ain't no use to no one! Kipper was wrong, Elsie'd been gone a month and she wasn't writing. Now swing her over, Spike was saying, which was our cue to haul the crate off the Toyota and let it drop on the concrete, the crabs crashing inside like flints. It was seven in the morning and the fisherman was looking down at us from the cab of the truck and cracking jokes because he'd been up since three and his day was done. There were perhaps twelve crates on the truck, and each one had about twenty crabs in it and they'd sit hulked down on their shells with their claws drawn in. The crabs were wide and flat and tried to get us only when we lifted them from the crate. The larger ones were peppered with barnacles, and those barnacles, perhaps mistaking the crabs for flints themselves, had made the wrong choice. Because they were going to die also.

Spike was the cruellest man I'd ever met. Never saw him without a fag hanging from the corner of his mouth – it just hung there, half-smoked, stuck to dry lips, and if a crab swung a pincer at him he'd burn the crab's eyes with the end of the cigarette. Did it to impress the fishermen, who thought he was the lowest of the low. They don't feel pain, he'd say, but when he burned them their claws would clench into one thick knuckled fist under their bodies and a large bubble of spit would foam from their mouths. He was a demon, torturing and roasting and boiling his victims, and in its own way the crab factory was a region of hell and that suited me.

I'll make some calls, Kipper had said, and that evening I'd heard him on the phone saying he won't be no trouble, he don't even talk, he just want to earn some cash. Kipper had shipped me off to Cromer into this inferno, swapping his smokehouse for the boiling tubs. But for me it was heading in the right direction – instead of hanging the dead in a smoking chimney, I was sliding the living into boiling water. Even at that stage I knew how this story would end for me.

So they came off the trucks and the crabs were lifted from their crates and pressed against a yardstick and graded for size. It was a quick process. Lift, measure, throw into a holding cart. And landing with the dry sound of skulls they'd slide against each other and rise up on one side and hold a pincer in the air. Pugilists, the lot of them. In the cart they'd spin and turn and overturn one another – enraged by the factory's sudden violence, claiming territories, seeking safety under each other and folding their legs in fury. Left in the cart they'd eventually huddle down and stop moving. They'd blow some spit, and something would dart in and out of their mouths with the speed of a snake's tongue. It gave the feeling they were watching you, judging, full of knowledge and knowing exactly what was coming next. Which was swift. Spike on one side of the cart and me on the other; we'd lift it to shoulder height and tip it in one motion into the boiling tank. Immediately the notorious shriek would emerge and I would think of the rising screech of Kipper's fireworks as the crabs fell sideways to the bottom, spinning past the bubbles, and it seemed that in some of those bubbles were the last parts of their screams – bursting on the surface and filling the shed like as many crabby souls making their final dash for the sea. And if you kept your head away from the steam, and if the water cleared at all, you could just make out the bottom of the tank and see the claws move tighter, then relax and not move again. Or was it just a trick of the water? I rarely looked. Spike was waiting for me to crack because all the others had over the years, but as for me, when I entered that factory I had no conscience and I wasn't going to let him have the monopoly on cruelty. Many before me had run off down Corner Street slamming brown-stained aprons into the gutter and I wouldn't be one of them. I'd play Spike at his own game. Show no emotion and no compassion and if I gave him no response then his cruelty was pointless and it might take time but that would eventually get him.

After a while a brown scum would rise to the surface which stank and Spike always claimed it was the crabs shitting themselves and when the scum formed a froth so thick it could blow off the surface the crabs were ready. We lifted them out by raising a cage sunk deep in the tank, and when it was clear of the water we left them hanging in the air, up in their gibbet. They cooled like boiled eggs – the water evaporating from their shells leaving them dry and salty and burnished with heat.

By half eight in the morning the crabs were done and the dressing-women were there, full of talk and no-nonsense and Mary you been at it? and whass up love don't fret so and juss comin' back the pub like he always do like nothin' ain't happened. Yeah? Need some ed-u-cation I reckon. Well him an' all just like Eddie and the rest them old dogs, yeah? And the knifes would go into the shells between the back legs and with a crack the crab would unhinge and the meat would pull up and be freed from the shell and the bottom of the crab would be put to one side. All I'm sayin' is he ain't worth it – I ain't havin' a pop love but thass how I see it . . . Despite the heat of the boiling tank it was cold in the factory and they'd rub their noses with the backs of their hands while still holding the filthy knives. Phyllis had been there twenty years and the wood on the bench in front of her had worn down like a butcher's block. Jayne and Karen were younger, but were toughening up from their forearms upwards. She's late by two weeks an' if it's thass made him piss about then he got it comin'. They changed the radio station and made their own tea and ignored us and we skulked about wiping and sweeping while the knives slid in and the flesh came out: dead man's fingers – the poisonous lungs of the crab – lifted from the bodies like wet grey leaves and thrown on the floor in front of the broom. The women cracked the pincers with the handles of their knives and those handles were so worn it looked like a dog had been chewing them. At any moment they might bring us in with a let's ask the quiet one here or ain't that right Spike or you still a virgin? We did the job no one else would do and in their eyes we were little more than the things we boiled.

A long winter, cold and draughty and filled with the struggle of forgetting what had happened. Forgetting the *Hansa* and Elsie and why she'd run away and whether any of it made any sense to me. Elsie, who had always been slightly beyond reach, whose hair colour even now could be seen in the burned shells of the crabs, and it was those crabs themselves – dying by the thousand – that saved me. Spike noticed it first. Instead of throwing them about like flints from one crate to another, I had begun to study them. I held them, dragged my fingernail across their dry-wood shells, stared into their eyes while their pincers snapped the air in front of my face. A crab's eye looks like a piece of shingle on its stalk. Somehow it watches you through that stone, without blinking. I tapped their shells and pulled their armoured joints and pressed my ear to them and heard nothing – not even a whisper of the waves in my mother's seashell.

Spike drew the air in between his teeth, waited for me to walk out, but knew he wasn't quite getting me and that unnerved him.

Like my father listening to the Red Poll bull at the Stow Bardolph Estate, I let those crabs teach me. At night, in the flat above the factory, I thought of how they lurked off the coast, deep underwater, waiting for the boats to come out. Spike and I shared the flat and he spent the evenings watching videos and sitting on a sofa which had already had thirty years of people like him sitting on it. When he went to bed I stared at the sofa, saw his shape pressed into its old cushions, the sweat-mark his head made on the wall behind it, and I imagined all those crabs off the coast, all facing the town that hung on to the cliffs above them. Flexing their knuckles. Waiting for the pots to lower on to the seabed. Down there they'd plot and plan and crawl into the cage to pinch the cod's head and wait till dawn. Others would watch a piece of bacon rind lower on the end of a string and they'd hang on to that bacon like it was life itself even though the fall from the pier's railings might kill them. It was as if they wanted to be caught, to be boiled by the hundred like martyrs. It made me wonder about Gideon's painting of the crab factory with the clouds of boiling steam and the vigorous shape of St Gengulf in its midst, rescuing crabs from certain death by reaching bare-armed into the boiling tank, then letting them crawl their way in a line down Corner Street like a persecuted nation, backing old ladies into shop doorways as they return to the sea. Back to the cod-headed pots once more. And I realized the crab would be caught and caught and would outlive us all. Because the hard-shelled crab can never be broken, despite any torture; it keeps its secrets inside its shell and when that shell is cracked open those secrets cannot be found.

Kipper sent me a postcard in September, telling me Goose was going to be put in a home. The Marge in Upper Shering-ham, where she'd have a view of the sea and three hot meals a day. That same morning I hung up my apron, caught the Coast Hopper minibus to Blakeney and put my bag in my old room at Kipper's house. He didn't seem pleased to see me but he knew he couldn't turn me away. Probably thought about sending me back to my father and his field of chickens again. By the afternoon I was walking down to Lane End across the saltmarsh, watching the hares thundering across the sea lavender. Her gate was off its hinges, pushed into the hedge, and the pile of driftwood she'd collected over the years now looked like the pile of off-cuts behind Bryn Pugh's *Thistle Dew* wreck. Tiles were lifting like the hard crust of Fenland mud at Three Holes when the tulips first broke through. The windows were grimy. The chimney had bent. Junk in the garden. After many years of being the person Morston ignored, Goose had obviously become the person they talked about. Junk like that was all right on a high watermark, but not on your own doorstep, and Morston, after all, was becoming popular with weekenders. It looked like the cottage had been washed up there by the dirty kiss of a spring tide.

Goose had been packed off in a hurry. Boots, tools, papers and the old tin bath lay in a mess on the tiles, as if the 1953 storm had only just gone out the door. I went to the range – just as Hands would have done in those last days of 1945. His nimble fingers might have lifted the cloth over a proving loaf, or dipped themselves in the sauce of Goose's fish pie, but for me there was nothing but the stains, splatters, burns and spills of many years' hard cooking. The mud brown of beef gravy, the flaking scales of an ancient hollandaise and I couldn't help but be there, thirty-odd years earlier, by Lil' Mardler's side as she stands on a stool to stir the pot while Goose looks on.

'Mind that don't stick.'

'I won't let it.'

'It's stickin'.'

'No it *isn't*.'

'There, thass stuck, you fool – you've done it now.'

And so it goes on. My mother growing up, noticing things on the marshes – how the samphire grows near the terns' nesting sites – how they might be served next to each other on the plate. How a mussel opens only when it's ready to eat. How the chickens try to avoid fish bones because they taint their eggs. She takes it all in and practises her art. Till one day she's ready to leave like Hands before her and me after her. The whole family line, hell-bent on running. And now it's Goose herself, the only one of us to have stuck it out, truly, without changing. Lane End would be sold to pay for her bills, and while I could stay with Kipper for the time being, I'd have to move on. Be like the crab – crawl into the pot, grip the cod's head.

Take whatever comes.

The dayroom was large and as hot as a greenhouse, with a TV facing no one in particular and large leatherette seats round the sides. I hadn't seen Goose for a long time, and now, everyone looked like Goose except Goose herself, because without the saltmarsh and the clouds rushing about her head she was just a little old lady slipping down a plastic-covered chair. Someone had finally persuaded her to have her hair cut. That must have been a scene all right. Holding her down while the clippers go in. Like shearing a sheep. She had a very small head now.

'That one,' she said to me in a loud whisper, 'that one by the window – she's that bitch from Bodham.'

I sat on the easy chair next to hers and looked across the room at a plump woman fussing with a newspaper, trying to fold it inside out.

'Ain't that right,' Goose said, 'messed with them clouds, live up the farm on the heath and she change them clouds – did it for years till we go sort her out.' The woman flapped the paper smartly. I remembered something my mother had told me – how Goose had spent a year believing someone inland was changing clouds as they passed overhead before they reached the saltmarsh. How Goose had taken my mother to see the woman, found her on the lawn hanging sheets out. They'd had a big row.

'Serve her right to come here to die,' Goose was saying, and the plump woman gave her a mean look over the paper. I wasn't sure Goose knew who I was any more.

That was with my mother, I wrote on a notelet, which I then didn't show to her.

Goose sat in the easy chair and started to laugh, showing off her uneven row of madwoman's teeth.

'Pip Langore, you remember the seal, don't you? Yes, you do, I can see you do, that seal I got us. That make me laugh still.'

She squinted at me with her flint-grey eyes, making me remember the day she'd brought back a dead seal to Lane End. She'd put it on the floor and had tapped the frame of my bed with her walking stick to wake me up. Look what I got us, boy, she'd said. Goose had the seal on a piece of newspaper like it was fishing bait, all greasy and very dead, and she had stood next to it in her thick wool socks. Willie Slater hit it, she'd said, her face creasing up in some poorly disguised glee.

Hit it off the Longs in that new speedboat, silly prat, what's he gone and done spendin' two thousand on a speedboat with a hun'erd horse power just to impress that girl he's got. Well, she weren't impressed when he hits the seal pup, were she?

She'd begun prodding the seal and telling me what had happened next. Willie Slater's slowin' the boat as he come to the mouth of Morston Creek. He's got one arm round that tart an' he's got this look of thunder about him 'cause this dead seal's on the back seat an' it's all bloody on the up-hol-estery. Goose had levered the seal's jaw open the way you do a cat when you get a pill down it, and she'd pulled out a strand of seaweed before going on. So Willie's cut the throttle out there an' he's havin' this blazing row. *We cain't take that pup in, you hair*, he'd said, Norfolk to the core despite his money. *Them's protected and I don't want no trouble*. End of, he was saying. But the girl's in the back of the boat stroking the bloody thing and saying *it's so young, so young* through her tears.

The long and short of it had been Willie got his way, because he'd killed the seal showing off and it was his corpse to get rid of.

Goose had described hearing the satisfying splash as the pup was thrown overboard, the engine restarting, and watching the ugly profiles of Willie Slater and the girl, who now hated him, passing in the lolly-red speedboat as it went down the channel.

'Had to wade out there I did, clothes an' all. Poor bugger just bobbin' up on the surface an' I pull it in by its tail.'

That was the story, that was how the seal found its way to Lane End, not for dignified burial, but for a pepper sauce. Wanted sealmeat all my days, she'd said. Her impatience had made her burn it, the sauce disguised that somewhat, and we'd eaten it like steak, with sharp knives and new potatoes.

But I think Goose loved this story so much because she'd

thrown the carcass, those few disjointed bones, out on the lawn 'for the foxes'. There are no foxes on the saltmarsh. Those bones had been for the villagers, and they saw them all right. The bloody woman's killed and eaten a seal. She's just gone and done the unimaginable. A woman like that could eat their children.

The wickedness of the memory was making Goose chuckle.

'We got us our stories all right, ain't we lad? They cain't do nothin' to take them off of us.' She reached for her stick and pointed out a place setting on the breakfast table on the other side of the room. There was a childlike label with 'kitty's place' written on it in lower-case letters, a cartoon cat leaning against the first k of her name.

'We've got music and movement after lunch,' Goose said. 'Bastards. I'm gonna flash my fanny.'

A carer marched in at that point and Goose resigned herself to being hauled up the chair. She shooed the woman off and leaned forward, whispering for the first time.

'Lissen hair,' she said, 'you watch out for Kipper Langore. I ain't saying that man's out to harm but he is a liability, you unnerstand? Closer you get to a man like that the worse it get. Ever'thing he touch turn to salt in the end.'

With that she sat back in her chair.

'Have to burn everythin' now,' she said quickly. 'Down Lane End – make a good fire, I ain't goin' back.'

And that's exactly what I did. When I'd finished pulling the furniture from the house I unlocked the shed and looked at the junk in there. A crab pot, spare transom and rudder, an overcoat, half a barrel, bags of garden ties, string, rags, wire, twine, netting. Beneath it, the snapped-off prow of a rowing boat, painted Oxford blue. It could only be one thing, kept and kept hidden in an outside shed. The *Pip*. My namesake. The boat Hands had apparently repaired, recaulked, revarnished, repainted, and sailed away in. The boat of Goose's original myth. I closed my eyes and thought of Hands raising the quilted sail, of his determined long-distance gaze and his mind set on Europe. And he looked at me and gave me a knowing wink.

It all went on the lawn where I doused it with paraffin, and as dusk fell I set light to it, the upturned prow of the *Pip* in the centre. It took until the flames were a man's height before the bees came out – one by one – their wings on fire, burning briefly, carried upward by the punch of heat into the black Norfolk sky. And mixing in with the bees I began to watch amaretto wrappers lifting as they burned, lit by candles at the fondue party at Stow Bardolph all those years ago. My mother's face full of the knowledge of what was going on with her husband and the younger woman, letting the wrappers cast a tragic light on her while my father tried to be the man he never was.

'What d'you want?' Kipper says, wreathed in smoke, leaning there in the smokehouse doorway. I just stand there while he rakes the oak chippings. He's in an odd mood.

He unthreads bloaters from the pipes, being careful not to break their gills, and calmly says, 'I don't reckon we'll be seeing Else again, and without her I don't reckon there's much reason you sticking around. I don't want you here no more.'

It's all lies. It's all a big lie.

'She had us good and proper,' he says.

He must have got rid of her, sent her away, arranged things – because he always arranges things because that's how the Langore brothers have always done it – pillar to post.

You got rid of her, I write.

'What – like May?' he says casually. 'Like your mother?' My

uncle has stopped doing the bloaters and is staring at me from in the smoke. 'That's why your mum and dad went to the Fens. It weren't some bright new beginning. It was 'cause she was knocked up. And it weren't you. It was your sister, Elsie Holbeach.'

He said that – I'm sure he said that. *Did he?* He told me Elsie was my sister and he told me he'd packed her off and I just stood there outside his smokehouse, holding the broken latch on the old door and above both of us the clouds started arranging themselves.

'Now, get away from me,' he said.

That evening I went to Cley and knocked on the flat where the twins lived. Cliff came to the door and I gave him my note: *I want to make dead man's fingers.*

21

Dead Man's Fingers

Whatever happen don't let it smoke or it'll have your face off, Cliff said, as we walked through the oak copse on the way to the field. The oak wood smelled dry and old like a church. Sandy lit a cigarette as we walked and Cliff told him to stub it out, bloody fool, and they both had a laugh at that. Through the trees the field raked up at an angle into the sky, and the shack was there, perched on its crest. 'We're stopping here by the hedge, all right?' Cliff said. They gave me the demijohns, and a newspaper filled with ice cubes. Remember how I told you, all right? Any trouble and we ain't going to be any part of this, OK? I nodded, but they were part of it all right, they were part of my plan.

Inside the shack it had the earthy smell of a potting shed. The first room had a dry-baked trestle table in front of a small sash window. There were cobwebs on the glass and a milky view of the field outside. Piled into particular order was the usual farming heap: scythes with thirty years' work on their blades, forks, picks, dibbers, plungers, blunted screwdrivers, paint tins hammered shut, jam jars full with nails, lengths of rope, twine, barbed wire, bands, sacking, chemical bags, seed bags, agricultural calendars, worming tablets. Throw nothing away, end up with nothing. Tools chucked down in frustration, treated with disregard and impatience, botched repairs, jobs half finished, problems half solved. The air was thick with the odour of damp soil, grass seeds, dead birds, old magazines, rat shit, diesel, Vaseline, turps, tea bags, apples and, through it all, the sharp smell of rusted iron as if the machinery had grown half vegetable.

A second room was tidier, though it too had a sour stink. By the window was another trestle table, this one held up by bricks at one end. This was where the twins had left the enamel bowl, the wax, goose feathers and, beside them, Kipper's firework journal. They'd stolen that from the Lab. His book of spells, yet when I opened it there were two sets of handwriting – the neat copperplate of my uncle and the lazily wandering letters of my father on loose sheets folded into the spine, from a time when his study and his science was an intriguing, secret world. This book was the combined dream of the Langore brothers' science, listing the instructions that could counter the stories the women peddled – the myths of clouds and sails and flowers and food and Ol' Norse and creek-diggers and spirits of the North Sea and the ghosts of ancient storms. All the things that kept us men from the straight and narrow. Read the Book and train your mind. Rationalize, concentrate, like Hands did with his sail.

Those brothers, swimming across the Pit to the *Hansa*; oh yes, Kipper you'd tied the knots all right, but Shrimp had thrown further and he could talk to the birds. I thought of all the jobs they'd both done here; of all those my father had done at Stow Bardolph Estate, the breeding tables, the weights and measures, the ledgers he'd tried to neaten up; and I thought of Kipper arriving at my parents' wedding with his bag of fireworks and his clothes beginning to smell of fish and smoke. They'd tried, both of them, breeding bulls and selling fish and curing hocks but really, it had all come to nothing. They'd never done anything but be the boys they always were.

I read my father's name in the journal and the date: 8 May 1968. My mother's birthday. Next to it, in his still-dreaming script: *The Manufacture of Artificial Amber*. From later years,

The Chicken's Nervous System, curious annotations . . . *watch it ferment but mind you don't breathe it in . . . a poker will do, though one of those three-quarter fencing posts is better . . . the cigarette does not burn the leaf* . . . I see him in his study, a threadbare rug beneath his desk, cool to touch, always slightly damp; I see him reaching for books off the shelf as the smell of a meat pie my mother's baked him rises from the plate on his desk. He's forgotten about it. He's nibbling the corners of the page as he thinks. The green desk lamplight on his face like a wartime code-breaker, and he turns to me and says *whatever happen don't let it smoke or it'll have your face off.*

Behind me something stirred and I thought it was my father the chicken man and I turned to see a rope pulling taut across the doorway. The rope pulled tighter and flecks of dust sprang out of the twine. Then it went slack, and in came a goat, chewing a magazine photo of Elvis, slipping as it trod across a pile of potato skins. The skins themselves were leather-dry, but still sprouting with the potato's ceaseless self-belief. An optimistic vegetable, that one. I sat next to the goat, just beyond the length of its tether. The goat didn't like this much, but knew the length of the rope and didn't bother to jab. It was an old billy, with long stained whiskers, a grey mottled ridge of hair down its back and hooves as dark as coal. Beyond the goat, a small room blackened by the fire that had once nearly burned the shack down. I realized that this was where the young boy from Cley had received his burns, not a firework blowing up in his face, but making the dead man's fingers for the twins, and it was Kipper who'd taken the blame. I sat at the table and stared across the field at the twins, both of them in dirty work jeans and T-shirts. It was getting hot out there. Sandy had taken off his Doc Martens and Cliff was reading a paper. Bloody dead man's fingers, I thought. I'd show them.

What time was it, half-nine – ten? A few miles away Goose would be banging her radio into life, knocking it against the easy chair till the batteries fell into place while the smell of poached eggs rose from the kitchens. She'd check the mealy Upper Sheringham clouds while a nurse beat the pillows and paced the floor and she'd squint at the nurse's arse and wonder whether she'd start her comments or leave them till later. My father dragging chickens off their eggs, Kipper beating the price down on fish. A vein of arrogance running through my family.

The walls were covered with snares, traps and poaching wires. Eight-strand snares with peg and tealers hung from nails in the roof, badger-tunnel snares along a wall, fox one-lever-release traps down by the window, and several mole-shaft traps in a wooden tray by the table. Their metal smelled of wild garlic. There were photos too, of a fat very dead pike being held over the side of a boat, a pile of rabbit corpses across the freshly ploughed furrows of a field. A fox with his hind leg broken and torn.

I have to do this. I have to see all this through.

On the table was a Swan Vesta matchbox, and as I slid it open something twitched from one side to the other. It was a queen bee, starved but alive, curled into the box lengthwise with its still-iridescent abdomen moving in some kind of agony. Its wings were paper dry and in pieces around it. I carefully slid it back into the box and began to make the dead man's fingers, carefully reading the method in Kipper's journal. *Never leave the mix*, it said, and then in his best writing my uncle had eulogized the chemicals:

Glycerine is made as a by-product of making soap. Uses: emollient and laxative.
$C_3H_8O_3$ *sulphuric acid: (containing sexivalent sulphur) dense and oily, colourless.*

H_2SO_4, nitric acid: (containing nitrogen in the quinquevalent state) (mix of five), colourless, poisonous.
HNO_3 (glycerine + OLI?).
Nitro-glycerine is yellowish. The colour of smoked fish skin!

I poured the liquids from the demijohns and began to stir with a glass rod, round the bowl, round the bowl, the sound of the rod on the enamel and I saw the folds of dough on a proving loaf, and then the flour dust on the soft hair of my mother's arms. Thin dark hairs covering in dust as if years and years were passing while I watched. Pass me the raisins, she says, and I see we're making a malt loaf together, to be ready when Elsie comes round with Mrs Holbeach. Flowers growing outside the kitchen window. Not all of them, she says, as I tip the bowl into the mix. She saves one or two and says these are special, these are ours, and she pops them into my mouth and I taste the salt and flour and butter on her fingers. Why did you walk out on to the ice? I say to her and it makes her laugh. Why? I ask again. Because that was the way out, wasn't it, my love, that was the path I'd never seen before.

The goat looked at me with the mean emptiness of its species. Beyond it, my father, looking up at me from the books on his desk in the pool of green light as I appeared in my pyjamas in the middle of the night at the door of his study, me, woken by bad dreams and now unable to understand the look of impatience he gave me, waiting for him to flick his pen to shoo me away from the door down the corridor to go pester my mother, and I thought, at that moment, how my entire life seemed to be an inexhaustible journey of wrong turns and unresolved moments. That I had to take charge now. I had to find my own way out.

And then something was stinging my eyes and I saw all the ice cubes were just water and rising out from the enamel bowl were the first wisps of smoke curling strangely and gently out of the liquid. What had my uncle written, don't let it smoke, never leave the mix, not what to do if it smoked. I stirred harder, then left it, then stirred again, softer this time. Whatever I did the smoke kept coming, growing stronger, following some rule deep within it that had nothing to do with me. I thought of the traps, which were like evil grinning mouths, and then, curiously, of Goose's hollandaise, the one she'd stirred in 1944 while Hands looked on, folding the mixture in so the egg didn't curdle, and a hollandaise has always curdled for me, even while my mother looked on and that was no use, just no use at all and then that damned goat was there by my elbow, tugging at my shirt and I tried to push it away and it butted me back and some of the mixture slopped up the side of the bowl. *Careful!* Each drip a fully-made bomb just waiting to go off.

The smell of the acids was filling the air, and as I looked down at the mix in the dim light of the trap room, I saw the strong silent curls of smoke rising from the colourless liquids and I sensed the profound beauty of science. Powerless to do anything but stare at the rising vapour, like I'd once gazed down the burning barrels of a shotgun and seen the heat haze rising from the metal, as if I was witnessing some dark, revealing miracle.

The mysterious fire was locking itself into the molecules of these densely coiled fluids. I was enthralled by it, and there, I wanted to plunge my hands into the mix and feel the violence of the acids. I took my lead from Kipper at that point, methodically arranging the goose feathers into rows, damping them into the mixture and carefully rolling them within the sheets of wax. Rolling them like firework tapers, a thin line of fuse cord down their centres like the spine of a wild animal. Dead man's fingers, the explosives those twins had never dared to make themselves, stacked on the side of the trestle table as the sun lowered over the field outside and its rays glowed through the window as if through the bars of a fire and I thought about this shack on the crest of its own hill and about how Norfolk's veins were filled with a deep, explosive fire just waiting to get out.

It was dusk when we walked back through the oak copse. The twins let me carry the dead man's fingers and Sandy led the goat ahead of us. It was sick and needed to be put down, Cliff reckoned, and he said he would have done it there and then at the shack except you should always make it walk to its grave before you killed it because then you didn't have to carry it, like George Langore, the dreamer boy, had been told all those years before when he'd had to kill his first sick calf. I held the dead man's fingers, smelled the fear in my shirt and looked up at the evening sky. Here come the clouds, I thought.

Here come the clouds.

Early morning, still dark across the marsh, and Kipper's standing on the lawn in a blue smock holding a mug of tea in his hands.

'You're joking,' he's saying, 'you can't think of going out today.'

Across the lawn the twins are standing with their fishing gear. 'Come on, Kipper,' Cliff says, 'you gotta do it some day and you ain't never caught a hound yet.'

'I know that, but it's gonna be bad weather coming and your boat ain't nothing but a floating wreck.'

That sounds like a compliment to the twins.

'Kipper, we'll bait you up, get you a hound and be back for lunch, how about it?'

'When's the tide?' Kipper asks.

'She'll float in a half-hour. If we stick to the channel then go wide off the Longs we'll get an extra run.'

'Pip's coming,' Sandy says, 'he's gonna catch his first hound.'

'No one should be on a boat today,' Kipper says, sniffing the air, a little hint of that old competitive edge in his voice. He looks at me in a calm, level way. He knows something is up. Things are still not straight between him and me. I'm unnerving him.

'All right,' he says.

All four of us crossed the saltmarsh towards the *Bastard*, which was tied up to a rough wooden staithe in a former oyster creek. The twins carried the heavy rods and bait bucket and bags and they were trying not to slip in the mud and they were scuffing their boots through the sea lavender. I was trailing, holding the dry-bag, and in it I'd secretly put the rough sticks of dead man's fingers, each one of them rolled and sealed in wax. They were further wrapped in cotton wool. Kipper came up to my side.

'What you up to?' he said, directly. 'Why are you suddenly hanging out with these two?'

I ignored him. Across the marshes the sky was filling with clouds. Ugly grey banks of storm clouds, and barging their way through the cumulus were coming the trickster fractonimbus – the rag clouds – wasp-like, quarrying the weather and stoking up a sky so filled with trouble it looked like a winterland of mountains and ice. A storm was coming. A hell of a storm.

The twins had noticed it by the time we reached the *Bastard*. Don't look pretty, Cliff said, always the first to talk, and Sandy said we shoun't go out 'cause the luggers are heading back in. Pussies, Cliff said, and they both laughed. Sandy pushed the cuddy down with the weight of one leg and said what d'ya reckon to his brother. I ain't going back, not with all this stuff, Cliff said, besides, boat's made out of wrecks, ain't it?

'This is madness,' Kipper said, beyond the point of turning back. We climbed in and Cliff towed the boat into the channel till the water was as high as his chest on the waders. He hauled himself on to the bow like he was scaling a wall, and Sandy dropped the outboard on the transom, fixed the wing nuts and pulled the cord. Three times, then it fired with a dirty cough of two-stroke exhaust. Sandy held the tiller, staring at the horizon in the manner of all boatmen, while Cliff pulled himself round the cabin dragging the trim of the boat so heavily on one side the rods fell and I grabbed the dry-bag in case it tipped. Sensing the sea, the eels coiled and writhed in their bucket like hoses filling with water. Kipper, looking for space on a small boat, edged his way front of the cabin till he was crouching near the bow itself.

'You staying there?' Cliff shouted above the racket of the engine.

Kipper nodded, crouching on the deck.

'Suit yerself!' Cliff shouted, then to his brother said, 'Well, how about that, he ain't got the nerve out here!' All three of us looked at Kipper, clutching the front of the cabin. After all this time, all his life living by the sea, put him on a boat and he was scared rigid.

'She's coming this way,' Cliff said of the storm.

'Got the primus?'

'Stowed. You know – I ain't gonna try the heavy line. I'm going for the 18-pound uptide.'

'Rod's a 40-pound.'

'Don't matter. I'm going uptide and use the water.'

'From the Banks?'

'What d'ya reckon?'

'Let's try it on the tide then take her further.'

And Sandy looked at me and said hounds love some weather anyhow. A hound being a male tope, the prize of their sea. So the twins settled into their fish-talk and were soon laughing about hooks and reels and traces and bait. They kept looking at Kipper, still clutching the front of the boat and looking nervous with it. That's one funny sight, Sandy said, then began to tell a story about a hound shark that got away – and not just the fish but the rod too, which had leaped from the tripod when a tope made its first charge and all he'd seen was his rod like a javelin skimming the water till the weight of the reel took it under.

'Got the rod clipped nowadays,' he said. 'He always make a charge and I let him go till he stop and then I hit him.'

Cliff disagreed. 'You fish uptide he go ten feet you got to hit.'

'Ten feet you reckon?'

''Specially if you've lip-hooked.'

Kipper kept staring at me, thin-lipped and uneasy, as the boat dipped and swayed into the deeper water. His time was coming. Beyond him the sky continued to deepen. The rag clouds were marshalling the storm and sending it higher. I began to make out the rudimentary shapes as they formed – Ol' Norse like a genie, wrapping his arms in vapours he pulled from the sea, spinning fish and animals and birds into his cloak. I was afraid to look. Everywhere the water was darkening and softening and I could smell the storm like a freshly cut onion.

We were beyond the Race by then and heading straight offshore. Blakeney, the Morston Meals, the Point and Holkham dunes were becoming a paper-thin line behind us, between sky and sea, as if a finger could wipe it clear.

'Talk about the one that got away,' Cliff said with a wink to his brother. 'Wonder who Elsie's screwing now.'

Just words, just words, I thought, remembering how the fire had locked itself into the acids in the enamel bowl. How the clear liquid had coiled and darkened and seemed to lose reflection, and I looked at the twins and Kipper and I knew I didn't have any fear any more, not of anything, and the twins seemed strangely uneasy and couldn't look back at me so they needlessly started to fuss with their tackle instead. Gradually the water became choppy beneath us. This was the shallow area they called the Banks.

'We got to head back in!' Kipper shouted from the front.

Cliff cut the engine and shook his head back. I'm enjoyin' this, he muttered to his brother, we're gonna laugh about this one. Cliff glanced at me and reached for an eel. It twisted quickly round his fist like he was binding a belt across his knuckles ready to fight. It made it hard for him to get at the tail so he whacked it against the keel housing and it fell off him, stunned. He trapped it under his foot and cut it in half, about six inches above the tail. The eel coiled so tightly it rose with the knot it made, and then it began to loosen and twist into the gaps between the planks. Dark red blood and oil slid away from its severed end.

I watched the eel die, and felt my fist clench round something in my pocket. And as Cliff threaded the eel on to the wire trace I looked to see what it was and I saw the unmistakable insignia of the charging bull on my father's switchblade razor.

I sat back against the cabin, then, while Cliff cast off and Sandy cut another chunk of the eel, I opened the blade a fraction, nicked the end of my thumb with it and saw a tiny bead of blood there.

The water shivered round the boat and grew expectant and suddenly all those storm clouds seemed to look familiar, all those wicked rag clouds had been whipping up the sky into the same one I'd seen once before, that day at Bedlam Fen.

Returning, again, like Goose always said it would, a North Sea storm caught in its own endless spin.

The twins were watching the rod tips and their lines and frying some butter on the primus for the rest of the eel. The cuddy fell silent apart from the hiss of the gas and the creaks of the screws and flathead nails that held the various parts of the boat together. Water sloshed around darkly under the deck boards, and occasionally one or other of them bailed with an empty margarine tub.

I opened the dry-bag and felt inside for the dead man's fingers. Each one had a smooth water-resistant taper attached to the end.

Sandy noticed the open bag and nudged his brother. Cliff looked at his line, then said what you got in there? I ignored him. He hadn't seen.

The butter started to spit and Sandy chucked in the eel. The smell of oily fish and butter and sea air made me think of Goose, how she used to stand by her stove in Lane End. I wondered whether she was standing in the dayroom, fascinated by the cloud-tops of the storm she could see rushing towards the land.

And at that point Cliff's rod tipped and the reel span with a high whiz. Both twins whooped and the line rushed and Sandy called *strike!* But Cliff waited and looked coolly at his twin as though he had all the time in the world. Gradually the line relaxed, and like a sniper Cliff lifted his rod from the tripod, wound a couple of turns on the reel to take the slack and jerked the rod backwards and suddenly he was shouting and reeling in and letting the shark fight the line and bite the trace and he knew he had it. Kipper was standing and beginning to edge his way round the side of the cabin, nervously. Sandy stamped delight and punched the gunwale with his knuckles and then punched Cliff on the arm and Cliff barged him back with his shoulder and both of them were laughing and standing up and really you shouldn't stand up on small boats and no one noticed the storm was hanging above our heads like the phantom mask of a giant with barred teeth and that in all that motion and ignoring everything around me I'd pulled out the razor and had placed it carefully on deck. My moment, my plan, the chance to finish. And now things were happening according to their own determined logic – I saw the fuses were all tying themselves together in a strange knot like the eels in the bucket and it was only halfway tied when I felt I knew what the knot was and it was none other than the clumsy granny-slip which Goose had tied in my mother's umbilical cord. And the knot made me laugh out loud and despite all that was going on both twins stopped what they were doing and stared strangely at me, knowing what was about to happen. Kipper too, nearly reaching me and his eyes wide in fear. But whether they realized it or not none of them moved when the knotted fuses passed through the flame of the primus and I held the sticks of dead man's fingers as they spat and fizzed in my hand like a bunch of frost-blackened carrots.

Though the twins acted in unison all their lives it was Sandy who screamed while Cliff looked on frozen in shock. Cliff continued to reel, even though he wasn't aware of doing so any more. And in my fist the fiery white flames of the fuses were burning chaotically round the knot and the sparks felt hot and painful on my skin. I remember seeing something darkly impenetrable and amazing in Kipper's eyes. Then Sandy jumped on me and was ramming my hand against the bulwark and somehow the sticks came loose and briefly they looked as if they were dancing about with their own excitement, their own explosive life they contained, till Cliff's boot lifted them on his toe and punted them over the side.

*

An instant later there was a deep *oomph* under the boat like the sea was suddenly as solid as soil and the whole cuddy lifted and broke and split around us. The sea peaked up like daggers between the boards and a rush of venomous noise spat out between the sharp edges of water and the steam of some liquid which wasn't water and wasn't air flew violently and stung me in my eyes, and my ears felt punched by a sound I hadn't quite heard. And all four of us were falling through the juddering boat like we'd been up in the air and there was nothing beneath us and bits of wood and plank were turning in front of us like we had to examine them, and I saw my father's switchblade razor flying once more like a beautiful sleek fish in front of me – the bull on its handle charging free.

The holes we fell through turned out to be full of the sea and there was no more explosion beneath us and the boat was rapidly nothing more than the cannibalized wreckage of all the boats it had once been, all sliding off on the waves as if they were trying to get back to their wrecks. Then in the middle of the wood and the splashing it felt oddly calm and I sensed a weird shape pass by me which wasn't wood and was as cold as the sea and I stared into the water and saw the long grey flank of the hound tope, its passionless eye and its shark's tail threading through the stunned wreckage.

It shouldn't have happened in the middle of the sea, but I was standing on tiptoes on a sandbank. Further away, the bucket of eels bobbed at an angle, beyond them, the sight of Kipper Langore, no thought for anyone else, swimming for his life in that no-nonsense front crawl of his, heading for Blakeney Point. Head down, a breath to the right after every four strokes. You bastard. Near me, the twins struggling to stand upright on the bank while their waders filled with water. Cliff spluttering in the choppy waves and shouting insults and trying to claw his way towards me, and Sandy pulling him back or trying to hold on and both of them dragging each other to where the sandbank seemed higher.

I clung to a piece of wood and started paddling for the Point, while around me the water began to boil under a hail of raindrops as heavy as lead shot. And yes, I did look back. Several times in fact. Each time, the twins were a little smaller, standing like broken staithe posts half-buried in the sandbank amid the steam and mist of the storm.

In the sea again – my family always ending up in deep water. But I'd never been this far out or this lost in the middle of such a storm. The piece of driftwood I clung to was painted dark blue. And as I paddled and splashed I put my face against its cold gloss and felt it lifting me clear from the water. I knew my legs were still moving, but the water was cold and I didn't really know whether I was going towards land or whether I was heading towards Dogger Bank and the swirl of North Sea, which had claimed my grandfather. If any of that story had been true. Blue gloss on the driftwood. Its colour seemed to be the only important thing. Above me, the storm hailed its heart out and pushed me further into the sea until I began to think the water might be some vast relaxing bed meant for sleep. My ears and eyes and mouth were full of water and my splashing legs sounded like the rain all round me. Dark blue wood. Yes, that's vital. The *Bastard* cuddy was built of many boats, but none of them was this colour. And this piece had been in the sea a long time. It was covered in a film of seaweed, moving like soft hair in the water. A long smooth piece of wood, the back half of a dinghy perhaps, and painted in a precise script by a delicate hand were the letters P and i.

P and i.

P and i.

The rhythm of my paddling. Lean my head on the wood; feel the barnacles and limpets, feel the sea, feel the whale, Elsie beside me, floating off, floating off. And as the cold swept over me in waves larger than the sea itself, I went in and out of consciousness, thinking back on my favourite memory of diving under water in the Pit, diving through the shafts of sunlight on a warm summer's day, the image of the *Hansa* refracting gently above me. Seals spinning and diving in the distance, the feel of the sandy bottom on my chest. I think of Hands's carvings along the wreck's gunwale: the gannet, the fish of the Dogger Bank, the storm petrels and the lobster.

And I remember that the the *Pip* had been painted Oxford blue. The *P-i-p*. The same shade of blue which was keeping me afloat now.

Nowhere to go but the bottom of the sea. Nowhere to go but the bottom of the sea. It went through my head because I'm sure that's what Hands must have been saying when he clung to the same bit of wood. And then strangely I wasn't on the *Pip* any more. The old smooth Oxford blue was gone, and in its place was the sharp dust of shingle and sand on my face. A wave which kept lifting me forward and pulling me back, dropping me on a beach and then rolling me off again. I slept some more, till the beach kept knocking me awake and I thumped it and tried to bang it quiet with my head. Why wouldn't it leave me alone? I was happy on the *Pip*. I'd been searching for it all my life. And now this beach with its sand as sharp as broken glass. I crawled out of the wave on to the shore and fell into a deep sleep. When I woke my mouth was full of sand and I couldn't – for a while – use my legs. But there they were, stretched out on the beach. There was the sea, and all around me the high-backed shore which could only be the Point. And the only thing which was missing was my piece of driftwood. It had disappeared. It wasn't by my side. It wasn't down the shoreline. Gradually I stood and started to look for it. Without my piece of the *Pip* I might always be lost.

But I never found it.

The storm had disappeared, leaving in its place a hot late-summer's day. Across the Point, over short-cropped grass, sea lavender blew gently, surrounded by the bright green of the year's new crop of samphire. Who would pick it this season, I thought, now Goose was in the home? The heatwave was continuing, the damp earth was steaming. Larks trilled their summer-meadow song – a sound so pure – all the times you've heard it before, all the times you hope to hear it again. And through the steamy air I saw the dark carcass of the *Hansa*. I walked to it and held its rotting hull. An old friend. I swam slowly across the channel and climbed out on the Morston side. The same spot where Hands had first appeared, buried up to his neck in mud.

Across the marsh, a man was hammering a SOLD banner over the FOR SALE sign outside Lane End, while a team of builders inside hacked off the old plaster with its tidemark from 1953.

The sun was low in the sky when I reached Kipper's house. I must have been in the water all day. Or had it been days? I kept thinking I saw the twins standing like posts in the reedbeds, but I knew they were just visions.

No one was in. I went to the window where Elsie had left her handprint and I placed my print on the other side of the glass. Hello. I searched the house. The muddy footprints from my own shoes were the only signs anyone had been in. The arm of his chair, pockmarked where he knocked the embers from his pipe. Even that pipe – an affectation. The calm dim shadows of his front room, the smell of tobacco, the hint of fish. The cave-like room of a man, a collector, a man wanting to possess and display.

I went outside again to find the whole marsh bathed in a soft sunset glow. Summer's so beautiful in Norfolk, I thought. Can this colour of light really exist anywhere else? I was sitting on the scrub lawn, and in front of me was the heavy wooden door of the smokehouse. Wisps of smoke curled out from the cracks like dark nails being pulled from the wood. I'd seen this before. In the clouds. A heavy door locked tight. I saw it in the clouds just after Kipper told me what he'd done with Elsie. What *had* he done with Elsie?

I tried to open the smokehouse door, but the latch had entirely gone. It had played up for years. Will someone please get that latch fixed! Kipper would say for the hundredth time – neither him nor the twins ever thinking it was necessary enough to do it. I put my finger in the hole where it had been but couldn't get the door open. Finally I prised it with a bloater pole, and through the roll of sickening grey smoke that came out I saw my uncle, sitting on the earth, muddy and covered with strands of seaweed, surrounded by still-glowing oak chips, as peaceful as a Buddha.

He'd tried to put the fire out, but he would have known the oak chips never really burned, they just smouldered, and it would take a week for them to go out naturally. He'd cleared the earth where he sat, and had crouched as low as possible in the hope that enough air might get in under the door for him to breathe, but there was no hope. Not really. I think he must have suffocated fairly quickly. In the minutes after the latch came away in his hand perhaps. So many times that had happened before, so many times me or one of the twins had pulled that door open.

Above him, the carving of Hands looked down like a

guardian angel, both of them silent, as if I'd interrupted a long and detailed conversation.

Lived all your life by the sea and when it came down to it how strange you were so terrified of it. I suppose it was the effect of being stranded up that tree when you were a boy, the night of the great storm. Looking down into those angry waves and thinking they'd be back to get you, one day. That front crawl of yours, a friend to the last, getting you back to dry land without even a look over your shoulder. And then crawling into the warmth of your smokehouse: the action of a rat. Well, you're dead now, Kipper, you deserve nothing less. You've done nothing but drive people away, force their hand, furnish your pocket, and where has it got you? Smoked with the bloaters, that's where.

I had to touch him. To be sure. I reached out and held his hand. Dead man's fingers all right. Odd that those grey eyes were shut and his mouth hung open, much like the bloaters themselves after five hours of smoking. And like them, his skin had taken on the waxy flypaper hue which said he was ready. Not quite smoked to the bone, as he would have said, but he wasn't far off it either.

He'd last for years in his grave.

22

Thistle Dew *(or, This'll Do)*

Hands, drowned; the same fate for his daughter over thirty years later, Lil' Mardler, below the ice. Can never break through. My father, pecked ragged by chickens, underneath the spitting electricity pylons. Elsie, so full of life and then nothing, no goodbye, just a handprint on a window which will be cleaned away one day. And now Kipper. All of them living and losing their way on this thin strip of saltmarsh which can never be called land and never be called sea. With a legacy of madness and hurt which must be out there among the creeks and samphire, blowing in the wind. This coastal living has formed them, made them extraordinary, and killed them off.

A thin vein of salt running though all these lives, unquenched and resolute, like a filigree of bone, growing in us all, connecting us with each other and the land that's made us. Salt marked our lives, the first thing to dry on our skin, the last thing to wash away, just as able to preserve as destroy. My family's story has been written in salt and it's lasted over the decades, but it's taken its toll on the people who have lived it. It's corroded their wills like the kiss of Ol' Norse on the ruined wood of the *Hansa*.

Kipper began to fall forwards and I caught him, his head resting briefly on my shoulder. I pushed him back and propped him against the wall of his smokehouse, where he belonged, then wiped some of the dirt from his face. His skin felt warm, whereas mine felt icy. Then I pushed the door of the smokehouse shut, with him behind it, and walked slowly away, the night closing in, until I reached the collapsing shape of the *Thistle Dew*, abandoned and damp, in the vague wide shadow of the Morston Marshes. Inside it was featureless and disgusting, without light, without warmth. Since Bryn Pugh had left it had clearly been used as a smoking den, there were porn mags scuffed across the floor, and there was a sweet smell of piss and a smell of dark leathery mud.

I wedged myself into the corner, bringing the card and papers around me for warmth. Hidden. Safe, for the moment. Wait for the morning, make a decision then, stay awake and wait. But a chill rising like a tide within me, stealthy and un-stoppable. The feeling of being drowned once again which wouldn't leave – how the water had peaked like daggers with the force of the explosion, and how I'd hit the sea with my mouth wide open and in the gulps of water I swallowed, I must have drowned as much as survived. Life avoiding its own traps. I began to shiver and cough as my mind raced with the images of the last few hours: those tapers passing through the primus flame, the umbilical knot catching fire, the sight of my uncle, sat like a Buddha and smoked like a herring, dead behind those coffin doors of his smokehouse – my family's story, with all its vanishings and exiles and secrets and lies, heading this way all along.

I fell into an exhausted sleep and began to dream that ice was growing alongside the wreck, inching its way along the hull with the sound of something feral and hungry. I saw it stretch-ing in one glowing sheet over the marshes, dusted with fresh snow. There was a single line of footprints across it, leading out to sea. I followed them, knowing they were my mother's, knowing all I had to do was catch up with her, reach her, not let her get away again. I trod in her steps, passing the Point, seeing the waves of the North Sea frozen eerily in mid movement, their long dark backs rising up in curls ready to break. Entombed in the ice, the frozen shapes of seals, all with Bryn Pugh's chisel marks on them. There were wrecks out there too, the *Pip*, gnawed by the dogfish, the *Mary Magdalene*, still technicolour bright with its painted clouds, the *Bastard* like a bric-a-brac stall. I mustn't let those footsteps get away. But I realized I was getting lost none the less, my mother was just too far away, and this would never be the way to reach her. The footsteps began to melt, the ice vanished, and I became aware that I was now standing in soil. Soft harvest soil – a giant field. This must be part of the map I now had to follow. I had a new direction. To return. Only a return can make sense, I thought. I must go back home.

As far as I could see were empty fields, windblown hedges and dusty tracks. The Norfolk Desert. Late-summer fragrances, a harvest where the land ripened into a bountiful larder. Pheasants braced in the trees, berries falling plump as raindrops, sweetcorn bursting from the husks. Roots growing fat in the ground as if the soil itself is turning edible and sweet: clay into carrots, stones into swedes.

But a harvest so quickly followed by slaughter. Shotguns filled with murder and lead, blasting into the air, the smells of wheat dust and diesel, of stubble burning in dark firestorms – men walking through the smoke dragging paraffin-soaked rags. Combines cutting long into the night, following their own headlamps, then being left, exhausted, covered in flour dust, the jaw of the cutting blade resting on the ground, full of a right to destroy.

I dreamed of all these things, returning, to the cold brick farmhouse on the edge of the Stow Bardolph Estate. Low outbuildings with their sinister black doorways and the pile of poaching traps spilling out like skeletal grins. The side door with its drab-painted porch and the room inside, never more than a place to heap boots, as chilly as a fridge. The thin damp carpets, the narrow stairs, the sense of something both unresolved and failed – a place which had never truly maintained a full and proper sense of life. Crusts of stale bread next to a cold mug of tea, still on the edge of the table. Here my mother washed the silverfish down the sink and grew her flowers in the garden, she repaired the decoy birds each evening, her heart slowly breaking, while my father learned his skills of bloodstock, became a man capable of attracting a younger, more hopeful woman, if only briefly. It was always a dismal spot, which could never have nurtured a family, how could we even have tried to do it there – it was destined to separate lives into threadbare elements.

And I knew my dream wouldn't end here, my return was not to this place, my return had to be further away than this damp plot of soil which had never quite belonged to any of us. I had to carry on, to go further, into the Fens, where it's so flat and huge it feels like you're not only alone but that even the hills, trees and hedgerows have given up too. Into the precise and rigid geometry of agriculture, soil as black as old lava, something dead and yet also new-formed about it. A blank slate. To the drainage channels, trying to keep fields from returning back to the sea – but the nature of the land itself seems to be the seabed none the less. Be untamed and uncharted. Grow your life there but be under no illusions, the land knows itself as something other than you do. Past the heavy iron sluice gates and a sense of recognition growing in me as I continue, knowing that I'm close now, close to the chicken farm at Four Gotes. I imagine my father would be slumped in an armchair, in an unlit room, the flickering colour of his television giving the room the glow of an aquarium. He's always there, frozen in time, hopeless, the sum of his failures, but he's everything too – he's my father. The sign to the egg farm would be falling off its hinges as I walk past. The chickens would murmur within their hencoops, another day closer to the butcher's block. The pylons would drape across the bungalow with their broad dark pulse of life. Then I would knock at the door, wait, try the handle and let myself in. There's a smell in there of neglect, but also a gentle familiarity too, the smell of Kipper's living room and my father's old study – his contribution to the house at the Saints I must have missed all these years. So familiar, like your own smell, so easy to overlook. I find the bungalow is all shadows and empty rooms, as if the pylons that straddle the building have drawn out its life in their ceaseless overhead flow.

My father is sitting in the armchair as I expected, his hair messy and sparse, like he's just pulled off a jumper. He has no need to smooth it down. He's asleep. The TV is on but it's just the test card, the girl with the red headband, playing noughts and crosses with the doll, so unfailingly hopeful and poignant, never moving, never ageing, neither noughts nor crosses. The sound coming from the set is a drawn-out distant whine coming deep from within the wires. Gull's asleep too, near my father's chequered slippers – a Christmas gift from my mother ten years before, they're grey and worn now but they still fit the feet, still keep a hint of the warmth of the original gift, the original moment he got them. Gull doesn't move, doesn't hear, doesn't make a sound. I only know he's alive because he's still in this room, not buried outside next to the chickens he hates.

I touch my father on his shoulder – the twill shirt he's wearing is worn soft and warm. He stirs and tries to focus his eyes and I know he's been drinking hard that evening. Ahh, Pip, he says, quietly, and smiles with the haze of a pleasant dream. A moment he's happy in. He's peaceful in this state, the dreamer boy he once was. Gradually he wakes more.

You're here, ain't you? he says. I nod, obedient and wanting to rest, feeling weary and just wanting to sit and watch the test card with him.

He continues to sit, wanting to keep his eyes closed, then jolts a little and clears his throat. He's embarrassed by his loneliness. He rubs his forehead with a dirty hand. I'll get you a drink, you must be thirsty. I'm glad you came. He rises stiffly from the chair and when he's standing I smell the old smell of the chair's cushions and the smell of chickens which is forever in his clothes. He grins, dry-lipped, but it passes, and he shuffles towards the kitchen. A switch is snapped on in there and a square of precise acid light is cast into the lounge. He lets out a yawn which almost sounds like he's chewing something, then he appears in the doorway, pale and small, peering at me. Pip, he says.

I go into the kitchen and he makes me a hot drink of something from a packet, which smells malty and sweet. He lets me take a few sips – it's far too hot to drink, then he says come through and he leads me to a room off the corridor I've never seen before. Inside is a single bed and a bookcase. The bed has the quilt I used to sleep under when I was a child. You're tall now, he says, you've grown quick this year. And I look round and see that this is a room for me, a room he's kept and made. It has all I left behind in the Saints, some of the crayon sketches I did when I was still a toddler, and other things I remembered, the cockchafer on its pin, the gyroscope he always had on his desk, things he would have given me one day; all left for me in this room. The same pair of curtains my mother used to revamp the spare room for herself. It's all right in here, ain't it, lad, it feel all right, don't it? He's tapping the bookcase with a sense of pride he doesn't have for the rest of the house. If you want, you know, if it don't bother you too much, you can stay in here, I don't need the room . . . The words trail off into an awkward silence, and he breaks it by handing me a card folder from a shelf – I been keeping a scrapbook about you. I look in it. He comes closer, I can see the spikes of his stubble, now grey, and smell the sweated alcohol on his breath. His eyes look pale and watery and on the verge of tears. It's a look he has permanently now.

Inside the scrapbook are various articles from regional papers. One headline says 'Gruesome find in Smokehouse', with a picture below it of Kipper's smokehouse doors and the faulty catch. Another reports the double drowning of the twins. Separated at last, Cliff went east to wash up dead on Runton Beach, while Sandy went west, almost making Scolt Head against the tide. And that one, my father says, pointing to a black-and-white photograph, that's me at Kipper's funeral. My father, only smart at funerals now, wearing the same tie he wore to see my mother off. He's leading Goose away from the grave, trying to jolly her along, repair their past. Weren't that many people there, in the end. And he's right, the grave-yard is almost empty. Still, it were a proper send-off, he adds, the duty giving his voice a hint of strength.

The overwhelming sadness that this homecoming is not real. It's not happening. And I feel like I'm falling and I can't help it but I put my arms round him and fall into him, on to his side, my father, and I reach up to his shoulder and almost hang there, for fear of letting go. I bury my face into his shirt and just stay still, unable to go any further, not wanting to move any more, I've come this far, this is as far as there is. Coming home is as far as you can go. He has to understand, this is all I have and all I am. I imagine his arm could go round me and the feel of him patting my back, gently, his gesture more important than anything he could say. We've been so apart, so estranged for so long, but now we are all there is, we are the ones who are left and we are the connection between what was and what is. It's that simple.

Quietly my father says you need to go now, you got more to see, ain't you? and I know it's all just a lonely fantasy, I could never truly belong here, and I walk, sadly, out of the strange little child's room he's made for me and into a much larger room than the corridor ever was outside, and I realize I'm no longer in my father's bungalow at all. I'm in a large bedroom in a Victorian building. There's a smell of disinfectant and starched cotton and I see, over by the window, my grandmother's bed, the one she insisted on having because from it there's a slanted view of the marshes. I walk to her bed and crouch down to her level, and see an old woman asleep there, but it's not Goose. It's some other woman, and I think that Goose must have died too. I didn't even know about it – Goose, who has always survived, lived through the storms, and the only one of us who never changed in all these years. Battling with clouds and telling endless stories, fighting off the worst thing of all – the temptation to give up. That was never an option for her. Drive people away, yes, but never give up. And now she's disappeared like all the others.

As I back away from the bed I almost don't see the figure of the old crow-like woman behind me, I turn and there she is, leaning on her stick, that flinty gleam of spirit in her eyes. I got my coat on, boy, she says, I've had this coat on three months waitin' for you to turn up. Thought you weren't never comin'. Thought you'd done a runner like your grandfather.

Goose puts her dry old hands on my shoulder. What you searching for, lad? she says. I ain't got nothin' to tell you 'cause there ain't a wise bone in my whole body. All I ever learned is you got to keep on goin'. Thass the sum of all I know. Juss keep goin'.

She lets that sink in. You know, I ain't comin' with you. I ain't goin' nowhere now. I'm in this place for the dur-a-tion.

I turn to look for my father, knowing he's not there either and never will be, and in his place I see a small impeccably neat man standing in the doorway. He must be about the same age as Goose. His hair is thin and parted tidily in a straight line across his head. He stands in a grey suit with smart creases, and he holds a simple bunch of sea lavender in his hand.

Well I never, Goose says, delighted. You came back.

Hands takes a single step into the room, smiles at her kindly, and holds his lavender out for the old marshwoman he never quite forgot.

The image doesn't last long. It fades unstoppably and in its place are the bare wooden hull boards of the *Thistle Dew*, dim and wet in the first light of day, like the ribcage of a dead animal.

My skin is clammy and my clothes are soaked through with sweat. My chest is freezing and my bones are aching. I hold out a hand and see it trembling. I feel hot and shivery, but I've made it through the night. That's important. I begin to crawl painfully to the doorway, though my vision is swimming and I keep feeling so dizzy I have to rest my head on the wood. It's dark outside, unnaturally dark, and coming across the marsh is a large cloud. It's so tall there's no sky above it. I recognize it for the rag cloud it has once been. A cloud which is about to burst with its own storm. The thunder crashes deeply in it, and as the first fat drops of rain fall on the mud near the wreck I hear pigs squealing from a nearby field. Through the hedge I see them, beginning to scatter in all directions, mad with fear as the lake of water starts to tip out of the cloud. Others walk confused through the storm, grunting as the rain stings their backs. And the rain falls with flashes of silver like fish scales hitting the mud and I realize that there *actually are fish falling*, whole shoals of sprats bouncing on the mud, and as soon as the pigs see this in their field they're eating them as fast as possible and not bothering to swallow but just cramming the fish into their mouths.

Then quickly the storm is gone. I start coughing, badly, and almost faint. My mouth is so dry. I try to wedge myself into a lying position among the corner beams of the wreck so I won't slip over, and instantly I fall asleep, then wake to discover the marsh has been covered in a large steaming fog. The marsh stains the fog a sick shade of green. I imagine the grey chimney of Kipper's smokehouse, looming out there like the wrecked mast of a boat, and I crawl back further into my own wreck, nervously, I can feel the uncertain waves of my fever coming on again and I begin to hum Bryn's song, the song I always think of when things go wrong . . .

'. . . of the winter time, and of the summer too,
   And of the many, many times that I held her in my arms,
   Just to keep her from the foggy, foggy dew.'

The fog creeps into the wreck and I watch it condensing into the oaky fumes of a smokehouse fire. I'm sinking into a faint again. My vision keeps going – patches of shadows seem to spread along the ceiling, and from them I watch the tarry shapes of the fish and eels growing downwards in sinister clutches, and when they have formed all round me they're so solid I reach out to touch them. I break off a piece of eel. It's as dark as charcoal, as thick as thumbs.

I cautiously taste it – and here they come, the dry spices we rubbed into the flesh and the warm wooded flavour of Kipper's smokehouse. It's one of his all right. The eels begin to shiver with life and I see a clutch of hair-like elvers wriggling out of blanket weed Elsie and I have hauled from the water at

Popham's Eau Canal. I follow them as they thread their way down the bank and realize I'm no longer looking at them but into the river itself, with its dark corners of water and weed. My mother comes to my side and places a calm hand on my shoulder. What are you looking for in there? she asks. I'm looking for you, I say back, I see you in every river now. It makes her sigh, kindly. But I'm not in there yet, I'm still here, with you. We stand there, gazing at the water. Mum, please don't leave me, don't take your hand away from my shoulder. I won't. But you will, you always will. She knows I'm right. I turn to look at her and see her hair is already wet, her eyes already glassy with the life she's losing. Why did you do it? I say to her. But I've told you love, I've told you already – it was the way out. It was the path I'd never seen before. I think you're on the same path yourself now, aren't you? She smiles as she begins to fade away. You're my love, remember that, you're everything I could have wanted.

And the eels return for me, taking me back with them to a meal my mother cooked, where I'm staring at an eel on my father's fork as it rises to his greasy lips. I look above him and see more eels, dozens of them, like tarred ropes – they're high up in Kipper's smokehouse like a brood of snakes coming in from the roof. More eels in the bucket on the tope cuddy, tying themselves in mysterious knots, excited by the scent of water and the promise of a storm, floating off through the wreckage. Eels knowing no boundaries and getting every-where, always returning, whatever the obstacle, finding you out, coming from the sea like the tide itself – up the rivers and drains and dykes and ponds and gutters, following the lines they made thousands of years before, and there, in the wreck, quarrying me like prey.

Again I woke up, feeling weak and light-headed. I'd been sick on the floor and I had no idea whether it was day or night or whether the fog was still there. It seemed cloudy in the wreck, and I thought it might be the smoke of one of the fires – one of the great fires like the elm tree or the poor *Mary Magdalene*. Thoughts and memories rushing at me as if a tide was flooding over the marsh. Hands on the *Pip* under its quilted sail, adrift above the Dogger Bank, his compass spinning as the boat spirals into an infernal whirlpool – a giant hole in the North Sea where cod and flounder stick their heads out of the walls of water like Gideon's painting *The Parting of the Wash*. A whirlpool so deep and wide it's begun to spin the entire North Sea round it. I know about these storms – the storms that have always circled, returning across the centuries in regular rhythm, bringing with them the dead and drowned back to the saltmarsh.

Inexplicably the air begins to still, and I return to that calm, that silence of my mother's room in the Quaker cottage hospital at Emneth Hungate. 1962. She's sitting on the edge of the bed in the middle of the night, listening to the fen and smelling the vegetables in the soil. She's so full of thoughts. In the corner of her hospital room I see the moth-eaten Andean condor, from the cage on Kelling Heath, rocking in misery. Something moves in my hand – and I know it's the queen bee, trapped in the Swann Vesta matchbox in the bomb-shack, twitching its once plump body from corner to corner, dying of hunger in a Norfolk hut which has forgotten she's ever existed. I see my mother again – rubbing her belly in the farmhouse at the Saints while it snows outside. A window growing colder by the second as the flakes settle – I see her place her hand on the glass and the print she leaves is Elsie's, a tiniest sign of warmth in a world so icy that my mother's going to be lost in it. The mile of footprints on a sheet of ice. How they melted – the impression of her feet somewhere, still, in the middle of the sea.

I'm sick again. I'm sweating, the fever begins to grow and tighten itself around me like the bars of a cage, and now I begin to see fondue sticks, crossing inappropriately over a party table. The sides of the *Thistle Dew* are no longer wood, but they're the dry bricks of the bull-pen at the Stow Bardolph Estate, only the bull's not there because I see it's the 'other woman', pressed against the bricks with her dress pulled to one side, biting her lower lip. I think of Elsie. I think of Elsie and she's naked, sitting astride me, and she too is biting her lower lip. We are on the whale. I press my fingers into Bryn's old bunk bed and feel the soft wood giving way because it has become the blubber and flesh of the sperm whale, and we are at sea again, under the brilliant stars, as the whale journeys across the ocean. And suddenly I'm staring into the liquid shadows of the wreck once more, and in those shadows I see two bright eyes looking back at me. The figure leans forward and I know it's Ol' Norse, finally revealing himself, as ancient as the sea, with weed for hair and scales for skin. His breath smells of salt as he tells me I am lost. I've lost my map in life. I've been looking at clouds all the time and they've got nothing to say. On land and at sea and I always wash up, shipwrecked, time after time.

Stories started in the mud here, they've grown over time, they're speaking with their own voices now, returning like the North Sea storms, changing each time, evolving, being added to, indefatigable like a cloud. *You'll never be free of them*, he says, and Ol' Norse grins at me and briefly, as he fades, I see the scales falling away from his skin to reveal my two-faced uncle, sitting in exactly the same posture. As calm as a Buddha once more as the smokehouse fire smoulders around him. Only it's my uncle dressed in the full regalia of Neptune himself. A brilliantly shining trident in his right hand, three herring speared on the tines. *You left me in there*, he says. *Left me in there with the damned fish while I banged on the door.* Till my hands bled. And I could see you through the crack, all soaking wet and not doing a damn thing to help. Well, it serves you right. Serves you right for being so messed up. Serves us all for the lies we've laid. And as he says this I see the thick mane of the Red Poll bull shaking his head while my father pours whispers into its ear. My father's voice, secret in that giant ear, but it's my uncle's voice I hear again, saying *your father! The chicken man!* Once a dreamer, always a dreamer. Spoke to the birds he did, spoke to the animals in the fields. Well he *Shoo arlo birds. Hi shoo all 'er birds!* And I see my father alone in a bungalow that smells of dead air, the double barrels of his Gallyon & Sons shotgun wedged into the roof of his mouth. His teeth chatter on the metal and he breathes in quick urgent gasps. He's remembering the day Elsie called there to see him, how he dropped three warm eggs into her hand, turned back to his bungalow, weeping there under the pylons because he's never told her, he just can't tell her she's his daughter. With blind Gull looking on, his fingers reaching for a trigger but he never pulls it and I look at the engraving on the stock and it's not of pheasants and grouse any more but it's of my father himself, broken by the chickens that mingle round his feet and peck his boots to shreds. Some of these things, but not all of them, broke my father's spirit, sent my mother through the ice. Details, and in all of them a record of pain and disappointment, or compromise. The greasy stain behind Goose's chair where she's leaned her head for forty years, the dry hard-working skin on the back on my father's neck, the farmer's hands he now has, the jobs never done, the life never quite lived, the sense of failure, everywhere, failure which is acceptable because it's just short of that other route, that of madness, which seems to have gone hand in hand with my family's history. Never far away, just beyond the horizon perhaps, a tide which rises every twenty years or so to overrun the marsh. And my uncle's laugh rings out and he starts to talk again about your mother and father – did a stupid thing, din't they? Got 'emselves kicked out of North Norfolk 'cause she was pregnant. *No!* Getting sent to that godforsaken fen farm and then when the time comes giving that child away. *You're lying!* My mother – her sad eyes in the Quaker hospital, looking back at me nodding. A little girl with red hair, he says. Go by the name of Elsie . . . *Get out!* I scream. *Get out of here!* Too late to talk now! my uncle shouts back, and with a fizz he lights a firework and the inside of the wreck shatters as it explodes and I am on the cuddy once more, with the jagged deck flying all around me and Cliff whispering *sisterfucker!* in my ear as he falls through the boat past the eels. I'm soaking wet, standing on the sandbank, and the tide's rising and pressing my face into the net of the oyster cage – and the tight-lipped oysters do nothing to help me. The sand eel passes through the cage like a phantom once more. And Bryn is there, fiddling with the knot, old and grey and telling me that Goose has lost her mind – that once a long time ago she'd lost her daughter and now she couldn't bear to lose me too and it was because of this she was going to be put in a home. A nice quiet home where she can relax and the nurses will know what to do. Briefly I glimpse Goose, swallowing a pill while a nurse tells her you're just seeing things, that's all, love. You've got a condition where you see things and this'll make you feel better. And when the nurse turns round she has a sheet of my five-year-old drawings in front of her. She tears it up and says you're going to start talking right now because I know you can and although she can't see it, behind her head the *Thistle Dew* is silently filling up with my childhood sketches. Bulls and goats and fish and fire surrounding my father's shotgun, poaching traps around his door, and across the roof the exquisite mural of clouds I drew inside the chicken coop. Stratus, cumulus nimbus, cirrus – and there, in the corner, the rag cloud, always there to catch me out.

I start to cry with fear – that I'll die in this wreck, that I'll die alone out here – and then I smell a gentle scent of vanilla. Of vanilla and scones and hard-boiled eggs, and when I look up there is Elsie, climbing clumsily into the *Thistle Dew* and sitting down on her haunches. I'm amazed to see her. Why did you leave? I ask her. I've been trying to sort things out. She smiles at that. We both have. It's so good to see her. Are you my sister? Elsie looks level-gazed at me. I see her in all her details: the multistranded woven colours of her hair, the thin slot of worry her mouth has become, the look of sleeplessness around her eyes, but a calmness there too, a new calmness that seems unusual in Elsie. I want to remember these things. Because she begins to fade away, like she always will, just too beyond reach for me, this time I am sure, the last time I'll ever see her. I touch the space where she'd been, and feel nothing but the cold waterlogged wood of the wreck. I lie down and give in to a thick numbing wave of sleep.

My fever had run its course. After dark I left the wrecked boat with my mother's seashell and a bag full of Kipper's fireworks I'd stolen from his house. It was a warm and quiet September night, and across the marsh in the car park at Blakeney there was a large bonfire burning.

I walked to the shore of the Pit, climbed into a dinghy and paddled over to the *Hansa*. The water was calm and at full tide, and the wreck looked once more like it was about to float off into the North Sea. I tied the boat to the gunwale, went to the wheelhouse and sat on the bones of the pilot's chair. Rusted metal as cold as the sea, salty with age. Finally I've come home, I thought – you don't need anything else, just the touch of something you understand in the middle of nowhere. A wrecked boat in the darkness. An acceptance. I leaned against the metal and for a moment felt my story in all its entirety, and all the stories that had made it, bending out into the night in calm pathways. And you keep on going. She's right, that's all there is to it.

When my fireworks went off, their multicoloured maroon shot up into the empty dome of the Norfolk sky. Find me. Across the saltmarshes I watched as the distant bonfire parted into a string of lights and torches, and this string began to stretch across the marsh like a faintly twinkling necklace. As it came nearer, the necklace split and reformed as it navigated the creeks and channels until it arrived at the Pit, where the lights collected in groups and climbed into boats to cross the water and take me back. Take me back. And I thought how beautiful it must have looked from the land – my little show of fireworks, a distant bloom of colour and smoke in a landscape so dark it's always drawn the light away and extinguished it like a blot.

Acknowledgements

Thanks to Kate Barker at Viking, for her calm steering, advice and friendship, and to Kate Jones at ICM, for being tremendous throughout. Thanks, too, to Kathryn Court and Sloan Harris.

Thanks to Cormac, for his knife-sharp pen, which never blunts, and the blood-red notes in the margins. Thank you Andrew, for our shared imagination and our humour, and thanks Mum, for your constant belief and love.

Thanks to C13. Also, to Norfolk.

Much thanks to you, my dear son Jacob, to whom this book is dedicated – you have shared so much of it with me, especially all of those mudwalks in the creeks. You are amazing.

And thank you Liz, for your sensitive reading, your shining soul, and for your boundless support.